FLETCHERS END

Shortly before Bel's marriage to Ellis, her friend Louise goes house hunting for the future Brownlees and discovers a charming yet neglected old stone cottage called Fletchers End. Bel adores the house and, keen to make her happy, Ellis buys the place from absent owner Lieutenant Commander Lestrange. Bel embarks on her new life as a devoted wife, loyally guiding Louise through her own romantic tribulations. She also enjoys sharing with Ellis the excitement and satisfaction of decorating their first home, as well as unravelling the mysteries of the old stone cottage. But with the unexpected arrival of Lieutenant Commander Lestrange, the peace of Fletchers End is suddenly threatened . . .

Books by D. E. Stevenson
Published in Ulverscroft Collections:

MUSIC IN THE HILLS
VITTORIA COTTAGE
WINTER AND ROUGH WEATHER
THE YOUNG CLEMENTINA
LISTENING VALLEY
THE FOUR GRACES
SPRING MAGIC
BEL LAMINGTON

D. E. STEVENSON

FLETCHERS END

Complete and Unabridged

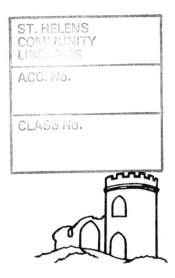

ULVERSCROFT
Leicester

First published in Great Britain in 1962

This Ulverscroft Edition
published 2020

A catalogue record for this book is available
from the British Library.

ISBN 978–1–4448–4437–5

Published by
Ulverscroft Limited
Anstey, Leicestershire

Set by Words & Graphics Ltd.
Anstey, Leicestershire
Printed and bound in Great Britain by
T. J. International Ltd., Padstow, Cornwall

This book is printed on acid-free paper

Contents

PART ONE   The Old House..................1

PART TWO   Winter in London...........95

PART THREE   The Brownlees
at Home.........................135

PART FOUR   Alarms and
Excursions.....................257

PART FIVE   Miss Lestrange's
Bureau............................335

PART ONE

The Old House

1

Mrs. Warmer often wondered how old the house was and who had lived in it. When she first took over the duty of caretaker she had been a little frightened of living in an empty house all by herself but she had got used to it quite soon. There was a friendly sort of feeling in the house. Mrs. Warmer was not an imaginative woman — one could see that at a glance — she was short and stout with thick legs and sandy hair and unexpectedly deep-blue eyes. Obviously she was not the sort of woman who had strange dreams and saw ghosts. All the same she had a feeling that there were things in the house which could not be accounted for in a rational way. There was a scent of violets in the drawing-room for instance. Sometimes the scent was quite strong and Mrs. Warmer would stand still for a few moments and sniff thoughtfully before she got down to the job of cleaning the windows and sweeping the floors.

The house was very solidly built of honey-coloured stone and was covered with creepers. The garden was a tangled mass of nettles and willow-herb and overgrown bushes and straggly trees — Mrs. Warmer was not responsible for keeping the garden in order — but there were no violets in the gardens. She had looked.

The house seemed isolated, it was in the Cotswold Country and very quiet, but it was not really as isolated as it seemed. The village of Archerfield was only a few hundred yards down the road. It was a very small village, consisting of a few cottages, a post-office (including a little shop which sold a heterogeneous collection of odds and ends) and an inn called The Green Man. Mrs. Warmer had several friends in the village, chief of whom was Mr. Carruthers the sweep. It was a great day for Mrs. Warmer when Mr. Carruthers came to sweep the chimneys at Fletchers End.

In the other direction little more than a mile distant was the much larger village of Shepherdsford with its shops and fine old Norman church. Mrs. Warmer could hear the clock on the tower of St. Julian's strike the hours — if the wind was in the right direction — and the sound of the bells on Sundays came drifting across the fields. Every Sunday Mrs. Warmer went to church at St. Julian's, either in the morning or the evening. There was a path along the bank of the stream which ran past the bottom of the garden. It was called The Church Walk because long ago all the inhabitants of Archerfield had walked over to St. Julian's to worship there. Now, alas, very few of the villagers attended church — or, if they did, they went by the bus which passed along the main road at convenient times for the services. Mrs. Warmer preferred to walk, for it was a pleasant walk, and unlike the bus, cost nothing at all.

Sometimes people said to Mrs. Warmer, 'It must be dull at Fletchers End. Aren't you lonely in that big empty house?' Mrs. Warmer was not lonely and she was never dull; there was far too much to do. She kept the house swept and garnished; she scrubbed and polished; she cooked her food and washed her clothes. Once a week she locked up the house securely and bicycled to Shepherdsford to receive her pay from Mr. Tennant's office and do her shopping. A van called at Fletchers End on Tuesdays. Every morning a bus passed along the road outside the house on its way to the town of Ernleigh, which was only five miles distant, and occasionally Mrs. Warmer boarded the bus, spent the day in Ernleigh and went to the pictures. Sometimes she went with her friend, Mrs. Stack, who lived at Archerfield, but more often she went alone for Mrs. Warmer was a woman who enjoyed her own company. She was of a contented nature.

The house was for sale and it was one of Mrs. Warmer's duties to show it to people who called and presented 'a card to view'. She was aware that her employer was very anxious to sell it, so obviously it was her duty to show it off and make the best of it to prospective buyers . . . and, as she had a high standard of integrity, she did so.

Sometimes she worried about what would happen to her if the house were sold. She would have to leave of course. She would have to go away and find some other job — the idea of leaving the dear old house was dreadful. The idea of going away and never seeing it again, of having no right to wander round the rooms, sweeping and dusting and polishing, of never

5

again smelling the violets ... Oh dear, it was almost unbearable!

But the months passed and the years passed and nobody showed the slightest desire to buy it. People came quite frequently with the necessary 'card to view' but they never stayed long. They looked round vaguely, asked a few questions and went away. Sometimes they were angry with the agent who had sent them to see it and most unjustly vented their rage upon Mrs. Warmer.

'What a dilapidated place!' they exclaimed. 'How dreadfully lonely and isolated! Who do you think would buy a house like this? Fancy coming all this way to see it! The agent must have been crazy to send us here. I told him the sort of house we wanted.'

'You'd like to see round the house, wouldn't you?' inquired Mrs. Warmer politely.

'No, indeed!' they replied crossly. 'It would just be a waste of time. I wouldn't have the place as a gift.' Then they went away and no more was heard of them.

The months passed and the years passed and the old house became more and more dilapidated. The woodwork round the windows rotted and the paint peeled off the front door; the gate was almost falling to pieces; the garden was wild and tangled, the creepers rioted over the walls and the roof. It was now quite usual for people with 'a card to view' to stop at the gate for a few moments and then drive on without getting out of their car.

If Mrs. Warmer saw them from a window she would run out and open the gate and try to persuade them to come in — in this way she performed her duty to the best of her ability — but she was seldom successful in her attempts.

Gradually the idea that anyone would ever buy the house faded from Mrs. Warmer's mind and Fletchers End became her settled home.

2

During all this time only one gentleman took an interest in the house. He presented a card from an agent in London, Messrs. Hook and Rook, upon which was written, 'Kindly give Mr. Rutherford every facility to view Fletchers End'. So Mrs. Warmer opened the front-door (not without difficulty for it had sunk on its hinges) and let the gentleman come in — and he went all over the house looking at everything very carefully and making notes in a little book.

'Are you thinking of buying it, sir?' asked Mrs. Warmer a trifle anxiously.

'Good heavens, no,' he replied. 'I'm interested in ruins, that's all.'

'Oh, it isn't a ruin!' exclaimed Mrs. Warmer, who could not bear to hear her home referred to in these terms. 'It's a very nice house. It's old, of course. I suppose it must be a hundred years old.'

'Multiply by three — possibly four,' said Mr. Rutherford smiling.

'All that?' asked Mrs. Warmer, opening her blue eyes very wide.

'All that,' he answered. 'You've only got to look at those huge oak beams in the ceilings; they had to be tremendously strong to sustain the weight of the stone roof. Those weren't made by machine; they were sawn by hand and chipped into shape. They're made of the same wood that was used to build Queen Elizabeth's Navy.'

Mrs. Warmer looked at the beams. She had seen them every day for years but now she saw them differently — not just as a hazard for tall people to bump their heads on (she always warned tall visitors of this danger), but put there by the men who built the house, chipped into shape by men's hands, set into the walls of the house to support the roof.

'What a big job! I wonder who did it,' said Mrs. Warmer wonderingly.

'Ah, that would be interesting to know. I should like to take a trip backwards in time and see this house under process of construction. It would be worth seeing. Those old johnnies knew how to build. The fabric is as sound as a bell — I was wrong when I called it a ruin. It has lasted about four hundred years and it'll still be standing when all the houses they're putting up now will have fallen as flat as pancakes.' He sighed and added, 'It's absolutely criminal for people to allow their property to deteriorate like this. Look at those window-frames, all rotting for want of a lick of paint!'

'The owner is a naval officer in forrin parts,' said Mrs. Warmer solemnly. 'He's a very nice young gentleman by all accounts.'

8

'He's nice, is he?' said Mr. Rutherford smiling. Already in their short acquaintance he had discovered that this was the caretaker's favourite word. 'Well, he doesn't keep his property in a very nice condition; you can tell him so from me the next time you see him.'

'I never seen him in my life,' declared Mrs. Warmer. 'I told you he's in forrin parts. I gets my wages every week from Mr. Tennant, the lawyer.'

They were coming down the stairs together by this time.

'I don't suppose you'd know what kind of people used to live here, sir?' Mrs. Warmer inquired. 'Funny kind of people they must of been to have three stairs, a little one at each end and a big one in the middle.'

'They were fletchers.'

'Fletchers?'

'People who made arrows and feathered them — I can tell you that much. The village down the road is called Archerfield, so it's only reasonable to suppose that they practised archery in that big meadow down by the stream.'

'And the people in this house made the arrows!'

'You've got it in one,' said Mr. Rutherford chuckling. 'As for the stairs: it's obvious that the house was originally built as two houses. Two families lived here and made arrows, see?' He took his coat which was hanging on the newel-post of the big central staircase which led into the hall.

'Three houses,' suggested Mrs. Warmer.

'No, no,' he replied, a trifle impatiently.

'Originally there were two small houses, each with a small staircase. Then someone came along and bought them and joined them together to make himself a good-sized residence. He turned the rooms round a bit and built a new staircase leading up from the hall.'

'How do you know all that?'

'I'm interested in old houses. I use my eyes.'

He put on his coat and made for the door, but Mrs. Warmer had not done with him yet. She followed him down the stone-paved path and helped him to open the gate which, like all the rest of the perishable material, was rapidly falling to pieces. It was difficult to open — or to shut — unless you knew its ways.

'I suppose,' said Mrs. Warmer. 'I suppose that's why it sunk — because it's so heavy, I mean.'

'Sunk?'

'Yes, right down to the very doorstep.'

Mr. Rutherford was annoyed; he had seen all he wanted and was anxious to get away. What a fool the woman was! Then he turned and, looking at the old house, he realised what she meant. A person who was accustomed to modern houses — boxes of brick with steps leading up to the front-door — might easily imagine that Fletchers had sunk. It had the appearance of an over-loaded ship sinking into a green sea of vegetation.

'Those old johnnies dug deep down before they started to build up,' said Mr. Rutherford, trying to explain the matter in words suited to his audience. 'That's one thing. Another thing is that, having originally been planned and built as two houses, the proportions are unusual . . . Well, never mind that. Here's something quite easy to understand: this place is getting buried by the weeds and bushes which have grown up all round it and are growing higher and thicker every year. That's why it looks as if it were sinking into the ground.'

'Oh, yes,' said Mrs. Warmer nodding.

Mr. Rutherford got into his car, switched on the engine and drove off, leaving a crisp crackly note in the hand which Mrs. Warmer had extended to bid him good-bye.

3

Mrs. Warmer never saw the gentleman again but he had given her something more valuable than the crackly note; he had given her food for thought. Indeed he had changed Mrs. Warmer, altered her whole outlook upon life. He had told her that he used his eyes and now Mrs. Warmer began to use hers. She had loved the house before, but now she loved it differently for she had begun to understand it. Instead of going round with a dust-pan thinking about the activities of the Women's Institute she went round with a dust-pan and thought about the house. She had always kept the place clean and tidy, it was her duty, but now she kept it scrubbed and polished as if she were expecting Queen Elizabeth herself to walk in at the door. Not the reigning Queen, of course, but the old one whose ships had been built of the same wood as the huge oaken beams.

One day when she was standing upon a ladder, poking about in the rafters searching for spiders' webs, she came across a little piece of polished stick; one end was sharp and tipped with metal; the other was jagged as if it had been broken in two. If it had not been for the gentleman Mrs. Warmer would have used it to light her fire . . . but the gentleman had said that long ago the people who lived in the house made arrows. Arrows! Well, of course, that was what it was! A bit of an arrow!

Mrs. Warmer was so excited that she forgot all about the spiders; she took her find down to the kitchen and put it away carefully in the drawer where she kept her mother's brooch and her Post Office Savings book and her National Insurance card. In other words the little piece of polished wood had become one of her treasures. Sometimes she took it out and held it in her hand and thought about the man who had made it, and wondered what he had looked like; (she had such a very hazy idea of history that she imagined him shaggy and attired in the skin of a bear). And she wondered how the arrow had got broken and where the other piece of it could be . . . but although she searched assiduously, high and low, she never found it.

2

Friday was the day for Mrs. Warmer's shopping expedition. It was a fine warm summer morning so the bicycle run to Shepherdsford was enjoyable. Coming back with a heavy basket on her handlebars was not quite so pleasant — it was uphill most of the way. As she turned the corner of the road which led past Fletchers End she was surprised to see a small car standing outside and a lady, young and slender and extremely pretty, struggling to open the gate.

'Did you want to come in?' asked Mrs. Warmer as she dismounted from her bicycle and leant it against the hedge.

'It's for sale, isn't it?' asked the young lady, shaking the gate violently.

'Don't do that, Miss!' exclaimed Mrs. Warmer in alarm. 'It'll fall to bits. I'll open it for you. It isn't difficult when you know how.'

The girl stepped back and looked up at the house.

She said doubtfully, 'It's in awfully bad repair, isn't it? They gave me a card to view but I don't know . . . perhaps it isn't worth bothering about.'

'You could see it, anyhow,' suggested Mrs. Warmer.

The 'card to view' was from Mr. Tennant instructing Mrs. Warmer to give Miss Louise Armstrong every facility to view Fletchers End.

'Are you the caretaker?' asked Miss Armstrong. 'Surely you don't live here all by yourself?'

'Yes, I live here.'

'How frightful. The place looks absolutely derelict.'

'It's a nice house, really. It's been let go a bit and the garden makes it look worse. There isn't nobody to keep the garden nice.'

'It isn't a garden at all. It's a jungle,' said Miss Armstrong with conviction.

By this time the gate had been opened and they were walking up the path to the front-door.

'If you wait a minute I'll go round and open it,' Mrs. Warmer said. 'You can't open this door from the outside, so I always use the back.'

'Goodness, look at it! The paint has all flaked off and the panels are loose. I don't think it's any good bothering to look at the place. I'm sure my friends would never think of buying a house like this.'

Mrs. Warmer was delighted to hear it, but she had her duty to do. 'Well, now you're here, you'd better come in and have a look round, hadn't you, Miss. It's an interesting old house.'

'All right, I'll wait,' said Miss Armstrong.

Mrs. Warmer wheeled her bicycle round the corner, let herself in at the back-door and took off her hat. She seized a moment to tidy her hair before going along the passage to the hall. When she opened the front-door she found Miss Armstrong staring up at the roof.

'What a pretty colour!' the girl exclaimed.

'It's made of stone; very heavy it is. That's why

14

there has to be oak beams.'

'The wood round the windows is absolutely rotten with damp.'

'Well, what could you expect? This house is three hundred years old.'

'You might expect the owner to paint it occasionally,' retorted Miss Armstrong with surprising asperity.

'You might if you didn't happen to know the owner was a naval officer in forrin parts.'

The girl laughed. Mrs. Warmer had no idea what had amused her but the laughter was so infectious that she was forced to smile.

'All the same,' said Miss Armstrong. 'All the same he ought to attend to his property. It's most important to paint all the outside woodwork every two years. We always do that.'

Mrs. Warmer did not pursue the subject. As a matter of fact she had pointed out to Mr. Tennant that the house ought to be painted but Mr. Tennant had shrugged his shoulders and replied that Lieutenant-Commander Lestrange had refused to spend any money on having the house painted; he had added ruefully that no money could be squeezed out of the young rapscallion for anything connected with the house ('Rapscallion' was a new word to Mrs. Warmer but she had a dictionary, in which she delighted, so she looked it up and was somewhat surprised).

Mrs. Warmer and her visitor were now in the hall.

'I suppose you wouldn't like a cup of tea before we go round the house?' suggested Mrs.

15

Warmer. She suggested it hopefully for she was an inveterate tea-drinker and she was pining for refreshment after her morning's shopping expedition to Shepherdsford.

'Wouldn't it be a bother?' asked Miss Armstrong.

This was an acceptance, of course. 'No bother at all,' declared Mrs. Warmer cheerfully. 'It won't take a minute — I'd just put a few drops of water in the kettle — it boils very quick.' And she hastened down the passage before Miss Armstrong had time to change her mind.

2

Louise Armstrong looked about the hall before following the caretaker to the kitchen, and was favourably impressed; she could not see much because, what with the tall bushes outside the window and the low roof supported by enormous black oak beams, it was dim and somewhat mysterious, but she noticed it was a pleasing shape, square and spacious, with doors opening off it on both sides, and she noticed the stone fireplace with its well-polished basket-grate and the oak staircase leading to the upper regions.

The kitchen was unexpectedly bright and cheerful; the walls were distempered in cream, not very expertly. Miss Armstrong was pretty certain that her hostess had done the job herself and on making tactful inquiries she learned that this was so. The Women's Institute had had a gentleman down from London to give a demonstration of 'Do it yourself'. Fired by this, Mrs. Warmer bought two tins of distemper and a large brush and 'had a go at it'.

'I daresay it might have been done better,' said Mrs. Warmer doubtfully. 'But it's made the kitchen nice and bright.'

'Very nice and bright,' agreed Louise Armstrong looking round admiringly.

There was a highly-coloured square of linoleum on the flagged floor; crisp curtains — checked blue and white — hanging at the windows and a row of gaily-patterned jugs on the chimney-piece. Everything was perfectly clean. Everything that could be polished had been polished within an inch of its life.

Tea was soon ready (not 'in a minute' as had been promised but in a surprisingly short time); Mrs. Warmer spread a blue and white checked cloth upon the well-scrubbed table, fetched cups and saucers, plates and knives, produced a dish of wholemeal scones and a slab of yellow farm butter, and the two sat down to the repast.

'Yes, it's nice and bright,' repeated Mrs. Warmer. 'I like things nice. I've got my own furniture of course. My bedroom's upstairs — I don't fancy sleeping on the ground floor. I've been here five — getting on for six years now. I was glad to get the job when my husband went away.'

'You mean — you mean he — died?'

'Just went away and left me sitting. Well, he wasn't much of a loss. Would you care for

17

another scone. Miss?'

'I wonder why it's called Fletchers End.'

'Because it's the end of the village where the fletchers used to live. They made arrows.'

'How do you know?'

'It was a gentleman told me . . . and it was *true* what he told me,' added Mrs. Warmer mysteriously. She hesitated for she had never shown her treasure to anyone — nor said a thing about it — but Miss Armstrong was such a nice young lady . . .

'Is it a secret?' asked the nice young lady.

Mrs. Warmer nodded. 'I'll show you if you promise to keep it dark.'

Of course Louise promised. Mrs. Warmer amused her enormously. It was a little difficult to 'place' the woman, thought Louise. She spoke well most of the time, but occasionally she lapsed into not-quite-so-good English. Probably she had educated herself by listening to programmes on the B.B.C. There was a radio standing on a table in the corner.

The piece of arrow was produced from the locked drawer and handed over for inspection. It was examined and admired and the story of how it had been found and when and where was received with interest.

'It's marvellous to think it had been lying there all those years — hundreds of years! No wonder you're proud of it,' declared Louise as she handed it back.

Mrs. Warmer offered her visitor another scone.

'I'm eating you out of house and home,' declared Louise as she took it. 'This is my third!

It's partly because they're so awfully good and partly because I'm hungry. I've looked at three houses this morning — none of them was any use at all. You see my greatest friend is going to be married in October and I want them to come and live in this district. We live in Ernleigh — at Coombe House.'

'You're Dr. Armstrong's daughter!' exclaimed Mrs. Warmer. 'Well, there now — I might have known! Fancy us talking all this time and me not knowing! I only saw the doctor once when I got a splinter in my finger. He took it out in a minute and I scarcely felt a thing! Very clever he is.'

'Yes, he is,' agreed his daughter proudly.

'I don't never have nothing wrong with me — very healthy I am — but, if I was ill, Dr. Armstrong's the one I'd go to.'

'You couldn't do better.'

They smiled at each other.

'When did you say your friend was getting married?' asked Mrs. Warmer after a slight pause.

'In October. We're having the wedding in Ernleigh and the reception at Coombe House. You see my friend has no relations and no proper home. She lives in a little flat in London.'

'I see,' said Mrs. Warmer nodding. 'You'll enjoy having the wedding, I'm sure.'

'Yes, and it's the right thing,' said Louise earnestly. 'Bel and I were at school together — we're just like sisters. Daddy is going to give her away. There was a certain amount of argument at first because Mr. Brownlee's mother

19

wanted to have the wedding at Beckenham — that's where she lives but I managed to persuade her tactfully that my plan was better, so she gave in and was quite kind and sensible about it.' Louise paused and looked at her audience to see if it were bored. Had she been talking too much?

Apparently not. 'Is it to be a big wedding?' inquired Mrs. Warmer eagerly.

'No, I'm afraid not. I wanted Bel to have a real proper wedding, but she's rather shy. She says she just wants a few friends. And she won't have a proper wedding dress because it wouldn't be any use afterwards. I wish she'd agree to have a real proper wedding,' added Louise with a sigh.

'I'm sure it will be nice.' Mrs. Warmer was perfectly certain it would be nice; she had decided that Miss Armstrong was an exceedingly capable young lady and that anything she undertook to do would be well carried out. It was somewhat surprising because very pretty young ladies were seldom capable — you did not expect it — but here was an exception to the rule.

3

The conversation had been so absorbing that the serious business which had brought Louise Armstrong to Fletchers End had been forgotten — but only temporarily of course. Louise remembered now that she had come to look at the house.

20

'I had better have a look round, hadn't I?' she said, rising as she spoke. 'It's been lovely having tea. I feel quite different. Thank you very much indeed.'

'It's been a pleasure,' declared Mrs. Warmer.

They began going round the house together. At first Louise examined the place casually for she had been 'put off' by the frightful condition of the gate and the window-frames and the front-door — not to speak of the garden — but after she had seen some of the bedrooms she became more interested. The bedrooms were really delightful; they were spacious and sunny and just the right size. Louise knew a good deal about old houses — her father's house was old — so she poked into cupboards and sniffed about for signs of dry-rot. She cast her eye over the plumbing, made pertinent inquiries about the electricity and asked whether the water supply was adequate.

All this amused Mrs. Warmer; she was happy and friendly, answering all the questions at length and laughing heartily at Miss Armstrong's jokes . . . but when Miss Armstrong emerged from the cupboard where the cistern was hidden, with her dark curls in disorder and her face flushed from her exertions, and said, 'This house isn't nearly as bad as it looks; I really believe it might do!' Mrs. Warmer felt a shiver of dismay run up her spine.

'I really believe it might do,' repeated Louise with shining eyes. 'Bel must come and see it! Oh, how lovely it would be if they liked it — and came to live here!'

21

Mrs. Warmer was torn in twain. She liked Miss Armstrong so much. Miss Armstrong was one of the nicest young ladies she had ever met — so friendly and kind and so amusing — and of course it would be lovely for her to have her greatest friend living within easy distance of Ernleigh — but, oh dear! what would happen if the house were to be sold? She would have to leave Fletchers End and go away! Where would she go? What would she do? Oh dear!

'It would have to have a lot of money spent on it,' said Mrs. Warmer.

'Oh, I know. But I've looked at so many houses and they were all quite hopeless — horrid cramped little villas or else enormous mansions full of dry-rot and smelling of damp. This house is perfectly dry — you said so, didn't you?'

Alas Mrs. Warmer had said so.

'I believe it might do,' Louise repeated. 'If Mr. Brownlee could buy it at a reasonable price . . . have you any idea . . . '

Mrs. Warmer shook her head.

'It's in such bad repair,' Louise pointed out.

'I'm sure Mr. Tennant would ask quite a lot for it. You see,' added Mrs. Warmer, remembering a phrase used by the gentleman who had been so interested. 'You see, Miss, the fabric is as sound as a bell.'

'But it's been empty for years and years.'

Mrs. Warmer was silent.

'I wonder,' said Louise, thoughtfully, 'it's much the best I've seen — and it's quite near Ernleigh. There are good trains from Ernleigh.'

'I don't know.'

'Oh, there are. I know several men who go up to town every morning. That's important because Mr. Brownlee will have to go up to his business; he's a partner in a big shipping-firm, you see.'

Mrs. Warmer said nothing.

Louise looked at her and smiled but no answering smile appeared upon the white face of Mrs. Warmer.

What's the matter with the woman? wondered Louise. She was so friendly — and now she isn't. What have I done wrong? Could she have taken offence because I asked the price? But surely it was a natural question. Why should she mind?

As they continued their tour of inspection Louise continued to wonder what she had done wrong. Mrs. Warmer showed her everything — she was given every facility — but the feeling of *rapprochement* had vanished.

Louise was quite upset. But of course it was silly to be upset. What did it matter? She had known this caretaker-woman for about an hour and probably would never see her again! All the same Louise was upset.

The fact was Louise Armstrong had a genius for acquiring friends. She exuded friendliness and sympathy, and nearly everyone responded to her charm: rich and poor, gentle and simple went down like ninepins when Louise smiled. Girls in shops, porters on the railway, char-women and plumbers, even policemen on point-duty thawed in the warmth of her personality. This woman had thawed rapidly — they had got on splendidly together — and

23

then, quite suddenly and for no apparent reason, she had frozen into a hard lump of ice.

However it was no use worrying about the woman; it was the house that mattered; and really and truly it might be the very thing for Bel and Ellis. Really and truly if they could get it cheap and spend money on it they could make it very comfortable indeed.

It isn't too big and it isn't too small, thought Louise. And it really is charming — I'd like it myself — I'd love it! This is a house you could love.

The tour was almost at an end; Louise had seen everything — everything except the drawing-room which was on the ground floor to the left of the front-door. If Mrs. Warmer could have avoided showing this room to her visitor she would have done so. She had left it to the last in the hope that her visitor might be short of time — or possibly overlook the fact that there was another room to see — but her visitor pointed to the door and said, 'I suppose that's the drawing-room?' and Mrs. Warmer was obliged to say, 'Yes.'

The door was opened and they went in.

'Oh, it's lovely!' exclaimed Louise rapturously.

It certainly was an attractive room — rectangular in shape with windows at each end. One of the windows looked out towards the front and the path which led to the gate, the other which was smaller looked out on to a little terrace and beyond to the garden. (At least they would have looked out in these two directions if they had not been masked by untrimmed creepers and overgrown bushes and tangles of briar). There was a big fireplace with a stone chimney-piece, and across the ceiling from side to side there were enormous oak beams; the floor was of the same dark wood, polished and shining.

'It's lovely,' repeated Louise. 'The loveliest room in the house. I'm sure Bel will adore it.'

'I daresay it could be made quite nice,' said Mrs. Warmer grudgingly.

'There are violets somewhere!'

'No.'

'But there must be! I can smell them.'

'It's the floor polish.'

'It's fresh violets. There must be some growing outside the window.'

Mrs. Warmer did not reply.

Louise sighed. 'Well I must go now,' she said, glancing at her watch. 'Thank you very much indeed. You've been so helpful and kind. I'll ring up my friend and tell her all about it. She could come and see it, couldn't she?'

'Yes, miss. Any time that suits. That's what I'm here for — to show people the house.'

Louise hesitated. Should she or should she not? Then, making up her mind that she should, she searched in her bag and produced a suitable reward.

'No, thank you, miss,' said Mrs. Warmer putting her hands behind her back.

'But I've taken up so much of your time. Please, won't you — '

'No, thank you. That's what I'm here for — to show people the house.'

Oh dear, I've made it worse! thought Louise as

she walked down the path to the gate where her little car was waiting. I've made it a hundred times worse. Oh, dear, what a pity!

3

Louise was not the girl to let grass grow beneath her feet so the moment she entered Coombe House she rushed to the telephone and rang up her friend's flat. The telephone in Bel Lamington's flat was newly installed — her fiancé had insisted that she should have one. Bel's flat was very small and not particularly comfortable but it was a useful *pied à terre*. The Armstrongs had wanted her to go and stay with them at Coombe House until she was married but she had refused because she liked being independent — and she liked being in London because of Ellis. Of course Ellis was busy at the office all day (Copping, Brownlee and Copping was a firm well-known in the City and owned large warehouses at the Pool of London) but he managed to call in at the flat nearly every evening and often stayed to supper before going home to his mother's house at Beckenham. Bel would not have seen him so often if she had been staying at Coombe House.

Louise got her connection quite easily and was delighted when she heard her friend's voice. 'Oh, good!' she exclaimed. 'I was afraid you might be out to lunch or something. Listen, Bel, I've seen a house. It's a dream of a house — especially the drawing-room — and it's just the right size. The only thing is it's in awfully bad repair, but if Ellis could buy it cheap he could afford to spend

27

money on it, couldn't he? You'd love it, Bel. Honestly you would — and it's only five miles away, between here and Shepherdsford. You remember Shepherdsford, don't you? It's a very nice little place with quite good shops. There's an excellent train service from Ernleigh so Ellis could get up to town quite easily. You must come down and see the house at once in case someone else takes a fancy to it. You had better come to-morrow.'

'We've seen a house at Beckenham,' said Bel when she could get a word in edgeways.

'Oh, no!' cried Louise in dismay. 'Oh, no, Bel — honestly — it wouldn't *do*. Mrs. Brownlee is a dear — I know you like her — but she's a bit possessive. She is, really. If you go and live on her doorstep Ellis won't belong to you at all.'

There was silence.

'Bel, are you there?' cried Louise frantically.

'Yes, of course I'm here.'

'Well, don't you see my point?'

'Yes, but — but I don't want to be selfish. Ellis is all she's got.'

'That's just why!' cried Louise more frantically than before. 'Bel, listen, I must see you. You must come down here to-morrow. You can talk to Daddy about it — see? Come by the early train and I'll meet you at Ernleigh. You will come, won't you?'

'Yes, all right, I'll come.'

Louise was just putting down the receiver when Dr. Armstrong came in.

'Hallo, something for me?' he asked.

'No. At least — '

'Not Mrs. White?'

'No,' said Louise. 'It's Bel. I've told her she must come down to-morrow. Perhaps she'll listen to you.'

It was obvious to the doctor that something was wrong and a glance at his daughter's face did not reassure him. 'Just a minute, Lou,' he said. 'Just give me a minute to wash my hands. You can tell me all about it while we're having lunch.'

2

Louise was not very good at telling people about things; she became too excited and her tongue ran away with her, but fortunately the doctor was used to this peculiarity and was pretty good at disentangling the muddle and putting two and two together; so he listened carefully and occasionally stemmed the flow of narrative with a judicious question and by the time he had finished his helping of veal and ham pie and was starting to eat his pudding he had a reasonably clear idea of the matter.

Dr. Armstrong had an orderly mind so he saw there were two problems: first, whether Bel and Ellis should live at Beckenham 'on Mrs. Brownlee's doorstep': second, whether they should live near Shepherdsford in a dilapidated mansion which Louise had seen that morning. As to the first problem Dr. Armstrong agreed with his daughter that it was a mistake for a newly-married couple to set up house too near their relations — especially in the case of an only son and an adoring mother. As to the second problem, he was not so sure. He pointed out that Ellis Brownlee was an exceedingly busy man and would have to travel daily, so it might be better for them to settle nearer town.

'But they both want to live in the country,' objected Louise. 'And you can't get proper country nearer town and the train service is very good. Lots of men who live in Shepherdsford go up to town daily. Joan's husband does — you know that, Daddy. Oh, Daddy, I wish you could see Fletchers End you would love it and it only wants — '

'Fletchers End! Oh, I know it well. It used to belong to an old lady called Miss Lestrange. When she died she left it to her nephew who is in the Navy.'

'I told you that, Daddy. I told you it belonged to 'a naval officer in forrin parts'.'

'So you did — but you didn't mention his name, nor the name of the house either,' said Dr. Armstrong smiling.

'What was she like? I mean Miss Lestrange, Did she live there all by herself? She wasn't a patient was she?'

This was another of Louise's little peculiarities. She often asked two or three — or sometimes four — questions one after another without stopping so that the questionee was left bewildered, not knowing which to answer first. The doctor had discovered that much the best plan was to answer the last question first. By so doing it was often unnecessary to answer the other questions at all.

'She was — latterly,' he said. 'Miss Lestrange was really Whittaker's patient but she fell out with him so she sent for me. I told Whittaker of course, and he said I was welcome to her; he could do nothing with the old lady and he was sick and tired of her vagaries.'

'But you soon had her eating out of your hand?'

He chuckled. 'Not on your life! She wasn't the sort of old lady to eat out of anyone's hand. She was very short-tempered and touchy, very obstinate and proud — but all the same you couldn't help admiring her.'

'You mean she was very good-looking?' asked Louise with interest.

'Yes, she was very good-looking indeed, but I didn't mean that. It was her courage I admired. She suffered a great deal of pain but it never got her down. I admire guts,' added the doctor vulgarly.

'I know you do,' said his daughter. 'Well, you'll speak to Bel, won't you? I shall take her to see Fletchers End in the afternoon.'

3

Louise met her friend as arranged at Ernleigh Station. They kissed each other and both exclaimed at the same moment: 'How nice you look, darling!' Then they laughed.

'But you do, really,' declared Louise. 'Every time I see you I think you're nicer to look at. It suits you to be happy.'

'I'm terribly happy,' said Bel with a little sigh.

'Ellis is simply perfect; I can't think why he wants to marry me.'

This modest opinion of her own worth was not shared by her friends. Although not exactly pretty she was delightful to look at; her bright brown hair was brushed back from her forehead in a big smooth wave, her eyes were grey and widely spaced; her mouth, though rather large, curved very prettily when she smiled, her skin was pale, but smooth and unblemished. Not exactly pretty — certainly not beautiful like Louise — but with her own unusual charm. Before her engagement to Ellis Brownlee her expression had been too serious, for she was a lonely creature and her life had been difficult and arduous; but it suited her to be happy, as Louise had told her. The knowledge that she was loved and treasured had given her poise and a gentle dignity — it had given her a glow.

'Silly old donkey,' said Louise giving her arm an affectionate squeeze. 'Ellis is a very lucky man — and he knows it. Listen Bel,' she added as she steered her friend to the car which was waiting in the station-yard. 'Listen to me. You'll make an awful mistake if you go and live near Mrs. Brownlee. Daddy thinks so too, and you know how wise he is — '

'Oh, that's all settled.'

'All settled!' cried Louise in consternation.

'I mean we've settled not to buy that house at Beckenham.'

'Thank goodness!'

They got into the car.

'It was awfully silly, really,' continued Bel. 'You

see I thought Ellis wanted to live at Beckenham and he thought I did. It was only last night when he came in to supper that we suddenly discovered neither of us wanted to live there. Weren't we idiots?'

'You were, rather,' said Louise frankly. 'What a good thing you discovered it in time!'

'Only just in time. Ellis had written the letter offering to buy the house and he brought it to show me. He said, 'You're pleased about it, aren't you? I mean you think you'll be happy there?' And I said I'd be happy anywhere if — if we were together. So then it was all cleared up. We both want to live in the country — real proper country — and although Ellis is very fond of his mother he thinks it would be better if we don't live too near. She can come and stay with us whenever she likes and we can go and see her quite often.'

'Much better,' declared Louise.

'I think so too,' agreed Bel. 'It was just that I didn't want to be selfish.'

'I shall take you to see Fletchers End this afternoon.'

'Fletchers End,' said Bel thoughtfully, savouring the name on her tongue. 'There's something very attractive about the name.'

'Oh, I *do* hope you'll like it!' exclaimed Louise. 'It would be almost too good to be true.'

4

It had been decided that Dr. Armstrong was to 'speak to Bel' at lunch about the inadvisability of living on Mrs. Brownlee's doorstep, but this was unnecessary of course. Instead he was urged on by his daughter to talk about Fletchers End. He explained that at one time the house and garden had been well-cared-for (Miss Lestrange kept her property in excellent order), but when she became ill and was unable to see to things herself the place had begun to go downhill. The gardener, a man called Fuller, who lived in a tiny cottage in Archerfield village, had been a very good gardener in his day but he was old and had become unfit for heavy work. Even before Miss Lestrange died the place had deteriorated considerably.

'Didn't she have anyone to live with her?' Louise wanted to know.

Dr. Armstrong shook his head. 'It would have been very difficult to live with her. I think most of her family were dead except her sister, Mrs. Harding. She was much younger than Miss Lestrange. She came and stayed at Fletchers End when the old lady had an attack of flu; she was quite different, a nice kind sensible sort of person. She was fond of the old place and spoke to me several times about the way it was being neglected — but of course she could do nothing about it. Then, after Miss Lestrange died, it went from bad to worse. The house stood empty and the garden became a tangle of weeds and over-grown bushes.'

'Poor garden!' said Bel sadly.

'But of course it can be cleared,' said Louise. 'It will be rather fun getting it all tidied up and put in order, won't it, Bel?'

Dr. Armstrong could not help smiling. He knew his daughter and he could see she had made up her mind that Bel and Ellis would come and live at Fletchers End. He hoped they would. It would be delightful for Lou to have her friend so near — and it would be delightful for Bel also. The two were devoted to one another and, being entirely different, they were exceedingly good for one another. Apart from anything else it would be delightful to see the old house put to rights and tenanted by people who would appreciate its charm. It had distressed the good doctor to pass the place when he went his rounds and to see it looking so sad and neglected. He felt slightly guilty about it, to tell the truth. Not that he could have helped it of course — it was not really his fault that the house had been left to a young man who did not care a pin about it — but all the same it made him uncomfortable. So much so that whenever possible, he went by another road to avoid passing Fletchers End.

'You're very silent, Daddy!' said Louise suddenly.

'I was just — thinking, and remembering things,' the doctor explained.

4

The sun was shining upon Fletchers End when Bel first saw it and the first thing she noticed was the beautiful colour of the roof. Then she saw the windows which, having been washed and polished by Mrs. Warmer, were all glittering in the golden light of the summer afternoon.

'You said it was in terribly bad repair!' exclaimed Bel in surprise.

'It is,' Louise told her. 'You'll see when you go in; but if you could get it cheap you could afford to spend money on it — ' She had begun to wrestle with the gate.

Mrs. Warmer had been watching from a window so she came out and opened it for them.

'This is Miss Lamington,' said Louise. 'I told you about her didn't I?'

'Yes, miss,' said Mrs. Warmer.

They all went in together and began to go round the house. Louise was distressed to find that the caretaker had not forgiven her for whatever it was that she had done — or left undone. The woman was quite agreeable, quite polite, but she looked like a woman under a cloud. If Louise had not sat at her kitchen-table and partaken of her hospitality, had not heard her laughing merrily and enjoying a good joke, had not experienced her friendliness, had not been shown her treasure, had not been taken into her confidence as it were, she would have thought it was the woman's nature to be taciturn. Some people were like that — some people, but fortunately not many.

As a matter of fact Louise was too busy showing Bel the house and trying to make Bel take an interest in it to bother very much about the woman. Unfortunately Bel seemed to be taking very little interest in the house. There was a dazed sort of look about Bel. She gazed about her in a casual manner, asked no questions and scarcely seemed to hear what Louise was saying. With two such silent and disinterested companions it was difficult — even for Louise — to keep the conversation going, so the tour of Fletchers End was accomplished in record time. Fortunately Louise remembered to ask about the septic tank; her father had told her to do so.

'Yes, miss, there's a skeptic tank at the end of the garden,' said Mrs. Warmer. 'Perhaps you would care to see it.'

Louise did not care to see it. What was the use of seeing it when Bel was not interested in the house? Besides even if she saw it she would not be any the wiser; she knew a good deal about houses but nothing whatever about septic tanks.

By this time they were in the kitchen. It had been left to the end. Here, upon the table, was a large bowl of roses at the sight of which Bel seemed to waken from her trance.

'What lovely roses!' said Bel.

'I like roses,' said Mrs. Warmer. 'Mr. Fuller brought me those. He grows them in his garden.'

Bel looked at Mrs. Warmer and suddenly became conscious of her as a person. During the tour of the house she had not been real to Bel — she had been the caretaker, that was all — but now quite suddenly she had become a human being who was fond of flowers.

'I love flowers — and roses are best of all,' said Bel. 'Mr. Brownlee, my fiancé, is terribly fond of roses. When we come to live here we shall have lots of roses — I mean IF we come to live here, of course.'

'That will be nice,' said Mrs. Warmer faintly. She felt as if a cold hand had gripped her heart.

Bel looked at her and their eyes met. 'What will you do if the house is sold?' asked Bel.

'I don't — know — miss. I've been here — such a long time.'

'I suppose — ' said Bel doubtfully. 'I suppose you wouldn't want to stay on? I mean if we — if someone bought the house.'

'Stay on, miss?'

'As a sort of — of housekeeper? No, of course you wouldn't.'

Mrs. Warmer moistened her dry lips and said huskily, 'I would — consider it.'

'We should want someone to be here,' explained Bel. 'I mean while the alterations were being done — to look after things for us. Some people might be frightened to stay here alone, but you're used to it, aren't you?'

'Yes, I'm used to it. I been here nearly six years.'

'And you don't mind?'

Mrs. Warmer swallowed a queer lump in her throat which seemed to be interfering with her breathing. 'I love it,' she said. 'I love Fletchers

End — every little bit of it. I love the nice thick walls and the big oak beams and I love the oak floors that takes such a nice polish — and all the funny little cupboards — and the handles on the doors — so, if you wants me to stay on, I'll — I'll consider it.'

Bel wondered what she meant. Did she mean she would think it over or did she mean that the offer was accepted? 'But of course it all depends upon whether Mr. Brownlee likes it,' said Bel hastily. 'You understand that, don't you?'

'But he *will* like it,' declared Mrs. Warmer. 'You'll come here I'm sure, and I'll stay on. I'll stay while the workmen are here and look after everything and see that they do their jobs, and when it's all nice and ready I'll stay and do the cooking and clean the house. It's a nice house — it really is. It's a friendly house. I'm sure you'll like it. I've been here nearly six years . . . '

They were now on their way to the gate and Mrs. Warmer was still talking breathlessly, talking about Fletchers End, explaining that the people who lived here long ago used to make arrows, pointing out to the future Mrs. Brownlee that it had once been two houses joined together before it had been made into one, assuring the future Mrs. Brownlee that in all the time she had lived here — nearly six years — never a drop of water had come in through the roof — not like these modern houses, put up all in a minute and so carelessly that the wind blew the tiles off and the rain poured in through the holes.

'There's a young man in the village that could make us a lovely new gate very reasonable,' declared Mrs. Warmer as she wrestled manfully with the old one.

They said good-bye, scrambled into the car and Louise drove away. She stopped suddenly when they had turned the corner and switched off the engine.

'What's the matter?' asked Bel, but Louise was laughing so immoderately that it was some time before she could reply.

'Oh, dear!' cried Louise at last. 'Oh, goodness, it was so funny. Oh, dear, I'm quite sore with laughing!'

'What was funny?'

'You were,' gasped Louise. 'I thought — you hated the place.'

'You thought I hated the place?'

'Yes, of course. You strolled round with a vacant expression and never looked at anything — and then — quite suddenly — you came to life — and — and not only bought the house — but — but engaged a cook — engaged a cook!' repeated Louise, her voice going up into a little squeak. 'Do you realise what you've done? You've — engaged — a — cook.'

'Louise, I didn't. I didn't buy the house — '

'Well, you practically bought it,' said Louise, mopping her streaming eyes. 'Obviously you intend Ellis to buy it which comes to the same thing.'

'It doesn't at all. If Ellis likes it he'll buy it, but I shan't try to persuade him.'

'He'll buy the house if you like it. You *did* like it, Bel?'

Bel sighed. 'I adored the house the moment I

saw it; when I walked in at the door I knew it was the house of my dreams. There was no need to look at it properly because I'd seen it before.'

'Seen it before?'

'In dreams,' said Bel vaguely. 'I suppose it must have been in dreams that I saw it all before. I felt as if I had lived there — I knew it so well, you see. I even remembered the scent of violets in the drawing-room.'

Louise was not laughing now. 'Oh, you noticed that?' she said. 'I noticed it yesterday but it was even stronger to-day.'

5

Bel had seen Fletchers End on a fine sunny afternoon; Ellis saw it for the first time on a wet Saturday morning. Unfortunately Bel was laid up with a cold so she could not go with him, and as Ellis did not want to go alone he took his friend Reggie Stephenson, who was an architect, to have a look at the house. Reggie was a good deal younger than Ellis, small and thin with a high forehead and sandy hair, rather insignificant in appearance, but there was a twinkle in his eye and Ellis liked him. He lived in Beckenham with his parents so the two knew each other pretty well and often played golf together. Ellis did not know much about his capabilities as an architect — probably they would need someone more experienced if they were going to buy the place — but there was no harm in taking Reggie and seeing what he thought of it.

Ellis arranged with Mr. Baker, the building contractor at Ernleigh, to meet them at Fletchers End and the two friends set off together in Ellis's car early in the morning.

Neither Ellis nor Reggie had ever been in the district before and there were so many little roads and twisting lanes that they lost their way and wasted a great deal of time wandering about the country. It was beautiful country, with tall trees, and little streams with willows growing on their banks, and meadows full of placid cows. In spite of the rain which had begun to fall with relentless persistency the two friends enjoyed their drive — it was pleasant and peaceful after the noise and bustle of town.

When at last they arrived at Fletchers End Mr. Baker was waiting for them at the gate, sheltering beneath a large black umbrella. He was a paunchy little man with a round chubby face and several chins. The chubby face wore a somewhat anxious expression, but when the car stopped and the visitors got out it broke into an enormous smile. Mr. Baker had been afraid they were not coming and was delighted to find his fear had been groundless. Mr. Baker was a shrewd business-man and he had decided that if he played his cards well this rich gentleman from London would buy the old house and give him the job of putting it in order. A big job it would be — a job that would take months and cost a mint of money — Mr. Baker was determined to get it.

Fletchers End was not looking its best that morning. Bel had told Ellis a great deal about it but somehow he had not expected the place to look so dreary and neglected. 'In bad repair' was a ridiculous understatement of its condition. However Bel seemed enchanted with the place so he and Reggie must have a look at it. There was nothing else to be done.

Mr. Baker introduced himself and began at once to explain the history of the house — or at least its recent history. Mr. Baker knew nothing of the fletchers, and cared less, but he knew that the place had been well kept when it had belonged to Miss Lestrange, it was only in the last few years that it had been neglected. Mr. Baker deplored the neglect, it was unpardonable in his opinion, but fortunately it was an old house, well and truly built. A modern house would have been utterly destroyed by such treatment.

Reggie Stephenson agreed that this was so. 'We'll see,' he said. 'Mr. Brownlee is interested, but he doesn't want to buy a ruin.'

'Quite so, quite so,' nodded Mr. Baker. 'I'll take you round. It's my belief you'll be pleasantly surprised when you've seen its condition, Mr. Stephenson.'

The gate stood open so they went in. Ellis saw the garden; a mass of vegetation, green and sodden, dripping with rain; the path up to the front door was slimy with some sort of unpleasant weed; the door itself was paintless, crooked, spongy with damp; the creepers hung down over the lintel in untidy swathes.

'Good heavens!' exclaimed Ellis under his breath.

'It was a bee-ootiful garden in Miss Lestrange's time,' declared Mr. Baker. 'Quite a sight it was. All it needs is a couple of men to tidy it up a bit. They'd do it in half no time.'

The stone-paved hall was dark and gloomy; nothing could be seen of it until Reggie switched on the light — a single bulb hanging from a beam in the ceiling.

'It isn't damp, anyhow,' said Reggie, sniffing like a terrier at a rat-hole. 'And, Ellis, look at those beams! Absolutely gorgeous!'

'There's beams like that all over the house,' said Mrs. Warmer appearing suddenly from the dim passages which led to the back premises. 'They're made of solid oak, that's what. It's the same kind of wood that was used to make ships for Queen Elizabeth's navy — in the Armada it was,' she added a trifle vaguely.

'That's right,' agreed Reggie, putting up his hand and stroking the well-polished surface. 'The wooden walls of England were made of stuff like this. You couldn't get it now for love nor money. I only wish you could.'

'What about dry rot and — and that sort of thing?' asked Ellis who had been listening to his friend's panegyrics with a good deal of misgiving. It was all very well to talk about Queen Elizabeth's navy and the wooden walls of England, but what Ellis wanted was a comfortable house to live in.

'That remains to be seen,' replied Reggie cheerfully. 'We'll start at the top. The condition of the roof is of the first importance.'

They started at the top. Reggie climbed up a ladder and disappeared from view. He was up there for half an hour or longer. The others waited; they could hear him tapping and probing. When he returned from his expedition he was dirty and there were cobwebs in his hair. 'Ugh, spiders!' said Reggie. 'Can't bear spiders — never could — but there's nothing much the matter with the roof. Those old fellows knew how to build.'

'They had the materials,' said Mr. Baker, who

felt this statement to be a reflection upon his own skill. 'Give me the materials — *and* the labour — *and* the time — and I'll guarantee to make as good a job any day, Mr. Stephenson.'

'Who's going to give you the materials — and the labour — and the time?' asked Reggie laughing.

Mr. Baker shook his head sadly.

After that they went into every room and Reggie crawled over the floors, sniffing and tapping; in several places he insisted that Mr. Baker should remove some boards in the flooring. Mr. Baker performed this little job reluctantly for his figure was not suited to stooping and his knees creaked alarmingly when he knelt down; he puffed and blew and perspiration broke out upon his forehead. To make matters worse Mr. Baker had attired himself in his best suit of navy blue worsted and a new pair of brown suede shoes — not the sort of garments he would have chosen for scrambling about on the floor.

Reggie leaned out of every window and stabbed the woodwork with his knife; he peered up chimneys, gazed into the cistern and questioned Mr. Baker about the drains.

Ellis followed round watching his friend's activities but at last he was so tired, and so bored with the proceedings, that he went and sat down on the stairs. He had satisfied himself that Reggie Stephenson knew his job and was carrying it out with commendable energy. If you call in an expert you can sit down and let him get on with the job, thought Ellis.

Ellis had been sitting on the step for some time, and had begun to wish it were not quite so hard, when Mrs. Warmer found him and hailed him into her kitchen and gave him a comfortable chair. She offered him a cup of tea, which he accepted with alacrity, and she gave him a great deal of interesting information about the district and the people who lived in the village of Archerfield and the cricket matches which took place in the meadow down by the stream. Revived by the refreshment and by Mrs. Warmer's conversation, Ellis began to feel a good deal more cheerful about the house. Perhaps it was not so bad after all . . . perhaps it might be made habitable. He was prepared to endure quite a lot of hardship and inconvenience if Bel thought she would be happy here.

Presently Reggie Stephenson looked in, 'Oh, there you are!' he exclaimed, 'I've been looking for you everywhere — I might have known you'd find the most comfortable place in the house! Our Mr. Baker has gone home to dinner. What are we doing about a meal?'

'There's ham and eggs, sir,' suggested Mrs. Warmer, ' — if that would suit.'

'Oh, no!' exclaimed Ellis. 'It would be far too much trouble. We can easily go to Shepherdsford; there's an inn called The Owl — '

'It would be no bother at all,' said Mrs. Warmer earnestly. 'It would be a pleasure — really it would. I just wish I had something nicer. A juicy bit of steak — underdone — is what gentlemen likes . . . and if only I'd known — '

Unlike Ellis, Reggie had partaken of no refreshment since breakfast — and breakfast seemed a long time ago. He had been taking a great deal of strenuous physical exercise and he was famished. The mere mention of a juicy bit of steak — underdone — made his mouth water. But, failing that, ham and eggs were not to be despised. It was nearly two o'clock by this time and quite possibly The Owl might refuse to give chance visitors a meal. Wasn't it better, demanded Reggie, wasn't it much wiser to accept Mrs. Warmer's kind invitation than to put their trust in the tender mercies of The Owl?

Mrs. Warmer added her persuasions and, after some argument, the two friends sat down together while their hostess set about the task of preparing their meal.

It was nice that they were staying, thought Mrs. Warmer. There were two reasons why it was nice. First and foremost she hoped to hear them discussing the house and to learn whether or not Mr. Brownlee was going to buy it. She wanted him to, of course; she wanted with all her heart to stay on at Fletchers End, and Mrs. Brownlee had said she could! (At least she wasn't Mrs. Brownlee yet, but Mrs. Warmer couldn't remember her name and she was going to be Mrs. Brownlee quite soon so it didn't matter). Second: here was a golden opportunity to impress Mr. Brownlee with her skill in cooking so that he would make no objections to his future wife's choice of a cook. Mrs. Warmer sighed when she thought of the juicy bit of steak which she might have got yesterday at the butcher's if only she had known . . . but it could not be helped and, as a matter of fact, Mrs. Warmer was extremely skilful in the preparation of ham and eggs; she made up her mind to give these two gentlemen the best ham and eggs they had ever tasted.

'Look here, Ellis,' said Reggie Stephenson, producing his notebook and flipping over the pages. 'I've been round this house pretty thoroughly and I can tell you this; the structure is sound. There are various small details that require attention, but — '

'What about dry-rot?'

'You've got dry-rot on the brain, haven't you?' said Reggie smiling. 'Well, I wouldn't stake my life on it — I mean it will need a much more thorough examination than I could give it this morning — but I shall be very much surprised if dry-rot is found in this house. There's wood-worm here and there, but it isn't extensive and can be dealt with fairly easily. Now for the plumbing,' said Reggie. 'Well, the plumbing leaves a good deal to be desired. Some of the pipes will have to be renewed, and all the fittings of course. You'll want another bathroom and — '

'And fixed basins of course.'

'I wouldn't think of it!' Reggie declared. 'My dear fellow, have you looked at the walls? If you start making holes for pipes in these solid stone walls you'll find yourself in serious trouble.'

'There are fixed basins in all the bedrooms at Rose Hill.'

'Rose Hill!' exclaimed Reggie scornfully. 'Good heavens, you can't compare that modern atrocity of your mother's with a place like Fletchers End! This is a HOUSE, Ellis. It was built by people who had the best materials in the world at their disposal — and the skill to use them — and pride in a good job of work. This is a house for gracious living.'

Ellis gazed at his friend in astonishment. Rose Hill was his mother's pride and joy and the envy of her friends, it was bright and cheerful; it was fitted with all the most modern inventions for labour-saving — including fixed basins in all the bedrooms — and it was kept in perfect condition inside and out. To hear Rose Hill referred to as 'that modern atrocity' positively took his breath away.

'Look here, Ellis,' continued Reggie after a short silence. 'I had better tell you the worst about this place. The window-frames are rotten; in fact practically all the outside woodwork is rotten for lack of paint and will have to be renewed. That will cost something. As regards the inside of the house I've got quite a number of suggestions — but we needn't go into that now. The important thing to settle is whether or not you want to make an offer for it. My advice is — ' he paused.

'Well, what's your advice?' asked Ellis impatiently.

'If you can get the house at a reasonable price and can afford to spend a good deal of money I advise you to buy it.' He hesitated and then added, 'If I could afford it I would buy the house

50

myself. It's a house I would be proud to own.'

Of course Mrs. Warmer had heard every word; she had been in the kitchen all the time, cooking and making toast. She had been heating her two best plates (lovely big plates, they were, with a picture of a bridge and a stream and willow trees and funny little men); she had been laying the table with a clean white cloth and setting out knives and forks and cups and saucers. Of course Mrs. Warmer had heard every word, she could not have helped hearing every word unless she had been deaf, but although she would dearly have loved to join in the conversation she remained silent. It's not for me to interfere, said Mrs. Warmer to herself and she fastened her lips together firmly.

3

The meal was ready now so Mrs. Warmer put it on the table; a rack of pale-brown toast; a slab of farm-butter, yellow as gold, with a raised pattern of buttercups on its pristine surface; half-a-dozen wholemeal scones on a plate with a design of roses; a large brown tea-pot, a milk jug and a bowl of sugar. Lastly she put down before each of her guests a large blue and white plate containing two perfectly fried eggs — their whites white as snow, their yolks orange-coloured — nestling amongst four crisp rashers of ham.

Reggie, who had been talking hard, was suddenly silent with astonishment and gazed at the vision which had appeared before his eyes with an expression of awe.

Ellis, not as hungry as his friend, was able to voice his admiration and exclaimed, 'That plate of ham and eggs is a picture! It's almost too beautiful to eat!'

'But not quite,' declared Reggie seizing his knife and fork.

'They're nice eggs,' said Mrs. Warmer smiling indulgently as she watched the results of her labours disappearing. 'You don't get eggs like that in town. I get my eggs from Mr. Carruthers. Lovely hens he has — all running about in a big green field — that's why the yolks is so dark. They've got quite a different taste from the eggs you buys in towns. Mr. Carruthers says he wouldn't eat batteries, nor he wouldn't keep his hens in prison even if they did lay two or three eggs a day. There's no good in them, no nourishment, Mr. Carruthers says.'

'How right he is!' said Reggie with his mouth full.

'He's a sweep,' said Mrs. Warmer. She added after a moment's silence, 'He sweeps chimbleys.'

'I'd like to meet Mr. Carruthers,' said Reggie. 'It would be interesting to hear what he has to say about these chimneys.'

'Oh, he'd tell you in a minute. Mr. Carruthers knows all about chimbleys. He comes here often. I has to keep the fires going to air the house so the chimbleys has to be swep' and I wouldn't have nobody else but Mr. Carruthers.' She leant on the table and continued. 'He says there used to be little boys that climbed up inside the chimbleys — that was how they was cleaned. I thought Mr. Carruthers was having me on when he told me that — but it's true. He shined his torch up some of the chimbleys and there was little rungs so the boys could climb up easily. I saw the little rungs with my own eyes. Cruel, I call it.'

'Mr. Dickens and Mr. Kingsley shared your opinion,' Reggie told her.

'Well, I don't know the gentlemen but they're right. Fancy making those poor little boys climb up inside dirty, sooty chimbleys! I said as much to Mr. Carruthers; it was downright cruel, I said.'

There was a short silence while Mrs. Warmer filled up the tea-pot and produced another plate of wholemeal scones.

'I should like a chat with your Mr. Carruthers,' repeated Reggie.

'Any time,' nodded Mrs. Warmer. 'Any time you like. If you just drop me a postcard I'll see he's here. The milk very kindly takes messages for me.'

'The milk of human kindness,' murmured Reggie.

'Everyone round here is very kind indeed,' Mrs. Warmer declared. 'All except Mr. Black that lives at the other end of the village near the post office. Mr. Black is a very disreputable man,' she added solemnly.

Reggie's eyes twinkled. 'The disreputable Mr. Black — rather a good title for a thriller, don't you think so, Ellis?'

Ellis shook his head at his ebullient friend and

the friend relapsed into silence.

The ice having been broken and a friendly atmosphere established Mrs. Warmer felt she could mention without impropriety the subject nearest her heart.

'You could buy the house cheap if you wanted,' she said.

Her two guests looked up from their almost empty plates with one accord. They were too surprised to speak.

Mrs. Warmer nodded two or three times. 'I been thinking about it a lot. It was what Mr. Tennant said last week when he came for a look round. He was talking about the windows, saying as how something better be done soon or the glass would fall out.'

'Exactly my opinion,' put in Reggie.

'Quite rotten, Mr. Tennant said the wood was. So I asked him why he didn't have them put right and he said 'I can't get no money out of that young rapscallion' — and he called the young gentleman a bad name that I wouldn't soil my lips with,' added Mrs. Warmer primly. 'Of course Mr. Tennant was angry — that was the reason, but still . . . '

'Very annoying for him,' Ellis suggested.

'Yes, it was no wonder he was angry. He's got to look after the house and get it sold, and there isn't many people would buy it — let alone look at it properly — the way it's been neglected. Mr. Tennant gets necessary things done, like mending a pipe that's leaking, but it's him that has to foot the bill. He said that to me with his own lips and he said, 'That young rapscallion

54

owes me something like four hundred pounds and I shan't get a penny unless the house is sold'.'

She paused for a moment but her audience was silent. It was hanging upon her words with flattering attention.

'So then,' continued Mrs. Warmer. 'So then I said, 'that's awful, Mr. Tennant. Why don't you write to him about it?' and he said he'd written over and over again and sometimes 'the young rapscallion' didn't answer at all and sometimes he wrote and said he was hard-up at the moment. 'He's always hard-up and always will be' said Mr. Tennant in a rage.'

'I hope you are paid regularly?' said Ellis who had been listening to this revelation in astonishment.

'Oh, yes, Mr. Tennant is a very nice gentleman; he gives me my money as regular as clockwork every Friday — except what he has to take off for National Health — but I never knew before that he pays me out of his own pocket. It doesn't seem right, does it?'

'It's very wrong,' declared Ellis. 'But of course he'll get it back from the young — er — '

'Mr. Lestrange his name is.'

'Oh, yes. Well, Mr. Lestrange will have to settle his lawyer's bill when the house is sold. No doubt Mr. Tennant will see that he gets what's due to him.'

'But if it isn't sold he won't get nothing,' said Mrs. Warmer significantly.

Reggie chuckled in appreciation. 'You see the point, don't you, Ellis?'

Of course Ellis had seen the point. 'We had better call upon Mr. Tennant at once if not sooner,' he declared. 'It's a good opportunity to see him while we're here.'

'On a Saturday afternoon!' exclaimed Mrs. Warmer. 'You won't find Mr. Tennant in his office on a Saturday; he likes his golf. Besides you didn't ought to seem too keen. You'd be better to write a letter and say you've seen the house and you're interested, but it needs so much doing to it — specially the windows and the drain-pipes — that you couldn't think about it unless you was to get it cheap.'

'At a reasonable figure,' murmured Reggie nodding.

'Yes, that's right. You know the right words to put.'

'You know the right way to go about it,' declared Reggie. He added, 'I take off my hat to you, Mrs. Warmer — or at least I would if I happened to be wearing a hat.'

Mrs. Warmer laughed. 'You *are* a one, Mr. Stephenson,' she said.

4

The drive home was very pleasant for the clouds had rolled away and the sun was shining. And, having received clear and detailed directions from Mrs. Warmer, the two friends found themselves on the main road ten minutes after leaving Fletchers End. As they whizzed along the fine smooth surface in Ellis's comfortable

Wolsley, he and Reggie discussed the old house thoroughly and Ellis decided quite definitely that if the surveyor's report was favourable and he could buy the place at 'a reasonable figure' he would do so.

'And if I buy it I hope you'll undertake the job of supervising the renovations,' added Ellis.

'Yes, of course I will!' exclaimed Reggie with enthusiasm. 'It would be a peach of a job — we could do wonders with that beautiful old house! I've got all sorts of plans simmering in my head. For one thing,' continued Reggie eagerly. 'If you could afford the money I'd like to put a bow-window in the drawing-room and a glass door leading on to the terrace. It would improve the room tremendously — and think how nice it would be to stroll out on to the terrace on a fine summer evening . . .'

Reggie went on talking about all the improvements which he had thought of for quite a long time and Ellis listened and agreed and said that they sounded grand — but of course they must ask Bel. It was only when they were quite near home that the subject was changed.

'Mrs. Warmer is a rum 'un, isn't she?' said Reggie. 'Why did you shut me up when I wanted to ask her about the disreputable Mr. Black?'

'Oh,' said Ellis, 'it was just that I didn't like you making fun of her when she was giving us such an excellent meal.'

'She didn't notice.'

'She might have noticed. She's a good deal more shrewd than she seems.'

Reggie agreed to this definition of Mrs.

Warmer. 'Oh, well, she didn't do badly out of us,' he said.

'What do you mean? I gave her ten bob as we were coming away, but that wasn't — '

'Yes, I saw you,' said Reggie chuckling. 'I'd just given her the same myself, so you see she didn't do badly out of us. What's going to become of the good lady when you buy the house? — IF you buy the house,' he added.

'She's staying on as cook. Bel arranged it with her.'

'What!' cried Reggie. 'My hat! Some people have all the luck. I hope you'll ask me to breakfast sometimes.'

'Yes, of course,' said Ellis laughing. 'Or perhaps you'd rather come to lunch; a juicy bit of steak — underdone — is what gentlemen likes.'

6

Ellis had decided to buy Fletchers End, but the negotiations took some time. Roy Lestrange was a Lieutenant-Commander in Her Majesty's Navy and was serving in an Aircraft Carrier based at Hong Kong. He wanted to sell the house, but he wanted to get as much for it as he possibly could — a not unnatural desire. Mr. Tennant was eager to sell the house at any reasonable price — as Mrs. Warmer had foretold. These divergent points of view were difficult to reconcile. If they could have sat down round a table and thrashed it out the matter could have been settled in an hour but letters took time to come and go and cables were found to be an unsatisfactory means of communication. With the best will in the world and regardless of expense it is difficult to explain anything complicated by cablegram.

Mr. Tennant started off by writing a long explanatory letter setting forth the advisability of getting the place off their hands before it deteriorated further. If the house were not sold immediately a great deal of money must be spent on the windows otherwise the panes of glass would begin to fall out of their frames. He mentioned that his account up to date for absolutely essential repairs and caretaker's wages was now four hundred and twenty-seven pounds thirteen shillings and sixpence and an early settlement would oblige. He went on to say it was his considered opinion that very few people would think of buying a place which had become so unattractive, but fortunately here was Mr. Ellis Brownlee, a partner in the well-known firm of Copping, Brownlee and Copping, who was willing to buy Fletchers End at a reasonable figure; therefore let it be sold immediately at a reasonable figure to Mr. Brownlee.

It was a well-thought-out letter and Mr. Tennant felt certain it would do the trick, so he was exceedingly disappointed when Mr. Lestrange replied quite shortly that the figure mentioned was not reasonable — in fact it was ludicrous. Mr. Brownlee must be made to pay more.

Several cablegrams were exchanged but no progress was made and at last Ellis became impatient. He rang up Mr. Tennant and informed him that there was another house in the same neighbourhood which had come into the market. He was arranging to see it next week.

Mr. Tennant was alarmed; he saw his four hundred and twenty-seven pounds receding into the distance! He composed a very expensive cable to 'that rapscallion' informing him of the new development, threatening to give up his management of Mr. Lestrange's affairs and to sue him for the payment of his account.

The rapscallion cabled back, *Sell the place for what you can get.*

Fletchers End was sold.

2

All this time Bel had been on tenterhooks, scarcely daring to hope that the house of her dreams would become her future home. Unlike Louise, whose passage through life had been smooth and pleasant, Bel's passage had been rough. Life had dealt her some hard blows; she was used to disappointments; she did not expect Fate to be kind. She had been amazed and almost incredulous when she had discovered that Ellis Brownlee loved her and wanted to marry her. The mere idea of living at Fletchers End — with Ellis — was overwhelming. Bel kept on telling herself that it could not happen — not possibly — and she had practically convinced herself of the fact; so when, just a week before the wedding, Ellis came in to supper at the flat and hugged her even more enthusiastically than usual and cried, 'Bel, guess what! *I've bought it!* Fletchers End belongs to us — to you and me. It's fixed. I did it this morning,' she almost swooned in his arms. She was going to be married to Ellis and live at Fletchers End! It was almost too much happiness to bear.

Ellis was excited too, for this time he had set his heart on the place (the arrangement to look at Woodhill had been made when he was angry and impatient with all the delays and had felt that something must be settled at once). It was not Woodhill he wanted, it was Fletchers End. Now he had got it, and had got it at a reasonable price, so they could make all the alterations that Reggie had suggested. They could put in central heating; they could renew the electric wiring; they could make the new bathroom; they could even build the bow-window in the drawing-room in place of the small window facing west.

'And the glass door opening on to the terrace?' asked Bel.

'Yes, there must certainly be a glass door.'

'Ellis, I can scarcely believe it!'

Ellis laughed. 'Neither can I,' he said. 'But it's true. You and I are going to live in that lovely old house together for the rest of our lives. Of course it will take months before it's all ready — goodness knows how long it will take!'

'It doesn't matter how long it takes,' said Bel with a little sigh.

They sat down to supper and began to talk more reasonably about their plans.

'I've phoned to Reggie,' said Ellis. 'He's delighted. He's going down to-morrow to see Baker and put things in hand. I wish I could go down myself and see to things but that's impossible at the moment. I'm much too busy at the office.'

Bel knew this of course. She knew a great deal about the firm for she had been a member of the staff. She had been employed first as a typist and afterwards as Ellis Brownlee's secretary — it was in the latter capacity that she had learnt so much about the way the business was conducted. It was a very interesting business — or so Bel thought — for the firm owned large warehouses at The Pool of London and ships came from all over the world bringing merchandise which was discharged at Copping Wharf and stored in the warehouses and afterwards distributed to traders all over the country. She and Ellis had often joked about the cargoes of 'ivory and apes and peacocks' which the 'triremes' brought to Copping Wharf. The cargoes of modern times were less romantic perhaps but a great deal more useful, consisting of tea and coffee and sugar, dried fruits of various kinds, rice and tapioca and other comestibles too numerous to mention.

When Bel was there the firm had been designated, Copping, Wills and Brownlee, but (Mr. Wills having been obliged to retire owing to a nervous breakdown) Mr. Copping's young son had now become the junior partner. Bel knew James Copping well. He had a talent for languages and quite often he had come into the office to translate foreign letters. She knew him and liked him but he was very young and inexperienced and, until he had settled down and learnt a great deal more, he would not be much help. The elder Mr. Copping was extremely clever and reliable but unfortunately he was getting old and suffered from an unusual form of heart-trouble. When he was able he came to the office daily and did his full share of the work but sometimes for long periods he was obliged to rest and the whole responsibility for the direction of affairs devolved upon Ellis Brownlee.

'Yes, I know you're terribly busy,' said Bel. 'But Mr. Copping is pretty well at the moment, isn't he? Do you think he'll manage all right while we're away.'

'I hope so. It's only for a week,' replied Ellis.

They had arranged to go to Paris for their honeymoon — but only for a week. Ellis did not feel he could be away for longer until Jim Copping had learnt the ropes and could take his proper place.

'It's a pity I can't take a fortnight,' Ellis continued, 'but it's impossible. Young Jim is tremendously keen but he knows practically nothing about running the business.' He hesitated and then added, 'We ought to have fixed up where we're going to spend the winter. Fletchers End won't be ready until the spring.'

'It would be better for you to be in town,' said Bel thoughtfully. 'I mean you're so busy — '

'Much better,' he agreed. 'Why shouldn't we live here, just temporarily? It's small but it's very convenient for the office and it would be difficult to find another flat.'

Bel was doubtful. She had lived in her flat for years and knew its disadvantages. 'I don't think it would be very comfortable for you,' she said.

'It would be better than a hotel (where we should have no privacy), and much less expensive. We want to save money for Fletchers End, don't we? Carpets and curtains and furniture and all sorts of things.'

Bel agreed, but she did not feel happy about the plan. She wanted Ellis to be *more* comfortable when he was married — not less — and however hard she tried it would be impossible to make Ellis more comfortable in the tiny flat than he had been in his mother's modern well-designed house at Beckenham.

The flat was in Mellington Street — a not very salubrious district — and was at the top of the house, high up amongst the roof-tops. It was reached by an ill-lighted stone-stair with doors on every landing. Presumably people lived behind all these doors, for there was rarely a vacant flat in the building, but in all the years Bel had lived there she had never become acquainted with any of her neighbours. The flats were said to be all alike but Bel was the fortunate possessor of a tiny roof-garden outside her sitting-room window. Here she grew plants in big stone troughs and window-boxes and here, on summer evenings, she would sit out on a deck chair. It was a pleasant place to sit — except for the smuts which fell from the smoking chimneys — and it made all the difference to Bel, who loved flowers, to have a few flowers of her own to enjoy.

The flat was cheap of course, which was the principal reason why Bel had rented it, and she was used to its inconveniences by this time — but how would Ellis like it? That was the question.

Bel explained all this to Ellis and he replied that he did not mind a few inconveniences as long as they could be together — he and Bel. It was a very satisfactory reply but it did not altogether banish Bel's apprehensions.

It was late that night when Ellis went away for they had so much to talk about and so many matters to arrange.

When he had said good-bye he hesitated at the

door and said, 'That's fixed, then. We'll come straight back here after our honeymoon . . . but don't mention it to Mother. I mean there's no need for her to know about it until we're settled. She might want us to spend the winter with her at Rose Hill.'

Bel had been thinking exactly the same thing. Indeed she had been wondering whether it was her duty to suggest that they should ask Mrs. Brownlee to have them. Mrs. Brownlee would be only too delighted and it would be a great deal more comfortable for Ellis, but still . . .

'We want to be together — just you and I — don't we?' said Ellis.

It was very strange how their ideas were always in accord.

7

Several days before the wedding Bel went to stay at Coombe House to help with the preparations. She was considerably alarmed to find preparations being made on such a large scale for she and Ellis both wanted a very quiet wedding. Louise had agreed. 'Just a few friends,' she had said and Bel had replied, 'That will be lovely.' But surely, thought Bel, surely if just a few friends were expected to attend the reception there was no need to clear the drawing-room and pile all the furniture in one of the upstairs bedrooms. Surely there was no need for the enormous number of champagne glasses which were being unpacked from a box in the attic and arranged upon the sideboard in the dining-room.

'They'll have to be washed,' said Louise. 'I'll get Joan to come and do it to-morrow morning. She asked if she could help — and it's the very job for Joan.'

'Are there a lot of people coming?'

'I'm not sure how many,' said Louise vaguely. 'Let me see. We had to ask the Musgraves of course. They live at Shepherdsford so it will be nice for you to know them. There's Mrs. Musgrave — she's a pet — and Rose, the youngest daughter. Rose lives with her mother at The Bridle House. The other daughter, Margaret, is married to Bernard Warren and they've got a darling little baby boy. Meg and Bernard are my greatest friends — next to you. Then there's Edward and Joan. She's coming to wash the glasses for me. And there's Sylvia Newbigging and her father. He's a retired colonel and a great friend of Daddy's. They play golf together sometimes so we had to ask him. We decided not to ask the new secretary of the golf-club, he isn't nearly as amusing as Freddie Stafford. Perhaps you remember me telling you that Freddie married Mrs. Winter and they've started a hotel somewhere near Cannes. I believe it's a very comfortable hotel — small but extremely well-run.'

Bel had no recollection of this. She said hopefully, 'Is that all?'

'Oh, no, not nearly,' replied Louise. 'We had to ask Mr. and Mrs. Mainwaring; they would have been frightfully hurt if we'd left them out . . . and of course Lady Steyne may not come — she's old, you see — but Miss Penney is coming to do the flowers in the church — isn't it kind of her?'

'Yes,' said Bel.

'Then there are all the people from Beckenham. Mrs. Brownlee and her sister Mrs. Playter, who lives at Bournemouth, and several friends and relations who have known Ellis all his life. And Ellis asked me to send an invitation to Reggie Stephenson, the man who is going to help you with the alterations at Fletchers End. He's going to be the best man, of course, isn't he? Then Daddy said we must ask Dr. Whittaker who is the doctor at Shepherdsford. I didn't want to ask him, really, but of course I had to . . . '

Louise paused for breath and then continued, 'I asked the Dering Johnstones — you like them, don't you Bel? Of course I never thought they would come — all the way from Drumburly! But Rhoda is coming. Isn't that fun? James is too busy with his sheep but Rhoda said in her letter that she can get away quite easily now that Flockie is back. She said, 'Tell Bel that I must see her safely married.' You're glad she's coming, aren't you?'

Bel nodded. She really was glad Rhoda was coming for Rhoda was a very special friend. If it had not been for Rhoda's encouragement Bel might have lost the chance of marrying Ellis. It was quite terrifying to look back on what had happened at Tassieknowe Farm and to think how foolish she had been, how easily she might have refused to marry Ellis. Oh, yes, Bel was very glad that Rhoda was coming 'to see her safely married.' She owed Rhoda more than she could ever repay.

'Then there's Mr. Nelson,' said Louise. 'You said I was to send an invitation to Mr. Nelson, the manager of Copping Wharf. And there's Ellis's partner, Mr. Copping, and Mrs. Copping of course. I asked their son too — Mr. James Copping — but he can't come. I think that's all . . . no wait a minute, there's a woman called Miss Snow who used to be a friend of yours when you worked in the office. Ellis told me that Miss Snow is very fond of you and would love to come to the wedding.'

'Fond of me! She's like an iceberg!' exclaimed Bel.

'Well, that's what he said, so of course I asked her. Oh, and you wanted me to ask Mrs. Warmer, didn't you? How many is that?'

Bel had no idea how many it was. She was speechless with dismay.

'Two Musgraves and two Warrens,' said Louise ticking them off on her fingers. 'The Newbiggings makes six. Dr. and Mrs. Whittaker — eight; Mrs. Warmer — nine; Mr. and Mrs. Copping — eleven; Mr. Nelson — twelve; Miss Snow — thirteen. Then there's Lady Steyne and Miss Penney . . . Oh, they said the Bucklands might be staying with them at Underwoods so of course I said be sure to bring them too. That's sixteen, isn't it? No, seventeen if Lady Steyne comes. The Mainwarings and the Winslows make twenty-one; Reggie Stephenson — twenty-two. Mrs. Brownlee and her sister twenty-four. Mrs. Brownlee's friends — she didn't say how many — call it five — that makes twenty-nine. Then there's Rhoda; that's thirty. Daddy and I and you and Ellis makes thirty-four. Is that right?'

'I — think so,' said Bel faintly.

'Don't be silly, Bel,' said Louise. 'I know you said you wanted just a few friends, but if you ask one you must ask another — or they're offended. You don't want to offend people, do you? It would be a pity — especially when you're coming to live so near.'

'Oh, Louise, don't think I'm ungrateful!' exclaimed Bel. 'You're terribly kind to do all this for me. It's only just — '

70

'I know,' said Louise nodding. 'I know all that, so don't worry . . . and you needn't be a bit grateful because I'm enjoying it all tremendously. It's fun making all the arrangements and it's going to be a lovely wedding.' She hesitated and then added, 'By the way I asked Mark to come.'

'You asked Mark!' exclaimed Bel incredulously.

'Much better to ask him,' said Louise. 'I know you felt you never wanted to see him again after the extraordinary way he behaved to you, but it's all over and done with long ago. It will do Mark a lot of good to come and see you being married to Ellis. Besides he's my cousin — Daddy's nephew — so Daddy would think it queer if we didn't ask him.'

'Is he coming?'

'Goodness knows,' said Louise cheerfully. 'Mark never answers invitations, nor letters either. If he feels like coming he'll arrive all toshed up in wedding garments, but if he's busy painting one of his queer pictures he'll forget all about it. That's Mark.'

'Yes, that's Mark,' Bel agreed — and smiled. It certainly had been a shock to hear that Mark Desborough had been invited to her wedding; but now, having thought about it, she realised that Louise was right. It would be quite a good thing for Mark to attend her wedding. She hoped he would come.

At one time — how long ago it seemed! — Bel had lost her heart to the young painter, but the foolish infatuation had not lasted long. It had lasted just a few days — just long enough for Bel

71

to discover that Mark was absolutely unreliable and selfish; quite literally he cared for nobody except himself. How long ago it seemed! So long ago that Bel could scarcely remember what Mark looked like.

'Where is he now?' asked Bel after a little silence.

'Hampstead Heath. Do you want his address?'

'No, of course not. I was only wondering — '

Louise laughed and said, 'You were wondering if he was going back to that flat near yours in Mellington Street. Well, he isn't.'

'Thank goodness!' exclaimed Bel.

2

Anyone who had met Louise at parties or at the Tennis Club; had seen her laughing merrily and had heard her talking nonsense to all and sundry, might easily have thought her a butterfly-girl — very lovely to look at but not much use in the stress and strain of life. Bel knew her better for she had stayed at Coombe House several times and admired the competent manner in which she ran her father's house and managed to make it very comfortable indeed with the help of a not very reliable daily. Louise answered the telephone, took messages for the doctor and soothed anxious patients. She kept her father's engagement book, worked out the best way for him to do his rounds, helped him with his accounts and filled up innumerable and extremely complicated forms. Yes, Louise was an extremely capable young woman. Bel knew that. Bel knew also that for all her light-hearted gaiety Louise was by no means superficial. She thought deeply about things that mattered and her standard of integrity was very high indeed. It was difficult to understand Louise because she was such a curious mixture; she had a way of surprising you — of doing something quite unexpected and thereby revealing a facet of her personality which you had not seen before.

After their chat about the wedding guests, Bel went upstairs and unpacked. Then Dr. Armstrong returned home for lunch. He ate his meal hastily for he had a good many visits to pay in the afternoon, but as he was going away he told Louise to rest.

'Do you know what this silly girl did?' he said to Bel. 'She heard me come home in the middle of the night and came down to make me a cup of Ovaltine.'

'It wasn't silly,' declared his daughter. 'If anyone is silly, it's you. You know perfectly well that I leave the tray ready on the kitchen-table but unless I come down and make it you just don't bother.'

Dr. Armstrong chuckled, he said, 'Well, you're looking tired — not as beautiful as usual — so you'd better rest.'

Bel was tired too, so they decided to take a couple of deck chairs and rest in the garden beneath the chestnut tree at the end of the lawn. They took rugs, for it was the beginning of October, but it was so warm and sunny that they scarcely needed them.

'We won't knit or read, we needn't even talk,' said Louise. 'We'll just be nice and peaceful.' She settled herself comfortably and yawned.

'We'll go to sleep,' said Bel.

She had scarcely spoken when the telephone-bell rang.

'Oh, blow! Likewise dash!' cried Louise leaping from her chair and running across the lawn at top speed.

Bel could do nothing, of course, so she wrapped herself up in the rug and lay down. It was very peaceful and pleasant.

Ten minutes passed and Bel was almost asleep when she heard Louise calling to her. Somewhat reluctantly she unwrapped herself and went in.

'I'm awfully sorry to bother you,' said Louise quickly. 'I wouldn't have disturbed you — but it's serious. I must find Daddy at once. Poor old Mr. Hart was hanging a picture and he fell off the ladder (he's over eighty so he shouldn't have been climbing a ladder). Mrs. Hart says he's unconscious, he's lying in a crumpled heap on the floor. She's all of a dither. She's been trying to pour whisky down his throat — and I don't know what. I've told her not to move him, and I've phoned the hospital, but Daddy isn't there. D'you think you could find him, Bel? Look, here's a list of all the houses he meant to visit this afternoon! Ring them up and go on trying until you find him. Can you do that?'

'Yes, of course, but — '

'I must go straight off,' explained Louise, seizing her hat and cramming it on her head anyhow. 'The old woman is there by herself

74

— she's a horrid cross old woman, but that's not the point. It's a frightfully isolated cottage. Get hold of Daddy and tell him I'm here — here's the address and here's the list of people to ring.' The next moment she had gone.

The instructions, though hurried, were perfectly clear, and Bel was a trained secretary, so she sat down at the telephone and began ringing up the houses on the list. In some cases the doctor had just gone, in others he had not yet arrived, but at the fifth attempt she found him and gave him the message.

'Hart, Willow Cottage,' said the doctor. 'Listen Bel, you might ring up the hospital and tell them to send the ambulance at once to Willow Cottage and prepare a bed in the emergency ward.' Bel repeated the instructions.

She heard the doctor give a little chuckle as he rang off. The chuckle surprised her considerably, for she could see nothing amusing in the matter — but perhaps it had not been a chuckle, perhaps her ears had deceived her.

Bel completed her job efficiently and, having done so, she sat back and thought about the exigences of a doctor's calling. Doctors were wonderful, thought Bel. They spent their lives going from house to house, helping people. It did not matter what time of night or day they were summoned — nor how tired they were — they went. Doctors' daughters were wonderful too.

Bel thought of the old woman alone in the little cottage with her husband lying on the floor in a crumpled heap; she thought of the door opening and Louise walking in — perhaps unable to do very much, but just being there, just standing by. Louise, calm and kind, giving confidence and reassurance, waiting for the doctor to come. There was no need for Louise to have gone to Willow Cottage. She could have done her job by ringing up the houses where the doctor might be found — nobody could expect her to do more — but Louise had not hesitated for a moment, she had crammed on her hat and had gone without hesitation to a fellow human-being in distress. The fellow human-being happened to be a horrid cross old woman but that was not the point. The point was the woman was 'all of a dither' and needed help.

That was just like Louise, thought Bel. Louise loved people. She loved them even when they were disagreeable, even when they were old and cross.

(Would I have gone? wondered Bel. Yes, I think so, but I'd have gone because I'd have felt it was my duty to go. I'd have been afraid that the old woman might not want me. I'd have been afraid of finding a situation I couldn't cope with. Louise didn't think of anything like that. She just went. It's born and bred in Louise that she's her brother's keeper).

It was tea-time when Louise returned from her errand of mercy. She looked quite exhausted so Bel made her sit down and prepared tea herself.

'I'm glad I went,' said Louise. 'She was terribly cross — even crosser than usual — but that was because she was frightened. Fortunately it isn't as bad as I expected — concussion and a fractured ankle — that's all. Daddy got him off to hospital and I helped the old woman to shut up the cottage and took her over to her sister's at Shepherdsford. She made an awful fuss about leaving the cottage empty, but she couldn't stay in the place alone — so I had to be quite firm with her.

'Daddy was amused,' added Louise smiling.

'Amused?' asked Bel in surprise.

'Amused at you and me. You see when Daddy discovered that the old man hadn't fractured a femur he was as jolly as a sandboy. He was in one of his teasing moods.'

'But why was he amused at me?'

'So efficient. So absolutely the perfect private secretary. He said,' declared Louise giggling. 'He said it was remarkable that two such bee-ootiful females should be so terrifically efficient. You can get a job at Coombe House any time you like,' she added.

Bel laughed and said it was very kind of Dr. Armstrong but she had got a job already and was taking up her duties on Wednesday.

8

Mrs. Warmer had been correct in thinking that anything taken in hand by Miss Armstrong would be well done. Louise had all the arrangements for the wedding under control; she had enlisted the help of her friends and assigned them their duties according to their capabilities. Most of Louise's friends lived in Shepherdsford and on the morning before the wedding, Rose Musgrave and Sylvia Newbigging arrived in Sylvia's small car and were given the task of arranging the flowers for the drawing-room. Joan Winslow was already hard at work washing the glasses and Bel was drying them. Margaret Warren came over by bus with her small son.

'What shall I do?' asked Margaret walking into the kitchen with her child in her arms. 'And what am I to do with Bernard? I couldn't leave him at home because my wretched daily never turned up this morning.'

'You can cut the sandwiches,' said Louise. 'We'll have no time to-morrow morning and they'll keep quite fresh in polythene bags. Bernard will be all right in this big chair, won't he?'

Bernard was settled comfortably in the chair with a piece of string round his waist to prevent him from falling out. He sat there contentedly playing with a wooden spoon and watching all that was going on. Everyone spoke to him of course, commenting on his beauty; his adorable chubby cheeks, his lovely complexion and his sea-blue eyes — but, most favourably of all, everyone commented upon his sweetly placid nature and declared they had never seen such a good sensible baby in all their lives.

Bernard smiled engagingly and enjoyed the admiration he so well deserved.

All these people were strangers to Bel — and she was never at her best with strangers — but they were so friendly and kind that she soon lost her shyness. They all knew that she was coming to live at Fletchers End and they seemed delighted.

'That nice old house!' said Margaret Warren. 'So lovely to think that it won't be empty and sad any longer. It's only about a mile from us by the Church Walk so we'll be able to meet quite often.'

Sylvia wanted to know if Bel were interested in Girl Guides.

'Shut up, Sylvia!' exclaimed Rose Musgrave. 'You don't suppose Miss Lamington wants to be drawn into your net the moment she arrives!'

'I think we should call her Bel — straight off,' said Margaret. 'I mean it's silly to get used to calling her 'Miss Lamington' and then having to change to Mrs. Brownlee.'

'No sense in it at all,' agreed Joan.

'Oh, please do!' exclaimed Bel. 'I mean please call me Bel. It sounds so much more friendly.'

'Are you going to have a daily?' inquired Margaret. 'You'll want someone to help you in that big house, won't you?'

'She has got a real live cook,' declared Louise.

'Golly, how did you manage that?' asked Sylvia. 'I'd give my back teeth for a real live cook.'

They had all paused in their work and were looking at Bel with interest — they all wanted to know how she had achieved the remarkable feat — so Bel began to explain about Mrs. Warmer, and Louise chipped in and made a joke of the manner in which Mrs. Warmer had been engaged, and everyone laughed.

Bernard laughed too, displaying some pearly-white teeth, and hammered on the edge of his chair with the wooden spoon.

Nobody could be shy with all this going on — not even Bel — so she emerged from her shell and became gay and cheerful.

Presently Mrs. Musgrave arrived and was greeted rapturously.

Margaret said, 'Mummie, this is Bel. Of course you know her already, because she's the only person you don't know, but I thought I'd better introduce her properly. We've decided . . . '

The rest of Margaret's sentence was drowned in shouts of laughter.

Bel and Mrs. Musgrave shook hands. 'They're all quite mad,' explained Mrs. Musgrave. 'But it's a harmless form of madness so there's no need to be alarmed.'

'I think they're all delightful,' replied Bel smiling.

'Oh, the pet! Oh, the darling lambkin!' cried Mrs. Musgrave, catching sight of her grandson and making a bee-line for him across the room.

'Come and talk to Gran,' she added, seizing him in her arms. 'Come and tell Gran what you've been doing — you dear soft bundle of loveliness! Helping the girls to cut the sandwiches and arrange the flowers?'

'Hindering them,' declared his mother — most unfairly. She added, 'There's no sense to be got out of Mummie when Bernard is anywhere about.'

'That's most unfair,' complained Mrs. Musgrave. 'Bernard and I understand each other perfectly and enjoy each other's company . . . and I've been working very hard this morning. I've been at St. Michael's helping Miss Penney to arrange the flowers. She brought a whole car-load of beautiful chrysanthemums from the garden at Underwoods. She says Lady Steyne is hoping to come to the wedding to-morrow if it's a fine day.'

'It will be a fine day,' said Dr Armstrong who, unperceived in all the bustle, had opened the door and was gazing round his kitchen with twinkling eyes.

There were more greetings and an increased noise of talking. The kitchen was full by this time.

'Dr. Armstrong, how do you know it will be a fine day?' somebody inquired.

'Because the glass is rising,' he replied solemnly.

Why this perfectly sensible and eminently logical answer should have made everyone laugh it is difficult to see, but everyone laughed merrily.

Everyone seemed busy except Mrs. Musgrave, so the doctor made his way through the crowd to where she was sitting with Bernard on her knee, and began to talk to her and to compliment her on the healthy appearance of her grandson. He liked Esther Musgrave; he was her doctor and had got to know her well during her husband's last illness. She had been quite young when Charles Musgrave died — young and pretty — but she had been extremely courageous. He decided that she still looked young and pretty, absurdly young to be a grandmother.

The preparations were now finished; the glasses had been washed and polished; the sandwiches cut and the flowers arranged, but the girls continued to chat.

Then suddenly Sylvia exclaimed, 'Heavens, look at the time!' and with that everyone rose hastily and went away.

Louise and Bel walked down to the gate to see them off and Bel was interested to notice that the Musgrave family had divided differently. Rose went away in her mother's car and Margaret Warren and Bernard with Sylvia Newbigging.

'It's because they live quite near,' explained Louise. 'The Warrens have a dear little house; it stands high and has a lovely view. You like Meg, don't you?'

'I like them all,' declared Bel.

2

Some time before, when Bel had been staying with Louise, the two girls had gone to St.

Michael's Church to the early morning Communion Service and Bel had been so impressed with the peace and beauty of the little church that she wanted her wedding to be there. Naturally, the church looked quite different when Bel arrived with Dr. Armstrong in the large Daimler lent for the occasion by Lady Steyne.

To begin with there was a striped awning outside the porch, and a crowd of sightseers who had gathered to see the bride. There were women with prams, errand-boys with baskets, and small children chewing gum or sucking lollipops; there was even a fairly large contingent of men — most of them ancient — in the crowd. They all gazed with interest at the bride and at the thrilling spectacle of their own dear Dr. Armstrong attired in morning-dress with a grey tall hat upon his head and a white carnation in his buttonhole.

The crowd alarmed Bel so much that she stumbled in getting out of the car and might have fallen if Dr. Armstrong had not been there to catch her.

'Cheer up! It'll soon be over,' he said encouragingly as he guided her up the steps.

One of the women in the crowd giggled hysterically and whispered to her companion. 'That's wot 'e sed ter me when I was 'aving my first.'

Louise was waiting at the door. She was the only bridesmaid, and looked even more ravishing than usual in a pale green frock and a black picture-hat. She seized Bel and arranged her dress and whispered to her father, 'The other side, Daddy.'

'What?' asked the doctor.

'You're the wrong side,' said Louise, taking hold of him and forcibly changing his position. 'Go on, they've begun,' she added.

The church was brightly lighted. It seemed full of people — all standing up and singing. The altar was a mass of flowers.

Bel was terrified. All these people had come to look at her. All the singing and the flowers were for her benefit. Her heart beat madly and her knees felt as if they were made of brown paper. She clung to the doctor's arm and they began to walk up the aisle together, with Louise close behind.

Then Bel saw Ellis. There he was, waiting for her, looking at her and smiling reassuringly — and suddenly it was all right. Suddenly there was nobody else in the church except Ellis — nobody else in the world.

3

After that it was all a dream. Bel felt quite different from her usual self, she felt big and brave and beautiful. This girl — who was not Bel, but someone else quite different — was able to take her proper part in the service and make her vows in a clear sweet voice which could be heard all over the church. In the vestry, which was small and full of people, this girl was not the slightest bit nervous. Someone put a pen in to her hand and she signed her name without a tremor: Beatrice Elizabeth Lamington. It wouldn't be Bel any more of course, thought Bel, looking at her signature rather wistfully.

The excited talk going on all round her did not trouble her in the least. Ellis kissed her — everyone kissed her. She was suddenly enveloped in a bear-like hug by an enormous man whom she had never seen in her life.

'It's only Uncle Bob,' whispered Ellis, seizing her hand and holding it in a warm encouraging clasp.

Soon after this the door was opened and the organ played and the bride and bridegroom walked down the aisle together, smiling happily, followed by their friends and relations, two by two in correct order — as arranged by Louise.

The crowd was still waiting at the porch, but it was not in the least alarming. The bride smiled at it in a friendly manner and waved her hand.

It was still a dream when the bride and bridegroom arrived at Coombe House. The drawing-room looked strange — as things always do in a dream. The comfortable furniture had vanished, the room was empty except for a few chairs and a sofa, pushed into the corner, a glistening wedding-cake and masses of flowers.

'Are you all right, darling?' inquired Ellis anxiously, for somehow or other his newly-acquired wife seemed rather unlike herself.

'Yes, of course,' she replied smiling happily.

'You didn't mind Uncle Bob kissing you like that?'

85

'No, of course not.'

There was no time to say more. People began to arrive: Louise with Reggie Stephenson; Dr. Armstrong with Mrs. Brownlee and Uncle Bob. After that a whole string of guests all talking and laughing excitedly; all kissing the bride and the bridegroom — or shaking hands — and wishing them long life and happiness.

It was all a dream, even when Bel looked up and saw Mark Desborough standing beside her. As a matter of fact she scarcely recognised him for she had never seen him all dressed up like this.

Mark did not voice the conventional good wishes; as he took her hand he said, 'The girl who married her boss!'

Bel was not angry nor embarrassed, she laughed merrily and exclaimed, 'Hallo Mark! Yes, he was such a good boss that she took him for better for worse.'

'As her boss, I suppose?'

'Yes, of course. Didn't you hear her say 'obey'?'

'Gosh, you're quite different!' said Mark in amazement.

He could say no more for he was pushed aside by a beautifully dressed young woman with dazzling golden hair.

'Rhoda darling!' cried Bel. 'How marvellous to see you!'

'I had to come,' declared Rhoda Dering Johnstone as she hugged Bel affectionately. 'I just abandoned my family. I had to make certain you were properly married. When I start something I like to see it through.'

'I hope you're certain we're properly married,' said Ellis laughing.

'Perfectly certain,' she replied. 'I heard every word. I heard you take each other for better for worse and I hope you'll be every bit as happy as James and I. It's the best thing I can wish you.' She added, 'I must kiss Ellis — he's such a lamb.'

'Of course you must kiss him!' cried Bel.

4

There had been some argument as to who should be asked to propose the healths of the bride and bridegroom. Mrs. Brownlee had suggested her brother, but Ellis had refused quite definitely to have him, saying that Uncle Bob would gas for hours and make a lot of idiotic jokes. Bel had wanted Dr. Armstrong, but the doctor pointed out that it was quite enough work to escort the bride to the altar and give her away. Someone else must propose the health — why not Mr. Copping?

Everyone agreed to this suggestion, so Mr. Copping had been asked to make the speech.

None of the other guests knew Mr. Copping, of course, but perhaps that was all to the good . . . and when he stood up to propose the toast it was obvious that he had been the right choice. Tall and thin with silver hair and light-blue eyes he looked so distinguished; he looked every inch the important personage which he undoubtedly was.

Mr. Copping began by saying it was a great honour to have been asked to propose this toast. It gave him great pleasure to do so because he knew the bride and bridegroom very well indeed. He had known Bel's parents years ago — her father, a distinguished officer in the army; her mother charming and as pretty as a picture. With parents like these it was not surprising that Bel was such a delightful girl. Mr. Copping said he was sure they would all agree that she was one of the prettiest brides they had ever seen, but he knew Bel and he could tell them that her beauty was not skin deep. She was beautiful all through. His friend and partner, Ellis Brownlee, was exceedingly clever and capable and had shown these qualities in his choice of a wife. Ellis was a lucky fellow to have won such a prize — there was no doubt of that — but Bel was fortunate too. One would have to travel far to find a better fellow than Ellis. These two were admirably suited to each other and they would be happy, he was sure.

'They are strangers to you,' declared Mr. Copping. 'But they are coming to live near you, so they won't be strangers for long, and when you get to know them you'll realise that every word I've said is true. I can't help feeling that you will be very fortunate to have them as neighbours at Fletchers End — and, as I look round the room, I feel certain that they too will be fortunate in their neighbours.'

Mr. Copping smiled and held up his glass. 'I ask you to join me in drinking the toast of health and happiness to these young people and may they live a long useful life together in their chosen home!'

The little speech was neither witty nor amusing but it was dignified and utterly sincere. It was received with applause.

'Dear old boy!' whispered Ellis to Bel.

'Yes, he's a pet,' she replied. 'I'm enjoying it all tremendously, aren't you?'

This was so unlike Bel, who usually was as shy as a mouse, that he became more anxious about her than before.

Ellis's speech was merely the conventional expressions of gratitude on behalf of himself and his wife to all the kind people who had helped to make this day so happy and memorable. He had prepared several little *bon mots* but unfortunately they had vanished from his mind in the agitation of the moment.

It was now Reggie's turn to play his part in the proceedings, but instead of reading the pile of telegrams, which was his duty as best man, he began to talk about Fletchers End, a subject which was occupying his mind to the exclusion of everything else. He talked about the exquisite beauty of the old house and the strength of its construction and about all his wonderful plans to make it still more beautiful. At first his audience was interested and amused but when Reggie forgot himself in his excitement, and talked about stresses and strains and other technical matters, which nobody present could understand, the bridegroom decided that it was time to call a halt.

'Dry up, Reggie,' said the bridegroom, poking

89

his friend in the back. 'You aren't supposed to be giving a lecture on architecture.'

Poor Reggie dried up suddenly in the middle of a sentence and everybody laughed.

The telegrams were forgotten, (which was just as well for no doubt they were quite as boring and repetitive as telegrams on these occasions usually are) so the wedding guests were free to enjoy themselves and did so without delay, chatting and laughing and making a tremendous din, drinking champagne, eating large chunks of indigestible cake and dropping the crumbs on the floor.

The bride was free to enjoy herself too, and, as she was still walking about in a dream, she was able to talk to all the guests and say the correct thing — thereby winning golden opinions. She spoke to Mr. Copping and congratulated him on his excellent speech and said how sorry she was that his son was unable to be here. She spoke to Mrs. Musgrave and said that Rose was looking charming — which was perfectly true. She had a pleasant chat with Mr. Whitehead, the vicar. (Mr. Whitehead had not been mentioned by Louise in her list of guests, which was curious considering that the wedding could not have been celebrated without him.) She had a few words with Miss Penney and thanked her for the flower arrangements in the church, which were perfectly beautiful, and expressed her regret that Lady Steyne had a slight cold and was not able to come. She was seized upon by her mother-in-law and introduced to 'Aunt Catherine' and to all the friends who had come from

Beckenham for the occasion. It was not very easy to detach herself from these kind people — she could never have managed it if she had been her ordinary everyday self — but to-day she managed it graciously. After that she had a talk with Rhoda and inquired after all the people at Tassieknowe Farm — not forgetting Mr. Sutherland, the shepherd, and his wife — and was glad to hear that they were flourishing.

Then the bride spoke to a short, stout cheerful-looking man, whom she afterwards discovered was Dr. Whittaker — the doctor whose practice was at Shepherdsford — he told her he knew Fletchers End well and had always admired the old house. She had a word with Mr. Nelson and Miss Snow, who seemed to have come together and were sticking together somewhat shyly. Both were impeccably turned out and looked quite different from their usual selves. After that she chatted to several other guests whose names she did not know and she was about to speak to Margaret Warren and her husband when suddenly she was swept away by Louise and conducted upstairs to change into the neat new coat and skirt, and a fur coat — a present from Dr. Armstrong — which she was wearing for the flight to Paris.

'Bel, are you feeling all right?' asked Louise.

'Yes, of course,' said Bel happily. 'It has been a lovely wedding, everyone is so nice.'

'You seem — different.'

'Yes, of course,' repeated Bel. 'I'm not me at all. I'm someone else.'

'But that's dreadful!' Louise exclaimed in

dismay. 'I don't want you to be someone else! I mean I want you to go on being you.'

'It's a dream, that's all,' said Bel reassuringly. 'I expect I shall wake up sooner or later and be just as shy and silly as ever.'

'But we'll always be friends, won't we?' asked Louise with sudden misgiving.

'Yes, of course,' replied Bel — she seemed to be saying the same thing over and over again but she could not help it — 'Yes, of course, darling Louise,' said Bel. 'Of course we'll always be the greatest friends. Next to Ellis I love you best in all the world.'

This delightful answer, accompanied by a loving hug, ought to have reassured Louise, but it did not assure her entirely for somehow it was unlike Bel to be able to put her inmost feelings into felicitous words.

Ellis was ready now so the bride and bridegroom ran downstairs together; they were seized and embraced by their friends and relations, patted on their backs and pelted with confetti in the usual uncomfortable manner. They managed to escape, fled out of the front-door, scrambled into the waiting car and drove away.

5

After the departure of the leading lady and gentleman the party seemed to sag; the usual feeling of anti-climax affected the guests and they began to drift away. They all said they had enjoyed themselves immensely and what a successful wedding it had been! Quite soon Louise and her father were left alone amongst the debris, alone with the remains of the wedding-cake and a few bottles of champagne. There were crumbs on the carpet and cigarette-ends in the ashtrays and an enormous number of empty glasses scattered about the room, but Louise was too tired to bother about them to-night.

'They all said it was a successful wedding,' said Louise, trying to chase away the forlorn feeling in her heart.

'Yes, they did,' agreed the doctor. 'I noticed they all said that. I wonder what an unsuccessful wedding is like.'

'Don't be silly, Daddy!'

'All sorts of things might happen,' said the doctor thoughtfully. 'For instance if you hadn't been there I might have taken the bride up the aisle on the wrong arm and got married to her by mistake. I wouldn't have minded, of course — I can think of worse fates than being married to Bel — but Ellis might have been annoyed.'

'Don't tease, Daddy.'

'I was only trying to cheer you up,' he explained. 'You look a bit under the weather, Lou. What's the matter?'

'Bel was different,' replied Louise sadly. 'I didn't realise that being married would make her different.'

Dr. Armstrong smiled. 'It will wear off,' he said. 'Don't worry, Lou. You'll get your own dear Bel back again, the same as ever — or very nearly.

'Very nearly?'

'Well — yes,' said the doctor, taking up his morning paper which until this moment he had been too busy to read. 'You can't expect her to be exactly the same. Marriage is a mysterious thing, you know. Perhaps you were too fussed to listen to the service this afternoon.'

'What do you mean, Daddy?' asked Louise in surprise.

'It's an excellent mystery,' said the doctor chuckling. 'Look it up and you'll see.'

PART TWO

Winter in London

9

When the Brownlees flew home from Paris where they had been spending their honeymoon they took up their abode in Bel's small flat.

Ellis had gone straight to the office to see what had been happening in his absence so Bel arrived at the flat alone. Her heart sank when she opened the door and went in for, after the palatial room in the Paris hotel, it seemed even smaller than usual; it seemed terribly cramped and shabby, and of course it was very dirty. The flat had been shut up for a fortnight and sooty dust from the neighbouring chimneys had filtered in through the ill-fitting window-frames.

Would Ellis be happy in this queer little place?

Of course Ellis knew the flat — he had been here often — and it was his idea that they should spend the winter here, but Bel was aware that it was one thing to visit the flat for supper and quite another thing to live in it, day in and day out.

However it was no good worrying; there was far too much to be done. Bel put on a large overall and set to work to clean the rooms and to prepare supper — she had stopped on the way home to buy necessary food. Fortunately she had cleaned up the flat so often that she knew exactly what to do; she lighted the fire, heated the water for the bath and flew round the place sweeping and dusting and polishing.

This was just a 'lick and a promise' thought Bel. (It must be ready for Ellis when he came, and she did not know how long he would be) to-morrow she would have to give the whole flat a thorough cleaning; there was no doubt about that.

When she had done all that was necessary she bathed and changed and sat down to wait.

'How nice this is!' were the first words uttered by Ellis as he came in at the door.

'It's very small,' said Bel. 'It seems smaller after that big room in the hotel — '

'That's what I mean. It's like a cosy little nest, high up in the tree-tops. We'll be happy here, you and I together. I can't think why we went to that noisy overcrowded hotel when we could have come here and been alone. Why did we?'

Bel giggled feebly. She said, 'Louise seemed to think Paris was the right place for a honeymoon, so — '

'She was wrong,' said Ellis firmly. 'What you need on your honeymoon is privacy so that you can kiss your wife whenever you feel inclined . . .'

When Bel had managed to disentangle herself she said, 'Supper will be ready in ten minutes.'

Ellis laughed. 'And I'll be ready for supper. It will just give me time to wash. Look at that!' he added holding out his hands. 'Absolutely filthy! That's London.'

'You can have a bath if you like. There's plenty of hot water,' Bel told him.

'I thought you said this flat was uncomfortable? Yes, of course I'd like a bath — give me a quarter of an hour, and you'll have a nice clean husband to sup with you.'

'And just put on your dressing-gown,' added Bel.

He looked back from the door and grinned. 'I see I'm going to be spoilt,' he declared.

There had been no time to prepare an elaborate meal; there was grilled steak and mushrooms and fried potatoes, followed by biscuits and Orkney Farm-House cheese; there was a plate of Cox's Orange Pippins and coffee in a brown jug, standing near the fire.

Ellis was completely satisfied with the meal. He said he had enjoyed it more than all the long expensive dinners in Paris.

'Good plain food is what I like,' he declared. 'Let's go on having good plain food and lots of fruit. These apples are delicious.'

'How did they get on at the office without you?' asked Bel.

'Very badly indeed,' replied Ellis. 'There were several serious muddles while I was away — Nelson is hopping mad. Of course it will be better when Jim has got into the way of things. At present he isn't much help; his father is very annoyed with him to tell you the truth.'

'That's a pity!'

'Yes. I'm beginning to think we made a mistake. Jim is much too young and inexperienced. He should have been sent to Oxford to read law before coming into the firm as a partner. It would have calmed him down and broadened his outlook — and the degree would have been very useful indeed. As a matter of fact

I suggested it to Mr. Copping some time ago but he didn't agree.'

'He wanted his son in the firm,' Bel pointed out.

'I know. That was his idea. Of course I would never have consented to have Jim in the firm — so young — if Mr. Copping hadn't been keen about it. Well, there you are,' added Ellis with a sigh. 'It's too late now. We've done it and we've got to make the best of it.'

Bel was looking very thoughtful. She said, 'You found an experienced secretary for him, didn't you?'

'She's absolutely useless — no good at all.'

Bel was silent.

'I suppose — ' began Ellis and paused.

'What do you suppose?' asked Bel, hiding a little smile.

'Well — I was just wondering whether you could possibly take the job. I mean just temporarily until Jim finds his feet.'

'Yes,' said Bel nodding.

'Really?' asked Ellis eagerly. 'Could you bear it? If you could come back — even for part-time — it would be splendid. You know the way things are run and you get on so well with Nelson. It would be a tremendous help if you could come back.'

'Shall I be paid a salary?'

Ellis roared with laughter. 'Certainly you will be paid. Do you think I would ask you to work for nothing?'

'I thought you might be asking me to work for love,' said Bel smiling. 'Yes, Ellis, I'll take the job.

I'm very fond of Mr. James and I shall enjoy being his secretary. Of course nothing would have induced me to do it if Miss Goudge were still there, but now that she has gone — and Mr. Wills as well — I should like to go back to the office. I'll come every morning but not in the afternoon.'

'You've been thinking about this!' exclaimed Ellis, gazing at her in surprise.

It was true. She had been thinking about it. She knew that the office was understaffed and Ellis had far too much to do, and she had been wondering how she could fill in the time while Ellis was at his work. The answer to these two problems was obvious. Bel had hoped to get some sort of job in the office; she had never thought of getting the job of secretary to the junior partner. That was a plum which had fallen into her lap and she was suitably grateful — it would be fun to be secretary to Mr. James. As regards the salary, she did not really need it, because Ellis was giving her a generous allowance, but all the same it would be pleasant to have money of her very own — money which she had earned herself — and she was aware that she could earn it creditably. When she was secretary to Ellis she had learnt a great deal about the business and had taken a tremendous interest in all that went on. She had felt that she belonged to the firm. Now she belonged to the firm again, not as an employee but as the wife of one of the partners. It was an honourable position but she was delighted at the idea of being both.

'I'll come every morning,' repeated Bel, 'but not in the afternoon. I want to be free in the afternoon to clean the flat and prepare your supper. How much am I to be paid?'

Ellis laughed again and named a salary which his wife was pleased to accept.

2

The newly married couple had not told their friends and relations that they were returning so soon from their honeymoon so they had a spell of perfect peace to settle down to their routine. Bel was surprised and touched at the welcome she received on her return to the office. Everyone seemed pleased to see her — everyone from Mr. Copping, the senior partner, down to the page-boy who ran errands and stoked the fires. Bel wondered whether there would have been as warm a reception if she had returned as Miss Lamington, but that was an unworthy thought. Now that Miss Goudge had gone there was a very different atmosphere in the place and everyone was happier. Miss Snow, who reigned in her stead, was cool and calm and pleasant to deal with, best of all she was absolutely just. Bel wondered where Miss Goudge had gone and whether she was creating trouble in some other place of business with her moody temperament and her bitter tongue. It seemed sad to think of it — all the more sad because she was an exceedingly capable woman and but for her unfortunate disposition could have been a valuable employee.

Mr. James was delighted to see Bel and welcomed her warmly. He looked just the same as ever; his rugged bony face seemed not a day older, his long legs and arms were still awkward and clumsy. Perhaps his straw-coloured hair was a little more orderly, for now that he had become a partner in his father's firm he brushed it more carefully and sleeked it down with oil.

'I say, Miss Lam — I mean Mrs. Brownlee!' exclaimed Mr. James shaking her hand with painful cordiality. 'It's simply grand having you as my secretary — I jumped for joy when Mr. Brownlee told me. All my troubles are over now.'

'All your troubles?'

'You know all about everything,' he explained. 'You'll be able to hold my hand and prevent me from making any more ghastly mistakes. Mr. Brownlee has been frightfully decent, but the Guv'nor is beginning to get a bit ratty.'

'Everyone makes mistakes sometimes,' said Bel in soothing tones.

'Yes, I daresay, but I've been making too many — and that woman didn't help. She was supposed to be an experienced secretary but she knew nothing and cared less. She just sat and goggled at me and wrote down everything I said in shorthand and typed it all out very neatly.'

'Wasn't that what she was here for?'

'I suppose so — in a way — but she didn't use her brains. It came to a head one day when I was translating a letter; I said, 'Dash it, this old boy doesn't know his own language!' Well, believe it

103

or not, she typed that too and dumped it with the other letters on the Guv'nor's table . . . and it wasn't 'dash' and it wasn't 'old boy',' added Mr. James ruefully. 'Lordy, what a ticking off I got! My boyish pranks were more suited to a Prep School was one of the least offensive remarks.'

Bel was horrified; too horrified to speak.

'I can see you think she did it on purpose,' said Mr. James, who certainly was no fool. 'But honestly, I don't think so. She was just a machine — you put a penny in the slot and out came a box of matches, see?'

Bel saw — but was still unconvinced. 'Anyhow it won't happen again,' she said.

'Not while you're here,' he agreed smiling at her affectionately. 'You'll keep me out of trouble. I got ticked off for my 'slovenly appearance' too. I do try to be neat and tidy but it's frightfully difficult. I don't seem to be made like other people. My suits get baggy and my collars go limp and my tie keeps on working round my neck until the knot is under my left ear. I daresay you've noticed that?'

Yes, she had noticed this peculiarity before and had often wondered about it.

'Other fellows' ties don't do that, so why does mine? I suppose my neck must be crooked or something,' said Mr. James sadly. 'It's a most awful nuisance, you know. Sometimes when I'm talking to people I suddenly see them gazing at me — and I never know whether it's better to haul it round into the proper position or leave it and pretend not to notice.'

The problem was too difficult for Bel. She said, 'I could tell you, couldn't I?'

'Yes, that's the idea,' he agreed. 'Just say 'tie' and then I'll know. Be sure to say it when I'm going into the Guv'nor's room or anything important like that.

'You know what's been happening in the office, don't you?' he continued. 'Old Wills went off his nut and had to retire, so I'm the junior partner. Copping, Brownlee and Copping sounds good doesn't it? I wish I was a success.'

'You need a little experience, that's all.'

'I need a lot of experience,' said Mr. James gloomily. Then his face brightened and he added. 'I've got old Wills's room for my very own. Come and see it.'

3

Mr. Wills's room held very unpleasant memories for Bel. Long before he had been forced to retire Mr. Wills had been very peculiar indeed and for some reason or other had taken a violent dislike to Miss Lamington . . . but there was no time to think of that now. Bel was to be here only in the morning so it behoved her to get to work with all speed. There was a large pile of letters on the table, most of them with foreign stamps, Bel began opening them and sorting them out.

'Are you doing all the translations, Mr. James?' she inquired.

'Yes, nobody else seems able to cope — and it's no bother to me. But look here, Miss Lam

— Mrs. Brownlee, I mean — you needn't go on calling me that.'

Bel hesitated. He had suggested before that she should call him 'Jim' and it would have been easy, for although he was such an immense size he was very young and boyish. She remembered the day they had gone to the Zoo together and he had fed the bears with buns — how he had enjoyed himself that day! Bel had enjoyed it too; she had told herself that she was his nursemaid and he was her 'great big enormous child.' Now she was to be his nursemaid again; she was to direct his faltering steps and train him in the way he should go ... but, in spite of this, the relationship between them should be correct.

'You can call me Jim, can't you?' he said wheedlingly.

Bel smiled — he really was a dear. She said, 'You're a partner in Copping, Brownlee and Copping and I'm your secretary. You see that, don't you?'

'Oh, well ... ' said Mr. James with a sigh.

'We mustn't waste time,' she reminded him.

'No — all right — I'll do the translations first. You can take them straight down on the typewriter if you like.'

Bel did like; her shorthand had always been her weak point and she had not practised it for months. She sat down at the typewriter and waited for him to begin.

'It's a new typewriter,' said Mr. James, coming over to the table and bending over her. 'Look, it's absolutely brand new! I thought you'd like it, so I bagged it out of the Guv'nor's room.'

'What!' exclaimed Bel in horrified tones.

'It's all right. His typewriter is hardly ever used, you know. He spends most of his time interviewing people — and all that. I put the old one in its place so he won't notice, and if Miss Wellworth notices she won't dare to say so. The old machine is frightfully stiff and clumsy; I wasn't going to have you hurting your fingers on the beastly thing.'

'It was very kind of you, but all the same — '

'It's all right,' repeated Mr. James. 'Not to worry. Look at this lovely new machine! This is the very latest, it's a slap-up job. See how nice and easy it runs — smooth as velvet! It's a pleasure to work with a machine like this.'

Bel agreed that it would be a pleasure and repeated her suggestion that they should start at once.

Some time later when Ellis looked in to see how they were getting on he beheld a scene of concentrated industry; the junior partner and his new secretary seemed to be getting on very well indeed.

10

The week passed quickly and on Saturday afternoon the Brownlees motored down to Fletchers End to see how things were progressing. Reggie had been notified of their intention and was waiting for them at the gate. The new gate — made by Mrs. Warmer's friend — was already in position and had been painted a deep shade of blue; the path up to the door had been treated with chemicals and was now clean and dry; the new front-door had been painted blue to match the gate. Some of the windows had been taken out and the rotten woodwork renewed.

All this looked like good progress and the owners of the house were pleased. They were not so pleased when they went inside the house for here the changes were all to the bad — or at least they appeared so to the uninstructed eye. Before the alterations had begun the inside of the house had been clean — now it was extremely dirty. There were holes in the floors where the central heating was being put in and holes in the walls where the faulty pipes had been taken out. There were heaps of wood and rubble everywhere and dirty footmarks on the stairs. A piercing wind was blowing in through some of the gaping windows and rustling amongst piles of dirty newspaper. The old bath had been torn from its moorings and heaved out on to the landing where it lay on its side amongst pieces of sacking and rusty pipes and pails half-full of scummy water.

It was all quite dreadful but the drawing-room was much the worst for here the masons had been at work. One end, where the bow-window was in process of construction, was a mass of rubble, everything was thickly coated with yellow dust . . .

'Oh, dear!' exclaimed Bel looking round in dismay.

'We're getting on splendidly,' declared Reggie. 'Our Mr. Baker is pretty good value — he knows his job. Just at the moment the place looks a bit messy but that can't be helped. Think how lovely it will be when it's finished.'

'Will it ever be finished?'

Reggie chuckled. 'Yes, and in good time, too. I'm staying at Shepherdsford and coming over nearly every day to keep Mr. Baker and his myrmidons up to the mark.'

'That's very good of you!' exclaimed Ellis. 'But what about your own business?'

'I've two partners,' Reggie replied. 'They're managing all right.' He paused and then added, 'As a matter of fact I'm on sick leave. I've got some new-fangled bug in my inside and the doctor said I was to have a holiday. 'A complete rest', that was what he said.'

'But you aren't resting!'

'I'm doing what I like. I'm having a complete rest from designing modern bungalows for ignorant idiots — people who want everything as cheap as they can get it. Sometimes it makes me wild. They don't realise that if it's all got to be 'on the cheap' you must make their wretched doors of unseasoned wood which will warp in a few years' time. All that sort of thing,' explained Reggie, waving his hand vaguely.

'I wish I could come down more often,' said Ellis, 'but the fact is I simply can't get away — neither can Bel. We're both working like Trojans. This winter is going to be particularly difficult with Mr. Copping laid up and young Jim so inexperienced. The business has to come first.'

'Yes, I see that,' agreed Reggie. 'But there isn't any need for you to worry. I'll look after all this.'

'You must put in a bill for all your time and trouble.'

'Oh, yes, I'll bill you,' said Reggie smiling. 'But it won't be a very big bill because I'm just doing it for fun. I've lost my heart to the dear old house — that's the truth of the matter.'

2

Bel did not see how it could be much fun pottering about in this scene of desolation, but she discovered that Mrs. Warmer had the same curious taste.

'It's fun, Mrs. Brownlee,' said Mrs. Warmer. 'There's such a lot going on — never a dull moment — and it's going to be so nice when it's all finished and we can get cleaned up. Of course it's a bit troublesome when they turns off the water — I grant you that — but that can't be helped. They've left me my kitchen in the

110

meantime and I've brought my bed down from the upstairs room. It wasn't very comfortable up there when they started making holes in the floors. Dear me no, Mrs. Brownlee, I don't want to move. I'd miss all the excitement if I wasn't here.

'That Mr. Stephenson is a very nice young gentleman,' she continued. 'So free and easy, he is. Not proud at all. He usually brings his dinner with him and I makes a pot of tea and we has it together in the kitchen as friendly as you like. That Mister Baker — as he calls himself — ' said Mrs. Warmer scornfully. 'He's a very different pair of shoes. Proud, that's what *he* is! And what's *he* got to be proud of I should like to know? His father was a day labourer, but he never did an honest day's work in his life. I knew Tim Baker. Just a lounger and a scrounger, he was. Drink was his trouble. So what's Mister Baker got to be proud of?'

Bel thought perhaps Mr. Baker might be proud of the fact that he had risen in the world by his own efforts and was now the proprietor of a flourishing firm of builders . . . but she did not say so to Mrs. Warmer. As a matter of fact she was aware that when Mrs. Warmer said 'proud' she really meant that Mr. Baker was a snob. She really meant that Mr. Baker would no sooner have thought of sitting down and having his dinner with her in her comfortable kitchen than he would have thought of flying by rocket to the moon. Bel thought about it seriously — it really was very interesting indeed. She decided she must talk to Ellis and

111

hear his views on the subject.

While Bel was chatting to Mrs. Warmer, sitting at her kitchen table and enjoying a very welcome cup of tea, Ellis and Reggie had been making a tour of the house; looking at the room which some day — one hoped — would be a clean and pleasant second bathroom, but which was now a hideous mess, and examining the new window-frames and the gutters.

'It will never be finished by March,' said Ellis lugubriously as they came down the stairs together.

'Oh, you'll be surprised,' Reggie told him. 'I've got it all under control. We're getting on very nice — as Mrs. Warmer would say. You can't do anything at this stage of the proceedings.'

Obviously this was true, so instead of staying the night at The Owl as they had intended the Brownlees returned to London. They had dinner at the Berkeley to cheer them up a bit and went home to their flat.

11

It was fortunate indeed that there were two such reliable people as Reggie Stephenson and Mrs. Warmer controlling matters at Fletchers End, for Ellis had never been so busy before — and that was saying a good deal. Old Mr. Copping had had another heart attack and, although it was not a severe one, the doctor refused to allow him to return to the office for at least a month. To add to their troubles several of the clerks went down with 'flu.

One day Bel was obliged to go down to Copping Wharf and see Mr. Nelson, who was manager there. When she was at the office before, it had been one of her duties to go to the Wharf with letters and messages. She had always enjoyed the outing; it was a welcome break in office-routine. Now she felt she knew him even better, for he had been to her wedding, so they greeted each other cordially.

'Fancy you coming back to the office!' exclaimed Mr. Nelson. 'I must say I was glad when I heard it; I could always depend on you to get things done. We had a bad time when you left. Everything was at sixes and sevens. You'll find a great change at the office now that Mr. Wills has gone . . . went off his head, you know. I wasn't surprised to tell you the truth. He'd been getting very queer for months.'

'Miss Goudge has gone too.'

'No loss,' declared Mr. Nelson. 'Good riddance of bad rubbish, that's what I said when I heard the news.'

2

Bel had told herself that she was to be secretary-nursemaid to Mr. James and very soon she discovered that this was indeed her position. If she had not been there to restrain him he would have made a great many mistakes, some of them serious and others of minor importance. Fortunately he was eager to learn; he was also very intelligent — much more clever than he looked — so he rarely made the same mistake twice. She noticed, too, that his mistakes always occurred because he was impulsive and over-keen, anxious to get things done quickly. These were the sins of youth and easily forgiven. Bel rectified his mistakes as best she could; she helped him to choose his clothes, mended his socks and was able to prevent him from inviting the new typist — who was very young and pretty but extraordinarily silly — to have lunch with him.

'It would be nice for the kid,' he explained.

'You can't do it,' Bel told him. 'You mustn't, really. It wouldn't be kind.'

'Wouldn't be kind? But I thought — '

'Not kind at all. It would cause the most frightful jealousy. Do remember that you're an important person in this office, Mr. James.'

'Oh, well . . . ' he said with a sigh. 'You know best, of course.'

After the first day he ceased to call her 'Miss Lam — Mrs. Brownlee' and asked permission to address her as 'Mrs. B.'

'It's like this, you see,' he explained. 'Mr. Brown-lee is Mr. Brownlee and somehow the name seems to belong to him. I'd like you to have a name of your very own. So if you don't mind . . . '

Bel did not mind in the least. She was amused to find the abbreviation adopted by other people in the office — by nearly everyone in fact — even the exceedingly prim and proper Miss Snow addressed her as 'Mrs. B.'

3

One morning Mr. James arrived at the office in particularly good form, he was positively effervescent. The Guv'nor had given him a new car for his birthday; a Moonbeam Sports car with a convertible hood and a super-charged engine. Naturally he wished to tell his secretary all about it and described it in detail.

Bel listened and nodded and tried to look intelligent but knowing nothing whatever about internal combustion engines she could not understand a word.

'What colour is it?' she asked.

'Sky blue,' he replied proudly. 'I thought of red at first and then I saw a red Moonbeam — exactly the same model — with two ghastly people in it. They had parked in a lay-by and they were hugging each other — on the main road, mark you! It was enough to put anyone off red cars for life. So I rang up the fellow at the garage and changed to sky blue.'

'It was lucky you were in time.'

He nodded. 'Yes, it was. My little bus is a dream.'

'And I suppose it goes like the wind?'

'Like the wind?' exclaimed Mr. James scornfully. 'We don't often get winds in this country with a velocity of over a hundred miles an hour. I tell you what, Mrs. B. I'll take you for a spin along M.1 and show you what she can do.'

'That would be lovely,' said Mrs. B. with a strange lack of enthusiasm.

A good deal of valuable time had been wasted discussing the new car, so it was necessary to get down to business. They were hard at work when one of the typists came in with two cups of coffee, and a couple of biscuits in each saucer. This was the usual routine (it occurred every morning) and as usual the coffee had slopped over into the saucers. The girl put the cups on the table and went away.

'Look at that!' exclaimed Mr. James. 'It's disgusting! It's unbearable! Careless slovenly creatures! The coffee is tepid and the biscuits are sodden. I'm jolly well going to tell those girls what I think of them.' He rose and made for the door.

Bel ran after him and caught hold of his arm. 'No,' she cried. 'No, Mr. James — '

'You said I was an important person in this office, so — '

'That's why,' declared Bel earnestly. 'You're too

116

important to go and make a row about the coffee. I'll speak to them and tell them you were very angry. That's the right way to do it.' She dragged him back into the room and shut the door.

'Oh, well . . . ' said Mr. James reluctantly. 'If that's the way to do it . . . but I must say I feel like giving them beans.'

'Not about coffee,' Bel told him shaking her head. She hesitated and then added, 'If you want to give them beans you might speak to them about the delay in sorting the letters. They ought to be on my table every morning when I arrive.'

Mr. James, who had been looking somewhat glum, brightened up immediately. 'That's the stuff,' he said. 'I'll go now while I'm feeling in the mood.'

'Tie,' said Bel.

'What? Oh, yes, of course.' He straightened his tie, shot out his cuffs and marched to the door.

Bel was smiling as she watched him go; she would dearly have loved to follow and hear what happened, but, alas, this was impossible.

After some time Mr. James returned looking very solemn indeed. He sat down at his table — and winked at his secretary.

'Ahem!' said Mr. James. 'In future the letters will be on your table within ten minutes of their delivery.'

'Good,' nodded his secretary.

'You're quite right,' declared Mr. James abandoning his solemnity and grinning from ear to ear. 'I *am* an important person in this office.' He added, 'Don't forget to tell them how angry I was about the coffee, will you?'

In these, and in other matters of greater consequences, Bel guided the steps of the junior partner. It was an interesting job, often amusing, but it took up a great deal of time. Bel had intended to go to the office only in the morning but she soon discovered that this would never do. Not only was there far too much work but also, and more important, was the fact that Mr. James was apt to get into serious muddles when she was not there to keep an eye on him. She was reluctant to give up her afternoons but it could not be helped.

Housekeeping was very much easier than Bel had expected for there was no lack of money — as there had been in the days when Bel was on her own. The allowance for housekeeping which Ellis was giving her was more than enough. She was able to get a woman to come in every morning for an hour to clean the flat — so when she and Ellis returned from the office it was spick and span — and she was able to buy the best pieces of meat and all sorts of luxuries to cook for supper. For lunch she and Ellis went to a restaurant, which was an excellent plan, not only because it saved the bother of thinking about food but also because it gave them an opportunity of discussing business affairs and arranging the afternoon's programme.

Sometimes in the evening they went out to dinner and to a play or a concert but they did not do this often, for as a matter of fact they were both tired by their day's work and preferred to settle down by the fire and chat or read or listen to the radio. One evening when they had settled down like this Ellis reminded Bel that she had warned him the flat would be very uncomfortable and added laughingly that he had never been so comfortable and well-looked-after in his life.

Bel was happy too; even the bad weather did not depress her as it used to do. She had hated setting out for the office on foggy mornings all by herself but now she had Ellis with her she did not mind.

Time passed quickly. Once or twice Bel managed to seize a day off from the office and attended sales and bought some good second-hand furniture (she and Ellis had decided that modern furniture would be quite the wrong thing for Fletchers End). Amongst other things she bought a large four-post bed for a few pounds — and a new interior-spring mattress to fit it, which cost a great deal more — she bought some carpets and wheel-back chairs and several large chests of drawers; an oak chest and an oval mirror which would be suitable for the hall.

Ellis got loose one afternoon and visited an antique shop where he spent a great deal of money upon a charming corner cupboard and some old oak stools.

Saturday was free of course and on several occasions Louise came up for the day and helped to choose blankets and pillows and linen and kitchen utensils and a great many other things which would be necessary when they moved into Fletchers End.

In addition to all her other commitments Bel felt obliged to go and see her mother-in-law whenever possible. Sometimes Ellis came too, but more often Bel went alone. Mrs. Brownlee was finding it dull at Beckenham without her wonderful son and Bel felt very sorry for her. In fact Bel felt guilty — it was a most uncomfortable feeling — for it was she who had stolen Ellis from his mother.

One day when Bel arrived at Rose Hill unexpectedly she found Mrs. Brownlee in tears.

'I know it's silly,' declared Mrs. Brownlee. 'But I can't bear it. You see I used to look forward all day to Ellis coming home in the evening. Now there's nothing to look forward to at all. I'm so lonely. I don't seem to have enough to do. I can't stand it any longer.'

Bel was aghast. She did not know what to say.

'I can't stand it any longer,' repeated Mrs. Brownlee. 'The only thing to do is to sell Rose Hill — it's much too big for me now. Perhaps I could find a little house at Shepherdsford and then I should be near you and Ellis.'

Bel thought this an excellent plan (she was very fond of her mother-in-law) so she promised to talk to Ellis about it.

'Yes, ask Ellis,' said Mrs. Brownlee. 'See what Ellis thinks. I'm sure we could sell Rose Hill quite easily.'

4

Bel was certain that Ellis would approve of Mrs. Brownlee's plan of coming to live at Shepherdsford so she was very much surprised to discover that he was dead against it.

'But, Ellis, she's so lonely!' exclaimed Bel.

'It wouldn't work,' said Ellis firmly. 'Mother wouldn't be happy.'

'Of course she would be happy — she would be near us.'

'Too near.'

'But Ellis, it would be nice — '

'Listen, Bel. I tell you it wouldn't work. She might like it for a bit but quite soon she'd be bored. Mother isn't really a country woman. She loves parties; she enjoys popping into town for a day's shopping; she's fond of bridge. What on earth would she do in Shepherdsford? I had better go and see her on Sunday afternoon and talk to her about it.'

'You'll be tactful, won't you?' said Bel anxiously. 'I mean we don't want her to think — '

'My dear girl, I know my Mother,' declared Ellis.

It was true that Ellis knew his mother — he had always been able to twist her round his little finger — so he went down to Beckenham the following Sunday and had a long talk with her. Obviously she could not stay on at Rose Hill if she were unhappy there, but what about Bournemouth? suggested Ellis. At Bournemouth she would be near her sister, Mrs. Player, who had lived in the place for years and knew everyone. There were good concerts at Bournemouth and fascinating shops — and the climate was delightful.

'Yes,' said Mrs. Brownlee doubtful. 'Yes, it would be nice to be near Catherine, but it would

121

be a long way from you and Bel.'

'Not really very far,' said Ellis. 'Bel and I could run over quite often and spend a week-end with you. It would be lovely for us to have a little change and a breath of sea air.'

'And of course it's a very healthy place for children,' said Mrs. Brownlee nodding. 'I mean after they've had whooping-cough or measles.'

Ellis was a little surprised. He knew of no children in whom his mother was particularly interested. 'It's a very healthy place for elderly ladies,' he said, giving her an affectionate hug. 'Let's write to Aunt Catherine and see what she thinks of the plan.'

'Yes, I'll write to her to-night,' agreed Mrs. Brownlee smiling cheerfully. 'You're quite right, Ellis. Bournemouth will be a delightful place to live — I always enjoy my visits to Catherine so much — it really is very strange that I never thought of it before.'

Naturally Mrs. Player was delighted at the idea of having her favourite sister settled so near; she set to work without delay to find a suitable residence and soon discovered an attractive bungalow which was being vacated shortly. Mrs. Brownlee went down to see it and decided it would do very well, so Rose Hill was sold, without any difficulty, and the bungalow bought forthwith.

In comparison with the trouble and delay which Ellis had experienced in the purchase of Fletchers End the matter was very easily dealt with. The whole transaction was accomplished in a few weeks.

Naturally the bungalow was smaller than Rose Hill so Mrs. Brownlee wrote to Ellis offering him some of her large furniture which would not be required. The letter containing the offer arrived when the young Brownlees were having breakfast.

'Look at that,' said Ellis, handing the letter to Bel. 'Very kind of Mother, but we don't want it, do we?'

'Don't want it!' exclaimed Bel in surprise.

'It's Victorian stuff — not a bit suitable for Fletchers End.'

'Oh, Ellis, we can't possibly refuse to have it! For one thing your mother would be frightfully hurt, and for another it will fill up the house very comfortably. We haven't got nearly enough furniture. She wants to get rid of her big sofa and it will do very nicely for the drawing-room. There are several easy chairs and two large wardrobes and all the dining-room furniture. We could do with some carpets, too — it costs the earth to buy carpets — so you must ring up your mother and tell her we'll be very grateful to have everything she can spare.'

Ellis laughed and did as he was told.

5

It was that same evening, when they had had supper and were sitting beside their comfortable fire, that Ellis looked up from his paper and remarked, 'Jim is coming on well. He's improved tremendously. He seems steadier, more civilised

123

— if you know what I mean.'

'Yes,' nodded Bel.

'I notice a great difference. His manners are better and his clothes are more suitable. I suppose you've been helping him a bit?'

'Yes.'

'D'you think he'll be all right when you leave?'

Bel hesitated. Although her child was growing up rapidly he still needed a great deal of care. She had not told Ellis about all the things she was doing for Mr. James nor of all the things she had prevented him from doing. Several times she had felt very much inclined to tell Ellis about some of the amusing scenes which had taken place in Mr. Wills's old room, but she had managed to refrain. It would not be fair to give away secrets — and, besides that, she had a feeling that Ellis might not be amused.

'Perhaps I had better look for a really good secretary for him,' said Ellis. 'She could come soon, before you leave, and learn the ropes.'

'Let me find someone, Ellis.'

'Let you? Wouldn't it be an awful bother for you?'

'I know the sort of person he needs.'

She knew exactly the sort of person he needed but whether or not she would be able to find that person was doubtful. However she realised that she would have to try. She could not possibly walk out and leave Mr. James to the tender mercies of an unknown young woman — even a very experienced young woman — it was unthinkable.

There was no difficulty in finding a young woman, for the office had a good name. Half-a-dozen experienced young women applied for the post. Bel interviewed them all but decided that none of them would do.

At last after endless troubles she succeeded in finding Mrs. Garry, a widow with a young son. Mrs. Garry was plump and cheerful; she was not experienced — or at least Ellis would not have thought her so. She had been a typist before she was married but, since then, she had not been working in an office at all, so she was finding some difficulty in getting a well-paid post. Although she had a small income, sufficient for her needs, it was not enough to pay for her son's training. He had always wanted to enter the medical profession and she was determined that he should have his wish. She explained all this to Bel.

Bel liked Mrs. Garry at once — and liked her even more when her duties had been explained to her. Mrs. Garry bubbled over with laughter and promised to do her best. She could come at once and learn how things were done; she would look after 'the poor young man' like a mother. Bel engaged Mrs. Garry on the spot and told her to come on the following Monday.

At first Mrs. Garry found it a little difficult to get into the way of office-work but she soon settled down and proved herself to be capable and intelligent — and the fact that she was not 'experienced' in the accepted sense of the word made her more adjustable, more willing to take on duties which do not usually come within the scope of the secretary of the junior partner of an important firm.

Mr. James would have preferred a younger and more attractive secretary, but he merely sighed and said, 'Oh, well . . . Of course you know best, Mrs. B. She certainly seems very keen.'

The advent of Mrs. Garry left Bel more time for her own affairs and she was able to turn her attention to Fletchers End. Louise had been over to see the house quite often and now rang up to say that Bel must come down and see it for herself. There were various matters to be decided upon which only Bel could decide. Bel must stay at Coombe House for the week-end and Ellis must go to his club. That was the best arrangement.

Louise's plans were nearly always sensible and well-thought-out — and this one was no exception to the rule — so the Brownlees agreed. They agreed somewhat reluctantly because this was the first time they had parted since their marriage and neither of them liked the idea at all.

'I shall be sorry to leave this cosy little nest,' announced Ellis as they were shutting up the flat, fastening the windows securely and covering the furniture with dust-sheets — a necessary precaution in an abode amongst the roof-tops and chimney-stacks.

'Will you, Ellis?' said Bel. 'I was so afraid you would find it very uncomfortable after Rose Hill — uncomfortable and cramped and dirty.'

'Dirty! Yes, but that's London,' declared Ellis smiling. 'If you've got to live in town you must make up your mind to put up with a few smuts. Anyhow I've been very happy here.'

'Oh, so have I!' exclaimed Bel. 'I've been terribly happy and I've enjoyed working at the office, but we shall be even happier at Fletchers End.'

12

Fletchers End was looking very different when Bel and Louise and Dr. Armstrong went to see it on Saturday afternoon. The window-frames had all been renewed and painted and the creepers cut back. Naturally this made all the difference to the exterior appearance of the house. (It would have looked a great deal better if some attempt had been made to clear the garden but it was difficult to get men to do it, so Ellis decided that this must wait until they came down themselves).

When Dr. Armstrong opened the front-door and they went in they found the hall pleasantly warm, for the central heating was now completed and had been turned on to dry up the plaster. The holes in the floors had vanished as if they had never been; the windows had been washed and the mess of dust and dirt cleaned up. They went into the drawing-room first and admired the bow-window — what a difference it made to the room! It looked so much larger and brighter. Bel was enchanted with it and was still exclaiming rapturously when Reggie Stephenson came in, followed by the painter with several large books of wall-paper patterns.

'Hallo, Reggie!' said Louise in surprise. 'I thought you had gone home.'

'Yes, I did,' he replied. 'They sent for me so I had to go, but when I heard that Bel was coming this morning I came over in the car. I wanted to be here when the wall-papers were chosen — and there are several other things to decide. Besides,' he added turning to Bel, 'I wanted to hear what you thought about everything.'

'It's marvellous,' declared Bel. 'I'm terribly grateful to you for all you've done and I know Ellis will be, too. I don't know what we should have done without you.'

'I've been happy here,' said Reggie. 'It's been a delightful job — the sort of job I like. The window is a success, isn't it?'

'Perfectly lovely,' declared Bel. 'It's all so lovely that I want to come and live here — soon.'

'Ask Mrs. Warmer,' said Reggie smiling. 'Mrs. Warmer knows about everything. We're bosom friends. She's borne all the discomforts, all the fuss and bother without turning a hair. She's a great old girl is Mrs. Warmer.'

While they were talking the painter had spread out the patterns and was waiting to hear which they would like. Everyone present took part in the discussion — even Dr. Armstrong had ideas to offer — so the choosing of the patterns for the different rooms took a considerable time.

Bel was extremely interested of course, but in spite of that she had time to notice that Reggie Stephenson and Louise had become very friendly indeed; they had been seeing a great deal of each other, meeting at Fletchers End and discussing plans. Reggie had said that he had lost his heart to the old house, but Bel felt increasingly certain that he had lost his heart to Louise.

It was more difficult to guess what Louise was feeling; her manner to Reggie was kind and friendly (but Louise was kind and friendly to everyone). Was it possible that here at last was the right man for Louise? Bel kept on wondering about it. She liked Reggie immensely; he was a dear — but he was not at all good-looking. Bel had always imagined that the right man for Louise would be tall and handsome — a sort of fairy prince — for Louise herself was so lovely . . . but of course you never knew, thought Bel as she watched them and heard them talking together Possibly Louise saw something attractive in this particular young man — something which was not apparent to other people.

The whole party moved from room to room choosing paint and papers and, as they did so, Bel made another discovery which interested her greatly. She discovered that Dr. Armstrong had been treating Reggie as a patient and had been trying to defeat 'the new-fangled bug' which had been causing Reggie so much trouble and playing havoc with his 'inside'. She overheard the doctor say, 'How's the tummy, Reggie?' and Reggie reply in a very cheerful voice, 'Absolutely O.K. thanks to you, sir. Those funny little yellow pills seem to have done the trick.'

Bel was exceedingly glad when she overheard this little aside for she had been worrying about Reggie's activities at Fletchers End. He had been told to rest and instead of resting he had been working for her and Ellis. Now that she looked at Reggie more carefully she noticed a great improvement since the last time she had seen

130

him. His colour was clearer, his eyes were brighter and he seemed more lively.

'Well, what's the verdict?' smiled Reggie.

'Oh, was I staring?' asked Bel. 'I was just thinking you looked a lot better, that's all.'

'Yes, he's better,' said Dr. Armstrong. 'But he must put on some weight. Lots of milk, Reggie — and no late nights.'

The new bathroom was still unfinished; so far nothing had been decided about the colour scheme. The painter suggested egg-shell blue and produced patterns.

'Peach colour would be better,' said Reggie firmly. 'The room has a north aspect so we want something warm and cosy.'

'But not all one colour,' objected Bel.

'Off-white for the walls and a peach-coloured bath,' said Louise. 'You could have a peach bath-mat and towels to match and gaily-coloured curtains.'

Reggie agreed at once. 'Yes that would be grand,' he said.

'What about the linoleum?' asked Dr. Armstrong. 'I think large squares of black and white would be very effective.'

'Black and white tiles,' nodded Reggie.

'And you'd like fish, wouldn't you?' asked Louise.

'Fish!' exclaimed Bel in surprise.

But Louise and Reggie were both laughing, so obviously it was a joke.

'Tell her about it,' said Louise.

'Louise is just being naughty,' explained Reggie. 'You see I've been asked to design a

131

modern bungalow for a retired fishmonger; he's a very nice fellow, really, but he has some quaint ideas — '

'He wants all sorts of fish swimming about on his bathroom walls,' put in Louise.

'Quite ghastly,' said Reggie with a sigh.

'Why shouldn't he have them if he wants them?' asked Louise. 'I mean if it makes him happy . . . '

'Because it would be frightful, that's why.'

'But it's his bathroom, Reggie — not yours.'

'I couldn't,' declared Reggie. 'You agree with me, don't you, Dr. Armstrong?'

'I'm afraid I see both sides of the question,' said the doctor smiling. 'The only thing I can suggest is that the bathroom should be completed without fish, and the owner should stick them on the walls afterwards with his own hands.'

'Solomon!' exclaimed Louise laughing gaily.

'Well that's fixed then,' said Reggie. 'I mean about this bathroom — not the fishmonger's. Off-white walls, black and white tiles and peach-coloured fittings. I think a full-length mirror would look well on that wall.'

'Oh, lovely!' exclaimed Louise. 'I'd like to come and have a bath in this bathroom when it's ready.'

2

When they had been all round the house Bel went into the kitchen to see Mrs. Warmer. She

132

was pleased to find that the electric stove had been installed and the new sink and cupboards.

'It's all splendid,' declared Mrs. Warmer enthusiastically. 'Mr. Stephenson has done wonders — he really has. He's been here nearly every day gingering up the men. It's a pity his holiday's over.'

'Not much of a holiday,' suggested Bel.

'Mr. Stephenson says a holiday is doing what you like, and he likes pottering about Fletchers End . . . and it's my belief there's another reason that the poor young gentleman likes being here,' added Mrs. Warmer nodding in a very knowing manner.

It was Bel's belief too.

'She's such a nice young lady,' Mrs. Warmer continued. 'As pretty as a picture is Miss Armstrong, and she couldn't get a nicer kinder husband — not if she was to search the whole of England. It would be nice if there was another wedding at Coombe House, wouldn't it?'

'Er — yes — but I don't think — ' began Bel. 'I mean Miss Armstrong is — I mean the doctor couldn't get on without her, could he?'

'Love laughs at locksmiths,' said Mrs. Warmer sententiously.

The saying was not very apt, but Bel knew what was meant. She changed the subject by asking when Mrs. Warmer thought it would be possible to move in.

'Well, that depends. If you want it all ready and lovely it would be the end of March,' said Mrs. Warmer in thoughtful tones. 'But if you didn't mind a bit of a mess I could get one or

133

two girls from the village to give me a hand and you could come a bit sooner.'

'I'll ask Mr. Brownlee and let you know,' said Bel. She said it calmly but she was not calm inside. Now that she had seen the old house again, and had seen it looking so much more pleasant, the enchantment had laid hold upon her with renewed force. Bel would have liked to stay here; she would have liked to take up her abode in the place this very day . . . but of course that was impossible. She could not leave Ellis by himself, she could not desert Mr. James.

But it won't be long, thought Bel. Perhaps we could manage to come in a fortnight if Ellis doesn't mind 'a bit of a mess.'

It was the end of February and there was a feeling of Spring in the air — the lovely fresh country air, so different from London! Already the days were beginning to lengthen; rooks were to be seen sitting on the roofs with little twigs in their beaks, and there were snowdrops scattered beneath the chestnut tree in the garden at Coombe House. Next year there would be snowdrops at Fletchers End — and crocuses too. Next year — at Fletchers End!

PART THREE

The Brownlees at Home

13

Ellis was standing on the little terrace outside the bow-window of the drawing-room at Fletchers End. He and Bel had arrived at tea-time and had had a busy time settling in, for although Mrs. Warmer and the two girls from the village had scrubbed and polished, laid carpets and moved furniture, there was still a great deal to be done. Mrs. Warmer had provided an exceedingly good dinner to which they had done full justice . . . it was now after nine o'clock and they had decided to do no more that night.

They had decided to do no more that night but Ellis could hear the voices of Bel and Mrs. Warmer upstairs in the bedroom, the window of which looked out over the garden, so they were still at work — and Bel was tired.

'Bel, come out!' he called.

'We're just making the bed,' explained Bel, putting her head out of the window. 'I'll come in a minute.'

Presently she came out through the glass door and slipped her hand through his arm. Neither of them said a word for a long time.

Although it was only the middle of March it was quite mild. The moon was very bright so the stars looked pale, twinkling feebly in the dark blue sky. The garden was still an almost impenetrable jungle of withered vegetation . . . but that could be dealt with when they had time.

'We're home,' said Ellis at last with a long sigh of pleasure.

Bel tightened her fingers on his arm. 'Yes, we're home,' she said softly. 'Dear Fletchers End! This is to be our home all our lives.'

An owl flew past on silent wings and disappeared amongst the trees.

'All our lives,' echoed Ellis thoughtfully. 'We'll grow old here; we'll be Darby and Joan. It will be pleasant to grow old in Fletchers End.'

After a bit they went into the drawing-room and sat down together on the sofa and began to talk.

'You had a great send-off this morning,' said Ellis smiling. 'Mrs. B. seems to have made herself extremely popular in the office.'

'They were all terribly kind; it almost made me cry. Mr. Copping sent for me to his room and thanked me.'

'So he should. Goodness knows what would have happened if you hadn't worked like a Trojan all winter. Things will be better now that we've got that new man — and your Mrs. Garry seems a sensible woman. Mr. Copping suggested I should take a week's holiday.'

'You certainly deserve it.'

'Yes, I think I do,' agreed Ellis with a smile. 'Now that Mr. Copping is back there's no reason why I shouldn't take a few days off.'

'A week at least,' said Bel firmly. She added, 'Look, Ellis. Mr. Copping gave me this.'

'This' was a small gold watch with a gold bracelet. She held up her wrist for Ellis to see it.

'I say, what a lovely one!' he exclaimed.

'Wasn't it kind? He said it was for 'looking after the boy.' He said all sorts of nice things; he said, 'If we get ourselves into trouble again we'll send for you.''

'What did you say?'

'Oh, I just said I'd always felt that I belonged to the firm and of course I still belonged and always would.'

'Very tactful.'

'It wasn't tactful at all; it was true,' said Bel earnestly.

'All right, it was both,' said Ellis, laughing at her. 'And now we'll go to bed.'

2

Ellis was having his holiday and Bel was anxious that he should take things easily. But there were pictures to be hung and shelves to be put up and furniture to be arranged more conveniently. With all this to be done it was impossible to get Ellis to rest.

'It is a rest,' Ellis told her as he came down the ladder and looked at the picture to see if it were straight. 'Reggie said it was a holiday to do what you liked and he was absolutely right. I'm not using my brains at all. I haven't got to dictate letters or answer the telephone or tell people off. You don't expect me to lie in bed all day, do you?'

Bel would have been quite pleased to keep him in bed all day or half the day — and bring him trays of food, but she realised that Ellis was not

139

the sort of person to enjoy idleness so she went away and left him to his task.

Gradually they got things straight and began to settle down; they began to learn something about the neighbourhood in which they intended to spend the rest of their lives. Mrs. Warmer knew everyone and was only too delighted to supply any information that was wanted. There were several very large houses round about Archerfield but these were no longer occupied by the families who had owned them for years. One of them had become a preparatory school for boys, another was a Rest Home for clergymen working in London parishes. Louise had said that they would be 'no use socially,' which was true of course, but Bel was not very sociably inclined; she was perfectly happy pottering about the house and was not at all anxious for visitors. Ellis had promised to buy her a little car and teach her how to drive; he realised that she would be rather stranded when his short holiday was over for he would have to take his car to Ernleigh every morning to catch his train to town and leave it there for his return journey in the evening. Meantime Bel got a bicycle which secretly she preferred (she knew nothing whatever about cars and was somewhat nervous of them). The bicycle was useful for shopping in Shepherdsford and later on when she was not so busy she could go over and see the Musgraves and Margaret Warren and other friends whom she had met at Coombe House. One fine morning she walked into Shepherdsford by the delightful path along the bank of the stream

140

which Mrs. Warmer had told her was called 'The Church Walk.'

The first Sunday that the Brownlees spent at Fletchers End was a bright breezy day with white fleecy clouds moving across the sky. Bel and Ellis decided to walk to St. Julian's for matins. They had expected to see quite a crowd making the expedition, but there were only a few people from the village, including Mr. Carruthers. They knew him, for he had swept their chimneys, but it was difficult to recognise the black and sooty sweep in the well-turned-out gentleman who overtook them and doffed his hat so politely.

'Er — Mr. Carruthers?' asked Ellis.

'That's right,' agreed Mr. Carruthers. 'Fine morning isn't it, Mr. Brownlee? I 'opes you're not 'aving no more trouble with that there chimbley.'

They walked along together chatting in a friendly manner and presently were joined by a very old man. He was small and bent, with a brown wrinkled face and quantities of very white hair.

'That's Mr. Fuller,' said Mr. Carruthers. 'If you wants to know about the garding at Fletchers End 'e's the chap to tell you. 'E used ter be the gard'ner — '

'The 'ead gard'ner,' said Mr. Fuller hastily. 'There was three of us, see? The garding was noice in those days an' we 'ad ter keep it neat as ninepence. Old Mr. Lestrange was very pertick-ler about the garding.'

Bel was very pleased to meet the old gardener for there were all sorts of things she wanted to know . . . and Mr. Fuller was delighted to inform her. He had a queer high-pitched voice which rambled on from one thing to another. He told her about the 'kitching-garding'; how to make an asparagus bed and how to grow celery.

'Celery's a 'eartbreak,' said Mr. Fuller sadly. 'You can't never depend on celery no matter 'ow much trouble you takes. It was Miss Lestrange that was so partial to celery — but it 'ad to be crisp. She used ter say celery weren't no good if it weren't crisp. 'Make it crisp, Fuller,' she used ter say. It weren't never crisp enough ter please 'er . . . '

'I was wondering about violets,' said Bel when she could get a word in edgeways. 'Did you grow violets in the garden at Fletchers End?'

'If *you* wants vilets,' said Mr. Fuller. '*You* get a cold frame and *you* put it in that sunny corner near that there skeptic tank, you'll 'ave vilets in March if you does that, see? Old Mrs. Lestrange — a very noice lady she was and very pretty too — she was a great one for vilets.'

'Mr. Brownlee is especially fond of roses,' said Bel.

'Ah, roses! Them's my fav'rites. Luverly roses we 'ad at Fletchers End. I got some in my garding too. They grow noice in this place, roses does.'

Bel was delighted to hear it for the roses at Rose Hill had been very fine indeed and she wanted them to grow even more beautifully — for Ellis — at Fletchers End. She made searching inquiries of Mr. Fuller as to where the rose-beds should be placed and what kind of manure was most effective.

'You let me know when you've got the garding dug,' said Mr. Fuller. 'I'll come and show you — and I'll come and plant the roses too, when you gets 'em, see? I can't do 'ard work now — I'm eighty four come Mickelmas — but I'll come and plant your roses and prune 'em too. Don't you go and let nobody else do it.'

Bel accepted the offer with gratitude.

The whole party had arrived at St. Julian's by this time. Mr. Carruthers led the way, Bel and Ellis followed.

'*You* 'urry up and get the garding cleared — sooner the better, see?' said Mr. Fuller in a creaky whisper as he took off his hat and followed the others in at the door.

3

Bel had been particularly interested in Mr. Fuller's information, not only about the roses but also about the 'vilets.' She supposed that old Mrs. Lestrange, who had been so fond of violets, must have been the mother of Miss Lestrange. Perhaps it was she who had left, as a gentle reminder of her presence, the scent of the violets in the drawing-room. Alas, the fragrance which had gone completely during the alterations had never returned. Bel hoped it might — someday — and said so to Ellis.

'I think you imagined it, darling,' he replied.

'Oh, no!' exclaimed Bel. 'It was quite strong. How could I have imagined it?'

'Perhaps you smelt violets in the house of your dreams and then when you came to Fletchers End and — and connected it with the house you had dreamt about so often you imagined the scent of violets.'

'But Louise smelt it too.'

'Just imagination,' said Ellis with conviction.

This seemed unlikely to say the least of it, but Bel did not pursue the subject any further. Ellis had never smelt violets in the drawing-room, neither had Reggie Stephenson — she had asked him. It did not occur to Bel to mention the matter to Mrs. Warmer; she was such a sensible practical sort of person — not at all the sort of person who would be likely to notice the fragrance of ghostly violets.

4

When the day came for Ellis to return to his work he went reluctantly, for already in one short week he had got thoroughly dug in to his new surroundings. But of course he would come home every evening and would be free to enjoy the amenities of Fletchers End on Saturdays and Sundays. Fortunately the daily journey did not worry him at all for the train was comfortable and he had time to read his morning paper before his arrival at Paddington and his evening paper on the way home.

Bel had not forgotten Mr. Fuller's injunction to hurry up and get the garden cleared. Indeed it had not been necessary for now that the house was getting settled and the days were becoming warmer and brighter her thoughts were turning more and more towards the garden. She had made all sorts of wonderful plans for the garden at Fletchers End but, before she could do anything at all, the place must be cleared. Ellis had made her promise faithfully to do nothing whatever in the garden until this was accomplished,

'But how are we to get it cleared?' asked Bel.

'It's a task for strong men,' replied Ellis.

Bel made a few inquiries in the village but everyone told her it was impossible to get labour. Most of the men worked on farms and those who did not were employed by Mr. Middleton who owned a nursery garden in the vicinity. Everyone told Bel that it might be possible to get a man once or twice a week in the evenings — but not if there happened to be a cricket match of course.

On Saturday morning Bel and Ellis went to the village together and Ellis mentioned his requirement to Mr. Smith, the postmaster.

'I want a few chaps to come and clear the garden,' explained Ellis.

'That won't be easy,' replied Mr. Smith. He smiled in a slightly unpleasant manner and added, 'P'raps you might get one or two if you paid 'em double.'

'I shan't overpay them,' said Ellis shortly.

'You won't get 'em then,' declared Mr. Smith.

Bel had a moment of sheer panic when she heard these fatal words. Were they to live in the depths of a jungle for the rest of their lives? Of

145

course Ellis was capable — nobody could direct his business more efficiently — but this was a different matter altogether.

14

Bel need not have worried about the capabilities of her husband. Once they were settled and Ellis was able to give his mind to the problem he solved it without much difficulty; within a few days of Mr. Smith's gloomy prophecy he produced strong men to clear the garden. They did not come every evening — even Ellis could not accomplish the impossible — but they came three times a week and every other Saturday afternoon. They came armed with axes and bill-hooks and scythes and spades and they built a bonfire which smoked sullenly for hours on end. After a week the garden looked a great deal worse, for instead of a jungle it had become a wilderness.

'It's awful,' said Bel in despair.

'It's got to be worse before it's better,' said Ellis cheerfully.

One might have thought it a miracle to have got labour in a place where no labour was to be had, but it was merely the result of a well-thought-out-scheme. Various factors contributed to Ellis's success. For one thing there is a savage streak in every man worth his salt which makes him revel in destruction. Hacking and sawing, tearing up bushes by the roots and burning them, is proper work for strong men. For another thing the jungle at Fletchers End had been a joke for years. In an odd sort of way the villagers were quite proud of the jungle; they discussed it over pints of ale at The Green Man; so in an odd sort of way it was satisfactory to wade into the jungle and hack it to pieces.

But that was after Ellis had accomplished his object and had got his strong men. How had he managed it?

One evening after his return from town Mr. Brownlee strolled into The Green Man; he treated the assembled company to a round of what they fancied and asked for a half pint of ale for himself. At first the company was shy and silent but Mr. Brownlee asked a few questions about the district: where was the quarry from which the stone had been taken to build Fletchers End — and all the other houses in the neighbourhood? Soon they were all talking and arguing about it. Unfortunately Mr. Brownlee could not understand all that was said — in fact not half that was said — and this was a pity because it was a subject that interested him.

When they had all said their say Mr. Brownlee looked about the room and asked if there were any strong men hereabouts. Several people sniggered, they knew what Mr. Brownlee was up to.

Old Mr. Fuller, who was sitting in the corner with his usual on the table before him, said in his squeaky voice, 'No, sir, not now there ain't. There ain't nobody 'ere to-night that's as strong as me when I was young.'

Hearty laughter greeted this sally and a lot of chaff followed. Mr. Brownlee wished he could understand the jokes; that they were very funny

148

and somewhat lewd he had no doubt whatever. He waited patiently, leaning on the bar counter, smiling and drinking his ale . . . and before very long several hefty young men sidled up to him and said bashfully that they 'didn't mind if they did.'

Mr. Brownlee had got his men — that was good enough to start with — he was quite pleased with his evening's work. The next thing was, could he keep them or would they fade away and leave the job half done? He did not think so, for he had liked the look of the chaps, but he was taking no chances. He had another scheme which he hoped would work and he proceeded to put it into operation.

Every evening when Mr. Brownlee returned from town and found his chaps at work he went out and spoke to them; he jollied them along, complimenting them on the progress they had made. Then, still in his conventional city-clothes, Mr. Brownlee took a hand with the saw or the barrow — he was not allowed to touch the scythe. The chaps thought this very funny indeed — and probably it was. When work was over Mr. Brownlee paid the amount due in silver, counting it out into each large horny hand. He had a small leather bag full of silver which he kept for the purpose. He made a joke of it and the joke was appreciated, partly because it was considered a good joke and partly because it was rather pleasant to go home with a pocket full of jingling coins.

When the business transaction was over everyone trooped into the back kitchen for a glass of ale, drawn from the barrel. This was pleasant too.

The chaps thought Mr. Brownlee was 'a rum 'un' but it was an endearing kind of rumness. Stories about what he had done and said were retained with advantages in The Green Man — and occasioned mirth. Mr. Brownlee's chaps discovered that their appearance at The Green Man was warmly welcomed. They were beset with questions, subjected to a round of not unpleasant teasing. How far into the jungle had they penetrated this evening? Had they seen any tigers? Why didn't Mr. Brownlee provide elephants to help with the job?

The chaps stood there and smiled and jingled their pockets and everyone laughed.

2

Bel often watched the ceremony of paying out (peeping from behind the curtain in the bow-window). It amused her considerably.

One night when Ellis came in she said to him, 'You're like that man in the Bible who engaged labourers to work in his vineyard.'

Ellis smiled. 'It's funny you should say that, Bel. That story gave me the idea of paying them every night. When you've worked hard, and sweated over it, I think it's very satisfactory to get paid on the nail.'

'With pennies.'

'Yes, they like going home with jingling pockets. It's a joke. But I'm not really like the man in the Bible because my chaps get paid by the hour — so many hours of work, so much pay. And it isn't a penny,' added Ellis somewhat ruefully. 'It's a whole heap of pennies and silver ones at that.'

'It wasn't a penny — even in those days — it was ever so much more. The New English Bible says it was 'a fair day's wage'.'

'A denarius,' agreed Ellis. He was silent and thoughtful for a few moments, and then continued, 'To tell you the truth that story has always puzzled me. I don't wonder that the fellows who had toiled all day were a bit fed up when they saw the others, who had only worked for an hour, were getting the same pay. I'd have been fed up myself,' said Ellis frankly. 'I'd have been so fed up I wouldn't have worked in that vineyard again.'

'Yes,' said Bel in doubtful tones. 'Yes, but I think you're missing the point. The point is that the first lot of men agreed to work all day for a penny and it was only when they saw the other men getting a penny that they thought they ought to be given more.'

'You mean they ought to have minded their own business?'

'Partly that — and partly because it was horrid of them to be annoyed at their friends' good fortune. They were jealous.'

'Well, I don't blame them,' declared Ellis. 'And anyhow whether it's right or wrong it isn't practical. It wouldn't work. Nobody would be pleased.'

'Surely the men who got a whole day's pay for

an hour's work would be pleased!'

'No, Bel. That's where you're mistaken. Perhaps it might have worked in Palestine, long ago, but it wouldn't work here and now. My chaps respect themselves too much. They tell me exactly how long they've worked and if I happen to miscalculate they point out the mistake and hand back a sixpence — or whatever it may be. No, it wouldn't work,' repeated Ellis thoughtfully. 'It would upset the labour market. You wouldn't get any man in his sane senses to work all day if he knew that other chaps who worked for an hour would get the same wages.'

'He wouldn't know,' suggested Bel.

'Of course he'd know,' declared Ellis smiling. 'The other chaps would boast about it in The Green Man.'

Bel laughed and said, 'I can't argue with you, Ellis. You're much too clever.'

'But it's fun arguing, isn't it?' said Ellis. He added, 'I must get some more silver pennies when I go to town to-morrow. This bag is nearly empty.'

15

Reggie Stephenson had been given a standing invitation to come and stay at Fletchers End whenever he liked. He came one Saturday afternoon and stayed the night and was suitably entertained with a juicy piece of steak and other delectable viands. Bel had wondered whether there was some sort of understanding between Reggie and Louise, and had asked Louise if she and the doctor would come and have lunch on Sunday, but Louise had refused the invitation saying she would rather come some other day when Bel was alone.

'I thought you liked Reggie,' said Bel in surprise.

'Of course I like him,' replied Louise. 'I like him very much — we were friends — but now he has got silly.' She sighed and added, 'It's such a pity. I don't know why people can't just be friends with me.'

There was no need to say more. The matter was perfectly clear to Bel. She was aware that Louise suffered considerably from the inability to 'just be friends' with the young men of her acquaintance.

To Bel's surprise Reggie seemed quite cheerful. He approved of all the furniture which had been bought at sales, but he did not approve of the furniture from Rose Hill and advised his host and hostess to get rid of it as soon as possible. The dining-room furniture was particularly obnoxious in Reggie's opinion. An oak refectory table would be the correct thing for Fletchers End.

'And wooden stools to sit on, I suppose?' asked Bel with a little smile.

'Yes, that would be correct, but I wouldn't object to oak chairs with cushions.'

'We'll keep a look-out for the right kind of stuff,' said Ellis.

'No, we can't change it,' said Bel. 'Your mother wouldn't like it if we sold the furniture she gave us. It would hurt her feelings to think we didn't appreciate her kindness. People's feelings are more important than refectory tables.'

Reggie did not agree. He would have liked to see Fletchers End furnished in the correct manner for its period (regardless of Mrs. Brownlee's feelings and equally regardless of the fact that it would have been uncomfortable and inconvenient) but he realised that nothing he could say would be the slightest use so he sighed and said nothing.

That was on Saturday evening, at dinner. On Sunday morning Bel rose early to go to Communion Service at St. Julian's. She came downstairs through the sleeping house and into the drawing-room; it was easier to go out through the glass door — she always did so — and she could leave it open for her return.

On this particular morning Bel found the glass door already open, which surprised her considerably for it was unlike Ellis to forget to lock it before coming up to bed . . . but of course he had been talking to Reggie so it must have slipped his memory. She went down the garden and through the gate which opened on to the Church Walk.

It was bright and sunshiny; there was a light mist rising from the stream and the birds were singing joyfully. Apart from the birds not a creature was to be seen. Bel and the birds had the morning all to themselves.

There were quite a lot of people in church and the service was even more beautiful and satisfying than usual. When Bel came out of the dim building into the bright sunshine she felt happy and at peace. She did not linger in the churchyard, as some of the other members of the congregation liked to do, but set out for home at a brisk pace.

Bel had not gone far when she heard someone call her by name and looking round she saw Reggie hurrying after her. Obviously he too had been to St. Julian's — it was surprising that she had not seen him. It was surprising to see him now, for she had imagined him slumbering peacefully in bed.

'Hallo, Bel,' said Reggie. 'Do you mind if I walk home with you, or would you rather be alone?'

'Let's walk home together,' said Bel smiling at him.

They fell into step and walked along companionably.

'Do you often do this?' asked Reggie.

'Yes, quite often. I enjoy it.'

155

'So do I,' he added, 'I could see you were a bit surprised to see me. As a matter of fact I was a bit surprised to see you. Funny, isn't it?'

'Funny?' asked Bel.

'I mean strange. It seems wrong that we shouldn't have known each other better. Neither of us knew that the other liked this sort of thing.'

'People don't talk about it. That's why. You can know people for years and yet not know in the very least what they think about religion.'

Reggie nodded. 'You know what they think about politics and sport and whether they like yachting. They'll tell you about their business, but . . . ' he hesitated.

'Go on,' said Bel. 'You're thinking about something, aren't you?'

'Yes, I am,' he admitted. 'I'm thinking about a sermon I heard some time ago. The text was, 'Then they that feared the Lord spake often one to another.' Why don't we speak often to one another about important things? I don't mean just you and me, I mean everyone. Why is religion kept shut up in a cupboard and only taken out on Sundays — put on like your best hat?'

'It should be a part of everyday life.'

'Yes,' said Reggie. 'Why don't we talk about it? Of course the answer is that it's 'not done.' Fellows would think you had gone a bit queer in the head if you started talking about the Lord.'

Bel could not help smiling.

'It's true, isn't it?' asked Reggie.

'Yes, it's perfectly true.'

They were now walking along by the side of

156

the stream. The mist had vanished completely and the sunlight was sparkling on the water as it rippled over the stones.

'Bel,' said Reggie. 'I've decided to enter the Church.'

'Really? Do you mean — '

'Yes, really. I've been thinking about it for months. I haven't told anyone else but I felt I'd like to tell you. Fortunately I have a little money of my own — not very much but enough to make it possible.'

'You'll go to Oxford to take your degree?'

'Yes, if I can. I must find out more about it. I suppose you think I'm a fool to throw up my career — '

'No, of course not!'

'Other people will, but I've made up my mind quite definitely.'

'Tell me about it, Reggie. What made you think of it?'

'The idea began with that text from Malachi: 'Then they that feared the Lord spake often one to another.' I've told you already how it stuck in my mind and what I thought about it. When I was here, looking after the renovation at Fletchers End, I thought about it more and more.'

'And you kept on wondering what had gone wrong with the world and why people had stopped talking about the Lord?'

'Yes, something like that,' Reggie agreed. 'You see I wasn't well, and I had to rest a good deal, so I had time to think. Fletchers End helped me to make up my mind.'

'Fletchers End helped you?' asked Bel in surprise.

'It's difficult to explain,' said Reggie thoughtfully. 'I think it was because the old house satisfied me. It satisfied something in me — a sort of hunger, if you know what I mean. The house was made by men who took a pride in their work and did it to the best of their ability. Everything in the house is good and beautiful. I got to know it well — poking about in hidden corners — and I found that even in hidden corners every joint in the woodwork fitted perfectly. You can see the same meticulous workmanship in old churches. They were made by men's hands for the glory of God.'

Bel nodded, 'It didn't matter whether or not their work was seen. They put their best into it.'

'Yes, that's what I mean. All this worked together in my mind until I felt that I must learn to tell other people about it. That's all, really,' added Reggie. 'Perhaps you don't see the connection between the two ideas — I don't see it clearly myself — but it's there, somewhere.'

They walked on together in silence.

At last Bel said, 'If you feel like that I'm sure it's the right thing for you to do. I hope you'll be very happy in your new life, Reggie.'

'I think I shall,' he said. 'I'm not at all happy in my present life — you know that, don't you? Making houses with shoddy materials, running them up as cheaply and quickly as possible — there's something very wrong about it, Bel.'

'You want perfection.'

He hesitated. 'Perfection is a big word, isn't it?

I want to do something that I can offer to God, and you can't offer Him anything less than your best.'

'That's a lovely idea,' Bel told him. 'I shall keep it safely and think about it.'

2

Reggie and Bel had arrived at the glass door by this time; here they paused for a few moments.

'You haven't told Ellis?' asked Bel.

'No, I'm afraid he'll be annoyed with me. He'll think it's foolish of me to chuck up my career just when I'm beginning to make headway. I don't want to argue with Ellis; nothing he can say will make me change my mind so the argument would be fruitless. You can tell him, if you like, but not until after I've gone.'

Bel nodded. She understood.

Ellis had started breakfast when they went in; obviously he was surprised to see them come in together.

'Hallo, Reggie,' he said. 'I didn't know you had gone with Bel. I thought you were still in bed and I've been creeping about like a thief in the night so as not to waken you. I'm afraid you'll have to wait a few minutes for your ham and eggs; Mrs. Warmer was holding back until you were ready.'

Reggie laughed and said Mrs. Warmer's ham and eggs were worth waiting for. After that they talked about other matters.

Apart from his dissatisfaction with the

159

furniture Reggie was very pleased with Fletchers End; he enjoyed his short visit and the excellent food provided for his benefit by Mrs. Warmer. Of course he renewed his friendship with the good lady and spent a long time in the kitchen chatting to her. Bel wondered if they had talked about Louise and hoped that if so Mrs. Warmer had been tactful. It was a very faint hope for she was aware that tact was not Mrs. Warmer's strong point.

Neither Bel nor Ellis mentioned the Armstrongs, but after they had bidden their guest good-bye and had watched him drive off from the gate, Ellis said, 'He's an awfully good chap. It's a pity about Louise, isn't it?'

'Oh, you know about that!' exclaimed Bel in surprise.

'It was pretty obvious,' replied Ellis smiling. 'Of course poor old Reggie isn't much to look at — I grant you that — but Louise might do a great deal worse.'

'I think he's got over it,' said Bel.

'Yes, he seems very cheerful. I suppose he's accepted the fact that she won't have him and decided to make the best of it.'

Bel thought so too. For a moment she wondered whether this was a good opportunity to tell Ellis about Reggie's plans, but she found it difficult to begin and while she was beginning Ellis started to talk about something else.

16

Louise came over to see Bel quite often, though not as often as she would have liked for it was difficult for her to get away from home. One morning when she had dropped in unexpectedly for a cup of coffee Bel reminded her that she had said she would like to have a bath in the new bathroom; it was all ready now, even to the peach-coloured mat and towels and the gaily-coloured curtains.

'Yes,' said Louise. 'I'd love to have a bath in your new bathroom — it's the prettiest bathroom I've ever seen — but I haven't time this morning.'

'Of course not, you donkey! You must come and stay for a week-end,' said Bel laughing.

'I don't see how I could.'

'Do try,' said Bel persuasively. 'I'm sure Dr. Armstrong would think it a good plan for you to have a little holiday.'

'Is there a special reason?' asked Louise.

There was a 'special reason' why Bel wanted her friend to come. She explained that Mrs. Brownlee was now comfortably settled in her bungalow at Bournemouth and was anxious for Ellis to pay her a little visit and see how delightful it was. She had asked Bel too, of course, but Bel thought it would be very much nicer for Mrs. Brownlee to have her son to herself.

'You're quite right,' declared Louise. 'When I have a son I'd like to have him all to myself occasionally. No matter how much I liked his wife I wouldn't want her hanging on to his coat-tails all the time.'

Bel could not help smiling at this glimpse into the faraway future when Louise would have not only a son but a daughter-in-law into the bargain.

'Ellis doesn't agree,' said Bel. 'Ellis doesn't like the idea of going without me — but I thought if you could come . . . '

'You want me to come and provide a good excuse for you to stay at home.'

'Partly that, but not only that,' explained Bel. 'It would be so lovely to have you — especially while Ellis is at Bournemouth — because we could talk all the time. We never seem to have time for a really good talk nowadays. No sooner have you arrived than you have to rush away.'

'Yes, that's true,' agreed Louise. 'It certainly would be fun. I wonder if I could possibly get Mrs. Morgan to come for a week-end. She came before, when I had appendicitis, and she was a great success. She cooked well and was very sensible about telephone messages and of course she adored Daddy — everyone does. I'm sure Mrs. Morgan would come if she could. I'll talk to Daddy and see what he thinks.'

Sometimes it is very difficult to arrange things to please everyone concerned and at other times things work out so easily that they may almost be said to arrange themselves. Louise's plan regarding her visit to Fletchers End was of the latter sort. Dr. Armstrong was delighted at the idea that Louise should have a little holiday; Mrs. Morgan was available and more than willing to oblige; Ellis agreed — though somewhat reluctantly — to go to Bournemouth alone. His mother was very fond of Bel but all the same perhaps it would be better if he went alone — just this once — and Bel would be perfectly happy at home with Louise to keep her company.

Bel was very much excited at the prospect of Louise's visit. She had been to stay with Louise so often — and now Louise was coming to stay with her! Nothing was too good for the eagerly expected guest and of course Bel had a staunch ally in Mrs. Warmer, for Mrs. Warmer was devoted to Miss Armstrong. They had long discussions about food, which in Mrs. Warmer's opinion was of primary importance.

It was decided that the guest should be given the room which looked out on to the front garden and the path to the gate. The front garden had now been cleared and the hedges trimmed, so it was more like a garden and less like a jungle.

Bel spent a long time arranging the room comfortably, while Mrs. Warmer busied herself putting clean white paper in the drawers. It was all ready in good time for Louise's arrival and on Friday afternoon Bel and Mrs. Warmer went in to have a last look round.

'A little vase on the dressing-table would just finish it off,' said Mrs. Warmer regretfully.

'Never mind,' said Bel in comforting tones.

163

'We can't help it. Miss Armstrong knows we haven't any flowers. Next year we'll have lots of flowers. Next year we'll have sweet peas and roses and everything you can think of.'

'And vilets,' suggested Mrs. Warmer.

'Are you very fond of violets?' asked Bel in surprise.

'They're not much to look at; it's the smell — ' began Mrs. Warmer.

At that very moment there was a loud hoot — a signal which always heralded the arrival of Louise at Fletchers End — so Bel turned and rushed downstairs at break-neck speed and reached the gate breathless, in time to welcome her guest.

They hugged each other ecstatically — as if they had not seen each other for months — and chattered and laughed like a couple of over-excited schoolgirls. Then, as they went up the path together, Louise dropped a curtsy very gracefully indeed and exclaimed, 'Good afternoon, Mr. Fletchers End! You're looking very handsome with your lovely new paint and shining windows,' and Bel, putting on a deep, gruff voice (the sort of voice which might conceivably belong to an elderly gentleman with side-whiskers) replied, 'Good afternoon, Miss Armstrong! You're in very good looks, yourself, if I may be permitted to say so.'

Mrs. Warmer, peeping at them from the bedroom window thought it was a crazy way for two grown-up ladies to behave — and one of them married! — but she could not help smiling all the same.

There was no doubt about it; Bel and Louise were just a bit crazy — a bit above themselves, as the saying is — but perhaps there was some excuse for their curious behaviour. They had the prospect of a whole week-end before them with nothing to do except enjoy each other's company — a whole week-end of idleness. Of course there was still a great deal to be done in the house, but Bel had been working hard ever since she and Ellis had arrived (and she had been working hard all winter in the office) so she had decided that she would do nothing at all while Louise was here; she felt she could idle with a clear conscience. As for Louise; she certainly was due a holiday from the hundred and one duties which filled her days. Her father had told her to enjoy herself and she was determined to do so . . . and what a relief it was to know that even if the telephone-bell shrilled forth a peremptory summons it would not be her duty to rush and answer it!

The afternoon was fine and warm so, after Louise had seen her room and admired all the preparations which had been made for her comfort, the two friends went out for a walk along the stream. The sunshine glanced on the rippling water; the trees were putting forth their tiny new green leaves; there were primroses and daffodils — and a scatter of bluebells in sheltered hollows.

It was so peaceful and beautiful that for a time they walked along in silence and then at last Bel said, 'Last Spring I was in London.'

'You were unhappy there, weren't you?'

'Yes, but I didn't really know how unhappy I was,' replied Bel thoughtfully. 'It's only now when I'm here with Ellis at Fletchers End that I realise what a wretched life I had. Everything is quite perfect now — so perfect that I'm almost frightened.'

'But we're meant to be happy, Bel,' said Louise in surprise.

'I wonder . . . yes, I suppose we are . . . but so many people are unhappy. That's the trouble.'

'Refugees.'

'Not only refugees but people here in our own country. When I lived in town and went to the office in the bus I used to look round at all the people. It was dreadful to see their faces — all so miserable and worried, so tired and careworn. When I think of them it seems wrong for me to be happy and safe.'

Louise did not reply. She understood, but only vaguely, for she had always been happy and safe.

They walked along in silence, but after a little they began to talk again and became more cheerful. It was impossible not to be cheerful on such a lovely afternoon. They picked little bunches of primroses and golden king cups to take home with them and presently Louise called Bel to come and see what she had found. It was a little cluster of violets, fresh and sweet, hiding amongst their moist green leaves.

'Aren't they darlings?' said Louise. 'We won't pick them, Bel. They wouldn't like to be picked and taken away.'

166

Although it was only a small cluster the scent of the little flowers was quite strong and the two girls looked at each other understandingly.

'It has gone, hasn't it?' asked Louise.

'Yes, I haven't smelt it since that first day when you and I looked over the house together.'

'It was the alterations to the room,' said Louise. 'It was the holes in the floor and the bow-window and all that frightful mess — but I hoped it would come back.'

'You don't think we just imagined it, do you?' asked Bel doubtfully. 'Nobody seems to have smelt it except you and me . . . unless perhaps Mrs. Warmer. I never thought of asking her, but funnily enough she said something about the scent of violets — '

'I asked her and she said it was floor polish.'

They smiled at each other.

'But it wasn't,' said Louise firmly. 'It wasn't floor polish and it wasn't imagination; it was the scent of fresh violets.'

17

It had been a warm day, very warm for April, but after dinner a breeze sprang up and it became cooler — cool enough for a fire to be very pleasant. As a matter of fact Bel liked to see a fire burning in the big stone fireplace in the drawing-room; it was comfortable to sit and watch it and chat. Fortunately Ellis shared this taste and, since their arrival they had had a fire every evening.

'Let me light it,' Louise said. 'You know I love fiddling about with fires.'

Bel smiled and gave her the matches and watched Louise at the task. She was such a pleasure to look at, so unconscious of her grace and charm. Her face was serious and absorbed.

'You don't mind if I alter it a bit,' said Louise. 'Mrs. Warmer is a gem — that soufflé was perfect — but obviously she doesn't understand fires. Too much paper for one thing.' Quickly her hands altered it, piling the sticks criss-cross and topping the heap with a few small lumps of coal. 'A fire needs lot of air,' she explained putting her head on one side and regarding the result of her work with satisfaction. 'One match should do the trick.'

One match did the trick. The paper was set alight, the little flames leapt up and the wood began to crackle.

Bel had sat down in the low chair beside the

fireplace and Louise leant against her knee. For a few minutes they watched the fire without speaking.

Presently Louise bent forward and put on a log. 'D'you remember the log fires at Drumburly?, Lovely, weren't they?'

'Lovely.'

'It was a happy holiday, wasn't it?'

'It was bliss,' said Bel. Every day, every hour of that wonderful holiday which she had spent with the Armstrongs at Mrs. Simpson's comfortable hotel was clear in her memory and would always remain so. The long walks over the hills where the heather was in flower, sweetly scented in the golden sunshine; the river flowing past beneath the windows of the hotel, its gentle splash and gurgle lulling her to sleep . . .

'You remember Alec Drummond?' asked Louise.

'Yes, of course. I liked him immensely. Where is he now? Do you ever hear from him?'

'I've had several letters — and I went up to London one day and met him for lunch, but afterwards I wished I hadn't.'

'Louise! Why?'

'He keeps on asking me to — to marry him,' said Louise in a very low voice.

Bel was not surprised. Alec Drummond had been staying at the hotel and had fallen in love with Louise. It was by no means unusual for young men to fall in love with Louise but Alec had done so in a spectacular way — head over heels.

'I keep on saying no,' continued Louise after a

169

little silence. 'I thought I had made him understand quite definitely when I saw him in London, but I had another letter from him this morning.'

'Where is he now?'

'At Loch Boisdale,' said Louise. 'Fishing, of course. He never does anything else — you know that, don't you? He says in his letter that he expects to be in London next month and he would like to come down to Ernleigh for a week-end. He says any time that would be convenient. He says he wants to see me.' She hesitated and then added rather wistfully, 'It's an awfully nice letter.'

'Do you want him to come?' asked Bel.

'I don't know,' admitted Louise. 'At least — yes — I'd like to see Alec, but of course I couldn't possibly have him for a week-end.'

'Why not, Louise?'

'Oh, because,' said Louise, trying to explain. 'Because it would be too long. He would just get silly again if I had him in the house for a whole week-end.'

Bel hesitated. Then she said, 'You like Alec very much, don't you?'

'Of course I like him!' Louise exclaimed. 'Alec is a dear. If only he were a little more keen on his business and a little less keen on fishing . . . '

'You would marry him.'

Louise sat up and looked at Bel defiantly. She said, 'Yes, I would — so there!'

'I wonder — ' began Bel in doubtful tones. 'Don't you think perhaps — I mean it seems such a pity, doesn't it? Oh, darling, I don't know what to say.'

'I don't know — what to *do*,' declared Louise with a little catch in her breath that was almost a sob.

'You'd like to see him, wouldn't you?'

'Yes, I would. Of course I want to see him, but I haven't changed my mind. It isn't fair to let him come to Ernleigh, is it?'

'Perhaps we could have him here for the week-end,' suggested Bel. 'He could go over and have lunch with you or something. How would that do?'

'Yes — perhaps,' said Louise thoughtfully. 'That might be quite a good plan . . . but I'm not sure that it would be fair to let him come at all.'

'Ask him to come as a friend. You could do that, couldn't you? You could make it quite clear that you would like to see him — but only as a friend. Tell him that you can't have him for the week-end but that we'll be delighted if he will come to us and he can go over to Coombe House to lunch.'

'Would it be fair?'

'Yes, I think so.'

'You think I'll change my mind,' said Louise accusingly. 'But I shan't change my mind. I'd rather marry Reggie.'

'But Louise — '

'Yes, I would, really. Reggie works hard and he takes pride in his work — but as a matter of fact I don't want to marry anyone. I'm quite happy with Daddy.'

'I know,' agreed Bel, 'but all the same you'd like to see Alec, so why not — '

'You think when I see Alec I'll change my

171

mind. Oh, yes you do. It's no use trying to pretend things to me.'

Bel knew this, of course. As a matter of fact she was not very good at 'pretending things' to anyone. Her face was the sort of face that discloses its owner's feelings only too clearly. She said, 'It's just that I like Alec so much, and it seems — '

'You think it's silly of me to mind about fishing, don't you?' demanded Louise.

'No, not really,' said Bel thoughtfully, 'It isn't so much his keenness on fishing that worried you, it's his slackness about his business. That's true, isn't it?'

'It's both. To Alec fishing is much more important than business. You saw that for yourself when we were at Drumburly.'

'He was having a fishing holiday,' Bel pointed out.

'Alec's whole life is a fishing holiday. He just goes from one place to another fishing all the time; when he isn't fishing he's shooting. He told me himself that his business gets along quite well without him.'

'Perhaps it does.'

'Listen Bel,' said Louise earnestly. 'I couldn't possibly marry a man I didn't respect — a man I couldn't be proud of! You're proud of Ellis so surely you can understand.'

Bel understood. She loved Ellis dearly; she admired him for his integrity and his tireless industry; of course she was proud of him.

'People ought to work,' continued Louise. 'Not when they get old, of course, but when they're young and strong. There isn't room for idlers and playboys in this modern world. People ought to find a job that suits them and stick into it and do it as well as they possibly can. You agree, don't you, Bel? Tell me honestly.'

'Yes, of course I agree.'

'I don't like slackers; I despise them,' said Louise. She added in a voice that was little more than a whisper, 'I despise Alec.'

After that there was silence for a long time.

2

Louise went up to bed early, for she had had a tiring day getting everything arranged at Coombe House before her departure. Bel sat by the fire for a little while longer thinking of all that had been said. It was a pity about Alec Drummond — he was such a dear — but it was no good at all if Louise felt like that about him . . . and of course Bel agreed with her friend. It was not enough to have a husband you could love, you must be able to admire him as well.

Presently Bel got up and tidied the drawing-room — she hated to leave it in an untidy condition for the night — she put on the guard and made sure that all the doors and windows were securely fastened. This was Ellis's task, of course; he had made her promise to see to it herself in his absence and not to leave it to Mrs. Warmer.

As she went up to bed Bel paused on the half-way landing and listened to the silence. She

173

loved the silence of Fletchers End. Then, after a few moments, she heard the old house whispering to itself . . . a curious sighing sound, a gentle creak . . . all the little secret sounds that an old house makes at night! You could imagine that you heard the rustle of a silken gown — but you knew it was really the soft night air in the leaves of the aspen tree outside the staircase window.

Bel heard another sound as she went on up the stairs; no ghostly sound this, but the splashing of water in the peach bathroom. She smiled to herself and knocked on the door. 'Are you enjoying your bath?' she called.

'Blissful!' was the reply.

'Don't hurry,' said Bel.

The injunction, kindly meant, was quite unnecessary. Louise never hurried over her bath. She was one of those people who delight in soaking for long periods in hot water. She was fond of saying that a hot bath was one of the pleasures of the civilised world — a simple pleasure perhaps, but none the less enjoyable. She was fond of saying that if you were worried or anxious you could soak it all away in hot water. Louise was enjoying her bath more than usual to-night — not only because it was such a pretty bathroom and Bel's violet-scented bath salts had such a delicious fragrance — but chiefly because there was no danger of interruption. At home there was always this danger. There was always the uncomfortable feeling that just at the moment when you had lowered yourself slowly into the lovely hot water the telephone-bell might ring. This did not happen very often of course, but it had happened more than once and Louise had been obliged to leap up and answer the summons, dripping wet and wrapped in a towel.

Here, at Fletchers End, there was absolute peace.

'Hurry? Not blooming likely!' said Louise to herself. She turned on the hot tap and let the water trickle slowly into the bath to warm it up.

3

The week-end passed very pleasantly. The two girls talked to their hearts' content. Every night Louise had a long luxurious bath and emerged pink and relaxed; every morning Mrs. Warmer brought her breakfast in bed. Several times the telephone-bell rang and Louise leapt to her feet and then sat down and laughed.

One of the telephone calls was from Ellis who was anxious to know if all was well and if Bel was remembering to lock up securely before going to bed. He said the weather was very pleasant and he would give Bel all the news when he got home on Monday night.

The weather was very pleasant at Fletchers End also. On Sunday the two girls went to St. Julian's in the morning and for a run in Louise's little car in the afternoon. On Monday Louise went home to Coombe House.

It was sad to part from Louise — Bel had enjoyed every moment of her visit — but it was joyful to welcome Ellis home. He arrived at his usual hour on Monday evening and having greeted one another rapturously, as if they had been parted for weeks, they settled down to talk. In answer to Bel's inquiries Ellis said his mother was well and happy in her new home. She had been to several concerts and had joined a bridge club and was seeing her sister nearly every day.

'It's a success?' asked Bel anxiously.

'Yes, it's a great success. The bungalow is very nice indeed.'

'When is she coming to stay at Fletchers End?'

'I asked her that,' said Ellis smiling. 'But she can't fix a date. She's helping to run a bazaar and she's frightfully busy. The telephone-bell rings all day and she's dashing about the place like a two-year-old.'

'I hope she isn't doing far too much!'

'The bazaar is a God-send,' declared Ellis. 'She's getting to know lots of people; she's getting thoroughly dug-in.' He laughed and added, 'Mother is never happy unless she is doing far too much.'

'Ellis!'

'It's true,' said Ellis seriously. 'That's why it would have been a great mistake for her to come to Shepherdsford. She would have been bored stiff in a little place like that. I know you thought it was rather unkind of me to veto the idea of Mother coming to live near us, but I happen to know her rather well, and — '

'I didn't think it unkind. It was only — '

'Yes, you did — and I know the reason why. You thought it would be nice for Mother,

176

because if you had been Mother you would have liked it. But you aren't Mother; you're quite a different sort of person. You see, Bel,' said Ellis very seriously indeed, 'if you undertake to make plans for other people it's absolutely essential to understand what the people are like. That's where Louise goes wrong.'

'Louise is a darling!' exclaimed Bel.

'Yes, of course she's a darling. I'm very fond of Louise — you know that. She's very sweet and very amusing, she's one of the kindest people on earth, but she's just a little too keen on making plans for her friends.'

'Louise makes very good plans.'

'Yes, sometimes they're very good, but not always. It's because she thinks other people are like herself.'

'You mean she doesn't understand other people?'

'She thinks other people are like herself,' repeated Ellis. 'So of course she thinks that what would be delightful for her would be equally delightful for them.'

Bel was silent. It was a new idea to her but she saw that there was a good deal of truth in what Ellis had said.

'There are lots of people like that,' added Ellis.

18

The weeks passed quickly. The Brownlees settled comfortably into their house and loved it more every day. Of course there were still a good many things to be done, Ellis wanted more room for his books and was putting up some shelves in his study; Bel wanted new curtains. The curtains which had come from Rose Hill had been hung up as a temporary measure but they were not really suitable, so Bel had decided to make new curtains herself and had written to London for patterns.

The large parcel containing the patterns arrived at Fletchers End one morning and Bel rang up Louise to ask her to come over and help to choose them; Louise said she would come after tea. Meanwhile Bel and Mrs. Warmer decided that they had better measure all the windows.

It was while they were thus engaged that they saw a man walking about in the garden and gazing up at the house.

'I wonder what he wants,' Bel exclaimed.

'He's got no business to be there,' declared Mrs. Warmer. 'Such cheek! He looks as if the place belongs to him. I'll run downstairs and tell him to go away.'

'I think I'd better go and see what he wants.'

The man was still there when Bel went through the glass door on to the terrace, still standing and gazing about in an interested sort of way. Now that she saw him properly she was pleasantly surprised for he was tall and good-looking with very dark hair and a brown clean-shaven face. When he saw Bel he came up to the terrace to speak to her.

'I hope you don't mind,' he said. 'Of course I've no right to come in and look at the place like this, but I'm interested to see what's being done. This house used to belong to me; I'm Roy Lestrange.'

'Oh, of course!' exclaimed Bel. 'We bought it from you — but I thought you were in Hong Kong.'

'I'm home on leave,' he explained. 'I didn't really mean to bother you but I'm staying for a few days with my cousin at Oxford and I couldn't resist coming over and having a look at the old place, so I managed to borrow a motor bike — and here I am. I used to stay here with my aunt when I was a boy.'

'It must be sad for you.'

'Sad?'

'I mean to have had to sell Fletchers End.'

He smiled in a charming way and said, 'I haven't very happy memories of Fletchers End — if that's what you mean. Aunt Helen was a bit of a tartar. I used to stay here in the holidays when my parents were abroad and I was always getting ticked off for muddy shoes and dirty hands — you know the sort of thing. Of course I can see now that it must have been pretty sickening for Aunt Helen to have a small boy dumped on her for the holidays but I didn't see it that way at the time.'

It was at this moment that Mrs. Warmer appeared in her usual sudden and unexpected fashion, and asked if the gentleman would be staying to tea.

'Oh, yes,' said Bel. 'Yes, of course. You'll stay and have tea won't you, Mr. Lestrange?'

Perhaps she did not say this very warmly for she had had no intention of asking him to tea and most certainly did not want him (Louise was coming to look at the patterns for the curtains and there would be no chance of looking at patterns if this young man were here) but Mrs. Warmer had forced her hand. What could she do but tender the invitation?

'No, really,' said Roy Lestrange. 'It's very kind of you, but I only meant to look in and see the old place — '

'It's all ready in the drawing-room,' said Mrs. Warmer hospitably. 'I've only to boil the kettle and that won't take a minute.'

'Oh, well — thanks awfully,' he said. 'If you're sure it won't be a nuisance. I must say a cup of tea would be very pleasant.'

2

As he followed his hostess into the drawing-room Roy Lestrange drew in his breath with a gasp of surprise. 'I say!' he exclaimed. 'This used to be rather a dark room in Aunt Helen's day!'

'We made a bow-window,' explained Bel. 'And

of course we trimmed the creepers and cut down one or two trees.'

'I hated this room,' he continued. 'I suppose it was because I had to be on my best behaviour — sit quietly and not fidget! I escaped to the kitchen whenever I could; they liked me in the kitchen. I suppose you've altered a lot of things in the house?'

'Yes, we had to,' said Bel. She was finding it difficult to respond for she was never at her best with strangers (she could chat to Louise by the hour, but with strangers she was practically dumb). In addition to this she was not very ready to be friendly with this young man because of the shameful way he had neglected Fletchers End. Other people might have disguised their feelings and produced a flow of conversation but to Bel this was impossible. Fortunately her guest had plenty to say.

'It will take some time to get the garden into order,' he continued as he sat down in the big arm-chair. 'Of course I ought to have had a man in once a week or something, but to tell the truth I never thought of it — and even if I *had* thought of it I couldn't have afforded to shell out money to pay him. It was as much as I could do to pay the old caretaker, Mrs. What's-her-name, to keep the place from going to rack and ruin.'

'You did let the house go to rack and ruin,' said Bel reproachfully.

He nodded. 'Yes, I'm afraid that's true, but what could I do? I'm a naval officer — and keen on my job — I have to go where I'm sent. How could I look after Fletchers End? I can't think

181

why Aunt Helen left it to me.'

'She must have been very fond of you,' suggested Bel.

'No. At least I never thought she was fond of me,' said Roy Lestrange thoughtfully. 'She really was quite nasty to me when I was a boy. Later when I was in the service and had been about the world and become a bit more civilised she changed her tune. I remember I was home on leave one Christmas, staying with some friends in town, and suddenly I thought it would be rather a joke to go and see the old lady. To tell the truth I thought I might be able to touch her for a fiver. So I borrowed a car and set out. I didn't tell her I was coming, I just walked into Fletchers End with a parcel.'

'A Christmas present?' asked Bel, who in spite of her annoyance with Mr. Lestrange was becoming interested in his story.

'Yes,' he said smiling. 'It was an Egyptian scarf which I had picked up when we called at Cairo — it was rather striking — all colours of the rainbow. As a matter of fact I got it for a girl I was keen on, but when I came home I found she'd gone and got engaged to another fellow, so I thought it would do for Aunt Helen — soften her heart if you see what I mean. Well, believe it or not, the poor old thing was tickled to bits with that scarf! She put it on then and there and looked at herself in the big mirror which used to hang at the end of the room. I must say it suited her; she looked magnificent,' he chuckled and added, 'She was a very good-looking old lady, you know: good features and white hair done in

182

curls on the top of her head and a straight back like a Guardee. You can imagine her, can't you?'

Curiously enough Bel found she could imagine the old lady quite clearly.

'In a way it was pathetic,' Roy declared. 'I mean she was so pleased to see me. She said nobody bothered to go and see her and she couldn't get about much. She said it was so kind of me to think of her when I was in Egypt and bring a present for her. I felt rather uncomfortable about that,' said Roy confidentially. 'I mean of course I hadn't thought about her — but I couldn't explain, could I?'

'No, you couldn't,' agreed Bel. 'She would have been terribly hurt and disappointed.'

He chuckled. 'She would probably have taken off the scarf and thrown it at me — she had a temper, you know. Well, I stayed to lunch and she gave me a dashed good meal and an excellent glass of claret. She said nobody appreciated good claret nowadays but her father used to say it was a gentleman's wine. She said I had become very like my father — he had always been her favourite brother. That pleased me because my father was a very fine man indeed. What with one thing and another we got on like a house on fire. Of course I had no idea she had made me her heir — I never thought of it for a moment. I always thought she would leave Fletchers End to Aunt Dora.' He laughed and added, 'Aunt Dora thought so too. Perhaps that was why she didn't get it.'

Bel thought this might quite well have been the reason why Miss Lestrange had left the

183

house to her nephew. An old lady with a temper and 'a straight back like a Guardee' might have preferred to leave her property to someone who did not expect to get it rather than to someone who did.

3

By this time Mrs. Warmer had brought in tea so Bel poured out. She was beginning to feel more comfortable now, for there was nothing alarming about her guest; he was friendly and pleasant and she found his conversation entertaining.

'You could have knocked me down with a feather when I heard from Mr. Tennant that Aunt Helen had left me Fletchers End,' continued Roy as he accepted a cup of tea. 'I was never so surprised in my life. I didn't want it — '

'You didn't want it!'

'What good was it to me? It was just a source of trouble and expense. It was a white elephant.' He hesitated and then added, 'I can see you're fed up with me, but honestly — '

'Oh, no, of course not,' said Bel hastily. 'I've no right to be fed up.'

'But you are.'

This was true. She was annoyed with him — or at least she had been very much annoyed. She was not so annoyed with him now. It was difficult to go on feeling annoyed with Roy Lestrange.

'Oh, well, perhaps I was a little annoyed with you,' admitted Bel. 'You see it's such a darling old house and it was so sad and neglected. If only you could have seen what it looked like — '

'But that's just the point!' he exclaimed. 'I didn't see it — and I didn't think about it often. I was much too busy. The only time I ever thought about it was when I got a bill from old Tennant for Mrs. What's-her-name's wages and what he referred to as 'absolutely essential repairs.' When I thought about Fletchers End I remembered it as a miserable prison where I spent my holidays with Aunt Helen.' He looked round again and added, 'You've made this room perfectly beautiful, Mrs. Brownlee. I can't believe it's the same place.'

Bel was pleased. She loved the whole house but the drawing-room was the pride of her heart for it had required more care and planning than the other rooms. She smiled at him and said she was glad he liked it.

'I want you to understand,' he said leaning forward and speaking very earnestly. 'There was I — hundreds and hundreds of miles away — living an entirely different sort of life. Lieutenant-Commanders in Her Majesty's Navy don't get unlimited pay and I needed every penny to go about and to — to have a reasonably good time and enjoy myself. I mean if you can't have a good time when you're young . . . ' He hesitated and looked at Bel.

Bel nodded. Obviously he was the sort of young man to make hay while the sun shone. She was aware that he had required a good deal more than his pay to enjoy himself in 'forrin parts' but naturally she did not say so.

'It was all so difficult,' he continued. 'I suppose I'm inclined to be a bit extravagant — all the Lestranges are. What happens is you run into debt, without meaning to, and then of course you've got to pay interest on it — and all that. I don't know why I'm telling you this; I expect you're frightfully shocked, aren't you? I mean I can see that it's very difficult for a girl like you who has always had plenty of money to understand.'

'I haven't always had plenty of money,' said Bel quickly. 'Before I was married I had to work hard — but I never got into debt.'

'Oh, well — I did,' he said sadly. 'And I can tell you this: once you get down you can never pull up again however hard you try.'

Bel said nothing. She could find nothing to say. Debt had always been a bugbear to Bel and she had scrimped and saved and cut down every unnecessary expense to avoid it.

19

Roy Lestrange knew a good deal about Fletchers End; he had heard about it from his aunt; and although he had not been interested at the time — but intensely bored with the old lady's reminiscences — he remembered quite a lot about it now and produced some information to amuse his hostess. Bel knew some of it already, but not all, and in any case she was so interested in Fletchers End that she did not mind hearing it again from a different angle. He told her that it was his great-grandfather who had bought the two houses and made them into one, and that the Lestrange family had lived in the place ever since.

'There were two little staircases,' he said. 'One of them used to be here in this room. It led up to my bedroom.'

'Come and see,' said Bel smiling. She rose and opened a door in the corner of the room, and there were the stairs — but instead of leading to the bedroom, which had once belonged to Roy Lestrange, the little twisty staircase had been made into a cupboard and on every step was an array of bottles and decanters of all shapes and sizes.

'By Jove, what a cracking idea!' exclaimed Roy Lestrange. 'I call that positively brilliant.'

'It belongs to Ellis. He thought of it and made it himself,' said Ellis's wife proudly.

They sat down again and continued their meal.

'Tell me more about Fletchers End,' said Bel as she refilled her guest's tea-cup. 'You must know a great deal about it.'

'I've told you all I remember,' he replied. 'But of course Aunt Helen knew lots more about its history. She had some old letters and diaries and things like that which she kept in the drawer of her bureau.'

'All about the house?' asked Bel eagerly. 'Oh, I should love to see them.'

He looked at her doubtfully. 'Yes, but I wonder where they are. Probably still in that drawer — and all the furniture is in store, so it's a bit hopeless.' He hesitated and then continued, 'I suppose I ought to go and have a look at the furniture while I'm here; there might be one or two decent pieces that I could sell. As a matter of fact I could use a little extra cash — things are terribly expensive nowadays, aren't they? Yes, perhaps I'd better go to the store and see what's there.'

'Don't you know what's there?'

'Oh, it's all there except for some silver and jewellery and things, which were special bequests mentioned in Aunt Helen's will. I was away at the time so old Tennant managed it. I told him to clear out the whole place. Afterwards when I began to get bills for the storage I wished I had told him to have a sale, but I never thought of it at the time.' He sighed and added, 'I was an awful fool. I mismanaged the whole affair.'

'But you sold the house eventually,' Bel reminded him.

He did not reply and for a few moments there was rather an awkward silence. Bel had an uncomfortable feeling that her visitor was regretting the sale of Fletchers End — or, more likely, he was thinking that he ought to have got a better price for the place. Seeing it now, when so much had been done to it, you could hardly blame him.

'It was in terribly bad repair,' she told him, 'We had to spend a lot of money on it, you know.'

'Well, I couldn't afford to spend a lot of money,' he said.

'I know,' agreed Bel. 'It was a pity. If the place had been in good repair it would have been sold long ago. Mrs. Warmer said a great many people came and looked at it — and went away.'

There was another short silence.

'Mrs. Warmer,' said Roy Lestrange at last. 'Yes, that was the old woman's name. What's become of her I wonder.'

'She's here. You saw her.'

'Oh, was that the good lady who invited me to tea?'

'I'm glad you stayed,' said Bel quickly.

He laughed rather mischievously.

'I mean — ' began Bel, who realised she had made a gaffe. 'I mean — '

'I know what you mean. You didn't want me a bit, but of course you had to ask me. You couldn't get out of it, could you? It was very wicked of me to stay — but I stayed. That's the whole thing in a nutshell.'

It was, of course. Bel could not help smiling.

She said, 'It would be rude to contradict you, wouldn't it?'

'Very rude and quite useless,' he replied. 'Your face gives you away every time. You should never play poker, Mrs. Brownlee.'

'Poker?' asked Bel in bewilderment. 'I don't know how to play poker.'

'Don't learn,' he said earnestly. 'It would be absolutely fatal for you to attempt it. Promise me faithfully that you'll never never learn to play poker.'

Bel did not know how to continue the conversation so she offered him the last scone — and he took it.

'A handsome wife or ten thousand a year?' asked Bel.

'Oh, both of course,' said Roy laughing. 'But if I've got to choose, it won't be the handsome wife. I could get her quite easily if I had ten thousand a year.'

2

When he had finished the last of Mrs. Warmer's wholemeal scones Roy Lestrange rose to take his departure.

'I must push along,' he declared glancing at the clock. 'It's been delightful meeting you, Mrs. Brownlee. I'm glad I was wicked enough to accept your cook's invitation. Sorry to dash off like this — but I'm staying with my cousin Leslie Harding. He's got a very nice little flat in Oxford; he lives there by himself and burrows about amongst old books and documents and sometimes gives lectures. He's rather an ass but quite harmless. As a matter of fact there's going to be a terrific binge to-night and I promised Leslie I wouldn't be late. The binge has been laid on for my benefit, you see.'

'Oh, you mustn't be late,' agreed Bel.

'No, and that means I shall have to get a move on,' he declared. 'The party is starting with drinks at Leslie's flat, then we all go in a body to some place where they give you Italian food — not an expensive restaurant, you know. After that I don't know what's happening — some sort of junketing, I suppose.'

'I expect you'll enjoy it.'

'Well, perhaps,' said Roy as they went towards the door together. 'Of course all Leslie's friends are frightfully young — even the older ones seem frightfully young and green — but it's quite fun to meet an entirely different crowd of people with different ideas from oneself . . . I say!' he exclaimed in surprise. 'This hall used to be ghastly; dim and dark and cluttered up with ugly furniture. It smelt of mice.'

'Mrs. Warmer got rid of all the mice.'

'Oh, look here! I ought to speak to the good lady. I mean I ought to shake her by the hand — and all that. Do you mind?'

Bel did not mind in the least. She thought it was kind of him to think of it. She was sure Mrs. Warmer would think he was nice. There was no need for her to show him the way to the kitchen so she waited in the hall while he disappeared through the green baize door, which Ellis had insisted was the correct thing to shut off the kitchen premises from the rest of the house.

Presently her guest returned, smiling cheerfully. 'Funny old bean,' he said. 'Very forthcoming. I think she liked me popping in to see her — I'm glad I remembered. Well, I'd better be getting along. I've got to go back to London to-morrow morning, and I'll see if I can find those diaries for you, Mrs. Brownlee.'

'Oh, yes, please do!' exclaimed Bel.

They were on the doorstep when the telephone-bell rang, so they said good-bye hastily and Bel ran to answer it. The telephone was in the hall and the front-door was open; as she took up the receiver, she saw her guest striding rapidly down the path to the gate. I wonder if he will remember, she thought.

It was Ellis on the phone to say that he had been delayed by important business and had lost his train so he would not be home until later. She was not to delay dinner for him; he would just have a snack at the station. Bel suggested that he should stay the night in town — it seemed a pity to come down late when he would have to go back early in the morning — he could stay at his club quite conveniently.

'But I want to come home,' objected Ellis. 'I don't mind the journey a bit. I like getting out of town — even for a few hours. You want me to come home, don't you?'

'Yes, of course. I was just trying to be sensible and unselfish,' declared Bel laughing.

They chatted for a few moments and then rang off.

When Bel went to shut the front-door she was surprised to hear voices and the sound of laughter. It was Louise laughing; there was no mistaking that gay, merry sound. Bel was expecting Louise but why didn't she come in?

Bel went down the path and — lo and behold! — there was Louise chatting to Roy Lestrange — Roy Lestrange, who should have been well on his way to Oxford! Roy Lestrange, who had promised his cousin not to be late for the party!

The two were so engrossed in conversation that they did not see Bel; so, after a moment's hesitation she turned and went back to the house. It was natural, of course, thought Bel. It was the most natural thing in the world for a young man to talk to Louise and to forget all his obligations in the delight of looking at her. His cousin at Oxford, who was expecting him; the terrific binge laid on for his benefit — all forgotten!

Bel went back to the drawing-room and unpacked the parcel of patterns so that they would be ready for Louise to look at when she decided to break off the conversation and come in. To tell the truth Bel was slightly worried. She did not know why she was worried but — somehow — she was. Of course it was silly to feel worried; Louise was friendly with everyone. It meant absolutely nothing. Beside, Bel liked Roy Lestrange. She had not liked him at first, but afterwards she had liked him. You couldn't help liking him; he was charming.

Perhaps that was why she was worried — because he was charming. Could that be the reason? He was charming but not altogether reliable, thought Bel. The more she thought about Roy Lestrange the more worried she became. His explanation for his neglect of Fletchers End had satisfied her completely and she had absolved him from his crimes, but now that she considered the matter seriously without the enchantment of his personality before her eyes, she realised that his behaviour had been irresponsible to say the least of it. Bel valued reliability very highly; she had got herself a thoroughly reliable husband. Would Ellis have enjoyed himself at Hong Kong — or wherever he happened to be — and spent every penny he earned and run himself into debt and neglected his property so shamefully?

No, Ellis would not.

How very odd! said Bel to herself. That young man must have bewitched me.

He had bewitched Mrs. Warmer also. Mrs. Warmer was full of his praises when she came in to clear away the tea-things. 'So handsome,' said Mrs. Warmer. 'Such a nice brown face — that's the sea-breezes — and he was so free and easy, so friendly and kind! I *do* think he's nice, don't you, Mrs. Brownlee?'

'He's certainly very attractive,' said Bel.

Of course Bel expected further eulogies from Louise, but when at last she appeared she seemed perfectly calm.

'Rather an entertaining bloke,' said Louise smiling. 'I met him at the gate and he said he

194

had been having tea with you. I suppose he was telling you all sorts of interesting things about Fletchers End. He used to stay here when he was a child. We had a little chat about one thing and another and then he went off to Oxford on a frightful old motor-bike. You never saw such a contraption — he said he had borrowed it from a friend. He's coming to lunch with us to-morrow — on the same bike.'

'But he's going back to London to-morrow morning!'

'No, darling, you've got it wrong. He's coming to lunch at Coombe House. As a matter of fact he sort of angled for the invitation. I didn't intend to ask him — but it doesn't matter; I think Daddy would like to talk to him. It's a change for Daddy to meet someone like Roy Lestrange who has travelled all over the world. At any rate I couldn't help asking him — it just sort of happened, if you know what I mean. I don't usually hand out invitations to stray young men.'

Bel was silent.

'Oh, are these the patterns?' exclaimed Louise. 'Some of them are good, aren't they? I like that one with the scarlet birds — it's very effective. We had better take them upstairs to your bedroom before we decide, hadn't we?'

After that they were both too engrossed upon the choosing of materials for bedroom curtains to spare a thought for the 'stray young man.'

20

Several days after the visit of Roy Lestrange, Louise rang up and asked Bel to go to Oxford with her.

'It's a party,' explained Louise. 'Roy is staying with his cousin, Leslie Harding, and they've asked us to go over to tea. It will be rather fun, won't it?'

'I thought Roy Lestrange was in London.'

'No, he's in Oxford staying with this cousin.'

'Why hasn't he gone to London?' asked Bel.

'I don't know, darling,' replied Louise. 'Perhaps he likes Oxford better or something. You can ask him about it this afternoon.'

'I didn't say I would go.'

'But you will, won't you? I'll fetch you about three. You must put on your best bib and tucker.'

'Yes, all right,' said Bel. She said it somewhat reluctantly for she was not fond of parties, but she decided that it would be better not to let Louise go alone. It was rather ridiculous to think of herself playing chaperone to Louise but that was what it came to.

As she dressed for the party — in her best bib and tucker as Louise had decreed — Bel wished with all her heart that Roy Lestrange had left Fletchers End a few minutes sooner or Louise had arrived a few minutes later so that they would not have met at the gate . . . but it was no use thinking about it now; the harm was done.

They had met at the gate and talked, and Roy Lestrange had wangled an invitation to lunch at Coombe House; worst of all, instead of going to London as he had intended, he was still hanging about in Oxford and Louise was seeing him again this afternoon.

Louise was always punctual, so at three o'clock precisely there was a loud hoot from the gate. Fortunately Bel possessed the same virtue so she was ready. She snatched up her bag, gave a last glance at herself in the large oval mirror which hung in the hall, and ran down the path.

'I say, you are smart!' exclaimed Louise admiringly.

'Do you like it?' asked Bel. 'It's new. I got it at Harrods — and the hat, too. I saved up quite a lot of money during the winter when I was working in the office so I decided to get some really nice clothes.' She climbed into the car and added, 'You're looking very smart yourself, but of course you always do.'

'The very best butter,' said Louise as she let in the clutch.

'Is it a big party?' Bel inquired somewhat anxiously.

'I don't think so. In fact I think it's just us.'

For a few minutes Bel was silent and then she said, 'You had him to lunch, didn't you? How did it go off?'

'Oh, it was a great success. Daddy liked him. Roy was very amusing about some of his experiences. He was in Egypt and then he went out to Australia — he's been to all sorts of places. You know, Bel, it's awfully interesting to

197

meet people like Roy who have travelled all over the world and seen so much — and done so many different things. People here are so frightfully narrow-minded and stodgy.'

Bel did not comment upon this somewhat sweeping statement. Certainly Roy Lestrange was not stodgy — whatever else he was.

The drive to Oxford was very pleasant indeed, the country was looking its best with new green leaves on the trees and lilac and laburnum in the cottage gardens. Here and there a slow-moving stream wound its way through meadows full of contentedly grazing cows. Louise was a good driver — perhaps just a trifle dashing, but as Bel had confidence in her judgment she was able to enjoy herself without any qualms.

It had been arranged that they were to meet at The Mitre, and Roy was there waiting for them. When he saw them he put his hand over his eyes and pretended to stagger.

'Two visions!' exclaimed Roy. 'Two bee-ootiful visions! It's quite — blinding. Get me some brandy!'

'Behave yourself, Roy,' said Louise giggling. 'Stop being a fool and tell me what I'm to do with the car.'

Roy stopped being a fool and took charge very efficiently. He showed Louise where she could park the car, locked it up for her and led the way to his cousin's flat.

This was Bel's first visit to Oxford; she was enchanted with the lovely buildings and would have liked to know all about them, but her companions were talking and laughing so she could not ask. She made up her mind to come here with Ellis; he had been at Balliol so he knew Oxford well and he would enjoy wandering round and showing her everything.

2

Leslie Harding lived in a side street not far from the river. The building was old, but had been converted into very comfortable flats. The sitting-room was panelled in oak, with rather a low ceiling and had a bay window with small panes of glass which looked out on to the street. There was a wide window-seat with fitted cushions, two large comfortable chairs and half a dozen old oak chairs with arms. All round the room there were bookcases filled with books and in the middle stood an oak gate-legged table spread with a white cloth. On it were plates of sandwiches, buns and cakes — enough to feed a large party — but only four places had been laid so obviously nobody else was expected.

Bel had imagined that Leslie Harding and Roy Lestrange would resemble each other — for of course they were cousins — but it would have been difficult to find two men so utterly and completely different. Roy Lestrange was tall and dark and strong; Leslie Harding was small and slender with a thin delicate face; his fair hair was smooth and silky and his round blue eyes peered at the world somewhat anxiously, through magnified lenses.

When the introductions had been made and a

few polite remarks exchanged Louise looked round and said, 'What a lovely room, Mr. Harding! I suppose this house is very old, isn't it?'

'Old as the hills,' said Roy before his cousin could answer. 'You see, Leslie likes old things — the more worm-eaten the better. He spends his whole life hunting for dirty old books.'

'Won't you sit down, Mrs. Brownlee and Miss Armstrong?' said Mr. Harding politely. 'I'm afraid I must leave you for a few moments to boil the kettle and make tea.'

'No, you won't!' exclaimed Roy laughing. 'I'll make the tea myself, and then it'll be worth drinking. Come on, Louise! You must help me.'

They went off together and Bel was left with her host.

She was shy at first, but soon she discovered that Mr. Harding was far more shy than she was, so she forgot her own shyness and endeavoured to put him at his ease, telling him that this was her first visit to the beautiful old city and saying how much she admired the lovely buildings. Evidently this was the right line to take for Mr. Harding emerged from his shell of reserve and began to talk quite comfortably. He told her that he did research and was interested in history — especially the history of Oxford — and then, quite suddenly he froze up again and said, 'But you wouldn't be interested.'

He was wrong, of course. Bel had always been fond of history and since she had come to live at Fletchers End she was even more interested in the past. She was in the middle of explaining this to Mr. Harding when the others returned with the tea-pot and the hot-water-jug and they all sat down to tea.

During the meal Mr. Harding was silent — he scarcely uttered a word — but Roy was equal to the occasion and entertained the party without the slightest difficulty. Louise also was in good form, her eyes sparkled and she teased Roy in an amusing manner. Bel put in a few words here and there but it was not really necessary for the conversation flowed on without a break.

Roy told some funny anecdotes about his experiences in foreign parts and told them well. Probably the stories were not entirely veracious but that did not matter, they all laughed heartily — except Mr. Harding. It was certainly a very successful and entertaining tea-party.

When they had finished Roy said, 'What about a stroll down to the river, Louise? You'd like that, wouldn't you?'

'Yes, lovely,' agreed Louise, rising.

Roy turned to his cousin and added, 'You and Mrs. Brownlee can amuse each other for a bit, can't you? We shan't be long.'

Bel had risen from her chair under the impression that the whole party was to stroll down to the river. Mr. Harding also had risen.

'It's a pleasant afternoon,' began Mr. Harding. 'Perhaps Mrs. Brownlee would like — '

Roy took no notice. 'Come on, Louise,' he said, opening the door.

The next moment they had gone.

'That's what he's like!' exclaimed Mr. Harding

201

in a queer strained voice. 'He takes what he wants. Other people don't count. Other people can go to the devil for all he cares.' There was a moment's uncomfortable silence.

'I expect you think he's amusing,' continued Mr. Harding. 'Well, of course he's amusing. He's good company — he can talk the hind leg off a donkey. Your cousin likes him, doesn't she?'

'Oh, she isn't my cousin!' exclaimed Bel. 'I wish she were. She's just a very great friend.'

'Why do you wish she were your cousin?' inquired Mr. Harding, peering at Bel through his large owlish spectacles. 'Friends are much better than cousins. You choose your friends. Do you think I would have chosen Roy as a friend?'

Bel was taken aback by this sudden heat in a man who had seemed so cold and lifeless. She said, 'No, perhaps not. You're quite different.'

'Different! I should hope so!' exclaimed Mr. Harding emphatically. He added, 'Perhaps you're wondering why I have him to stay?'

Bel had been wondering just that. She said, 'Why do you?'

'I don't often,' replied Mr. Harding. 'In fact I hadn't seen him for years and I'd forgotten what he was like — more or less — so when he rang up and asked if he could come and stay with me for the week-end I was quite pleased. I thought it would be amusing to have him — just for a weekend — but he's been here for a week and it feels like a month. He's just making use of me because he's short of money, that's all.'

3

They were still standing by the table, but now Mr. Harding remembered his duties as host and invited Bel to come and sit on the window-seat.

'I'm sorry you're having such an uncomfortable time,' said Bel.

'Oh, it wasn't bad at first,' he replied. 'We got on all right and he was very pleasant, but the last few days have been frightful. You heard what he said about tea? Well, he's like that all the time — making me look a fool in front of other people. Yesterday I took him to a bookshop — it's a very nice little place and I often go there to browse about and buy second-hand books. There's a girl there that I know very well; she's a friend of mine. Of course Roy talked in his usual idiotic way, but I took no notice. There was a book that I wanted on a high shelf — I was just going to ask the girl to bring a ladder when suddenly Roy seized me by the waist and lifted me off the floor so that I could get it. He was laughing all the time. He just did it to show how strong he was, that was the reason. The girl laughed — so did the other people in the shop. I suppose it must have looked very funny, but it didn't seem funny to me. It made me look a fool. You see that, don't you?'

Bel nodded. She did not know what to say.

'You see that, don't you?' he repeated. 'It made me look an absolute fool — in front of all the people in the shop.' He paused for a moment and then added thoughtfully, 'Perhaps I ought to have taken it as a joke, but the fact is I'm not that sort of person.'

Bel realised that this was true. She said, 'People are different, aren't they? Perhaps he'll go away soon.'

'Oh, he's going to-morrow.'

'To-morrow?'

'Yes, it all came to a head at breakfast this morning. He was in a bad mood — quite unbearable! First he crabbed the food — said it wasn't fit to eat — and then he started talking about my mother in a silly way.' Mr. Harding drew a long breath. 'Well, I wasn't going to stand *that*. I've stood a lot, but that was beyond everything. I told him what I thought of him. I said he was nothing but a sponge. I said he wasn't fit to clean my mother's shoes — neither he is!' declared Mr. Harding with violence. 'Neither he is!'

Bel gazed at him in alarm. His face, which normally was very pale, had become exceedingly red and there were little beads of perspiration on his forehead.

'So that was that,' he continued. 'We had a blazing row and I told him I was sick of the sight of him. 'All right I'll go,' he said. 'I'd walk out here and now if those girls weren't coming to tea. I'll go to-morrow.' . . . so you see it isn't all joy having cousins.'

Mr. Harding took a large white handkerchief out of his pocket and mopping his face. 'Sorry,' he mumbled. 'Shouldn't have bothered you with all that. It was because you were kind. We'd better talk about something else.'

There is no more stultifying suggestion. Bel

cast about wildly for something else to talk about but could find nothing. Her mind was a blank.

Silence endured for about half a minute. It seemed a great deal longer.

'You've bought Fletchers End, haven't you?' said Mr. Harding at last.

Bel was thankful; she could talk about Fletchers End for hours. 'Oh, yes, it's a beautiful old house,' she began. 'We thought — '

'I know it well,' he told her. 'My mother and I often went and stayed there — it was my mother's old home. She was born and brought up at Fletchers End. I liked staying there when I was a child — when my grandmother was alive — but afterwards I didn't like staying there at all. Aunt Helen hated me.'

'Miss Lestrange hated you!'

He nodded. 'Yes. The only person she loved was my mother and she was very selfish and possessive so she was jealous of me. She wanted Mother to go and live with her and she thought that Mother would have done it if it hadn't been for me . . . but it would have been a frightful mistake. You see Aunt Helen was a domineering character and Mother would just have become a doormat. You see that, don't you, Mrs. Brownlee?' said Mr. Harding earnestly.

'Yes, of course,' said Bel. She was feeling uncomfortable at being made the recipient of these confidences, which seemed rather private to be given away to a perfect stranger, but what could she do but listen?

'Mother decided not to go and live with Aunt Helen, but she often went and stayed with her.

Whenever Aunt Helen was ill she sent for Mother and, no matter how inconvenient it might be, Mother always went and looked after her. Aunt Helen always said that when she died Mother was to have Fletchers End — 'but I don't intend to die just yet,' she used to say. She told Mother the same thing over and over again.'

By this time Bel was feeling very uncomfortable indeed — but it was no use worrying. Obviously Mr. Harding was one of those people who either talk all the time or else are completely dumb. Ordinary conversation was not within his powers. But in spite of his queer behaviour Bel could not help liking the little man and sympathising with all his various troubles and trials.

'And after all that,' said Mr. Harding bitterly, 'after all that she broke her promise. She left it to Roy and he let it go to rack and ruin. Mother was fond of the old place, she would have lived there and taken care of it — and I could have lived there with her. Doesn't it seem unfair?'

Bel did not answer. It certainly did seem unfair — it seemed all wrong — but she could not bring herself to say so. As a matter of fact Mr. Harding's words had given her a sensation of uneasiness . . . supposing things had happened otherwise and Miss Lestrange had left the house to her sister, as she had promised, what then? But of course it was silly to think of what might have happened. The house had been left to Roy Lestrange and he had sold it to Ellis.

'Mother wasn't there when she died,' continued Mr. Harding. 'She died very suddenly. We were in Guernsey at the time, but of course we flew home for the funeral. Then, when the will was read, we discovered that Aunt Helen had broken her promise. It was a frightful shock to us. You can understand that, can't you?'

'Yes,' said Bel. 'Yes, of course.'

'Roy wasn't there — he was on his way to Australia — but several other relations turned up. My cousin Olivia and her husband and their married daughter, and my cousin Mary. They are all much older than I am, of course. Mother and I hadn't seen them for years — they live in Ireland — but there they were at the funeral! They had all been hoping for something, but all they got was a few pieces of jewellery and some old silver. Olivia was quite nasty about it — and so was her husband. It was very unpleasant.'

Bel could well believe it. The whole affair sounded very unpleasant indeed. Miss Lestrange's relations had not bothered much about her while she was alive — she had been a lonely old lady — but the moment she died they had gathered like vultures, 'hoping for something' . . . and they were nasty about it when they discovered that nothing substantial had been left to them! Of course you could see their side of it too, thought Bel. It was natural to hope for something from a rich aunt, but all the same . . .

Bel decided that wills were horrible things. They were rather frightening, really.

Mr. Harding was still talking — he was making up for his silence at tea-time — 'I went to see the old place about a year ago,' he said. 'I haven't got a car, but I enjoy going out for long

207

bicycle rides; it's good exercise and you can see the country better when you're riding along slowly on a bike. I could have wept when I saw the poor old house, looking so sad and neglected and buried in a wilderness of weeds. I meant to go in and have a look round but I couldn't bear it so I just turned and came home.' He sighed heavily and added, 'Well, I'm glad it has been bought by someone who can appreciate it.'

'We love Fletchers End,' said Bel simply.

'Yes, I can see that. I must tell Mother — she'll be pleased. It made her sad to think of it standing empty.'

'Perhaps you would like to come over to lunch some day,' suggested Bel. 'But perhaps you'd rather not,' she added hastily.

'That's very kind of you, Mrs. Brownlee! Yes, I'd like to come. I suppose you've made a good many alterations?'

Bel could not help smiling; 'alterations' was scarcely the word. 'It was in terribly bad repair,' Bel told him. 'We had to take out nearly every window and renew the wood. We made a second bathroom and a bow-window in the drawing-room and we — '

'Oh, you shouldn't have done that! It was a lovely room.'

'Everyone thinks it a great improvement,' declared Bel. 'We got a very good architect to design it, and it looks charming.'

'Oh, well, if you had a good architect — ' said Mr. Harding grudgingly.

There was another silence. As a matter of fact Bel wanted to ask Mr. Harding a question. She had been wanting to ask it ever since the beginning of their talk, but she did not know how to put it. She wanted to say, 'Was your grandmother fond of violets?' but it seemed a queer thing to ask straight out like that.

At last she said, 'I was talking to old Mr. Fuller. He remembers your grandmother.'

'Fuller? Oh, he was the gardener, of course!'

'Yes, he was telling me how to grow violets; he said your grandmother was fond of them.'

Mr. Harding rose to the bait, 'Oh, yes, my grandmother loved violets. Her name was Violet, you see. She nearly always had a little jar of fresh violets standing on her writing-desk. There was a greenhouse at Fletchers End in those days and sometimes even in winter the head-gardener used to bring in a little bunch of violets for her. All the people on the place were very fond of her so they liked doing things to please her. I can remember the scent of Grandmother's violets in the drawing-room — it's funny how clearly you can remember things that made an impression upon you when you were a child.'

'Yes, it is,' agreed Bel.

'She was a dear old lady,' continued Mr. Harding in reminiscent tones. 'I must have been about six or seven years old when she died but I can remember her quite well. When she was young she was very pretty; there was a portrait of her, hanging on the wall above the fireplace in the drawing-room. It was a lovely picture. Mother would have liked to have it, but Roy got everything and I expect he sold it all — he would sell his soul for money,' added Mr. Harding bitterly. 'Mother didn't get a single thing; not even a piece of furniture to remind her of her old home.'

'How dreadful! Did they quarrel — or something?'

'You mean Mother and Aunt Helen? No, indeed!' he exclaimed. 'Mother never quarrelled with anyone in her life. She's almost too good and kind. I mean when people are like that, other people take advantage of them.'

Bel agreed that this was true. She was about to tell Mr. Harding that all the furniture from Fletchers End was in store, somewhere in London, when the door opened and the other two came in.

Louise looked happy and excited. 'We had a lovely walk,' she said. 'I wish you had come, Bel. You would have enjoyed it.'

'We might have come if we had been asked,' said Mr. Harding.

Louise seemed surprised. 'But I thought — ' she began.

'Well, never mind!' exclaimed Roy laughing. 'They didn't come, and it's over now. What about drinks, Leslie?'

'Not for me,' said Louise quickly. 'I never drink when I'm going to drive — besides, we must go home.'

'You needn't go yet,' declared Roy. 'And just one little cocktail wouldn't do you any harm at all.'

'Yes and no,' Louise told him. 'We must go at once and I don't want a cocktail, see? I must be home in time to get Daddy's supper ready. I shall have to drive like Jehu, he was the man who drove furiously, wasn't he? Come on, Bel.'

Bel was quite ready to go; she liked to be at home when Ellis arrived back from town, so she gathered up her gloves and her bag, said good-bye to her host (who had once more become an oyster) and went away quickly after the others.

21

Louise and Roy Lestrange were already in the street when Bel joined them. As usual they were talking gaily and for a few minutes Bel was silent, but presently she plucked up her courage and broke into the conversation.

'Mr. Lestrange,' she said. 'What about the diaries?'

'Diaries?' he asked in surprise.

'The diaries and letters about Fletchers End.'

'Oh, gosh! I'd forgotten. I don't see what I can do about it now. I'm sure they must be in the drawer of Aunt Helen's bureau; but of course it's in the store — as I told you.'

'I know, but you said — '

'You aren't in a hurry for them, are you? If I go to the store I'll have a look for them. There, that's a promise,' said Roy gaily. 'If I go to the store I'll see what I can do.'

Bel knew already what his promises were worth and the hope of ever seeing the letters and diaries vanished from her mind. It was very disappointing but it could not be helped.

'There's another thing I want to ask you,' said Bel. 'I wonder if you still have the picture which used to hang above the chimney-piece in the drawing-room.'

'I expect so,' he replied. 'It's probably in the store with all the other things.'

'It's a portrait of your grandmother,' Bel

explained; she added, 'I was wondering if you would sell it.'

'Sell it?' he asked in surprise. 'Who would buy it?'

'Well — I would,' she told him. 'I mean if you thought you would like to sell it.'

Roy laughed. 'Yes, of course I'll sell my grandmother if I can get good money for her! I was just a bit surprised that anyone should want to buy the lady. What will you give for my grandmother, Mrs. Brownlee?'

Bel had no idea what to offer — and she was not sure if he were serious in saying that he was willing to sell the picture or whether it was a joke.

'Do you really want it?' asked Roy.

'Yes,' said Bel. 'I mean if you don't mind selling it.'

'Why should I mind? It's no use to me. I couldn't hang it up in my cabin, could I? Come on, Mrs. Brownlee. What will you give me?'

'Would ten pounds be enough?' asked Bel doubtfully.

'Couldn't you make it guineas?'

'No, I couldn't. I mean — '

'Going — going — gone!' cried Roy. 'Grandmother knocked down to the highest bidder. Bought by Mrs. Brownlee of Fletchers End for ten pounds.'

'Roy, you're absolutely incorrigible,' declared Louise laughing.

'Anything else you'd like?' asked Roy. 'What about Grandfather? Gentleman in a cravat with side-whiskers. Side-whiskers are very valuable, you know. I tell you what, Mrs. Brownlee, you can have the two for fifteen. There's a bargain for you!'

Bel shook her head. She did not want the gentleman with the side-whiskers; she only wanted the lady who had loved violets. Mr. Harding had told Bel that the picture used to hang on the wall above the fireplace — and that was where she would put it. Perhaps when Mrs. Lestrange was back in her proper place the fragrance of her favourite flowers would return to Fletchers End.

Bel had offered ten pounds — and had refused to make it guineas — because ten pounds was all that remained of her very own money, the money she had earned during the winter. Of course Ellis would have bought the picture for her if she had asked him, but she wanted to buy it herself.

By this time they had reached the place where they had parked the car and the two girls had got in. Roy was standing beside the car with his hand on the door.

'Don't delay us, Roy,' said Louise. 'We must go; I don't want to be late.'

'Just a minute,' he said. 'I want to ask you something Mrs. Brownlee. Would you mind buying it now?'

'You mean — paying you for the picture?' asked Bel in surprise.

He nodded. 'The fact is I'm a bit short of cash at the moment and I don't want to borrow from Leslie. If you pay me for the picture now, I'll write straight off to the fellow at the store and tell him to pack it up and send it. You'll get it in

214

two or three days.' He hesitated and then added, 'It seems a bit odd, but — well — it would save a lot of bother, wouldn't it?'

It certainly seemed a bit odd, but Bel was so delighted at having bought the picture, and at the prospect of getting it in two or three days, that she made no objections except to say that she was doubtful whether she had enough money with her.

'Well, just give me as much as you can,' said Roy. 'You can send me the balance later.'

'I've got some money with me,' said Louise.

The two girls opened their handbags and between them managed to produce nine pounds nineteen shillings and two pence.

'Never mind about the ten pence,' said Roy cheerfully as he collected the money and put it into the inside pocket of his jacket.

This curious transaction having been completed they said good-bye and the girls drove off. Roy stood watching them and waving.

'I hope we shan't get stuck or anything,' said Louise.

'Stuck?'

'Neither of us has got a farthing.'

'Oh, I never thought of that.'

'Not to worry,' Louise told her. 'There's always somebody about.'

Certainly Louise was not worrying. She had discovered that if by any chance she happened to 'get stuck' there were always people ready to help her. People of the male sex, young or old, welcomed the opportunity to rescue a beautiful damsel in distress.

Little more was said by the two friends until they were out of the town, for Louise was obliged to concentrate on driving through the traffic, but once on the main road there was more opportunity to talk.

'I suppose you're annoyed with me,' said Louise.

'Annoyed with you? Why should I be annoyed?'

'For going off with Roy and leaving you. I'm sorry, but I couldn't help it. Roy loves to have his own way. I thought of you several times and wondered what you were doing.'

'Just talking, that's all.'

'Talking? That silly owl never opened his mouth!'

'That's what you think! As a matter of fact he's very interesting.'

'Interesting!' exclaimed Louise incredulously.

'Yes, I rather liked him.' She hesitated and then added, 'I liked him because he's so fond of his mother.'

Louise was silent. Perhaps she did not think this a sufficient reason for liking Mr. Harding.

'He's coming over to lunch one day,' added Bel.

'You asked him to lunch? You must be crazy!' exclaimed Louise. 'I couldn't bear the man and Roy says he's an absolute sap — no sense of humour at all. Roy says he can't think why he was afflicted with a cousin so unlike himself.'

'Mr. Harding feels exactly the same.'

Louise did not comment upon this — perhaps she did not realise the implications — instead she said, 'Roy is terribly attractive isn't he? He's so big and strong. There's so much life about him. He makes me feel on top of the world. He makes my blood run faster. It's a curious sort of feeling — quite thrilling. Of course you wouldn't understand.'

Bel understood very well; she had noticed how Louise's eyes had sparkled — Louise had been on top of the world all the afternoon, but it was no good saying anything so she held her peace.

22

Time passed quickly and happily at Fletchers End; it was real summer now and how delightful it was to be in the country! How different from the summers Bel had spent in town! She felt very sorry for Ellis who was obliged to travel daily to his office and spend so much of his time in the hot over-crowded city. She tried to persuade him to take a short holiday. Ellis replied that he would take a holiday soon; it would be easier now because 'Mr. James' was getting into the way of things and was pulling his weight. Ellis did not mind the daily journey — even in the heat of summer — it was worth while to get out into the country and breathe the fresh air. He had said this before and continued to say it whenever Bel commiserated with him.

There were no near neighbours round about Archerfield, but there were quite a number of people at Shepherdsford and Ernleigh, some of whom had been to Bel's wedding. They were friends of the Armstrongs of course and Louise said they were all anxious to be friendly with the new arrivals. She had mentioned this several times and Bel had replied that she was much too busy getting settled to be bothered with visitors.

One day when Louise came in to have a cup of coffee she reopened the subject.

'You're settled now,' said Louise. 'It will be

nice for you to get to know some people, won't it?'

'I'd rather not,' replied Bel. 'Ellis and I are perfectly happy here together. We don't want to know a lot of people.'

'Don't be silly!' Louise exclaimed. 'You can't live at Fletchers End like a couple of hermits.'

'Why not?'

'It's so dull,' declared Louise. 'Besides, you said you liked my friends. You liked the Musgraves and Margaret Warren and Sylvia Newbigging, didn't you?'

It was true that Bel had liked them but it was also true that she was perfectly happy without them.

Soon after this conversation Margaret Warren rang up and said Louise had told her that Bel was ready for visitors.

'I should like to come and see you,' said Margaret in a friendly voice. 'I would have come before but Louise said you were too busy. Would it be all right if I came this afternoon.'

'Yes, do come,' said Bel. 'Come to tea.'

'I shall have to bring Bernard.'

'Yes, of course you must bring him.'

'All right. If you're sure you can bear it I'll come over this afternoon by The Church Walk and bring him in his pram.'

It was a lovely day, so when she had helped Mrs. Warmer to prepare for her visitors Bel set out to meet them and before she had gone far she saw them coming towards her. They met near the little bridge. It was nearly nine months since Bel had seen Margaret, and so much had happened that it seemed a great deal longer; but Margaret was just the same, kind and friendly and easy to get on with. She greeted Bel as if they had known each other for years.

Margaret was exactly the same but Bernard was quite different. She remembered him as a baby, he had now become a little boy.

'Goodness, how he has grown!' Bel exclaimed.

'Well, I should hope so,' said his mother. 'It's nearly nine months since you saw him. Did you expect to see him looking exactly the same?'

'Yes,' admitted Bel. She laughed and added, 'Silly of me, wasn't it? I don't know much about babies, you see.'

'I wish he would grow faster,' Margaret told her. 'I'm longing for him to grow up. It will be such fun when he's a proper boy.'

'Will it?' said Bel doubtfully. Her experience of boys had not been very happy, they were rough and noisy and tiresome. In her opinion Bernard was delightful as he was, rosy and chubby and beautifully clean in his pale yellow linen suit, smiling happily and talking nonsense. It seemed a pity that such an attractive little creature should grow up and become 'a proper boy.'

They had tea together in the drawing-room. Bernard behaved very nicely indeed; he drank his milk and ate large quantities of bread and butter. He was no bother at all.

'Yes, he's quite good,' said his mother in answer to Bel's extravagant praises . . . but in spite of her off-hand manner it was obvious that Margaret's son was the apple of her eye.

'He's quite useful too,' continued Margaret.

'My daily adores Bernard. That's why she stays with me.'

'Is it difficult to get dailies in Shepherdsford?' Bel inquired.

'It's difficult to keep them,' replied Margaret. 'They get bored and they like changing about from one place to another . . . and of course they know everything.'

'Know everything!' echoed Bel in surprise.

Margaret smiled. 'They know everything about everybody. They know more about you than you know about yourself. They're all friends, you see, and they discuss people's affairs with each other. Talk about grape-vines!' exclaimed Margaret. 'The grape-vine in Shepherdsford is a very flourishing plant indeed, and Louise says it's the same in Ernleigh. I suppose it's much the same in all small places. I don't encourage my daily to talk, because I think gossip is horrible, but sometimes it's difficult to prevent her from telling me things I'd rather not know.'

'Mrs. Warmer talks too,' said Bel smiling. 'She hears everything at the Women's Institute and comes home full of news.'

2

Bel and Margaret found they had a great deal in common; both were young and happily married, both adored their husbands, both were interested in their houses. Bel's house was old and Margaret's house was new, but it was interesting

221

to compare notes. The conversation flowed along very easily. Bel discovered, somewhat to her surprise, that it was just as easy to talk to Margaret as it was to talk to Louise; in fact in some ways it was easier. Bel and Louise had always been friends (and still were, of course) but now that Bel was married — and Louise not — there could not be the same sharing of every thought as there had been before. Between the married and the unmarried, in the case of feminine friendships, there is always a slight barrier. There are things not to be talked about, things that cannot be understood, and the chief of these is the mysterious bond of a happy marriage which binds two people together for the rest of their lives.

Things not to be talked about, thought Bel. Well, of course you didn't talk about them — even to Margaret — but they were there in the background which was their proper place; mysteries shared and understood and taken for granted as a part of ordinary everyday life.

Obviously Margaret had been thinking the same for after a short companionable silence she said, 'We'll be friends, won't we, Bel? Real friends. It's awfully nice to have a friend like you — I mean somebody young and married. Sylvia is my greatest friend — and always will be, of course, just like you and Louise — but she isn't married. Somehow it makes a difference; I don't know why, really.'

'Yes, it makes a difference,' agreed Bel, smiling at her guest affectionately.

The bond was sealed.

They talked of other things after that. Margaret admired the drawing-room. 'It's tremendously improved,' she said. 'I can scarcely believe it's the same room.'

'Have you been here before?' asked Bel in surprise.

'Yes. It was ages ago — I suppose I must have been about twelve years old. I was selling poppies, and Fletchers End was on my list of houses to call at for a donation to the fund. Everyone told me it was no good asking Miss Lestrange — Daddy said she would bite me — but I thought I'd have a try, so I bicycled over one Saturday afternoon with the tray of poppies and my collecting tin.'

'Did she bite you?' asked Bel smiling.

'No, she was frightfully kind. She asked me to come in and gave me ten pounds — wasn't it amazing? When I tried to thank her she shut me up and said she wasn't giving it to me, she was giving it to the soldiers and sailors who were wounded in the war, fighting for their country, so it was silly of me to say thank you.'

'Yes, I see what she meant,' said Bel thoughtfully.

'She asked me to stay to tea,' continued Margaret. 'It was funny of her to ask me but I think the old lady was lonely and wanted someone to talk to. As a matter of fact I would much rather have gone home but I didn't know how to get out of it — you know how it is when you're twelve — and anyhow she had just given me ten pounds. Even though it wasn't for me, I was very pleased to get it because I wanted to

223

give in a nice fat sum of money — more than Sylvia, if possible,' added Margaret chuckling.

'It's like that when you're twelve.'

'Exactly. And when you're twelve you enjoy a good tea, don't you? Well, it wasn't a good tea at all,' said Margaret regretfully. 'Thin little sandwiches with some sort of savoury paste in them and a cake with caraway seeds — quite horrid! All the same I enjoyed myself because it was interesting to listen to her talking. She talked to me as if I were the same age as she was. It made me feel grown-up.'

'Did she talk about the house?' asked Bel eagerly.

'Yes, quite a lot. She was born and brought up at Fletchers End and she was very proud of it. She said her father had left it to her, because she was the eldest of the family, so it was her very own — to do what she liked with. She said she would live here till she died and bequeath it to one of her family. Then she laughed in a mischievous sort of way and said, 'They all want it, but I can leave it to anyone I like and I haven't made up my mind yet. It's fun to keep them guessing, Miss Musgrave.'

'I was thrilled to bits at being called 'Miss Musgrave,'' added Margaret with one of her infectious chuckles.

Bel laughed. 'Go on, Margaret, tell me more.'

'You're like the 'satiable' elephant's child,' Margaret declared. 'Well, then she said did I think she should leave it to her nephew or to her sister, Dora? I thought from the way she spoke that she wanted me to say she should leave it to

224

her sister, so of course I said it but it was quite the wrong thing. All of a sudden she was very angry and exclaimed, 'This house has belonged to the Lestrange family for a hundred years and if I leave it to Dora it won't belong to a Lestrange any more.''

'That was true, wasn't it?' said Bel nodding.

'I tried to pacify her,' continued Margaret. 'She soon calmed down. She said she would think about it — perhaps she wouldn't leave it to either of them — and anyhow there was no hurry because she didn't intend to die just yet. Then she smiled quite nicely and asked if I were frightened of her. 'I suppose you think I'm mad,' she said.'

'But you weren't frightened?'

'No, not a bit. And she certainly wasn't mad — just different from other people.'

'Eccentric?'

'Yes, that's the word. Awfully queer and unpredictable — you never knew what she was going to say next. Presently I said I must go home, so she came out to the gate with me and when she saw my bike she said, 'That's a new bicycle, isn't it? Has it got a free-wheel?' I didn't know what on earth she meant. She explained that when she was a girl she had a bicycle with fixed pedals; there weren't any free-wheels in those days. She said, 'If you wanted to free-wheel downhill you had to put your feet on the handlebars; I suppose you can't believe I ever did anything so wicked.''

'It sounds frightfully dangerous!' exclaimed Bel.

'Yes, but I could believe it quite easily. There was something dangerous about Miss Lestrange; she was rather a wicked old lady.'

'Did you tell her so?'

Margaret smiled. 'I said 'daring.' It seemed more polite. She liked that. She laughed and said she was more daring than her brothers. 'I was the ring-leader,' she said. 'I used to lead them into awful scrapes.''

'How amusing!'

'Yes, but I'll tell you something even more amusing,' said Margaret. 'Just as I was getting on to my bike she said, 'Do you know Isabel?' I knew several girls called Isabel so I said, 'Isabel who?' and she said quite solemnly, 'Is a bell necessary on a bicycle?''

Bel laughed. She thought it very funny.

'Yes,' agreed Margaret. 'I thought it was an awfully good joke. I told her I'd try it on Daddy — he loved jokes. So then she laughed and said, 'Your Daddy will know it.' And he did,' said Margaret, nodding. 'He said it was a hoary old chestnut . . . but I tried it on some of the girls at school and caught them out properly!'

All this time Bernard had behaved beautifully; he had been sitting on the floor playing with some empty cotton reels and a couple of little boxes which was all that Bel could produce in the way of toys, but now he began to get restless.

'It's time for his bath,' said Margaret rising. 'Bath and supper, and bed. He's exactly like a clock,' she added. 'And an alarm clock at that. Come on, my bunny! We'll have to go home.'

Bernard was tucked securely into his pram

and they set off briskly; Bel walked with them as far as the bridge.

3

Margaret Warren was the first of Bel's visitors; after that quite a number of people called at Fletchers End. Sometimes Bel was out when they called and was told about them by Mrs. Warmer when she returned; sometimes she was in and entertained her visitors to tea. Many of Bel's visitors had known Miss Lestrange and were induced to talk about her. (Bel had become very interested in Miss Lestrange.) The queer thing was that everyone had something different to say about her — one might have thought that Miss Lestrange was half-a-dozen different people instead of one lonely old lady 'with a straight back like a Guardee.'

Mrs. Warmer was delighted with all the visitors, she welcomed them cordially and when Bel was not at home she tried to persuade them to stay and offered them tea. She took their visits as a tribute to Fletchers End. For years and years her beloved house had stood empty and neglected; nobody had been near it except the people who thought of buying it and had looked round casually and gone away in disgust. It was a different matter now. Everyone who came admired the house, praising its old-world beauty, marvelling at the huge oak beams. Fletchers End had taken its proper place in the world according to Mrs. Warmer.

There was one visitor who came nearly every day and was always welcome. Bel had told Mr. Fuller to come into the garden whenever he liked and he took full advantage of the invitation. Often when she looked out of the window she saw the small bent figure with the snow-white hair prowling about, walking along the paths, stopping every now and then and looking round with pleasure at the bare beds as if they were full of 'luvverly' flowers — as they had been long ago.

In the far corner of the garden near the little gate which opened on to The Church Walk there was a stone seat; it had been discovered when the jungle was cleared. The stone was stained and discoloured, covered with green slime, but when Mrs. Warmer had 'had a go at it' with a scrubbing-brush it proved itself to be an ornament to the garden. One morning when Bel looked out of the window she saw Mr. Fuller sitting there so she hurried out with a rug for him to sit on, a small attention which pleased him immensely. She told him that if he wanted to sit there he was to call at the house and get the rug — the stone was much too cold and hard. After that he often called for the rug.

Sometimes Bel went out and talked to him — or to be more exact she sat and listened to him talking. She found it pleasant and peaceful to sit there in the sunshine and listen to his funny squeaky voice flowing on and on like the stream. It was his thoughts flowing out, thoughts about the old days, thoughts about Miss Lestrange and the garden.

'There was 'olly 'ocks over there up against

228

that wall,' said Mr. Fuller. 'I can see 'em now, tall and straight, all sorts of different colours. Miss Lestrange used ter say that when 'olly 'ocks grew 'igh it meant that a woman was the boss of the 'ouse . . . and I never seen 'olly 'ocks grow 'igher than they did at Fletchers End. He — he!' chuckled Mr. Fuller. 'That was all right, that was. Miss Lestrange was the boss and she didn't never let you forget it. I can see 'er now coming down that path in a grey dress with a red thing round 'er neck and calling out, 'Fuller, where are you?, Why 'aven't you picked the peas? Why 'aven't you weeded the rockery? Why 'aven't you planted out the vi-olas?' Very impatient she was. Wanted everything done quick. She used ter stand at the kitching door and ring a bell — clang — clang — clang — and I 'ad ter go quick and see what she wanted. She used ter 'ave a letter she wanted posted or she wanted strawbries or a cabbage and she wanted it quick. 'Do it now, Fuller,' she used ter say. Sometimes she wanted me to write my name on a paper. She used ter say, 'Clean your boots on the mat and wash your 'ands. Be quick about it, Fuller.' Then I went into the droring-room and wrote my name on the paper and she give me ten bob. He, he!' chuckled Mr. Fuller. 'I did that two or three times. There was one time Dr. Whittaker was there and 'e wrote 'is name too. There 'ad ter be two people, see? Dr. Whittaker sed ter me, he sed, 'That there siggature of yours is a lot neater than mine, Fuller.' And it was, too. I was always a neat writer — got a prize for writing at school. He, he, he! That weren't yesterday, nor the day before neither . . .

'There was pee-onies over there,' continued Mr. Fuller pointing out the place. 'Miss Lestrange was a great one for pee-onies. I didn't like pee-onies much. They're pretty when they're in bloom — all red and pink and white — but you get a 'eavy shower and see what 'appens! And they ain't got no smell. There's something unnatural about a flower that ain't got no smell . . . '

The squeaky voice flowed on; Bel was only half listening. Presently she would have to go in and get ready for lunch, because Louise was coming over, but there was plenty of time.

'That south wall would be a good place for apricocks,' continued Mr. Fuller. 'Apricocks would grow noice up against that brick wall.'

'Apricocks,' thought Bel. 'Go bind thou up those dangling apricocks, Which, like unruly children, make their sire Stoop with oppression of their prodigal weight . . . '

Yes, of course, thought Bel; it was a Shakespearean word and how natural it was to hear it fall from the lips of old Mr. Fuller, who had lived all his life within measurable distance of Shakespeare's home!

'Oh, yes, we must have apricocks!' exclaimed Bel, envisaging the south wall with the little trees spread out upon it, their branches bowed down with the weight of dangling fruit.

'You get 'em from Mr. Middleton at the nursery garding,' said Mr. Fuller. 'I'll come and see that they puts them in proper. That's what to do.'

23

In Dr. Armstrong's opinion the best time of the day was after supper when he could settle down comfortably with a book of travel or memoirs with his daughter sitting opposite to him reading or sewing some feminine garment or knitting a little jacket for one of the numerous babies in whom she took an interest. Of course they could not depend upon a peaceful evening; quite often they were disturbed by the telephone-bell, but that was one of the annoyances that had to be borne.

Sometimes the two sat together in companionable silence, and at other times they talked of what they had been doing during the day. Louise was very interested in the affairs of her father's patients and although he was discreet — as be-fitted his calling — he told her a good deal. There was no harm in telling Louise — she was perfectly safe — and as a matter of fact she knew so much already in her capacity as secretary that he saw no object in withholding information from her.

On this particular evening he had told Louise about old Mr. Hart, who had fallen off a ladder and fractured a bone in his ankle, but had now recovered and was perfectly fit. He and his cross old wife had returned to Willow Cottage and were pursuing their usual avocations.

'Quarrelling like cat and dog,' said Louise nodding.

Dr. Armstrong chuckled and agreed.

'It's funny,' said Louise thoughtfully. 'I mean she was frightfully upset when he had that accident, so I suppose she must be fond of him.'

'Of course she's fond of him.'

'Well, why is she so beastly to him, then?'

Dr. Armstrong did not feel capable of answering this extremely penetrating question, so he did not try to do so.

There was a short silence.

'Daddy,' said Louise. 'Is it possible to love a person when you despise them?'

For some reason this question gave the doctor a shock, but he answered quite calmly, 'I shouldn't think so, Lou.'

'No,' she agreed in a low voice. 'Not properly — love.'

'Or else not properly despise,' suggested her father. 'Despise is an ugly word, Lou.'

'It's an ugly thing,' said Louise sadly. She was about to say more when the telephone-bell rang and as usual she jumped up and ran to answer it.

'If it's the pneumonia case at the hospital tell them I'll come at once!' exclaimed the doctor.

Louise had left the door open so he could hear what she was saying — and he listened with a good deal of anxiety. If it were not the pneumonia case it might be Mrs. Ringbolt's baby . . . but no, obviously it was not.

'Oh, Roy, it's you, is it?' Louise was saying. 'No, of course not. We thought it was one of Daddy's patients with a pain in his tummy or something . . . '

The conversation continued. Dr. Armstrong

232

could hear only one side of it but he had no difficulty whatever in following its trend. Indeed he could have filled in the pauses — almost word for word.

'In London?' Louise was saying. 'Oh, I see . . . Yes, I thought you were getting a bit bored with your cousin . . . No, I can't say I found him wildly amusing . . . Yes, of course — ages ago. Bel always pays her debts; she's that sort of person. I hope you've sent the picture . . . What? That's too bad of you, Roy. You promised you would send it at once . . . Yes, you'd better.'

There was a long pause.

'Oh, yes,' said Louise in a pleased sort of voice. 'Yes, I'd like to, Roy. It would be fun . . . No, I couldn't possibly stay the night in town. It will have to be a matinée . . . Well, I can't help that. I've got nowhere to stay . . . Roy, you really are the limit! I don't know why I like you . . . Well, naturally. You don't suppose I'd go up to town and go to a Show with you if I disliked you! . . . No, only a little . . . What did you say? . . . Yes, of course I'm laughing . . . Yes, all right I'll come up on Saturday . . . No, don't do that . . . No, I'd rather you didn't meet me at Paddington. I'll come up by the early train and do some shopping . . . But I don't like people trailing about after me when I'm shopping, see? . . . Don't be silly, Roy . . . All right, twelve-thirty at Fortnum's . . . Yes, it will be fun. Bye for now.'

Dr. Armstrong was disturbed. It was Roy Lestrange of course. Could it be he who was loved and despised? Doctor Armstrong sincerely hoped not. It had been amusing having the

233

young fellow to lunch; he talked well and was extremely entertaining, but it was one thing to enjoy the conversation of a luncheon guest and quite another when suddenly you were forced to consider him as a possible future son-in-law. Loved and despised, thought Dr. Armstrong frowning. Yes, that fitted in with the facts. It was natural that Lou should despise a man who had inherited a valuable property and had allowed it to deteriorate until it was little better than a ruin — as Lestrange had done. Perhaps it was natural also that Lou should be very much attracted by the young fellow's personality, his charm and vivacity, his undeniable good looks.

His undeniable good looks, thought Dr. Armstrong. Certainly nobody could deny that he was a good-looking young fellow, but he was very irresponsible to say the least of it. Dr. Armstrong had been told about the purchase of the picture — told about it as a joke — but for various reasons he had not been amused. He knew the picture well; he had seen it hanging above the chimney-piece when he visited Miss Lestrange, and had always admired it, so he was horrified to hear of the light-hearted manner in which it had been sold. He was horrified also that the young man had taken all the money that the girls possessed and allowed them to drive home penniless. Very irresponsible to say the least of it, thought Dr. Armstrong.

Louise returned to the study full of her news. 'It was Roy Lestrange,' she said. 'He wants me to go up to town on Saturday and have lunch with him and go to a Show. You don't mind, do you,

Daddy? I'll get Mrs. Morgan to come for the day . . .'

Dr. Armstrong had known it all before but he listened and nodded and said he did not mind. Lou could come home by the last train and he would meet her at the station.

At first when Louise returned from school — grown-up and beautiful — Dr. Armstrong had seen in every young man who lost his heart to Louise a potential son-in-law, but there had been so many (and Lou had lost her heart to none of them) that he had become hardened to it.

Some of them were extremely good fellows. There was that nice chap they had met at Drumburly — Alec Drummond. Dr. Armstrong had liked him immensely but Lou had turned him down; there was Reggie Stephenson, who, although not particularly attractive to look at, was good and kind and thoroughly sound. There were at least half-a-dozen others — it was difficult to keep track of them all — but apparently the right one had not appeared. Occasionally Dr. Armstrong wondered what on earth he would do without Lou when the right one appeared — but of course he would accept it cheerfully; he loved his daughter far too dearly to be selfish.

Dr. Armstrong wanted the best in life for Lou and, in his opinion, the best thing in life was a happy marriage. Of course the man who was going to marry Lou must be a very special sort of man, with all the attributes of a good husband: someone kind and considerate and absolutely reliable; someone who could be trusted to love and cherish his darling child; someone with a sense of humour to match her own. If he were strong and healthy and good to look at — all the better.

Dr. Armstrong hoped that this very special sort of man would not turn up too soon, for it would be nice to keep Lou just a little bit longer — and, as a matter of fact, he did not approve of people marrying when they were very young. In his experience, which was wide, marriages were better and happier when the two people concerned had reached an age of discretion. On the other hand it was a pity to leave it too late.

Dr. Armstrong thought of the Warrens. Theirs was an ideal marriage. Bernard was thoroughly sound. He was quiet and reserved with people he did not know well, but there was an engaging twinkle in his eye. Margaret was a perfect dear. She had been a little unhappy for a time because they had been married for several years before a child arrived, but now that she had managed to produce a fine lusty son she had nothing left to wish for.

Although the Musgraves lived in Shepherds-ford they were Dr. Armstrong's patients; he had attended Mr. Musgrave during his last illness, so he got to know Mrs. Musgrave very well and to admire her profoundly. Of course she worried too much about her family, but that was natural because it had not been an easy family to manage. Now they had all settled down so there was no need for Esther Musgrave to worry any more.

It struck Dr. Armstrong that he had not seen the Musgraves for some time — in fact not since Bel's wedding. This was good in some ways, for it meant they were perfectly healthy, but it would be pleasant to meet Esther Musgrave — to meet her socially not professionally of course. He decided to ask Lou about it. Perhaps Esther Musgrave and Rose could come to supper some evening.

24

The packing-case containing the picture of Mrs. Lestrange arrived at Fletchers End late one afternoon. The men carried it into the hall and stood it in the corner. Bel was delighted to see it for she had begun to wonder if Roy Lestrange had forgotten about it — as he had forgotten about the diaries. She would have liked to unpack it immediately, but the carpenter had come from Archerfield and was busy making the cold frame for the violets which Mr. Fuller had advised. The frame was to be put in the sunny corner near the 'skeptic tank' and it was essential that Bel should be on the spot to see that it was properly constructed.

Things always seemed to happen like that, thought Bel regretfully. Some days nothing happened and other days too many things happened all at once . . . but her duty was obvious. The picture was here, so there was no hurry about it; the cold frame must come first. Bel went out to the garden.

When Ellis returned from town the first thing he saw was the packing-case, which presumably contained Bel's picture; he decided to open it at once so he fetched the necessary tools and set to work. If Mrs. Warmer had known of his intention she would not have allowed him to open it in the hall, but Mrs. Warmer was in the kitchen cooking the dinner with the radio going full blast.

Ellis enjoyed himself immensely opening the packing-case. He piled the dirty straw in a heap on the floor and hummed as he worked for he was happy. It had amused him immeasurably when Bel told him about her purchase; it was so like Bel, sentimental darling, to want the picture of Mrs. Lestrange and it was so like the dear little innocent to think you could buy an oil painting for ten pounds. Of course it would be a ghastly daub — bound to be — but, whatever it was like, he would hang it for her exactly where she wanted it to be hung, thought Ellis smiling indulgently.

The picture was in a large oval gilt frame and when he had removed all the paper wrapping he propped it on the oak chest which stood in the hall and took a good look at it . . .

The indulgent smile faded. 'Whew!' exclaimed Ellis in a long-drawn whistle of astonishment.

It was no wonder that Ellis was astonished. The picture which had been bought by his wife for ten pounds — or to be strictly accurate nine pounds, nineteen shillings and two pence — was a perfectly beautiful portrait of a perfectly beautiful woman. The woman was young, with smooth shining hair and little ringlets on each side of her face . . . and what a lovely face it was! What a gentle, innocent expression! She was wearing a rose-coloured dress with a fichu of fine lace, fastened with a diamond brooch, and there was a little posy of violets tucked into her low-swept corsage.

Ellis did not know much about pictures but he was quite certain that this was a very good picture indeed. There was a velvety richness about it, a sort of glow. The picture gave him a feeling of satisfaction.

When he had finished admiring it from a distance Ellis went and looked at the picture closely. He looked to see if there was a name in the corner of it — he would not have been a bit surprised if he had found a famous name — but the painter had not signed it. Ellis tried to remember what famous painters had been alive when Mrs. Lestrange was young but he knew too little about the period. Of course an expert would be able to tell who had painted the picture. Ellis was no expert but he knew that a picture need not be signed with the painter's name — a famous painter signed his pictures with every stroke of his brush.

Someone must come and look at it, thought Ellis . . . or perhaps it might be better to take the picture to London and get it thoroughly examined by that queer old chap at the Welcome Galleries. He would know . . . but first he must show it to Bel.

Ellis picked up the picture and carried it into the drawing-room and stood it on the sofa. He had expected Bel to be there, but she was out in the garden — he could hear her voice — so he went on to the terrace and called to her to come in.

'Allow me to introduce Mrs. Brownlee, Mrs. Lestrange!' said Ellis with a little bow.

'Oh, isn't she lovely!' exclaimed Bel rapturously. 'Oh, Ellis, isn't she a darling!'

'She's very beautiful indeed. If you bought her

for ten pounds you got a bargain.'

'Yes, I told you — ten pounds. At least it was really — '

'I know,' said Ellis laughing. 'It was really nine pounds nineteen shillings and twopence. Well, she's worth a good deal more than that — or I'm a Dutchman. I've been wondering who painted the lady.'

'It doesn't matter.'

'What do you mean?'

'It's the lady that matters — the violet lady — not the painter. Look, Ellis, she's got a little posy of violets! That makes it simply perfect.'

'We must get an expert opinion about the picture.'

'No, Ellis. I don't want an expert opinion. She's beautiful — and she's mine. She's my very own.'

'I know, darling,' agreed Ellis. 'Of course she belongs to you, but you'd like to know who painted her. The picture may be very valuable for all we know.'

Bel went nearer and looked at the violet lady lovingly. 'She's glad to be back in her own room — I know she is. You'll hang her over the chimney-piece in her proper place, won't you, Ellis?'

'Yes, of course, but — '

'No buts,' said Bel looking up at him and smiling. 'Let's hang her up in her proper place and enjoy her. I don't want to know who painted her and I don't care a bit whether she's valuable or not, I just love her for herself. Quite honestly I'd rather she wasn't valuable.'

241

'Why?' asked Ellis in bewilderment.

'I'm not quite sure. Perhaps it's because if she were very valuable I wouldn't feel she belonged to me in the same way.'

Ellis could not understand that. He said, 'Perhaps it's because you bought her for ten pounds. Your conscience is pricking you, Bel.'

'It isn't a bit,' declared Bel emphatically. 'Roy was only too delighted to sell his grandmother — he thought it was a good joke. He was horrid about it, Ellis. It wasn't funny at all.'

It did not seem funny to Ellis either, so he said no more about having an expert opinion but went away and fetched the steps and hung Mrs. Lestrange above the chimney-piece in her accustomed place. She certainly looked delightful there and her presence gave a graceful finish to the room.

It was only afterwards when Ellis went upstairs to change out of his town clothes and get ready for dinner that he began to feel uncomfortable about it. Of course he saw Bel's point of view; Roy Lestrange had been 'only too delighted to sell his grandmother,' he had been 'horrid about it' so Bel felt perfectly justified in having acquired the picture for that ridiculous sum. Bel's conscience was more troublesome. He was almost certain that the picture was valuable — almost certain but not quite — he did not know enough about pictures to be quite certain; but he was aware that if an expert pronounced the picture to be valuable he would feel very uncomfortable indeed. In fact he would feel bound to offer Roy Lestrange the correct price.

He would not grudge it, for he admired the picture immensely and was perfectly willing to pay the correct price for it — but Bel might not like the idea.

How complicated it was! thought Ellis. What was the best thing to do? Should he see that fellow Roy Lestrange and talk to him about it or would it be better to get an expert opinion first? But of course he could do nothing unless Bel agreed — after all it was her picture.

Ellis sighed heavily and decided to have a serious talk with his wife and try to win her round to his point of view.

When Ellis went downstairs he found Bel standing in the drawing-room gazing at the picture entranced. She turned when she heard him come in and slipped her hand through his arm.

'Oh, Ellis, I'm so happy!' she exclaimed. 'I'm happy because she's here in her proper place, and I'm happy because she's my very own — bought with my very own money. You see I've never owned anything so beautiful before. You understand don't you?'

'Yes, darling. I understand,' said Ellis; and with that he kicked Roy Lestrange downstairs — metaphorically speaking of course — and the matter was settled.

2

The matter was settled. No expert would be invited to look at the picture; it belonged to Bel

243

and the transaction between her and Roy Lestrange by which it had been acquired was their affair entirely and had nothing whatever to do with Ellis — so Ellis decided. But the incident had given Ellis an idea and, while they were having dinner, he proceeded to disclose it to his wife.

Ellis had been told about the diaries and letters which were in the drawer of Miss Lestrange's bureau and he was almost as keen as Bel to have a look at them. He had never met Roy Lestrange but from what he had heard about the fellow he thought it unlikely that the fellow would take the trouble to go to the store and look for them.

Bel agreed with this. 'He has probably forgotten about them again,' said Bel nodding.

'Shall we offer to buy the bureau?' suggested Ellis. 'I mean if the fellow wants money he would probably sell it to us, wouldn't he? That would be the best way to get hold of those diaries.'

'Ellis, what a good idea!'

'It seems queer,' continued Ellis thoughtfully. 'Why should he want money so badly when he has just got the price for the house?'

'I think he used it to pay his debts.'

'All that!' exclaimed Ellis in shocked tones. 'Surely he couldn't have been so badly in debt!'

Bel did not know. All she knew was that Roy Lestrange was pushed for money. He had said things were very expensive nowadays.

'Well, that's settled,' said Ellis. 'I'll write and ask what he wants for the bureau.'

'The bureau and its contents,' said Bel nodding.

Ellis smiled. It always amused him when his wife disclosed a grasp of business matters. He said, 'Yes, I'll mention the contents. If the bureau belonged to old Miss Lestrange it's sure to be a good piece of furniture and it would be nice to have it.'

'It's a marvellous idea,' said Bel, smiling affectionately at her clever husband.

'Do you know his address?'

'No, but I expect Louise knows it. I'll ask her.'

Ellis was silent for a moment or two and then he said, 'I hope Louise isn't seeing too much of that fellow.'

'I'm afraid she is — seeing him — quite a lot,' said Bel. 'She went up to town on Saturday and met him for lunch, and he's coming to Coombe House on Friday to spend the day.'

'You ought to warn her.'

Bel had been thinking about this herself, wondering whether she could say anything to Louise about her new friend, but it was not an easy thing to do.

'You ought to warn her about him,' repeated Ellis.

'I will, if I get an opportunity,' said Bel doubtfully. 'It's not the sort of thing you can blurt out all in a minute . . . and the worst of it is he's really very attractive. You haven't seen him, have you?'

'No, and I don't want to,' replied Ellis emphatically.

Bel said nothing to this — there was nothing

to say — but she hoped most sincerely that Ellis and Roy would never meet.

They had finished dinner by this time so they went into the drawing-room and out on to the terrace by the glass door. Bel had bought a teak-wood seat for the terrace and they often sat here on fine evenings.

'We've made good use of Reggie's glass door,' said Ellis as they went out together. He laughed and added, 'I remember him saying how lovely it would be to stroll out into the garden. He was absolutely right. There are no flies on Reggie.'

'He's going into the Church,' said Bel.

She had been trying to tell Ellis this news for some time — indeed she had been trying to make up her mind to broach the subject ever since Reggie's visit — but somehow it had been difficult to find the right moment, and she had been afraid of what Ellis would say. She was still afraid of what Ellis would say and she waited rather nervously for his reaction to her news.

For a few moments Ellis said nothing. His arms were full of cushions and he arranged them on the seat before he spoke.

'Going into the Church? You mean he's giving up his partnership in that firm?'

'Yes, he's going to Oxford to take his degree.'

'I thought he was tremendously keen on architecture.'

'He's too keen on architecture,' said Bel thoughtfully. 'I think that's one of the reasons. He doesn't like building shoddy houses. Reggie wants perfection.'

'Perfection!' exclaimed Ellis. 'None of us can have that.'

'I know, but we can do our best, can't we? Reggie isn't free to do his best.'

'I suppose he told you all this when he was here. Why didn't the silly little blighter talk to me about it? That's what I should like to know.'

Bel was silent for a few moments. She realised that Ellis was hurt . . . and she had not expected this reaction. It was foolish of her of course, because the two were close friends so it would have been natural for Reggie to talk to Ellis about his plans.

'I'm not sure,' said Bel slowly, trying to feel her way. 'I think it was because Reggie admires you so much and has such confidence in your judgment.'

'That's a funny reason!'

'It isn't really,' she told him. 'Reggie was afraid you would think it very unwise to throw up his career. He was afraid you might be able to persuade him not to do it.'

'I wouldn't have tried to persuade him.'

'You think it's the right thing?' asked Bel eagerly.

'The right thing?' asked Ellis, turning his head and smiling at her. 'It depends what you mean when you say 'the right thing.' It certainly wouldn't be the right thing for me, but if Reggie is quite certain that that's what he wants to do — '

'Yes, absolutely certain.'

'Then, obviously, it's the right thing for him.'

'Yes,' said Bel with a sigh of relief.

There was a short silence. Bel was thinking

247

how very foolish she had been; first, in not realising that Ellis would feel hurt at being shut out from Reggie's confidence and, second, in being afraid that Ellis would try to arrange Reggie's life for him. She ought to have known Ellis better than that. It had been a difficult corner — all the more alarming because she and Ellis had never before had any difficult corners to negotiate . . . but it had been negotiated safely and no harm done.

'Of course there's more to it, isn't there?' said Ellis at last. 'It isn't just that Reggie is fed up with shoddy houses.'

'There's a lot more,' Bel said. 'I'll tell you all about it and you'll see that it really is the right thing.'

'I must write to him,' said Ellis thoughtfully. 'It will be a difficult letter to write but you can help me with it, can't you?' He added, 'It will be nice when he's at Oxford.'

'Yes, he'll be able to come over quite often,' Bel agreed.

3

A few days after the arrival of the picture Bel decided to spend an afternoon in the garden. She had got some plants from Mr. Middleton's nursery and wanted to put them in. Planting was a job she enjoyed and so far she had not been able to do very much herself, but now some of the beds were ready and the little plants had come.

She was in the middle of her task when Mrs. Warmer came dashing out of the kitchen-door in a tremendous state of excitement.

'Quick!' cried Mrs. Warmer breathlessly. 'It's Lady Steyne — her car has just stopped at the gate! She's come to see Fletchers End.'

'Lady Steyne? It can't be!' said Bel, looking up in surprise. (Louise had told her that Lady Steyne never called on anyone, she was too old and delicate). 'It can't be Lady Steyne,' repeated Bel.

'It is! It is!' cried Mrs. Warmer. 'And look at you — all dirty and mucky in your old tweed skirt! You better run up the back stairs and put on your nice new blue dress and your nylons — what a good thing I made that choclit cake this morning! Quick — there's the front-door bell!'

It was amazing how Mrs. Warmer always seemed to know when a car stopped at the gate. It was not that she wasted time gazing out of the windows, for she got through more work than two ordinary women. As Bel rose from her knees she wondered whether Mrs. Warmer possessed a sixth sense which warned her of the approach of visitors to Fletchers End.

Mrs. Warmer's idea of running up the back stairs and putting on her new dress to receive her visitor made Bel smile. It would be most discourteous to keep Lady Steyne waiting while she changed. Lady Steyne would not mind in the least what she was wearing; she had come to see Bel not her new blue dress (according to Mrs. Warmer she had come to see Fletchers End). Bel was still smiling as she rinsed her hands at the garden-tap and went in to greet her visitor.

Lady Steyne was a delightful old lady, fragile and dainty as a Dresden China figurine and very kind and friendly. She explained that she was too old to go about much nowadays but she had been so anxious to meet Mrs. Brownlee that she had broken her rule.

'Penney has gone up to town for the day,' said her ladyship, smiling mischievously. 'So I'm as free as air — and it was such a lovely afternoon that I decided to come and see you.'

'I'm so glad,' declared Bel.

'I hope I haven't interrupted you in the middle of doing something very important.'

'Gardening, that's all,' said Bel smiling. 'That's why I'm in rather a mess.' She hesitated and then added, 'My housekeeper wanted me to change into my new blue dress for you.'

'How delightful!' cried Lady Steyne. 'She must be a character! Will you get into trouble for not changing?'

'I'm afraid she'll be a little bit annoyed,' admitted Bel. They laughed together.

At first they talked about Bel's wedding. Lady Steyne said she was so sorry she had not been able to come, but she had heard all about it from her niece, Barbie Buckland, and from Miss Penney.

'Barbie is a dear, isn't she?' said Lady Steyne.

'I don't think I know her — '

'Oh, Barbie said you spoke to her at the wedding . . . but of course you wouldn't know who she was.'

'No,' said Bel. 'To tell you the truth I don't really remember much about the wedding. It's very queer.'

'Not queer at all,' replied her ladyship, smiling very kindly. 'I'm sure lots of people go through their weddings in a sort of dream — I know I did — and it must have been even more dream-like for you because there were so many people you didn't know.' Lady Steyne laughed and added, 'Anyhow there's no need for you to worry, everyone says you looked very sweet and behaved beautifully.'

Bel did not know what to say to this. Perhaps she should have taken it as a joke, but somehow she felt that it had not been intended as a joke. She was aware that she was blushing.

'I'm so glad you've got that lovely portrait of Violet Lestrange,' said Lady Steyne, looking up at it. 'I've always admired it so much. Did you buy it with the house?'

'No, I bought it just the other day from Roy Lestrange.'

'Oh, I see,' said Lady Steyne. 'It seems funny that none of the family wanted to keep it — but just as well. She's there in her proper place.'

'That's why I wanted her so much.'

Lady Steyne nodded. 'Yes, she's in her proper place. Who was the painter, Mrs. Brownlee? I used to think the picture was a Romney — it's very much like his work — but of course it can't be, because he died before Violet was born.'

'Oh, no!' exclaimed Bel. 'I mean it isn't by anyone well-known. It isn't at all valuable, Lady Steyne.'

'Isn't valuable?'

'I don't know who painted her — and I don't really want to know,' declared Bel earnestly. 'Ellis thought we ought to get someone who knows about pictures to look at it, but I just like to enjoy her because she's beautiful and sweet.'

'Oh, yes — I see,' said Lady Steyne in thoughtful tones. She herself knew a good deal about pictures and, although it certainly could not be a Romney, she felt sure it was a valuable painting. However, if Mrs. Brownlee did not want to know, there was no object in telling her. Like a wise woman Lady Steyne held her peace.

'Did you know Mrs. Lestrange well?' asked Bel.

'Yes, I knew her and loved her. Of course she was a great deal older than I was but that didn't matter; she remained young at heart till the end of her life.'

Bel continued to ask questions about Mrs. Lestrange — it was exciting to meet someone who had really known her — and Lady Steyne seemed pleased to talk about her friend of long ago. She told Bel that 'Violet' was nearly eighty when she died but was still beautiful and still had the same sweet expression.

'Her family was very difficult,' said Lady Steyne. 'They were all Lestranges — not like their mother at all. They were quarrelsome and wild — people used to talk of them as 'the wild Lestranges'! The two boys were very extravagant which led to all sorts of trouble — so you can imagine what it was like for Violet. She spent all her time getting them out of scrapes and trying to keep the peace.'

Bel glanced up at the picture.

'She looks peaceful doesn't she?' said Lady Steyne. 'She had wonderful faith which gave her inward peace, that was her secret. For the last few years of her life she was an invalid and I used to come and see her and bring her books — so I missed her dreadfully when she died.'

Lady Steyne paused and looked at Bel. Then she smiled and continued, 'I can see you're interested — and it's quite natural that you should be interested in the people who lived in Fletchers End. I have never talked about them to anyone, but it's all so long ago that I don't think it matters now.'

'I'm terribly interested because I love the old house.'

'Violet loved it dearly,' said Lady Steyne nodding. 'She often talked to me about it — to her it was almost human, if you know what I mean. I understood, of course, because I'm quite silly about Underwoods. You must come and see Underwoods some day, Mrs. Brownlee.'

Bel said she would love to see Underwoods, which was perfectly true because she had heard a great deal about it. Louise had told her that it was a Queen Anne house and full of beautiful things and the garden was marvellous. All the same she wanted Lady Steyne to tell her more about the Lestrange family.

Lady Steyne must have guessed her thoughts for she smiled and said, 'I wonder what to tell you. There's so much I could tell you about the

253

place. It was left to Helen, of course. She was the eldest of the family and her father's pet — he spoilt her dreadfully. Violet was sorry that the place was left to Helen; I remember her saying to me that it was a family house and ought to belong to a married couple who would settle down and have children. 'I want Fletchers End to be a happy home' she said. She knew that none of her family would settle down and make a proper home of the old house. The boys were wild and restless and it was most unlikely that Helen would marry. Poor Helen had a very unfortunate disposition.'

'Perhaps Mrs. Lestrange would have liked her other daughter to have it?' suggested Bel.

'Well — perhaps,' said Lady Steyne doubtfully. 'Dora was much younger than the others and quite different. To tell you the truth when I think of the Lestranges I don't think of Dora at all. Somehow she didn't seem to belong to the family — the others were all more or less grown-up when Dora was born. Have you met Dora Harding?'

'No,' said Bel. 'I've heard about her, that's all.'

'She's rather dull,' said Lady Steyne smiling. 'There, isn't that terribly wicked of me?'

Bel would have liked to hear more about 'the wild Lestranges,' but her ladyship began to talk of other things — perhaps she was regretting her wickedness. She was interested in the bow-window and the glass door leading out to the terrace, but when she saw the garden she was horrified.

'How dreadful!' she exclaimed. 'It used to be

such a lovely garden! Sometimes when I came to see Violet we sat out on the terrace and . . . but never mind, Mrs. Brownlee. It will be lovely again.'

'I hope so,' said Bel rather hopelessly.

'Of course it will. Perhaps you would like some herbaceous plants. We're going to dig up the border at Underwoods and divide up some of the plants so there will be plenty to spare if you would care to have them.'

Bel accepted gratefully. She had had several offers of plants from her other visitors and had got some already from Coombe House but she could not have too many.

Lady Steyne refused to stay to tea, saying that Penney would be coming back from town and would be horrified to find she had gone out instead of having her usual afternoon rest.

'I hope you won't be too tired,' said Bel anxiously, as she walked with her guest to the gate.

'Of course not! It has done me a lot of good. Penney is a dear kind creature, I should be absolutely lost without her, but she fusses about me far too much.'

The large Daimler, which had been lent to Bel for her wedding, was standing at the gate waiting for its mistress, but no chauffeur was to be seen.

'What on earth has happened to Stubbs!' exclaimed her ladyship impatiently.

'I expect he's having tea with Mrs. Warmer,' said Bel, trying to hide a smile. 'You mustn't blame him, Lady Steyne. You see, Mrs. Warmer is frightfully hospitable. She can't bear anyone to come to Fletchers End without being fed. She'll be very angry with me for letting you go without having a cup of tea.'

'Will she?' asked Lady Steyne smiling. 'You're in for a good deal of trouble this afternoon, one way and another.' She blew the horn violently and added, 'It's a funny world, isn't it, Mrs. Brownlee? I'm ruled with a rod of iron by Penney and you're brow-beaten by Mrs. Warmer.'

'But we're lucky,' said Bel laughing.

'Oh, yes, frightfully lucky,' agreed her ladyship.

Stubbs came running out of the house, wiping his mouth. 'Sorry, my lady,' he murmured. 'She said you'd be staying to tea.'

Bel stood and watched the car drive away. She simply could not believe that Lady Steyne was ruled by Miss Penney with a rod of iron.

PART FOUR

Alarms and Excursions

25

It was now September and the garden at Fletchers End had been cleared ready for planting. Paths had been discovered and treated with weed-killer and you could actually see where the flower beds had been. There were no flowers left — no garden plants — all had been choked to death by the powerful willow-herb, but it was now possible to envisage a rough plan.

Bel had been so busy with one thing and another that she had forgotten her suggestion that Alec Drummond should come to Fletchers End for a short visit; so she was very much surprised to receive a letter from him one morning at breakfast. The letter was from Edinburgh, from his house in Buckingham Terrace where he lived with his sister and read as follows:

Dear Bel,
It was so very good of you to offer to have me to stay for a week-end. Louise told me about your kind invitation some time ago. Of course I ought to have answered before and would have done so if I had not been rather worried about business affairs. I am wondering if the invitation is still open? I find I have to be in London next week and I should very much like to come to you, but you must be sure to say quite honestly if it

would be convenient to have me. I feel it is a liberty writing to you like this but you were kind to me when I met you at Drumburly so perhaps you will be kind to me again. That is the worst of being kind to people, isn't it? They are apt to become a nuisance!

Yours very sincerely,

Alec Drummond

Having read the letter Bel passed it across the table to Ellis.

'It's a very nice letter,' said Ellis. 'He sounds a good chap. I remember you told me about him; you said he was rather keen on Louise — I suppose that's why he wants to come.'

'Yes,' said Bel.

'Oh, well, all's fair in love and war,' said Ellis smiling. 'You had better write and tell him to come, hadn't you?'

'You wouldn't mind having him?'

'No, of course not. We could meet in town and come down together. That would be the best way.'

2

It was arranged that Alec Drummond should come on Friday and go over to Coombe House to lunch the following day. Bel was a trifle anxious about Alec's visit — she wondered whether Ellis would like him — and as she waited for the sound of the car she began to wish she had not asked him. The invitation conveyed through Louise, had been a momentary impulse and really it had been quite unnecessary. Louise did not want him to stay at Coombe House — which was understandable in the circumstances — but he could easily have gone to a hotel for he was extremely well-off. Money was no object to Alec. Perhaps it was foolish to worry, thought Bel. Ellis got on with most people and Alec was a dear — but all the same she was a little uneasy. The fact was they had not had many visitors. Reggie Stephenson had come but he was Ellis's friend and Louise had come when Ellis was at Bournemouth, so Alec was in quite a different category.

Bel was sitting in the drawing-room when she heard the car draw up at the gate. She went to the window and looked out and she heard their voices: Alec's deep voice, with its slight and rather attractive Scottish accent, saying, 'By Jove, what a wonderful colour there is in that roof!' and Ellis replying, 'Yes, Cotswold stone goes that colour when it has weathered. This house is about four hundred years old — we don't know exactly. We're trying to find out about its history. I'll bring your suitcase.'

'Nonsense! Give it to me!'

They both laughed — perhaps they were struggling for possession of the suitcase — and then the gate opened and they were coming up the path.

How foolish to worry! thought Bel as she hurried to the door to meet them.

Alec Drummond was just as she remembered him; tall and slenderly built with dark hair and eyes the colour of the peaty rivers in which he loved to fish. His smile was very friendly as he took Bel's hand and thanked her for having him to stay. He was taller than Ellis, so she warned him about the oak beams and the low doorways — a warning which was given as a matter of course to every tall visitor who came to Fletchers End.

'It's about time for a glass of sherry,' said Ellis as he followed them into the drawing-room. 'Or perhaps you'd rather have a cocktail. Come and see my cupboard, Drummond.'

As usual the cupboard called forth admiration. 'What a grand idea!' said the guest. 'Sherry, please. One shouldn't drink cocktails in a house like this.'

'That's true,' agreed Ellis. 'I suppose one shouldn't drink sherry either, it ought to be ale or something, but we'll risk it. You'll have some, won't you, Bel?'

They sat down and talked. Bel listened to them with interest, putting in a word when required. This was what she liked for she was not much good at talking, she preferred to play the part of listener. They were discussing wine — which was natural under the circumstances — Alec was saying that wine was his business. Drummond's of Edinburgh was his firm.

'Oh, you're *that* Drummond!' exclaimed Ellis. 'I've got you now. It's a very well-known firm.'

3

As Bel listened to the conversation and hemmed her curtains she reflected that she had known very little about Alex Drummond. She had met him at Drumburly, had stayed in the same hotel and had been in his company a good deal, but for all that she had had very little conversation with him and she had not had the vaguest idea what his business was. The only time she had talked to him seriously was one evening when they had met unexpectedly on the upper landing of the hotel and Alec had pleaded with her to speak to Louise on his behalf. She had almost forgotten the incident but now that she saw him again and heard his deep voice in conversation with Ellis she remembered it clearly — and remembered all he had said. She remembered how he had raved about Louise: he would do anything for Louise; she was the most wonderful girl he had ever seen; she was so beautiful and so good! And what a beautiful name it was — Louise — how well it suited her! She could not be called anything else but Louise! Yes, poor Alec had been quite crazy that evening. He had asked Bel over and over again what he was to do. Should he give up the struggle and go away and console himself by catching quantities of brown trout in Loch Leven or stay at Drumburly and keep on trying to capture the elusive Louise? Bel had thought of him as Orlando — a modern version of that love-sick swain — and had tried to imagine him wandering about in the woods, carving the name of his beloved upon trees.

Looking at him now, talking to Ellis quite calmly and sensibly, she could scarcely believe he had let himself go like that.

Bel was so preoccupied with her own thoughts

— about the modern Orlando — that she lost touch with the conversation. She was recalled by the sound of her own name.

'Bel will sew it on for you,' said Ellis. 'Give it to Bel.'

'No, certainly not!' Alec exclaimed. 'Why should she be bothered with the wretched thing!'

It was a button which had come off his jacket — that was all. Of course Bel was delighted to sew it on for him, and as she had her work-basket beside her on the sofa it was the easiest thing in the world.

Ellis made Alec take off his jacket and brought it over to her. He laughed as he did so and said, 'That's what wives are for. They sew on buttons and mend holes in socks — it's quite useful to have one in the house.'

'I shall have to get one,' said Alec lightly.

Bel was searching in her basket for a suitable reel of cotton; she smiled and said, 'If you had a wife she'd make you buy a new jacket. This one is a disgrace.'

'Can't afford it,' declared Alec in the same light tone.

They laughed at the joke.

'What about a turn round the garden?' suggested Ellis. 'It would be nice to have a breath of fresh air before dinner. Our sweet-peas are a dream.'

'I'm very fond of sweet-peas,' said Alec, rising as he spoke.

'Really, Ellis!' exclaimed Bel. 'You know the garden is nothing but a wilderness. We haven't got any sweet-peas.'

'I never said we had,' replied Ellis. 'I said our sweet-peas were a dream — and that's exactly what they are. I dreamt about them last night and they were beautiful — with five blooms on every stalk. They'll be real next year, of course, Drummond must come back and see them, meanwhile I can show him the bare patch in the middle of the wilderness where the chaps made the bonfire.'

'Wait a minute,' said Bel. 'Alec can't go out without his jacket.'

'His jacket!' Ellis exclaimed. 'It's quite warm — and he's come from Scotland!'

The subject of the argument was laughing heartily by this time. He agreed that the Scots were a hardy race and a jacket would be quite unnecessary for a walk in the garden.

The two men went out through the glass door and disappeared.

When they had gone Bel sewed on the button and mended several tears in the lining of Alec's jacket; she wondered what his sister was thinking of to allow him to wear such a disreputable garment.

It was a pity that Ellis had made that joke about wives, thought Bel . . . and she, herself, had made it a great deal worse. Somehow the words had slipped out without thinking. Alec had been upset! What a fool I am, thought Bel remorsefully. She was all the more remorseful because Alec was looking tired. Perhaps the noise and bustle of London had tired him. He had claimed to be a hardy Scot — and she was aware that this was true for at Drumburly he had

265

fished all day and every day with tremendous energy — but hardy Scots were not used to the noise and bustle of town.

Bel wondered what would happen to-morrow when he went over to Coombe House to lunch. Perhaps Louise would relent when she saw him and agree to make him a happy man. Bel hoped so with all her heart.

Bel hoped so with all her heart because she liked Alec — very much indeed — and, even more important, Ellis liked him. Ellis could be trusted in his judgment of men; Bel had never known him at fault.

When Bel had finished mending the torn jacket she took it up to Alec's bedroom and discovered that all his things had been unpacked and laid out for him; his dinner-jacket and trousers and other suitable garments on the bed, his hair-brushes and shaving tackle on the dressing-table. She peeped into the drawers and saw that everything had been arranged in the best possible manner.

What a woman! thought Bel, smiling to herself.

The fact was Bel knew very little about Mrs. Warmer. They talked together a great deal but, about her past history, Mrs. Warmer was silent. It was obvious that she had been well trained in a good house, and Bel was aware that she had married a man who had proved himself to be an unsatisfactory husband — but she knew no more.

The dinner-jacket on the bed showed that Mrs. Warmer expected everyone to dress for dinner in the conventional manner — doubtless Ellis would find the same garments laid out for him in his dressing-room. Usually the Brownlees did not dress for dinner when they were alone for Ellis liked to go out in the evening and get some fresh air after his day in town; usually Ellis had a bath before dinner and attired himself in grey slacks and a pullover . . . but although Mrs. Warmer never mentioned the matter Bel was fully aware of her disapproval. Mrs. Warmer thought it was letting down Fletchers End.

'Brow-beaten by Mrs. Warmer' thought Bel — remembering Lady Steyne. Well, not exactly 'brow-beaten' nor 'ruled with a rod of iron' but just directed gently into the right path.

Ellis and Alec would have to change, thought Bel smiling to herself. There was no getting out of it — they would have to wear the correct dress for dinner. Ellis would rebel, of course, but it would be good for him to conform to Mrs. Warmer's ruling . . . besides, Bel liked to see him in his dinner-jacket; he looked so nice.

She hung the shabby old jacket in the cupboard and went off to her bedroom to see what Mrs. Warmer considered the correct attire for herself.

26

The day had been hot, as Ellis had said, but it was cooler after dinner so Mrs. Warmer had lighted the fire. She was aware that Bel liked to have a fire in the drawing-room unless it was really very warm indeed.

Ellis had work to do. He had brought home a brief-case full of papers so he retired to his study while Bel and Alec went into the drawing-room to chat

'That's a lovely picture,' said Alec as he sat down in the big chair by the fire. 'It's your mother, I suppose — or perhaps your grand-mother.'

'Why should you think that?' asked Bel in surprise.

'It's like you — in a way,' replied Alec thoughtfully. 'The eyes and the hair and most of all the expression.'

'But she's beautiful!'

Alec laughed and agreed that she was very beautiful and asked who she was and who had painted her.

Thus prompted Bel told him the history of the picture and how she had bought it — but not what she had paid for it — and Alec listened with interest.

'It's a beautiful portrait,' said Alec when the tale was told. 'The violets in her bodice are extraordinarily real. I can almost smell them. In fact when I came into the room I imagined that I could smell the scent of violets. Curious, wasn't it?'

'Yes,' said Bel.

Since the arrival of the portrait Bel had been hoping that the scent of violets would return to the drawing-room, but so far it had not done so — or at least she had not been aware of it. Several times she had tried to imagine that she smelt the fragrance, she had sat down quietly and waited for it to come . . . but it had been no use at all. She had not spoken about it to anyone, for even Ellis, who was usually so understanding, could not be depended upon to understand this. He had said before that she had imagined the scent of violets and probably would say the same again . . . but it was really rather curious that Alec had noticed the scent.

'It was just imagination, of course,' said Alec after a short silence. 'It was just seeing the violets so beautifully painted in the picture — that's all.'

'Yes, of course,' said Bel with a little sigh. She realised that it was no use saying any more about it so she changed the subject. 'I'm sorry Ellis has all that work to do to-night when you're here, but it can't be helped. You understand, don't you, Alec?'

Alec nodded. 'He works hard, doesn't he? I can see he's tremendously keen and capable. He was telling me about his business before dinner and it's obvious that he's got all the threads in his own hands.'

'Yes,' agreed Bel. 'One of his partners is old and the other is very young so Ellis has far too much responsibility.'

'But he can take it — that's the important thing.'

Bel nodded. She was still busy hemming curtains and was becoming very bored with the monotonous task. Several pairs had been finished, and hung up by Mrs. Warmer in the appropriate windows, but there were quite a number still to do . . . and Bel was determined to complete the job herself.

'It was very good of you to mend my jacket,' said Alec after a little silence. 'It's a shabby old jacket — you were right about that. You thought it was a joke when I said I couldn't afford to buy a new one, didn't you, Bel?'

'Yes, of course!'

'It wasn't a joke.'

'Alec! What do you mean?'

'It was true — or at least very nearly true. The fact is I'm pretty well broke.'

'Alec!' exclaimed Bel in dismay.

'Yes,' he said. 'I'm on the rocks. It's grim, isn't it? Of course it's entirely my own fault — but that doesn't make it any better. I've been a fool.'

He was leaning forward gazing at the fire, his hands clasped between his knees — long thin fingers twisted together in a hard knot.

Bel pushed her sewing aside and said, 'What happened, Alec?'

'I'm afraid it's a long story and not very interesting.'

'Please tell me.'

Alec hesitated for a moment, then he said, 'It's really all about the firm. 'Drummond's' began

270

nearly a hundred years ago. My grandfather began it. He imported wine and built up the business very successfully, then my father took over the management and enlarged it. I was dedicated to 'Drummond's' from the day I was born and grew up with the tradition. When I had finished my education I went abroad and learnt about wine, travelling in Germany and France and studying the subject intensively. I was very interested and learnt a great deal and, as a matter of fact, I should have liked to become a vine-grower — that side of the business appealed to me — but when at last I was obliged to return home and start work in the office it didn't appeal to me at all. I was just doing routine work and it seemed terribly dull. My father was getting old and his health was failing. My mother had died some years before and Jean was running the house — you met my sister at Drumburly, didn't you, Bel?'

'Yes,' said Bel. She remembered Miss Drummond — tall and dark like Alec but a good deal older and not nearly so friendly — Bel had not liked Miss Drummond and had avoided her as much as possible.

'Jean ran the house and Campbell ran the office,' continued Alec. 'Campbell was the business manager, he had been in the firm for years. My father had always relied upon Campbell and when his health began to fail he relied upon him more and more. Campbell knew the whole business inside out. When my father died I suggested to Campbell that he should come into partnership with me but to my astonishment he refused.'

Alec remembered the little scene clearly. Campbell had come into his room with some papers for him to sign and had stood beside him at the desk . . . Campbell with his round cheerful face; his iron-grey hair, parted and brushed smoothly to one side; his neat dark suit; his white collar, his navy blue tie, his well-polished black shoes.

'Look here, Campbell,' Alec had said. 'You've been in 'Drummond's' for more years than I can remember. You're the man who knows all about the business — what about coming into partnership with me?'

'Oh, no, Mr. Alec!'

'I mean it, really. I'm sure my father would have approved of the idea. He depended upon you so much.'

'Oh, Mr. Alec!' exclaimed Campbell. 'It's a great honour — a very great honour. I appreciate it more than I can say, but I'm better as I am. Yes, I'm better as I am, Mr. Alec.'

'Listen, Campbell — '

'As for your father,' Campbell continued. 'Well, we can't tell what he would have said. Somehow I don't think he would have approved. No, somehow I don't think so. It's 'Drummond's' you see. That's the point. It's been 'Drummond's' for nearly a hundred years. No, no, Mr. Alec, we'll not change things. We'll just go on as we are.'

'We can't go on as we are,' Alec pointed out. 'Now that my father isn't here I'll have to get down to work in real earnest. At present you're doing far more than your share.'

'I'm not complaining, Mr. Alec.'

'I know, but it isn't right. I want to pull my weight.'

'Just as you say, Mr. Alec. You're the boss,' declared Campbell smiling. 'I can show you the ropes — no difficulty about that — but it wouldn't be my advice.'

'What do you mean?' asked Alec in surprise.

Campbell was perfectly serious now. He said, 'This is what I mean, Mr. Alec. To my mind you're not suited to an office chair. Some folk are and others are not. We're all made differently and it takes all kinds of different members to make a body, as Paul said in his epistle to the Corinthians. The Reverend Struthers was preaching from the text only last Sunday — a very powerful preacher he is. There's some folk that have the gift of tongues — the body must have a tongue to speak with. The body must have eyes and ears and hands and feet if it's to be a whole complete body. It was a very interesting sermon — the way he put it — and I sat there thinking about 'Drummond's' all the time.'

'But I don't see — '

''Drummond's' is like a body, Mr. Alec. That's what I was thinking,' explained Campbell. 'I was thinking that you would be better going about and meeting people and bringing in orders for the firm than sitting in an office chair. You could be the eyes and ears of 'Drummond's' and the tongue as well; I could be the right hand.

'See here, Mr. Alec,' continued Campbell

earnestly. 'I'll put it plain: I'm ready and willing to run the office. I've done it for years. Your father trusted me to do it and I'm proud to think he never had cause to find fault with me. You'll go about the country and make friends with people and bring in the orders. Of course it's for you to say whether that's what's to be, but you wanted my advice and there it is.'

Perhaps it was strange that Alec should remember his conversation with Campbell so clearly — or perhaps it was not really very strange. A prisoner in a dungeon, immured for life, would be unlikely to forget the terms of his release. Alec felt just like that. Alec had envisaged himself spending all his days sitting in a chair in the office surrounded by dusty old ledgers and suddenly he had been given his freedom.

'Campbell!' he exclaimed. 'Do you really think — '

'I do indeed, Mr. Alec. I do indeed. I've been thinking about the matter very seriously and I'm sure it's the right thing. You're a good-looking young fellow — if I may be allowed to say so — and you'll be a grand advertisement for the firm. Away you go with your gun and your fishing gear and make friends with people. You can stay at hotels all over the country and take your expenses out of the firm. That's the way it's done nowadays. Wherever you go you'll make a point of having a nice wee chat with the proprietor of the hotel and advise him about his cellar. You'll meet other folk as well — maybe you'll meet lairds with big properties and they'll

274

ask you to shoot their grouse and fish their rivers.'

'But Campbell, I don't think I could — '

'I know, I know,' declared Campbell, smiling all over his broad chubby face. 'I'm not asking you to ram 'Drummond's' down people's throats. I'm just asking you to make friends with people — all sorts and kinds of people — I'm just suggesting you should go about and enjoy yourself. That'll not be difficult.'

It was far too easy. That was the trouble.

3

'So that's what you did!' exclaimed Bel who had been listening enthralled to Alec's story.

'That's what I did,' nodded Alec. 'Of course I called in at the office every now and then and had a chat with Campbell, but most of the time I went about shooting and fishing and having a rattling good time. Incidentally, and without much trouble, I brought in a considerable number of orders for the firm.'

'So it was all right.'

'It was all wrong,' said Alec gloomily.

'But why? I mean you were doing good business — '

'Yes, but you see it wasn't my proper job. It's all very well for a junior member of a firm to be absent from the office and go about and bring in orders but I was the head of the firm. I should have been there at headquarters. I should have had all the threads in my hands.' He paused and looked down at his hands. 'All the threads in my hands,' he repeated.

Bel waited. There was nothing she could say.

'I knew that — in my heart of hearts,' continued Alec miserably. 'I knew perfectly well that it wasn't the right thing. As a matter of fact I tried several times — went back to the office and tried a spell of concentrated work — but I couldn't get the hang of it at all. I just got muddled and made some stupid mistakes . . . and Campbell gave me another of his lectures about eyes and ears and hands and feet. Jean got on to me too. Jean said I hadn't a good business head. Perhaps I haven't but I'm not really stupid, you know. I can see now that Campbell bamboozled me on purpose.'

'What!' cried Bel.

'Yes,' said Alec nodding. 'He made things more difficult for me. He wanted to get rid of me so that he could keep everything in his own hands. Campbell was false — he was an out and out blackguard.'

'Alec!'

'False all through,' continued Alec in a strained voice. 'His smooth cheerful face was a mask, and all that talk about eyes and ears and hands and feet was nothing but a ruse to get me out of the way.'

Bel was appalled. She said, 'I can scarcely believe it!'

'I could scarcely believe it myself — even when I had all the evidence before my eyes. I trusted him completely. It's an awful shock when somebody you've trusted lets you down like that.

I thought Campbell was absolutely faithful to 'Drummond's,' I thought he was heart and soul in the business. To tell the truth I thought 'Drummond's' meant more to him than it did to me. Now I've discovered that he'd been embezzling the funds for years. Not just small sums but chunks of capital — '

'Alec, how frightful!'

'No wonder he didn't want a partnership,' said Alec bitterly. 'The firm is on its beam ends.'

Bel was too horrified to speak.

'Well, there you are,' said Alec after a short silence. 'Now you know. It was good of you to listen — '

'Alec, where is he? Campbell, I mean.'

'Oh, gone, of course! Vamoosed, vanished from the face of the earth! He's probably somewhere in South America, living on his ill-gotten gains. Anyway he can't be found.'

'You told the police?'

'Yes. They can't trace him. Oh, Bel!' cried Alec. 'You don't know what an awful time I've had. It's been too ghastly for words. I was fishing at Loch Boisdale when I got a wire from one of the clerks in the office telling me to come at once, and when I got home Campbell had gone. He simply walked out of the office one evening and never returned. Everything was in the most frightful muddle and it was some time before I realised the truth. I couldn't believe Campbell was a thief — I just couldn't believe it. So by the time I got the police it was too late to catch him. They'll never catch him, I'm sure of that. He's much too clever.'

Bel tried to think of something helpful to say but could find nothing.

After a few moments Alec continued. 'I knew so little about the business that I was helpless, so I got a firm of chartered accountants to tackle it. They got on to it at once, but it took them days and days to get to the bottom of it and clear up the muddle. Campbell had altered figures and juggled about with returns in a most amazing way. The chartered accountants told me that they had never tackled such a difficult job before; they said Campbell must have been brilliantly clever . . . ' Alec's voice died away and he was silent.

'Alec,' said Bel earnestly, 'I've worked in an office, you know, and I can't understand how he managed to get away with it. I mean some of the clerks must have known what he was doing.'

'I'm certain that the head clerk was in it up to the neck. He says not, of course, and I've no proof; I can't bring it home to him. I expect he got a good rake-off from Campbell to keep his mouth shut. I sacked him, of course. There was nothing else I could do.'

'Surely some of the others must have suspected.'

'Well, I don't know,' said Alec thoughtfully. 'You see Campbell had full control of the office and none of the clerks stayed long. Campbell could sack whom he pleased and he made good use of his prerogative; there were new faces in the office whenever I went to the place.'

'You never had the slightest suspicion of Campbell?' asked Bel incredulously.

'It seems strange,' admitted Alec. 'But you see I'd known the man for years — ever since I was a child — and I trusted him completely. As a matter of fact one rather curious thing happened; I didn't think anything of it at the time, but I've thought about it since.' He paused and looked at Bel. 'You're not bored with all this?' he asked.

'No, of course not. Tell me about it, Alec.'

'There was a queer old fellow called Bates. He was a clerk and came to the office just before Christmas — last Christmas I mean. One morning when I happened to be in my room he brought in a letter for me to sign. I can see him now — a wizened little creature with a yellow face and a wee thin neck like a drawn chicken. I said I hadn't seen him before and he said he had only been in 'Drummond's' for six weeks. Then he asked if I were interested in history and I said I was — what else could I say? Then he said in a low voice, 'Mr. Drummond, did you ever read about the massacre of Glencoe?' Of course I thought the fellow was a bit mad, but there was something nice about him, too. I couldn't help liking him — if you know what I mean. 'Listen, Mr. Drummond,' he said earnestly. 'You'll no doubt remember what the Campbells did that night. The MacDonalds took the Campbells into their homes and gave them hospitality, and in the night when it was dark — black as pitch — the Campbells rose up and killed the MacDonalds — every one of them, man, woman and child! Was that not an awful thing, Mr. Drummond?'

'I said that it was a terrible thing.

'"It was a traitorous thing," he said, shaking his head. 'My mother was a MacDonald and she used to tell us about it when we were children, so it made a great impression on my mind . . . but the MacDonalds were to blame. They had only themselves to thank for what happened.'

'I asked him what on earth he meant and he came nearer and said in a whisper, 'You should never trust a Campbell.'

'He said it in such a queer way that it gave me the creeps. I don't know what I might have said — I was struck dumb for a moment — and then the telephone-bell rang and interrupted the extraordinary conversation and he went away. As I told you I thought he was queer in the head. Afterwards I mentioned it to Campbell as a joke. I said, 'Old Bates has a down on you. His mother was a MacDonald. He's been telling me about the massacre of Glencoe.' I thought Campbell would be amused but he was not amused at all. He looked quite taken aback. I said, 'It's a good joke, isn't it?' Then he pulled himself together and laughed, but all the same I could see he didn't like it. I never saw Bates again.'

'Alec, what do you mean!' exclaimed Bel in dismay.

'I mean he was sacked, that's all,' said Alec with a wan smile. 'You didn't suppose there was another massacre, did you?'

'No, of course not.'

'I believe you did, I believe you thought Campbell rose up in the night when it was dark — black as pitch — and slit his throat. Well, anyway it didn't happen like that. Bates just

280

disappeared and when I asked Campbell what had become of him he replied that the man was a silly old fool, always half-asleep, so he had paid him up and dismissed him. Campbell had the right to do it of course. He had complete control of the office. I told you that, didn't I?'

4

There was a short silence. Then Bel said, 'What are you going to do, Alec? Will you be able to carry on?'

He nodded. 'I think so,' he replied. 'At first it seemed absolutely hopeless. I thought 'Drummond's' was completely bust. Then I got a letter from a friend of my father's asking me to come to London and see him. That's the reason I came to London. I saw him yesterday and he has offered to lend me enough money to tide me over the next few months. I shall sell the house in Buckingham Terrace and go into cheap lodgings and try to get things straight. Fortunately Jean is all right — she has money of her own — so I don't need to worry about her.'

'Couldn't she help you?'

'I wouldn't dream of asking her,' declared Alec. 'No, I'll see it through myself. 'Drummond's' is my responsibility, it has nothing to do with Jean. She's in New Zealand at the moment staying with some friends, so she doesn't know anything about it and I don't intend to tell her. She'll have to know sooner or later, but I'll put it off as long as I can.'

He hesitated for a moment and then continued thoughtfully, 'It's a funny thing; I never cared for the business before, I thought it was dull; it didn't mean anything to me, but now, quite suddenly, it has begun to mean a lot. My grandfather started 'Drummond's' and my father built it up and I've wrecked it. That's not a pretty thought, is it? I lie awake at night and think about it. You can understand, can't you?'

Bel nodded.

'But that's all past,' declared Alec, sitting up and squaring his shoulders. 'It's no use crying over spilt milk. I've made up my mind to work night and day and put 'Drummond's' on its feet. 'Drummond's' is going to be bigger than ever before.'

'Good!' cried Bel, clapping her hands. 'That's the spirit! Splendid, Alec! You'll do it — I know you will.'

'Oh, Bel!' he said in a choked voice.

She looked at him and saw that his eyes were shining with tears. She held out her hand and he took it and gave it a little squeeze.

'Bel, you're a dear,' he said huskily. 'Forgive me for being so silly but I've had such a wretched time — I've been so miserable. When I came to London I felt absolutely down and out. I felt like chucking myself out of the train. Then yesterday I saw Sir Arthur and he made his wonderful offer, and to-night there's you — both of you believing in me! It's put new life into me and I shall go home to-morrow feeling a different man.'

'I'm glad,' she whispered. 'I'm awfully glad.'

'Do you think I could talk to your husband about it?'

'Yes, do talk to Ellis. I'm sure he would help you.'

'I should like his advice,' Alex explained. 'You see I've been wondering how to cut down office expenses. I shall have as few clerks as possible and do most of the work myself.'

'You must have one thoroughly reliable man.'

'I'm a bit chary of 'thoroughly reliable' men.'

'But you must, Alec. You might be ill or something. There simply must be someone in the office upon whom you can depend.'

'Yes, I see that,' agreed Alec. 'But the only thing is — '

'I wonder,' said Bel thoughtfully. 'What about that queer little man you were telling me about? I mean the one who talked to you about Glencoe.'

'You mean Bates?' asked Alec in surprise. 'He wouldn't be any good at all. He was a bit queer in the head; he was incompetent and half-asleep all the time.'

'But was he really? Was he incompetent and half-asleep? Perhaps he was too clever. Perhaps he was too wide awake.'

Alec looked at her doubtfully. 'You mean that was the reason Campbell got rid of him?'

'Yes, of course. He had discovered there was something wrong.'

'But why didn't he warn me?'

'He did warn you. He said you should never trust a Campbell. What more could he have said? You didn't take his warning, Alec.'

'All that talk about the massacre!'

'It was clever,' said Bel earnestly. 'The man was a clerk and had only been with you for a few weeks. Could he have walked into your room and said, 'Campbell is robbing you?' Don't you see, Alec? The man had to lead up to it and from what you've told me he seems to have led up to it very cleverly.'

'That's true,' admitted Alec in a thoughtful tone. 'Perhaps he suspected that there was something fishy going on.'

'Yes, he tried to give you a hint.'

Alec sighed. He said, 'I can see now that it was a pretty broad hint. If I hadn't been so besotted with Campbell I might have taken it.'

'I'm sure that man is clever and honest,' declared Bel. 'If he hadn't been honest he could have gone to Campbell and threatened him, couldn't he?'

'You mean blackmail?' asked Alec looking at her in astonishment. 'Goodness, Bel, what an extraordinary idea for you to have! You — of all people!'

Bel smiled; she could not help smiling at Alec's horrified expression. She said, 'Call it that if you like. At any rate he didn't try to get money out of Campbell; he came straight to you. He risked a great deal by doing so. He risked losing his job, and that's a big risk for a man in his position. I know, because I've been in that position myself — when the mere idea of losing my job gave me cold shivers up my spine.'

'You've made a good case for Bates.'

She nodded. 'Yes, I think Bates would be useful to you.'

'I believe you're right. It would be worth trying at any rate. I wonder if I could find him.'

'Do you know his other name?'

'Yes, Wilkie. I don't know why I should remember it, but that was what it was.'

'Wilkie Bates — I like it,' said Bel. 'Try to find him, Alec.'

'Yes, I'll try. I'll start inquiries the moment I get home.'

27

Having settled this problem — as much as it could be settled — Bel changed the subject. She said, 'Alec, you spoke of going home to-morrow. You didn't mean it, did you? We were hoping to have you here for several days at least.'

'It's very kind of you, but I must go home. If I could get a train from here in the morning I could go north by the midday Scot. I really must go home, I've got such a lot to do. You understand, don't you?'

'But Alec, you're going to Coombe House to lunch!'

'I've decided not to go.'

'But Louise is expecting you! It's all arranged. She said she would fetch you in her car to-morrow morning.'

'I mustn't go,' said Alec in a low miserable voice. 'It wouldn't be right. I can't think why I said I would go. I suppose it was because I wanted to see her for the last time.'

'For the last time?'

He nodded. 'You know what I feel about her, don't you? I made an ass of myself that night at Drumburly so — so you know what I feel. I loved Louise the moment I saw her and I shall go on loving her until I die, but I can't marry her. I can't marry her now.'

'Alec, don't you think — ' began Bel.

He took no notice. 'I've asked her twice,' he

continued. 'I was quite hopeful the second time — it was when I was in London last January and she came up and had lunch with me. She had written me such a nice letter and I was so hopeful that I bought a ring and had it all ready in my pocket to slip on to her dear little finger. Wasn't I a fool?' He paused and shook his head. 'Well, I asked her and she said no. She said she liked me very much and she wanted me to be her friend but she couldn't marry me. 'Never, never, never,' she said. She was so firm about it that I thought perhaps she loved somebody else — I was silly enough to ask. She said, 'Yes, I love Daddy. I love him better than anyone else in the world.' At the time I was nearly demented but I see now it was all for the best. Supposing we had been married — and this had happened!, Just think how awful it would have been!'

Bel did not know how to answer this. She said, 'Louise will be disappointed if you don't go over to Coombe House to-morrow.'

'She won't be very disappointed. She just likes me in a friendly sort of way, that's all. It's better not to see her again. It's quite hopeless. I'm a pauper. I shall have to toil and moil and economise in every possible way. I couldn't afford to marry — even if Louise would have me. I've told you that I've asked her and she has refused me quite definitely. Oh, it's no use talking about it,' he added in a desperate sort of voice. 'I keep on saying the same thing. You're a perfect saint to listen to all this drivel.'

'I'm terribly sorry. I wish I could do something to help you.'

'I was going to ask you to do something for me,' he replied. 'That's really why I came. I've written a little note to Louise — just a few lines to say I can't come to lunch — she'll get it to-morrow morning. I tried to write her a letter telling her what had happened but it was too difficult to explain. I thought perhaps you would give her a message for me.'

'Yes, of course I will.'

'Just tell her that my business is in ruins and I've got to set to work and build it up. That's all. She won't want to see me again.'

'She won't want to see you again!' echoed Bel in astonishment.

'No, it will put her off completely. It would put anybody off to know what a fool I've been. Louise was always a bit scornful about the way I amused myself instead of attending to my business. You know that, don't you.'

'She thought you were a little too keen on fishing,' admitted Bel.

'How right she was!' Alec exclaimed. 'How — right — she — was! Well, anyway, I've had my lesson. I never want to see a fishing-rod again. I shall sell my tackle — it's pretty good so I ought to get a decent price for it. Perhaps I'll get enough to buy a new jacket,' he added with a feeble sort of smile.

Bel was glad he could smile, however feebly. She said, 'You'll get a lot more than that. Enough to buy a couple of jackets and a really good suit as well. You mustn't go about looking shabby.'

'No, I mustn't,' agreed Alec. 'You're right. It

288

wouldn't be a good advertisement for the firm.'

'I'll go over to Ernleigh and see Louise to-morrow.'

'Yes, that will be very kind of you, Bel. It will be ever so much better than writing. I tried to write but the letter was just one long moan — so I tore it up. You understand, don't you?' he added. 'I don't want you to tell her the whole story. She wouldn't be interested.'

Bel was silent for a few moments and then she said, 'But, Alec, she'll ask me about it.'

'Oh, well, if she asks you about it you must use your own discretion, but I don't want her to be bored with a long recital of all my woes — see?'

'Yes, I see, but — ' she hesitated.

'What were you going to say?' Alec inquired.

'Nothing special. You might put another log on the fire for me. I expect Ellis will have finished his work and will be coming in soon. I'll just go off to bed and leave you to have a good talk. That will be the best way.'

'Yes — if you don't think he'll be bored.'

'He won't be bored,' said Bel with conviction.

2

On her way up to bed Bel went into the study and found Ellis gathering up his papers.

'Off to bed?' he asked.

'M'm,' said Bel, putting her arms round his neck and kissing the tip of his ear. 'Alec wants to talk to you about something important.'

'All right. I'm not surprised, really. I thought

the fellow had something on his mind.'

'Clever, aren't you?'

'So you say,' replied Ellis chuckling. He added, 'I'll draw some beer. It might help our deliberations.'

'Don't be too late.'

'Am I likely to be late?'

'Yes, I'm afraid so.'

'Oh, well, can't be helped,' said Ellis. 'Let's have breakfast at half-past nine. I haven't got to go up to town to-morrow.'

Bel gave him another little kiss and ran upstairs to get ready for bed.

This was marriage, thought Bel. It was absolute bliss. This was her life now — and always would be — cosy and comfortable and safe. Sometimes she thought about her life before she was married to Ellis; she thought of the loneliness and the wretched economies which she had been obliged to practise to make ends meet. She thought of how she had lain awake at night full of apprehension about the future. She thought of how she had risen early and rushed off to the office in the chill morning air; she remembered the crowded bus; people with tired white faces; mornings of pouring rain, when the bus was full of soaking umbrellas; or, worse still, mornings of dense, choking yellow fog.

All that was over now and she was lapped in the luxury of her husband's love, but all the same it was right to think about it and remember what it had been like because it prevented her from taking her blessings for granted. Bel had so many blessings and Ellis was the greatest of them all. But for Ellis she would still be lonely and miserable and frightened, she would still be one of that sad crowd with drooping shoulders and anxious faces travelling to their daily toil in offices and shops.

Bel had made up her mind that she must never forget it never, never forget it. She must never forget to say a prayer every night for all the lonely people in the world.

3

Breakfast was at nine-thirty, as Ellis had decreed. They had it together in the dining-room with the bright morning sun shining in through the open windows. Nothing was said about Alec's troubles. He seemed cheerful: he looked rested and refreshed; some of the tired lines had been smoothed out of his face. In answer to his host's inquiries he said he had slept like a top and dreamed about sweet peas.

'Ha, ha!' exclaimed Ellis. 'That was my joke. Alec. You see, when Bel and I were married we decided that we were both too serious. We decided that we must cultivate a sense of humour. We both had a sense of humour but we hadn't been exercising it properly — we hadn't much chance — but now that we're comfortably settled with no more worries we're getting on with the job. It's true, isn't it, Bel.'

'Yes,' said Bel smiling, 'we started with one joke a day but we're improving rapidly.'

Alec laughed — as had been intended. He said, 'That's a grand idea. It's a pity more people don't keep their sense of humour in good training. Have you patented the invention, Ellis?'

'No, it's free,' replied Ellis. 'You can use it if you like.'

Bel noticed that, whereas last night they had called each other 'Brownlee' and 'Drummond,' it was now 'Ellis' and 'Alec.' She was aware that this meant a great deal and she was pleased about it for she had wanted them to be friends ... men were so funny, thought Bel, hiding a little smile.

28

Alec was still firm in his intention to return to London by the morning train so Ellis ran out the car and took him to Ernleigh station. Meanwhile Bel did some necessary chores, chatted to Mrs. Warmer about food and then went out to the garden.

Below the terrace was a wide strip of ground which had been cleared and dug, ready for planting. Bel planned to have a mass of colour here where it could be seen from the drawing-room window. She was standing and looking at it with a seedsman's catalogue in her hand when the glass door opened and Louise came rushing out like a whirl-wind.

'Where is he?' demanded Louise.

Bel turned in surprise. She was even more surprised when she saw that Louise was panting — as if she had run a mile — her face was flushed and her eyes were blazing.

'Where is he?' repeated Louise. 'Where's Alec?'

'Louise, what's the matter?'

'Can't you answer a plain question? Where's Alec? That's what I want to know.'

'I thought he wrote you a letter — '

'I got a note — a few lines, that's all — saying he was sorry he couldn't come to lunch because he was obliged to return home on business.'

'Yes, he had to go this morning.'

'He had to go this morning!' cried Louise furiously. 'Why did he have to go this morning? When did he leave here? Where is he now?'

'Ellis took him to the station.'

'You let him go!' cried Louise. 'You let him — go away!'

'But Louise, I couldn't help it. He said — '

'You knew I was expecting him to lunch. It was all arranged. I was coming over to fetch him.'

'Yes, I know, but — '

'But!' cried Louise. 'What's the good of standing there and saying, 'but'?'

'Louise, listen — '

'I won't listen. You've deceived me! I thought you were my friend! You said you would have him to stay for the week-end — it was all arranged. You knew quite well that I wanted to see him — and you — you let him go away. Oh, Bel, how could you! How could you be — so — so cruel!' Suddenly she was in tears. 'And I had — such a nice — lunch — for him!' she sobbed. For a few moments Bel had been quite frightened — she had never seen Louise in such a rage — but now she was no longer frightened. She almost smiled, almost but not quite.

'Darling, come and sit down,' said Bel in soothing tones. 'You've got it all wrong — really you have. I told Alec you were expecting him. I couldn't do more.' She led Louise into the drawing-room and drew her down on to the sofa. 'I couldn't make him stay, could I?' asked Bel.

'You knew I wanted to see him — very much,' said Louise, mopping her eyes. 'You knew I was longing to see him, didn't you?'

'Not really,' said Bel doubtfully.

'What do you mean?'

It was difficult to explain what she meant. Of course she had known that Louise was expecting Alec to lunch, but she certainly had had no idea that Louise was 'longing to see him.'

'What do you mean?' repeated Louise.

'Well, as a matter of fact I thought — I thought you were — rather — interested — in Roy.'

'Roy!' exclaimed Louise. 'You thought I was 'interested' in him. Of course I like Roy; he's very amusing — we have fun together — but I suppose when you say 'interested' you mean more than that.' She hesitated and then added in an incredulous tone, 'You thought I was in love with that pirate!'

'Pirate?'

'That's what he is — a pirate. Charming and entertaining, quite thrilling in a way, but absolutely selfish and unreliable. He's ruthless,' added Louise. 'If he wants something he takes it.'

Bel remembered Leslie Harding saying, 'He takes what he wants. Other people can go to the devil for all he cares.' She said, 'Yes, I think he is a bit ruthless.'

'Well, never mind about Roy,' said Louise. 'I've told you I'm not 'interested' in him. Tell me about Alec. Why did he rush off like that?'

'Alec said I was to tell you that his business is

in ruins and he's got to set to work and build it
up.'

'Bel!' exclaimed Louise in horrified accents.
'Bel, how absolutely frightful! What happened?
Did he tell you about it?'

'Yes.'

'Well, go on. I suppose he wanted you to tell
me — '

'No,' said Bel, shaking her head. 'He said it
would bore you. He said you would never want
to see him again.'

'Never want to see him again?'

'That's what he said.'

'Alec must be mad! What sort of a person does
he think I am? Does he think I'd give him up
and never want to see him again because he's
lost all his money?'

'Yes, that's what he thinks.'

'And you think so to, I suppose,' said Louise
bitterly. 'You've got the same foul opinion of me.'

'Nobody has got a foul opinion of you,'
declared Bel, putting her arm round her friend's
waist and giving her an affectionate squeeze.
'Louise darling, you're all upset — you're just
being silly. There's no earthly need to be upset.
Poor Alec is terribly in love with you. You know
that, don't you?'

'He used to be.'

'He still is.'

'Did he say so?'

'He said he loved you the moment he saw you
and he would go on loving you until he died.'

'Oh!' said Louise with a little sigh. She leant
her head against Bel's shoulder. 'Tell me more.'

'You want a lot, don't you?'

'Don't tease. Just tell me all he said — everything — every single word.'

2

Bel had been given permission to use her own discretion as to what she told Louise and it seemed to her that the best thing was to tell the whole story from beginning to end. So she set to work without more ado. She began with the shabby old jacket and its torn lining and went on from there. Louise kept on interrupting and asking questions so the story took a long time to tell, but at last Bel came to the end — to the very end when Alec had announced his intention of selling his house, going into cheap lodgings and working day and night to put 'Drummond's' on its feet again and making it bigger and better than ever before.

'Oh, Bel!' cried Louise with shining eyes. 'Oh, Bel, that's splendid.'

'He'll do it.'

'Yes, of course he'll do it. We'll do it together.'

'Together?'

'Yes, together. It will be a worthwhile thing to do. Alec can't possibly live in cheap lodgings all by himself; he'd be frightfully lonely and miserable. He wouldn't get proper food — or anything.'

'He can't afford to marry. He said so.'

'I know — but he's a silly fool,' said Louise tenderly. 'It will be just as cheap to have a tiny flat — and ever so much nicer. I can cook his food and look after him properly, you see.'

'But Louise, I don't think — '

'I shall write to him to-night — no, I won't,' said Louise in thoughtful tones. 'Letters are useless. I couldn't possibly explain everything properly in a letter. It will be better to go and see him. Yes, I shall go to Edinburgh and see him. I shall have to get hold of Mrs. Morgan to look after Daddy while I'm away. I wonder how soon she could come. Perhaps she might be able to come on Wednesday.'

'Louise, listen — ' began Bel.

Louise was not ready to listen. She was far too busy making plans. 'I can stay at the Caledonian Hotel,' she continued. 'I've stayed there once or twice with Daddy and we were very comfortable. I shan't tell Alec I'm coming, I'll just go and see him. That's much the best plan.'

Bel's feelings were so mixed that she did not know what to say. She realised that Louise really loved Alec dearly and had loved him all the time. As a matter of fact Louise had said so. She had loved him but she had despised him — she had said she could not marry a man she despised. Now that Alec was going to work hard and pull his business together and make it bigger and better than ever before Louise could despise him no longer. Bel was glad about that — very glad indeed — because Alec was exactly the right man for Louise.

But was it all right? wondered Bel. Alec had said quite definitely that he could not afford to marry. Somehow Bel did not believe that he would marry Louise and take her to live in a tiny flat — a cheap uncomfortable flat. He had said he would have to economise in every possible way. Bel knew what that meant. It meant counting your pennies, buying cheap food, doing without new clothes, doing without holidays; it meant walking for miles in the rain to save a threepenny bus-fare. Would Alec agree to marry Louise and condemn her to that sort of life?

And how awful it would be if Louise went all the way to Edinburgh and Alec refused to agree to her plans!

It would be all the more awful because Louise was Louise. She was used to getting exactly what she wanted. She was not selfish — not a bit — for Louise always wanted happiness for the people she loved. She saw what was best for them and arranged their affairs in the best possible way. Obviously it would be best for Alec to have a home to return to after his day's work and a loving wife waiting for him with a well-cooked meal. Louise wanted that for Alec; she would be absolutely shattered if Alec refused to agree to such a sensible plan.

'Bel,' said Louise after a little silence. 'You haven't told me what you think of my plan.'

'I'm not sure,' replied Bel. 'Quite honestly I think it would be better to write. You see Alec said quite definitely — '

'Oh, I'm sure it will be all right,' interrupted Louise. 'Alec will be terribly pleased when he sees me. He'll do anything I say . . . and it's such a sensible plan, isn't it?'

'I'll come with you to Edinburgh,' said Bel.

'You'll come! Oh, darling, how marvellous of you! I never thought of that for a moment ... but it would make everything so much easier. Daddy won't make such a fuss if he knows you're going with me. Oh, Bel, what a dear you are! What an absolute angel! Do you think Ellis will mind?'

Bel did not reply. Of course Ellis would mind but he would realise that she could not let Louise go to Edinburgh alone. She could always depend upon Ellis to understand.

29

When Dr. Armstrong was informed of his daughter's plan he was naturally very much against it — any father would have been against such an extraordinary plan — but Louise used all her persuasions, so at last the doctor gave in.

The doctor would not have given in if he had not known Alec Drummond and liked him very much indeed. Alec Drummond was an exceedingly good fellow. They had gone fishing together at Drumburly. They had fished the river together and they had fished the loch from a boat. It is impossible to spend a whole day in a small boat without getting to know one's companion pretty thoroughly, so the doctor felt he knew Alec Drummond very well indeed . . . and he liked him. The doctor did not like Roy Lestrange. If the doctor had to choose between these two men as a husband for his darling child there was no doubt at all which of them he would choose.

The doctor would not have given in if Louise were going alone to Edinburgh, but Bel was going with her which made the expedition more tolerable. Bel was sensible and could be trusted to keep her friend's impulsive nature in check.

'Oh, well, if you're determined to go, you must just go,' said Dr. Armstrong at last. 'I think it's mad, but — '

'You like Alec, don't you, darling?'

'Yes, I like him very much indeed.'

'You'd like me to marry Alec, wouldn't you?'

Dr. Armstrong did not want her to marry anyone — but that was selfish. He pulled himself together and replied, 'I'd much rather you married him than — than someone else.'

'That's lovely,' declared Louise, kissing her father affectionately. 'That couldn't be better. You'd rather I married Alec than anyone else.'

This was not exactly what he had said; it was not what he had meant either, but he could not explain.

'I know you'll miss me,' continued Louise. 'And I shall miss you quite horribly, but you don't want your only daughter to be an old maid, do you?'

'No, of course not . . . but I can't understand why you didn't accept the man when he asked you to marry him; and why rush off to Edinburgh like this to tell him you've changed your mind? A letter would do just as well.'

'No, Daddy. It wouldn't do at all.'

'I've told you I think it's mad.'

'I suppose it is a bit mad,' agreed Louise. 'I'm rather a mad sort of person, I'm afraid.'

'And why did you have to wait until his business had gone to the dogs?' complained the doctor.

'Oh, Daddy, it hasn't gone to the dogs! It's a very good business — Ellis says so — and it only needs a little care to make it bigger and better than ever before. We shall have to economise very strictly at first but Alec will soon put things straight. Anyhow you wouldn't want me to marry for money, would you?'

The doctor sighed deeply and said, 'Of course not, you silly girl, but all the same it's a pity that he — '

'I don't mind a bit,' declared Louise. 'It will be fun economising and saving money. Alec and I love each other. That's the main thing, isn't it?'

Dr. Armstrong agreed that it was.

Having won her father's consent it was necessary to engage Mrs. Morgan, so Louise went to see her in the little cottage near Newbury where she lived with her daughter and her son-in-law. Louise had not expected any difficulty here for Mrs. Morgan was always delighted to come to Coombe House whenever she was wanted (it was a pleasant change from her somewhat monotonous life) but on this occasion she was not very anxious to come. Her daughter was expecting a baby and Mrs. Morgan was busy helping her in the house. However, after some persuasions, she agreed to come on Wednesday until Friday.

It seemed rather foolish to go so far for such a short period but Louise was determined to see Alec and get everything fixed up, so she decided to travel north on Wednesday night and return by day on Friday.

Ellis made all the arrangements for the expedition and on Wednesday evening he met the two girls at Paddington, took them in a taxi to Euston and saw them safely into the north-bound train. He was extremely efficient so there was no trouble of any kind whatever. He had their tickets, and gave them to the Sleeping-Car attendant with a substantial tip.

'You'll look after the two ladies, won't you?' said Ellis.

'Aye, that I will, sir,' was the reply.

'We're in Scotland already!' exclaimed Louise.

Ellis smiled and agreed, 'This platform is a little bit of Scotland.'

'You mean a wee bit of Scotland,' said Louise, giggling. She was in wildest spirits.

There was still five minutes before the train was due to start, so Bel went to the door of the coach and leaned out of the window. She stretched out her hand to Ellis who was standing on the platform.

'You understand why I've got to go,' she said.

'You know I understand,' he replied. 'Louise is your friend; you couldn't let her go alone. You and I are so happy that we've got to do what we can for other people.'

'Yes, that's what I feel too . . . but you'll take care of yourself, won't you?'

'What do you think could happen to me at Fletchers End?' asked Ellis smiling. He added, 'You'll take care of yourself, I hope. That's much more to the point.'

'Don't forget to lock the window in the bathroom,' said Bel anxiously.

Ellis was about to reply to this injunction when a man in a Burberry pushed him aside and leapt into the train; a porter came flying after him with a suitcase. The door was slammed; the train began to move.

'Ellis!' cried Bel. 'It's only for two days!'

Ellis took off his hat and shouted, 'I'll meet you on Friday!'

'Friday!' cried Bel, waving her handkerchief.

2

When Bel returned to her sleeper she found Louise there, sitting on the bed.

'Let's talk for a few minutes,' said Louise. 'I'm so excited I shan't sleep a wink. I keep on thinking about Alec all the time. Dear Alec, I wonder what he'll say when I walk into his room to-morrow. He'll be terribly surprised, won't he? What fun it will be to see his face! Poor Alec, I can't bear to think of him being lonely and unhappy. You said he was unhappy, didn't you?'

'Yes, I'm afraid he is. He's very worried about his business.'

'That's why I felt I had to see him at once. Troubles aren't nearly so bad when you've got someone to share them. I want to share his troubles, Bel.'

'Yes, I know.'

'I wish we could stay a bit longer in Edinburgh, but of course we can't — and anyhow there isn't much object in staying any longer. Once I have fixed everything with Alec I shall have to find someone to look after Daddy.'

'He'll miss you frightfully.'

Louise smiled. She said, 'I'll tell you a secret. I believe I've found someone for him. Of course it will take time — you can't rush things like that, can you?'

305

'Things like what?' asked Bel in bewilderment. 'I don't know what you're talking about.'

'I'm talking about Mrs. Musgrave.'

'Mrs. Musgrave?'

'Yes, Daddy likes her quite a lot,' said Louise giggling. 'He does, really. They're tremendous friends. I had no idea they were so friendly until the other night when Mrs. Musgrave and Rose came to supper. When I saw Mrs. Musgrave and Daddy talking to each other so happily and getting on with each other so well, I suddenly thought what a good thing it would be. It would be lovely for both of them, wouldn't it?'

'Yes,' said Bel, but she said it doubtfully for the idea seemed so strange . . . and then she remembered the morning before her wedding when they had all been in the kitchen and Dr. Armstrong had come in. She remembered that he had made straight for Mrs. Musgrave and talked to her.

'You don't sound very enthusiastic,' said Louise. 'I think it's a marvellous plan. Of course, as I said, you can't rush a thing like that. I shall have to find a housekeeper for Daddy — just a temporary one — until they get used to the idea. My plans usually come off all right,' she added.

Bel was aware of this.

'There's such a lot to arrange,' continued Louise thoughtfully. 'I expect Alec and I will have to be married in Edinburgh because Alec won't be able to get away from his business. I'd have liked a real proper wedding at Ernleigh . . . but the important thing is to be married as soon as possible so that I can look after Alec and

306

keep him happy. We shall have to find a little flat — just a teeny tiny flat and very cheap. It will be fun to go shopping in the morning and find the cheapest places to buy food — the cheapest pieces of meat. Shin of beef, for instance; you can make a very nourishing soup with shin of beef. They call it gigot in Scotland, so — '

'They call it hough,' said Bel, who had learnt quite a lot about housekeeping in Scotland while she was staying with the Dering Johnstones.

'Oh, well, I'll soon learn,' said Louise cheerfully. 'I shall make friends with the butcher. Butchers are always nice and friendly so there won't be any difficulty about that.'

Bel listened to all this and wondered. Would it be all right? Would Alec agree to everything that Louise had planned? Perhaps he would — it was difficult to deny Louise anything she had set her heart on — and he had said quite definitely that he would do anything for Louise. He had said so that night in the hotel at Drumburly — she remembered his very words and the tone in which they had been uttered. Yes, perhaps it would be all right.

Bel listened for a little while longer. At last she said, 'You had better go to bed. You'll be an absolute wreck to-morrow if you don't get any sleep — and Alec won't love you at all.'

'You wretch!' exclaimed Louise laughing. 'I suppose you want to go to bed yourself!'

'Yes, I do,' said Bel firmly. 'And what on earth was the good of Ellis getting sleepers for us if we aren't going to sleep?'

30

It had been decided after some argument that the best time for Louise to visit Alec would be after tea. Bel knew a good deal about office routine and she assured her friend that it would be a great mistake to call at the office in the morning or the early afternoon. Alec would be busy and not in the mood for interruption, however welcome his visitor might be.

Louise had intended to go and see Alec in the morning as early as possible, but she saw the point and agreed somewhat reluctantly to wait. Yes, perhaps it would be better for they would have so much to say — so many things to arrange. She would go after tea and they could stay together in the office after the staff had left; she would bring Alec back to the hotel for dinner.

The train arrived in good time so, having had breakfast and unpacked, they went for a stroll along Princes Street and looked at the shops. Louise bought a hat — a delightful piece of nonsense made of flowers — which became her greatly. She was so pleased with her purchase and with the shop assistant's assurance that she suited it a treat that she decided to wear it when she went to see Alec. Bel bought a silk scarf for herself and a tartan shopping bag for Mrs. Warmer. They visited a bookshop and each bought a paperback thriller to read in bed.

What with one thing and another the morning passed very pleasantly and after lunch they went up to their room and rested. They were sharing a double-bedded room so they chatted for a little and then went fast asleep.

It was tea-time when Bel awoke; she roused Louise, who was slumbering sweetly, and after they had dressed they went downstairs to the lounge and ordered tea.

2

By this time Louise was so excited that she could neither speak nor eat. She drank a cup of tea like a woman in a dream; her lips moved as if she were talking, every now and then she smiled vaguely at nothing at all. Certainly she looked extremely pretty — the new hat, perched coquettishly on her dark curls, suited her to perfection — but Bel had a feeling that under the circumstances it would have been better if she had gone to see Alec dressed in her oldest clothes (she looks too — too *expensive*, thought Bel, searching for the right word). It was no good saying so, of course, for even if Bel could have explained her feelings, which would have been difficult, Louise would not have listened. Louise would have thought her mad to make such an extraordinary suggestion.

'I'm going now,' said Louise suddenly. 'I can't put it off a moment longer.'

Bel watched her walk across the lounge and disappear through the door.

Would it be all right — or not? wondered Bel. She felt quite sick with apprehension. Louise had told her to go out for a walk; she had explained that she would be away for hours so it was no good for Bel to wait. All the same Bel waited.

People passed to and fro; some of them came in, talking and laughing cheerfully, they looked round and found a table and sat down to have tea; others seemed in a hurry, their faces were anxious and distraught. A man, sitting at the table near Bel, was reading an evening paper but he did not seem interested in the news for he kept putting it down and glancing at his watch. Bel saw two women meet suddenly face to face; they exclaimed in surprise, kissed each other affectionately and sat down to chat.

Bel's thoughts wandered. What was happening in Alec's office? What were they saying to each other? How long would she have to wait? Possibly she would have to wait for hours — as Louise had said — but it did not matter. That was why she had come with Louise to Edinburgh — just to wait — just to be here in case — in case she might be wanted.

Bel looked at her watch and saw to her amazement that she had waited less than twenty minutes. It was no use expecting Louise yet. It was silly to keep on watching the door . . . but she kept on watching the door. A man came in with a suitcase; a woman came in with a large black poodle . . . then the door opened again and it was Louise.

For a few moments Bel thought it was all right because Louise was smiling; but when she came nearer, wending her way between the tables towards the corner where Bel was sitting, it became apparent that the smile was not real. It was a smiling mask fixed tightly on to her face.

'Hallo, Bel, have you been waiting long?' she asked as she sat down and pulled off her gloves. She smoothed them out and added, 'Well, I've been turned down. Isn't it a joke?'

'Louise! What happened? Did you see him?'

'Of course I saw him. The clerk showed me into his room and there he was, alone in his glory. I thought he'd be pleased to see me, but he wasn't — not a bit. I asked him to marry me and he turned me down flat. That's all that happened.'

Bel gazed at her in silence.

'Why don't you say, 'I told you so'?' asked Louise.

'I didn't — tell you — ' whispered Bel.

'But you thought it, didn't you? You knew I'd get a slap in the face. That's why you came — to pick up the pieces — but there ain't going to be no pieces to pick up. See?'

Bel was silent. What could she say? If they had been alone — if they had been alone in the drawing-room at Fletchers End she could have put her arms round Louise and held her tightly — but you couldn't do that in the busy lounge of a station hotel! You couldn't do anything, you just had to sit and listen like a dummy while Louise put on her act.

'I'd forgotten it wasn't Leap Year,' continued Louise brightly. 'Silly of me, wasn't it? You might have reminded me about that. Oh, well, it doesn't matter. Alec isn't the only pebble on the beach. There's always Roy, isn't there?' She laughed in a hard brittle sort of way and added, 'I wouldn't have to ask him twice.'

'Louise! What did he say?'

'Who? Oh, you mean Alec! He just said, 'No thank you, I'm too busy to get married. I can't afford a wife.''

'I'm sure he didn't mean — '

'He was — quite different,' said Louise with a little catch in her breath. 'He was cold and hard — like a stone. I couldn't — get near him. He wouldn't listen — he wouldn't listen to anything I said.' Suddenly the bright smile went out (like a turned-off light) and her lips trembled.

'Let's go upstairs,' said Bel, rising. 'We can't talk here.'

'There's nothing to — talk about,' said Louise but she followed Bel to the lift.

They said no more — not a single word — until Bel opened the door of the room and they went in.

Louise threw her hat on the bed and walked over to the window. 'Lovely view of the Castle from here,' she said. 'I'm so glad they gave us a room this side, aren't you?'

'Louise — '

'No, I don't want to talk. There will be quite enough talk in Ernleigh when I go home.'

'Talk in Ernleigh? But people don't know — '

'Everyone knows. You can't move a finger in a place like that without everyone knowing. The dailies chat to each other about everything that happens and this will be a particularly spicy piece of news. People will say, 'Have you heard the latest? Louise Armstrong went all the way to Edinburgh to ask that man to marry her and he wouldn't have her as a gift.' Well, it will give them a good laugh.'

'Oh, darling, I'm sure — '

'You had better have dinner. I'm not hungry. I wonder why I'm not hungry. The air here is so bracing, isn't it?'

Curiously enough Bel was not hungry either, in spite of the bracing air. She hesitated for a moment or two wondering what to do. Louise's back was as straight as a ramrod.

'Would you rather I went away?' she asked doubtfully.

'Yes, I would. I know it's rude and — and unkind, but you could go and have dinner, couldn't you?'

'I'll tell them to bring you a glass of milk and some biscuits.'

'All right, you can tell them to bring it later. I don't want anything now. I shall sit here and read my book.'

3

The room was cold — or at least it seemed cold to Bel — so she switched on the electric radiator and, after another anxious glance at Louise who was still gazing out of the window, she went away, closing the door behind her. The chambermaid was on the landing so she explained that her friend was not feeling well and

313

ordered the milk and biscuits to be brought later. Then she went downstairs to the lounge.

For a few minutes Bel sat there, wondering what she should do; then she went to the hall-porter's desk and asked him to order a taxi.

It was nearly eight o'clock by this time, cold and cloudy; a thin drizzle had begun to fall. Bel wished she had thought of bringing her coat, but it could not be helped. She had no hat, but that could not be helped either.

The office was in George Street. She decided to try there first, for it was possible that Alec might be working late. If not she could go on to the house in Buckingham Terrace. If Alec were not there . . . but it was no good thinking about that.

The taxi came quite soon. The hall-porter saw her into it. He said, 'It's not a very nice evening, Miss. You should have put on a coat.'

Bel smiled and thanked him and said she was not going far. As a matter of fact she had no idea how far she was going for she did not know Edinburgh at all. She had expected quite a long drive — long enough to get her thoughts in order — but it took only a few moments to negotiate the complicated West End roundabout. Before she had time to think the taxi turned into George Street, and drew up at the office door. There were steps up to the door and over the top of the fan-light she saw DRUMMOND in big brass letters.

'Is this right?' asked the taxi driver. 'It's an office. I doubt you'll not find anybody in the place at this time of night.'

314

'I'll try,' said Bel. 'Wait for me, please. If there isn't anyone here I shall want you to take me somewhere else.'

He looked rather doubtful so she added, 'It's very important.'

'Very well, I'll wait on you,' he said. 'I'll take a read at my paper.'

Bel went up the steps and rang the bell. She felt sick and her knees were knocking together . . . and the rain had begun to fall quite hard. Fortunately she had not long to wait. The door was opened by a very small man with a wrinkled sallow face; he looked at her in surprise.

'Is Mr. Drummond here?' asked Bel.

'He's here, but he's not available. He's very busy.'

'It's important,' said Bel earnestly. 'I must see him.'

'I'm sorry but Mr. Drummond is not wanting to see anybody. It's after business hours. You'll need to come back in the morning.'

He was about to shut the door when Bel made a last effort. 'Mr. Bates, I must see him,' she said.

The man was so astonished at hearing his name on the lips of a completely strange young woman that he paused and gazed at her speechless.

'You are Mr. Bates, aren't you?' said Bel. 'Mr. Drummond told me about you. I know you and Mr. Drummond are both very busy getting the books in order but I've come all the way from London to see him, and I must see him to-night.'

While she was speaking she had slipped past the man and was in the hall (he stood there, hesitating, not knowing what to do). The hall was dark, but a door on the right was ajar and showed a chink of light . . . Bel pushed it open and went in, shutting it behind her.

31

Alec Drummond was sitting at a desk at the other end of the room with several big ledgers open in front of him. He did not look up from his work, but said in an abstracted tone of voice, 'Who was it, Wilkie? Did you get rid of him?'

'It was me,' said Bel.

Alec swung round. 'Bel!' he exclaimed incredulously.

'He tried to get rid of me but I dodged him. I had to see you, Alec.'

'Where on earth have you come from?' cried Alec. 'What are you doing here?'

'I had to see you,' repeated Bel, speaking very quickly. 'I know you're frightfully busy but you must listen to me — just for a few minutes — please, Alec!'

He had risen and was placing a chair for her. 'Goodness, you're all wet!' he exclaimed. 'Why haven't you got a coat?'

'I just — came — suddenly. I had to see you. There wasn't time to get a coat.'

'You're shivering! Come and sit near the fire for goodness' sake! You'll get your death of cold.'

Bel was shivering uncontrollably — but not with cold. All the same she was glad to sit near the fire.

Alec seized the poker and poked it into a blaze. 'I suppose it's about Louise,' he said. 'If so, you're wasting your time.'

'She's in a frightful state.'

'I can't help it, Bel. I can't really. It's absolutely impossible.'

At this moment the door opened and Wilkie Bates looked in, 'Mr. Drummond — ' he began.

'All right, Wilkie. You had better go home.'

'But Mr. Drummond — '

'We can't do any more to-night,' said Alec, waving him away.

The door closed softly.

'I explained to her,' said Alec. 'I told her marriage was out of the question for me. I've got to stick into this job with all my strength. I've got neither the time nor the money to get married.'

'Louise loves you — '

'No, she doesn't. She's sorry for me. She's so kind-hearted that she'd be sorry for a blind beggar or a lost dog! That's what I am,' declared Alec bitterly. 'That's all I am to Louise. I'm a blind beggar.'

'Alec, listen, she's — '

'Do you think I could marry her?' demanded Alec. 'Do you think I would take her from a comfortable home and put her into a wretched flat — which would be all I could afford — and have her slaving for me, cooking my meals and mending my socks. Louise is used to pretty clothes, she likes things to be nice. I wouldn't be able to give her anything she was used to — not even decent food. Don't you understand, Bel? I shall have to pinch and scrape and save every penny to get the business going again and pay back Sir Arthur's loan. Do you think I could accept such a sacrifice from Louise? Do you

318

think I would be happy?'

'No, I don't,' said Bel. 'I think you would both be miserable.'

Alec gazed at her in surprise.

'You couldn't possibly marry her,' Bel added.

'But I thought you came here to-night to persuade me to — '

'No, I didn't,' declared Bel. 'I've known all along that you wouldn't agree to her plans. That's why I came to Edinburgh with her. I couldn't let her come alone.'

'You came with her?'

'Yes, and it's just as well I did. She's in a terrible state.'

'Bel, look here — '

'She said you were quite different, 'Cold and hard like a stone.' She said you had given her a slap in the face.'

'Bel!' cried Alec in dismay.

'Well, it isn't awfully nice to — to offer to marry a man, and be told he doesn't want you.'

'Bel! It wasn't that at all!'

'She's in a terrible state,' repeated Bel. 'You've no idea what a state she's in. She might do something — something silly. She talked so wildly that I was frightened.'

'Talked wildly? What did she say?'

'She said, 'Well Alec isn't the only pebble on the beach. There's always Roy.''

'Who the hell is Roy?' exclaimed Alec in consternation.

'He's a naval officer — very good-looking and attractive. Louise has been seeing a lot of him lately.'

'Does she love him?'

'Of course she doesn't love him. She loves you.'

'She doesn't,' declared Alec in a low miserable voice. 'I asked Louise to marry me before, when I was reasonably well off, and she refused. I told you she said, 'never, never, never.' That's pretty definite, isn't it? Now, when I'm in the soup, she's sorry for me so she wants to help me. Don't you understand, Bel? I'm a blind beggar, that's all it is.'

'It's you who doesn't understand,' Bel told him. 'You don't understand Louise in the least. Louise has loved you all the time; she was in love with you at Drumburly.'

'That's nonsense!' he exclaimed. 'I did all I could — '

'Listen, Alec. Louise loved you all the time but she didn't feel — she didn't feel she could — respect you. There, Alec, that's the truth.'

'She didn't respect me!' exclaimed Alec in horrified tones.

'You see,' continued Bel hastily. 'You see Louise admires people who work hard and pull their weight in the world. For instance she admires her father. He's busy all the time, helping people, going from house to house wherever he's wanted. Quite often, he's out half the night. Louise thinks the world of her father.'

'So do I!' exclaimed Alec impulsively. 'A better man than Dr. Armstrong never stepped!' He hesitated for a moment and then nodded. 'I see,' he said. 'Louise thought I was a slacker. She was right, of course. It was unpardonable to neglect the business as I did. No wonder she compared me unfavourably with her father! No wonder she didn't want to marry me! Oh, Bel, what a fool I've been! I've lost everything — absolutely everything — and it's all my own fault.'

'Alec!' she cried. 'Don't talk like that! It isn't too late. You can still get it all back. 'Drummond's' has a good name and Ellis says that's half the battle. Ellis is willing to help you if you need help. He's willing to put money into your business. He said I was to tell you that.'

'How decent of him!' said Alec in a husky voice. 'How frightfully kind!'

'It isn't kind — at least not in the way you mean. Ellis is very shrewd. He wouldn't offer to put money into 'Drummond's' unless he was pretty certain you could pull through.'

'That makes it better.'

Bel nodded. 'I thought you'd feel that.'

'I think we're going to pull through,' Alec told her 'We're beginning to get things straightened out. It will take a long time, but I'm more hopeful. I've got Wilkie Bates — you told me to get him if I could and I never had better advice — we're working together every evening and he's teaching me a lot. Honestly, he's marvellous! He's an absolute genius in his own line — '

'But Alec, if he's as wonderful as all that why isn't he in a better position?'

Alec hesitated for a moment and then said, in a low voice, 'Drink is his trouble, poor chap.'

'Drink!' exclaimed Bel in dismay.

'Yes, he told me about it quite frankly when I engaged him. Every now and then the craving gets hold of him and he goes on the bust — and of course he loses his job. I said I'd take the risk. If he goes on the bust I shall wait until he recovers and take him back. The man is worth his weight in gold — at least he is to me. If it were not for drink Wilkie Bates might have made his mark in the world as a great financier. Ghastly, isn't it?'

'Yes, it is,' said Bel sadly.

'But look here!' exclaimed Alec. 'Why on earth are we wasting time talking about Wilkie Bates? It's Louise that matters. What are we to do about Louise? I mean — what about that naval man?'

'I've told you about him already,' said Bel impatiently. 'He's most attractive. Louise says he's thrilling — and I know what she means. The first time I saw him he — sort of — bewitched me, and — '

'Bel!' cried Alec in alarm. 'He sounds an absolute bounder — but you don't think there's any danger, do you?'

Bel did not think so — not really. She was aware that when people are badly hurt they say all sorts of foolish things — things that they do not mean — Louise had been very badly hurt so she had said the first thing that came into her head: 'There's always Roy,' and had added bitterly, 'I wouldn't have to ask him twice.'

But although Bel did not really think there was any danger — or at least not much — she decided not to answer Alec's question so she remained silent.

'Good heavens!' exclaimed Alec, looking at her

in alarm. 'You really think . . . but what can I do? I can't marry her, you know.'

'You could be engaged,' said Bel.

2

For a few moments Alec was silent. He was standing leaning upon the chimney-piece and gazing down at the fire. At last he said, 'I never thought of that.'

'I've thought of it,' declared Bel. 'I thought of it from the very beginning; it seems to me a very good plan: It solves all the problems and difficulties. Louise will be quite satisfied if you're engaged.'

'It wouldn't be right.'

'Why not?' asked Bel speaking urgently. 'Why wouldn't it be right? You can explain to Louise that you can't be married now and ask her if she'll wait until you've managed to pull your business together and get it going again. Tell her you love her dearly and you'll work night and day to — to get things straight. Tell her about Wilkie Bates — tell her everything.'

'It might be years before I could offer her a decent home.'

'It might be a year.'

'Well, perhaps,' said Alec doubtfully. 'But a year is a long time. Would it be fair to tie her down like that?'

'She wants to be tied down.'

'But would it be fair?' repeated Alec.

'Yes,' said Bel firmly. 'Yes and yes and yes. If

you love someone, and you know he loves you, it doesn't matter having to wait. I would have waited for Ellis for years and years. Please believe me, Alec. I know I'm right.'

'Bel, are you sure? Do you think — '

'You must do it properly, of course,' she told him. 'You must be properly engaged or it won't be any use at all.'

'Properly? What do you mean, Bel?'

'I mean it would be no use having a vague sort of understanding. It must be quite definite. You had better buy a ring. It needn't be an expensive one. Louise won't mind.'

Alec smiled. He took a little case out of his pocket and held it out to her. 'Will that do?' he asked.

The case contained a diamond ring — one large diamond surrounded by a cluster of small diamonds — the light winked and glittered on the shining stones so that they sparkled with rainbow colours.

'Alec!' exclaimed Bel in amazement. 'Alec, how lovely! What a beautiful stone! Where did you get it? Is this the ring you told me about? The one that you got for Louise when you — '

'Yes, I got it in London. I bought it when I was a rich man — or thought I was. Now that I'm a poor man I decided to sell it. That's why I had it in my pocket.'

'You mustn't sell it!'

'No — well — if you think Louise would like it. I mean if you think it's fair to — to ask her — '

'I've told you what I think.' She rose as she

spoke and added, 'We'll go now. Come on, Alec, get your coat.'

'But I can't come *now!*'

'You must,' declared Bel. 'The taxi has been waiting all this time. I can't keep it waiting any longer.'

As a matter of fact she had forgotten all about the taxi and, now that she remembered, she was filled with dismay. She felt as if she had been talking to Alec for hours.

'Hurry up,' she said urgently. 'Put on your coat and come.'

'It's far too late. I'll see Louise to-morrow.'

'You'll see Louise now,' said Bel firmly. 'I'm sharing a room with her and I want some sleep to-night.'

Alec laughed. Perhaps the laughter was somewhat hysterical but for all that Bel was quite pleased to hear it. She waited impatiently while Alec locked up the office and put on his coat.

The taxi was still there, standing at the kerb; the taxi man was inside it, fast asleep.

'What are we to do?' asked Alec looking at the slumbering man in surprise.

'Waken him of course,' said Bel impatiently. 'Give him a poke or something. We can't wait here all night.'

32

Bel's mind had been so set upon persuading Alec to agree to her plan and making him come with her to the hotel that she had thought no farther, but as they went into the lounge she suddenly realised that her troubles were by no means over. By this time Louise had probably got tired of sitting alone in the bedroom and gone to bed. Even if she had not gone to bed could she be persuaded to come downstairs and talk to Alec? And supposing she agreed — supposing she were willing to talk to him — how could they talk to each other properly in the lounge?

Apparently Alec had been thinking on the same lines. He said doubtfully, 'We can't talk here, can we? What are we to do?'

Bel had no ready answer to the question. However it was no use dallying. She had succeeded in getting Alec to come and was determined to see the affair through to a satisfactory conclusion, so after a moment's hesitation she said, 'You'll have to talk here. I'll go and fetch her.'

She had expected Alec to wait in the lounge but instead of doing so he followed her to the lift and they went up together.

'Alec, I don't think — ' began Bel.

'It's the only way.'

'What do you mean?'

'She may not want to come down.'

They were talking quickly in low tones for there were several other people in the small compartment.

'But, Alec. She may have gone to bed.'

'I don't care if she has. I'm going to see her and speak to her.'

'But, Alec. You can't possibly — '

'It's your own fault. You've brought me here and I'm not going away without seeing her.'

Bel relapsed into silence.

They arrived at the landing, got out and walked along the passage. The door was locked of course. Bel knocked upon it gently. She called out, 'Louise, it's me! It's Bel!'

There was no reply.

'Knock louder,' said Alec.

She knocked louder. She knocked several times and called 'Louise!' Nothing happened; there was not a sound.

Bel began to feel frightened. Could Louise have gone to sleep? It was most unlikely — and only a very sound sleeper could have failed to waken at the peremptory hammering on the door.

'Are you sure she's in the room?' asked Alec.

'Yes. At least — where else can she be?'

'She must have gone out.'

'Gone out! It's a horrible night. It's pouring with rain.'

'We must get the chambermaid to open the door,' exclaimed Alec in alarm.

They were just turning away to look for a chambermaid when they saw Louise coming along the passage towards them. She was clad in a pink nylon dressing-gown and was carrying a sponge-bag in her hand. Her dark curls were screwed up on to the top of her head and secured by a tortoise-shell pin. Her face was pink. She looked like a little girl who has just been thoroughly scrubbed by a competent Nannie.

For a few moments Louise did not see them standing outside the door. Then she saw them — and stopped — and turned.

'Louise!' cried Bel.

Alec said nothing, he ran after her with long strides; he caught her in his arms and kissed her. It was a very thorough kiss and took quite a long time. Louise seemed to be enjoying it; she had dropped her sponge-bag and the key of the door. Her arms were round Alec's neck.

Fortunately there was nobody about; the passage was empty. Bel was glad of this for she had a feeling that her two friends would have behaved in exactly the same way if the passage had been thronged with people. There was nobody about but at any moment someone might appear; one of the doors might open or someone might emerge from the lift. Bel went forward and picked up the key; she opened the bedroom door, pushed her two friends inside and shut it firmly.

2

There was a little alcove just opposite the door with a small sofa and a table in it. Bel sat down on the sofa and waited. Being somewhat old-fashioned in her ideas she felt a trifle uneasy. I'm a nice kind of chaperone, she thought. And then she thought, but it's Alec — so it's all right. If it were Roy — but of course I wouldn't have done it if it had been Roy.

She leant back with a sigh of relief. She was very tired and — yes — she was very hungry. She remembered that she had had no dinner and not very much tea. Oh, well, it couldn't be helped. She intended to give them half-an-hour — that ought to be enough to discuss their problems and get themselves properly engaged. She would give them half-an-hour and then knock on the door.

The minutes passed slowly. Presently the chambermaid came along the passage carrying a small tray with a glass of milk and a plate of biscuits. She paused when she saw Bel and said, 'Will I take it in to the lady now?'

'Oh,' said Bel. 'No, just leave it here, please.'

The girl smiled and put the tray beside Bel on the table. 'I hope your friend is feeling a bit better, Miss,' she said.

'Oh, yes, ever so much better, thank you.'

'That's good.'

'I wonder,' said Bel doubtfully. 'Do you think you could bring another glass of milk for me? I haven't had any dinner.'

'No dinner!' exclaimed the girl. 'That's dreadful . . . but you could get something now in the Postillion Restrong. They're always open late for people coming back from the theatre.'

'I'd rather have a glass of milk.'

The girl looked doubtful. She said, 'You'll need to wait a bit. I'm busy just now. There's a lot to do.'

Bel gave her a tip. 'Just when it's convenient,' she said.

The tray with the glass of milk and the biscuits was standing on the table and for several minutes Bel sat and looked at it. She felt the glass — it was warm. It was just right for drinking. What a pity to let it get cold! Bel decided it would be silly to let it get cold. She sipped it slowly. It was lovely creamy milk and the biscuits were delicious. She felt much better when she had finished, she felt warmed and comforted.

Half-an-hour had passed by this time; Bel was about to rise when she saw the door open and Alec come out. Louise came out after him; they were both smiling rapturously.

'Bel, we're engaged!' exclaimed Louise. She made the announcement as if it were the most astonishing news. 'Look, Bel,' she added. 'Look what Alec has given me! Isn't it lovely?'

The diamonds were flashing on her finger.

Bel looked at the ring in admiration. 'How beautiful!' she said.

'It's much too beautiful,' declared Louise earnestly. 'I've told him it's much too good. I've told him he ought to sell it and buy a cheap one — '

Alec laughed. He said, 'I've told her I'm not in the habit of giving my fiancées cheap rings.'

They looked at each other with their hearts in their eyes.

'I'm terribly glad,' said Bel. 'I hope you'll be

very, very happy — I'm sure you will be.'

'I'm sure we shall be,' said Louise with a sigh of bliss. 'Alec and I love each other frightfully much — so of course we'll be happy.' She hesitated and then exclaimed, 'Oh, Bel, I was so miserable! I was all horrid inside, that's why I was horrid to you. Every bit of me was as horrid as could be! You understand, don't you?'

'Of course I understand. I knew exactly what you were feeling. It doesn't matter a bit.'

'I was miserable,' repeated Louise. 'Utterly miserable — and then Alec came. You see he just guessed I would be feeling miserable, so he came.'

'I didn't say that,' objected Alec. 'It was really Bel — '

'No, you didn't say it, but I know that's how it was. You just suddenly felt you had to come.'

'Of course that's how it was,' said Bel firmly.

'It's all cleared up now,' Louise continued. 'It was just a silly misunderstanding, that's all. We're both perfectly happy, aren't we Alec? We'll have to wait, of course. We may have to wait quite a long time, but it doesn't matter how long we have to wait. We can write to each other and we shall see each other sometimes. When Alec comes south on business he can stay with us for a week-end. That will be something to look forward to.'

'And you've got Alec's ring.'

'Yes, I've got his ring,' agreed Louise, looking at it in delight. 'I shall show it to everyone and they'll all think it's perfectly lovely.' She looked up and smiled and added, 'It's all too marvellous for words.'

'And it's all due to Bel,' said Alec. 'If it hadn't been for Bel — '

'No, Alec,' said Bel, shaking her head significantly.

'If it hadn't been for Bel I don't know what would have happened,' declared Alec, and with that he put his hand on Bel's shoulder and stooped and kissed her very gently on the forehead.

Louise looked a little surprised. She said, 'Yes, of course. Bel is a darling.'

'She's the best friend anybody ever had.'

'Yes, of course,' repeated Louise. 'She's my very best friend. If she hadn't come with me to Edinburgh it would have been frightful.'

'It would have been absolutely frightful,' Alec agreed.

There was a short silence.

'I think Alec had better go home now,' said Bel.

Alec agreed at once. 'You must both be tired,' he said. 'I'll see you to-morrow — perhaps we could meet for lunch.'

'No,' said Louise, shaking her head sadly. 'We're going south to-morrow by the ten o'clock train.'

'Oh, Louise!'

'We must, really,' she told him. 'Mrs. Morgan only came 'to oblige.' Her daughter is going to have a baby at any moment and I promised faithfully I would be home to-morrow night. I must be there to look after Daddy and answer the telephone. It's my job.'

'Louise, couldn't you — '

'No, I couldn't,' said Louise firmly. 'I've told you it's my job. You wouldn't want me to neglect my job, would you, Alec?'

Alec was very red in the face. 'No Louise, I wouldn't,' he replied.

3

When Alec had gone — after a prolonged farewell — Louise sighed and said, 'I'm frightfully hungry. I wonder why that girl hasn't brought my milk.'

Bel pointed to the empty glass.

'You drank it!' cried Louise. 'Well, I like that! You had an enormous dinner — you were away for hours — and now you've drunk my milk!'

'You said the air was so bracing,' explained Bel, giggling feebly.

'Bracing!' cried Louise, half laughing and half in earnest. 'I should think it must be extremely bracing. It's just as well we're going home to-morrow; if you stayed here much longer you'd be as fat as a prize pig. There you sit, giggling! You don't seem to care about me. Am I to go to bed starving?'

Bel was laughing so much that she could not reply, but fortunately the chambermaid appeared with another glass of milk and another plate of biscuits so Louise was pacified and they went to bed.

They went to bed, but not to sleep. Louise was too happy and excited to sleep and Bel was obliged to listen to a long recital of Alec's charms. How good he was! How absolutely wonderful! How kind and understanding! How terribly hard he was working to put his business in order!

Bel listened sympathetically, but her eyelids were so heavy that her eyes kept shutting, no matter how hard she tried to keep them open. Presently they closed and remained closed.

Louise still had lots more to say — she could have gone on talking about Alec for hours — but it is impossible to go on talking to a person who is lying fast asleep with tightly closed eyes, breathing gently and rhythmically through her nose.

'Good night, dear darling Bel,' said Louise very softly.

There was no reply. So Louise turned out the bedside lamp and went to sleep herself.

PART FIVE

Miss Lestrange's Bureau

33

The Brownlees arrived home on Friday evening.

The two girls had been seen off by Alec and met at Euston by Ellis. Louise had been dropped at Coombe House in time to say good-bye to Mrs. Morgan and had been warmly welcomed by the doctor; everything had gone off according to plan.

Bel was delighted to get home — Fletchers End was looking even more beautiful than usual — she felt as if she had been away for weeks. Ellis had exactly the same feeling.

'You needn't have gone, need you?' said Ellis as they sat down to a belated meal.

'Needn't have gone?' asked Bel in astonishment.

'I mean you went to Edinburgh with Louise because you were afraid there might be trouble — I thought the same to tell you the truth — but it was all right, wasn't it? Louise seems blissfully happy.'

'Yes.'

'I'm not in favour of long engagements but in this case it's the best solution.'

'Yes, that's what I thought.'

'At any rate it will keep her out of the clutches of that fellow Lestrange.'

'Yes,' said Bel. She hesitated for a moment wondering if she should tell Ellis or not. Was it right to keep secrets from your husband?

'It isn't right,' said Ellis. 'Wives should tell their husbands everything.'

'Ellis, what do you mean? I never said — '

'No, but you thought,' said Ellis chuckling. 'I've been married to you for nearly a year, you know.'

'Bother my face!'

'It's a delightful face,' declared Ellis. 'It's the most beautiful face in the whole world . . . '

'Ellis, what nonsense!'

' . . . but you should never play poker.'

'Play poker!' echoed Bel in surprise. 'That's what Roy Lestrange said.'

'Roy Lestrange!' cried Ellis in sudden rage. 'What the devil has Roy Lestrange got to do with it! How dare he say a thing like that to you! I'll twist his neck if I ever get hold of him . . . '

Bel was giggling. It was funny how the mere mention of that man's name made other men so angry. Alec had been angry too.

When Ellis had finished describing all the unpleasant things he would do to Roy Lestrange if he ever got hold of him he drew a deep breath and said, 'Oh, well, I suppose it is rather funny. You seem to think so, anyhow. But we've strayed away from the point. We were talking about your trip to Edinburgh. Have you decided whether or not to tell me why your journey was really necessary?'

'Yes, but it's a long story. Let's go into the drawing-room,' said Bel.

When they were comfortably settled on the sofa together — very close together indeed — Bel told him all that had happened, or at least most of what had happened. Naturally she did not tell him what Louise had said about Roy, nor about the 'terrible state' she had been in. (There are some things that even the most devoted wife should not reveal to her husband.)

Ellis listened and made suitable comments and at last he said, 'You've been very clever indeed — and very brave. I've missed you terribly, but I'm glad you went. I'm sure those two friends of ours will be happy together.'

'I'm sure they will,' Bel agreed. 'If they're as happy as we are it will be all right, won't it, Ellis?'

'They couldn't possibly be happier,' he replied.

It was now Ellis's turn to relate what had been happening at Fletchers End during Bel's absence. The herbaceous plants had come from Underwoods and the 'chaps' had been busy putting them into the border. Ellis had made out an order for roses and sent it away. He had received a letter from 'that fellow' asking twenty-five pounds for Miss Lestrange's bureau and had sent him a cheque by return of post.

'Twenty-five pounds!' exclaimed Bel in horrified tones. 'But it may not be worth all that! We haven't seen it — or anything!'

'I know, but — '

'If he asked that amount he would have taken less. You should have bargained with him, Ellis. Why did you send him a cheque straight off without finding out its proper value! It isn't like you a bit.'

Ellis did not reply to this question. (There are

some things that even the most devoted husband should not reveal to his wife.) As a matter of fact he would have found it difficult to explain. It certainly was not like Ellis to buy a pig in a poke but on this occasion he had done just that. He had no idea what the bureau was worth and he had not tried to bargain with 'that fellow.' The reason for this unbusiness-like behaviour on the part of the business-like Ellis was really a vague sort of feeling that if he paid 'that fellow' what he wanted for the bureau — probably far too much — it would make up for the fact that Bel had paid far too little for the picture. It was illogical, of course — Ellis knew that. It was merely a sop to his troublesome conscience.

'You should have bargained with him, Ellis,' repeated Bel.

'The less I have to do with that fellow the better,' Ellis replied. He was rather pleased with himself at having found the right thing to say. Not only was the statement truthful but it satisfied Bel completely. The subject was closed.

'I wonder if the manure has come,' said Bel.

'It came yesterday morning,' replied Ellis.

After that the conversation was concerned with horticultural matters until they went up to bed.

2

The morning after her return from Edinburgh Bel was awakened early by strange noises in the house. Ellis was still slumbering peacefully so she put on her dressing-gown and went downstairs to see what was happening. The sounds seemed to be coming from Ellis's study and after a few moments hesitation she opened the door and peeped in. All the furniture in the room was swathed in dust sheets — that was the first thing she noticed — and of course she remembered now that Mrs. Warmer was expecting Mr. Carruthers to come and examine the 'chimbley' which was inclined to smoke when the wind was in the east. Mrs. Warmer had been looking forward to his visit for some time and Bel certainly would not have forgotten about it if her mind had not been so full of other, more important matters.

She went a little farther into the room and now perceived the hind-quarters of a man in the fireplace. His head and shoulders were half-way up the chimney, so it was impossible to tell whether this was actually Mr. Carruthers himself or Mr. Crouch, his assistant, but as Bel particularly wanted to speak to Mr. Carruthers about the unsatisfactory condition of the chimney she decided to chance it. She was in her dressing-gown of course but she did not think Mr. Carruthers would mind.

'Mr. Carruthers!' said Bel loudly.

The man came backwards out of the chimney and looked up at her from his kneeling position on the floor. Even then Bel was not quite certain, for the face that looked up at her was unfamiliar — the skin quite black and the eyes curiously white.

'Good morning, Mrs. Brownlee,' said the voice

of Mr. Carruthers — the same voice which so often greeted her on the way to church.

'Oh, good morning, Mr. Carruthers,' said Bel. 'I see you're having a look at that chimney. We can't understand what's the matter with it. All the other chimneys in the house are so good, they never give any trouble at all, but this one — '

'Ah, this one,' said Mr. Carruthers, shaking his head sadly. 'This chimbley 'as always given trouble and always will — more trouble than all the other chimbleys put together.'

'Always will?' asked Bel.

'Always will,' nodded Mr. Carruthers. 'It's the construction, Mrs. Brownlee.'

'Can't you do anything about it?'

'Not unless I was to pull down the 'ouse.'

'Oh, dear!' cried Bel in dismay. 'You mean — '

'I mean it's crooked,' he explained. 'That's the 'ole trouble, and we can't do nothing about that. It's like this, you see; if you was to put your 'ead up the droring-room chimbley you would see right up to the sky, but if you was to put your 'ead up this chimbley you wouldn't see nothing — because it's crooked.'

This explanation cleared up the matter, but distressed Bel considerably. 'Oh, how dreadful!' she exclaimed. 'I wonder why they made it like that.'

'Ah, now you're asking,' declared Mr. Carruthers, blinking at her with his queer white eyes. 'Chimbleys is like people, Mrs. Brownlee. There's some that's made crooked with awk-ard corners that gets choked up with soot — they

342

gives a lot of trouble in the world — and there's some that's made straight and draw as pretty as you please. They don't give no trouble at all — the straight ones don't. They go up from the sitting-room to 'eaven. Just like chimbleys, people are — some crooked and some straight — and you won't make the crooked ones straight no matter 'ow 'ard you try. Of course you could put on a cowl. That 'elps sometimes.'

Bel was bewildered. She was not sure whether Mr. Carruthers was still talking about people ('It is not the cowl that makes the monk,' she thought). She was still trying to see how it applied when Mr. Carruthers made a sudden decision.

'That's what to do,' he declared. 'I might 'ave thought of that before. I'll put on a cowl. If it don't do no good it won't do no 'arm — as the barber said when 'e sold the bald-'eaded customer a bottle of 'air-oil. Ha, ha!' exclaimed Mr. Carruthers opening a very red mouth and displaying a set of very white teeth. 'Ha, ha, ha! That's a good 'un!'

Bel laughed too, she thought it an excellent joke; so when she had arranged with Mr. Carruthers to get a cowl and put it on the 'chimbley' as soon as possible, she ran upstairs to see if Ellis were awake and if so to tell him all about it.

Fortunately Ellis had wakened some time ago and had been wondering where she had gone, so he was quite ready to listen to the whole story and to enjoy the joke. They agreed that one of the charms of living in the country was the

343

contact with country people — people who were unusual and interesting and, best of all, absolutely natural.

'Chimbleys,' said Ellis thoughtfully. 'It's a nice word, isn't it? — and so much easier to say.'

Bel smiled. 'It's frightfully infectious,' she declared. 'I almost said chimbley to Mr. Carruthers. I wonder whether he would have noticed.'

34

Roy Lestrange was considerably astonished when he received the cheque for twenty-five pounds by return of post. The sum he had named as an acceptable price for the bureau had been a shot in the dark; he had no idea of the value of furniture and could not be bothered to find out. He would have accepted less quite cheerfully. For a few moments Roy hesitated, cheque in hand, wondering whether he should have asked more, wondering whether it was now too late to sting that fellow Brownlee for another fiver. However the cheque was here, so perhaps it would be safer to keep it ('a bird in the hand is worth two in the bush,' thought Roy). Besides he needed the money — when did he not need money? so the matter settled itself.

The matter being settled, Roy decided that it might be just as well to complete the transaction without delay, so he cashed the cheque, made arrangements to send off the bureau as soon as possible and thought no more about it.

Of course Bel was tremendously excited when she saw the British Railways van draw up at the gate and the packing-case being unloaded. She had been looking forward to reading the letters and diaries. Indeed she had waited so long — ever since the first day she had seen Roy Lestrange and given him tea in the drawing-room — that she had almost given up hope of ever seeing them.

Bel called to Mrs. Warmer and ran out to the gate.

'Shall we carry it in, Miss?' asked the driver.

'Oh, yes,' said Bel breathlessly. 'Yes. Please carry it in.'

'No,' said Mrs. Warmer who had followed her from the house.

'Yes or no?' asked the man, smiling.

'No,' repeated Mrs. Warmer firmly. 'Just put it down here on the path. I don't want that dirty old crate in my nice clean hall.'

Although her manner was forbidding Mrs. Warmer was delighted at the arrival of the bureau (everything and everybody that arrived at Fletchers End was welcomed with joy by Mrs. Warmer) so the moment the men had put down the packing-case on the path outside the front-door she fetched a hammer and a chisel and proceeded to open it.

'Just look at that, Mrs. Brownlee' Mrs. Warmer exclaimed. 'Did you ever see such dirt? It's a good thing I was here or they'd have brought it into the house. Mr. Brownlee made a fine old mess when he opened that picture, but this is worse.'

Bel was obliged to admit that Mrs. Warmer was right. The packing-case was extremely dirty, the straw was dirty and smelt of mice, and when the bureau was revealed it presented a very sorry appearance. Bel was horrified when she saw it. Was this miserable-looking object the bureau for which Ellis had paid twenty-five pounds?

'Don't you worry,' said Mrs. Warmer. 'It's been in that dirty old store for years. A good wash is what it wants. When I've washed it and given it a nice polish-up it'll look quite different — you'll be surprised. You go and have a nice sit down with a book,' said Mrs. Warmer.

In spite of her disappointment at the appearance of the bureau Bel could not help smiling, for this was Mrs. Warmer's stock phrase when she wanted a clear field of action. It would have been rude to say, 'Go away. I can get on quicker without you' — and Mrs. Warmer was never rude. 'You go and have a nice sit down with a book' was polite and pleasant. Who could take exception to a suggestion so considerate and kind?

Of course Bel never sat down with a book in the morning — there was far too much to do — and Mrs. Warmer knew this perfectly well. Nobody would have been more surprised than Mrs. Warmer if she had found her employer sitting down with a book — the bed unmade and the drawing-room undusted — but all the same she said it. She said it when she was making jam and Bel went into the kitchen and offered to stir the preserving-pan; she said it when Bel offered to clean the silver. She had said it so often that the words had ceased to have any meaning and all ran together as they issued from her mouth. 'You-go-and-have-a-nice-sit-down-with-a-book,' said Mrs. Warmer as she wrung out a cloth in a pail of soapy water and started on her task.

Bel went upstairs and made the bed.

Mrs. Warmer's prediction was correct. When Bel saw the bureau nicely cleaned and polished she was delighted; it was a charming piece of furniture and it suited the old house. Reggie would not have agreed with this, of course, for writing-desks of elegant design were unknown in the days of Queen Elizabeth, but Bel was not so pernickety.

They carried it into the drawing-room and tried to decide where to put it. Where had it stood before?

'Over by the window,' said Mrs. Warmer. 'The house was empty when I took over but there was a patch on the wall-paper near the window just about the right size.'

They carried it over to the window and stood back to look at it.

'Yes,' said Bel. 'That's the best place for it — with the light coming in on the left.'

'That's where it was,' declared Mrs. Warmer and so saying she went away.

Left alone, Bel examined her new treasure more carefully. The drawers were locked but the keys, tied together, were hanging on one of the handles. Bel was almost afraid to open the drawers — how awful if they were empty! However she plucked up her courage and tried the keys in the locks.

The top drawer was full of papers; papers of all kinds and bundles of letters and receipted bills ... and, yes, here were the diaries, half-a-dozen fat little books fastened together with an elastic band. Bel's eyes sparkled with pleasure when she saw her trove; here she would find all sorts of interesting things about the old house. She would find interesting things about Miss Lestrange as well — and perhaps about old Mrs. Lestrange, the lady of the picture. It would take a long time to sort out all the papers, for they had been jumbled up together when the bureau had been moved, but there was no hurry, thought Bel. She could take her time about it, reading carefully, making notes and tearing up the rubbish as she went along. It would be a delightful job for a wet afternoon.

35

Ellis returned from town at the usual hour and was taken straight into the drawing-room.

'Hallo, it's come!' he exclaimed. 'That fellow didn't take long in sending it.'

'Isn't it lovely?'

Ellis agreed. He was pleasantly surprised at the appearance of the bureau; had it been in perfect condition it would have been well worth the twenty-five pounds which he had paid for it. Unfortunately it was not in perfect condition; there was a chip off the corner, one of the legs was cracked and the leather on the writing flap was badly stained with ink. Bel had not noticed these defects.

'It doesn't matter,' said Ellis cheerfully. 'It looks very nice and fits in well with the room. The leg can easily be mended and we can put some brown stain on that chip. It will hardly show at all — '

'But Ellis! You paid far too much for it!'

'Yes, but it doesn't matter,' he repeated. 'We've got the diaries and letters, haven't we? They're sure to be interesting.'

Bel said no more. As a matter of fact she was puzzled; Ellis's behaviour was completely out of character; she could not understand it at all.

Bel had decided that the task of sorting out the papers should be kept for a wet afternoon but Ellis was more impatient. He sat down at

350

once and opened the drawer.

'I say, what a mess!' he exclaimed. 'There isn't time to go through all these papers now, but here's something rather interesting. It's an extract from the Lestranges' family-tree. At least it's just a few rough notes, but it tells you when your 'violet lady' was born.'

They looked at the paper together:

Violet Harris. Born 1853. Died 1933.

Married Reginald Lestrange in 1876 (Four children).

1. Their daughter, Helen — born 1878.
2. Their son — Reginald — born 1880 — two daughters, Olivia and Mary.
3. Their son — Eric — born 1881 — one son, Roy, born 1926.
4. Their daughter, Dora — born 1895 — one son, Leslie, born 1927.

'It isn't a proper family-tree,' said Bel in disappointed tones.

'No, but it's quite interesting. Your friend Roy Lestrange seems to be thirty-five. I thought he was younger from what you told me about him.'

Bel was not surprised, for Roy was a man of the world, but she was surprised to discover Leslie Harding's age; she would have guessed him to be not more than thirty at the outside.

Ellis was still studying the paper; he said, 'Their daughter, Dora, seems to have been an afterthought.'

'Yes,' said Bel. 'Lady Steyne told me that the others were all more or less grown-up when she was born.'

'I expect you'll find out a lot more about your

351

'wild Lestranges' when you have time to get down to the job,' said Ellis smiling.

2

The next day was Saturday. It had been arranged that Jim Copping should come down to lunch. He had been asked before, several times, but what with one thing and another his visit had been postponed. Now, at last, he was coming and Bel was looking forward immensely to seeing him again.

Unfortunately the day was cold and cloudy, not at all the sort of weather Bel would have chosen for her eagerly expected guest. She could do nothing about the weather of course but she could and did arrange to have a particularly good and substantial lunch for him.

The sky blue sports car drew up at the gate soon after twelve o'clock and its owner unfolded his long legs and got out. Bel, who had been watching for its arrival, ran down to the gate, Ellis followed more slowly.

'Hallo, Mrs. B.!' exclaimed Jim Copping, taking her two hands and shaking them up and down vigorously. 'You're looking simply grand. Country life seems to suit you. What fun, seeing you again!'

'It seems ages,' declared Bel, smiling at him affectionately.

'It is ages,' he replied. 'You left in March, didn't you? Why haven't you been to see us at the office before this?'

'Why haven't you been to see us? I thought you had forgotten all about me.'

'Not likely,' he said with one of his wide grins. 'There are all sorts of things that remind me of you. For instance I've still got that nice bit of rubber in the green plastic case.'

Bel laughed. It amused her to be remembered by a piece of india-rubber.

'Oh, other things too,' he said hastily.

This was so like him, thought Bel. Mr. James, in spite of his immense size and awkward appearance, was very sensitive about people's feelings.

Ellis had told her that he had 'grown up' and now that she had time to look at him she realised that he looked more mature. He was not so gawky and his arms and legs seemed less unmanageable.

'I meant to come and see you before,' he continued, 'but I've been very busy, you know — and I've learnt a lot. I don't make so many idiotic mistakes nowadays.'

'Ellis says you're doing splendidly, Mr. James.'

Bel had intended to call him 'Jim,' as Ellis did, for she was no longer his secretary — she was the wife of his partner — but she had known him so long and so intimately as 'Mr. James' that the name had slipped out without thinking. It was going to be difficult to change, thought Bel, and was it necesary? After a moment's hesitation she decided that he was her very own Mr. James and would always remain so.

By this time Ellis had greeted the visitor, saying, 'Hallo, Jim! Glad you were able to come,'

353

and they all went into the house together.

'Look out for the beam,' said Ellis giving the usual warning.

'What beam?' asked Mr. James, turning suddenly and giving his head a resounding crack.

'That beam,' said Ellis laughing somewhat unfeelingly.

'Oh, goodness!' exclaimed Bel in dismay. 'We should have warned you properly. There are beams like that all over the house, so please be careful.'

Mr. James was rubbing his head ruefully. 'Why do you have them? They're frightfully dangerous,' he said.

'We have them to hold up the roof,' explained Ellis with elaborate sarcasm.

'Oh, yes, I see,' agreed Mr. James, looking carefully at the construction. 'They're fixed to the walls so it would be a bit difficult to have them removed . . . unless you were to put in steel girders. How about that?'

His host and hostess were dumb.

'It would cost a good deal,' admitted Mr. James thoughtfully. 'Failing that — I mean if it was too expensive — you could paint the beams white. It would be safer because people would be able to see them.'

Ellis was still speechless. Bel had begun to giggle.

'It would make the hall much lighter, you know. Have you ever thought of doing that?' inquired their guest.

'No, Jim,' said Ellis who had managed to find his tongue. 'It has never crossed our minds for a moment.'

'And nobody ever suggested it?' asked Mr. James incredulously.

'No, your suggestion is unique.'

'You might think about it.'

'Oh, yes, we'll think about it,' said Ellis nodding. 'When we're feeling a bit down in the mouth we'll say to each other, 'What about painting the beams?''

'I suppose I've said something funny, but it seems a very sensible idea to me.'

'It's only — ' began Bel trying to control her giggles. 'It's only because all our other visitors go into ecstasies over our beautiful oak beams.'

'Oh, well . . . ' said Mr. James with a sigh. He looked at the beams again, more carefully, and added, 'But I still think they're ugly — so rough and badly finished.'

'Never mind, Jim,' said Ellis kindly. 'Come into the drawing-room and have a glass of sherry before lunch, but for goodness' sake look out for your head as you go in at the door.'

3

'It seems funny to me,' said Mr. James when he was safely seated on the sofa. 'I mean why did they build houses with low beams and doorways?'

'The fletchers were small men,' Ellis told him.

'The fletchers? Oh, I see — Fletchers End.'

'Bar jokes, they really were smaller in those days,' Ellis explained. 'Someone once told me that those old suits of armour that you see in museums are much too small for an average-sized modern man — and you're not average-sized, are you?'

'No, worse luck,' said Mr. James. 'It's absolutely sickening. I have to pay much more than other people for my suits.'

'That's a very nice suit,' said Bel.

'Oh, do you like it?' he asked. 'It's new. I put it on specially for you to see. Mrs. Garry helped me to choose the stuff.'

There were all sorts of things that Bel wanted to know so she took advantage of a pause in the conversation.

'How are things going in the office?' she inquired. 'What about the letters? No slackness in sorting them, I hope.'

'Oh, that's all right. It's been all right ever since I got on to them and made a row about it. I enjoyed that row,' added Mr. James, smiling reminiscently.

'I know you did,' nodded Bel.

'Yes, it was a good row and most effective. The letters are on your table — I mean Mrs. Garry's table — every morning before she arrives.'

'Good!'

'Oh, by the way, you remember old Branksome, don't you? That queer old beaver who kicked up such a shindy about a consignment of sugar.'

Bel nodded, she remembered him well. It had been one of Mr. James's most unfortunate mistakes and it had taken his secretary all her time to soothe Mr. Branksome's justifiable rage and fury and to put things right with Mr. Nelson.

'Well, he's quite nice now,' declared Mr. James. 'He isn't a bit sorry. He drops in to the office every now and then and sits and tells me smutty stories. Some of them are very funny.' Mr. James chuckled and added, 'I saw him yesterday and he sent you his love.'

'What!' exclaimed Bel incredulously. 'Mr. Branksome sent — '

'Well, not exactly,' admitted Mr. James. 'He just said where was that nice little bit of fluff that I used to have as a secretary.'

Bel laughed immoderately but Ellis did not seem amused.

'Mrs. Garry isn't much to look at,' continued Mr. James, following his line of thought. 'But she's really very good value. Her typing is still a bit erratic but she's useful in other ways. Have you noticed this, Mrs. B.?' He pointed to his tie.

Bel smiled and nodded. Of course she had noticed. Instead of working round his neck until the knot was under his left ear his tie had remained in the correct position with the knot beneath his chin.

'That's Mrs. Garry,' he explained. 'She sews little loops on all my ties and I fasten them on to my back collar-stud. It's a marvellous idea.'

'What on earth is the use of that?' asked Ellis, a trifle irritably for he was feeling left out in the cold. He added 'Loops on your ties! It seems a crazy idea to me.'

'It's a secret, isn't it, Mr. James?' said Bel laughing.

He nodded, 'You bet it's a secret. The fact is Mrs. Garry's idea has made things much more comfortable for me. I don't have to worry; I know it's all right, you see.'

'No need for anyone to say 'tie,'' suggested Bel.

'No need at all. I'll tell you another thing, Mrs. B. Our coffee comes on a tray every morning: two cups and saucers and a plate of biscuits! What d'you think of that?'

'Grand!'

'It's because I'm so important of course.'

'Look here!' said Ellis. 'What's all this about?'

'He's jealous, Mrs. B.,' declared Mr. James screwing up his face and winking broadly at his erstwhile secretary. 'He doesn't get his coffee on a tray. I was in his room yesterday morning and in came the last-joined typist — not a bad-looking wench, but don't worry I shan't ask her out to lunch — '

'I should hope not!' put in Bel.

'In she came,' continued Mr. James. 'Smiling like a Cheshire cat, and she put down two slopping cups with the saucers full of sodden biscuits on Mr. Brownlee's table.'

'Why don't I get a tray?' demanded Ellis. 'I shall tell them — '

'No, no, you mustn't tell them!' cried Mr. James in horrified tones. 'It would never do to tell them yourself — frightfully undignified and all that! The right thing is for your secretary to tell them that you're a very important person, isn't it, Mrs. B.?'

'Really Jim!' exclaimed Ellis, half laughing and half annoyed. 'I don't know what's come over you to-day. You never talk like this in the office.'

'Good gracious, no! Of course not. What do you take me for?' cried Mr. James. He grinned and added, 'I'm on the loose to-day. You wait till you see me on Monday morning and you'll find me full of respect for your exalted position.'

'Cheek!' exclaimed Ellis.

Bel was somewhat alarmed. She decided it was time to change the subject so she asked hastily how the blue car was going, a question which certainly had the desired effect for it brought forth a flood of eulogies on her performance and a technical description of her engine which neither of the hearers could understand. However Mr. James finished his disquisition by saying, 'Girls like going out for a spin' which Bel understood quite well.

'Any special girl?' she inquired with interest.

'No, just girls,' replied Mr. James. 'I haven't got a steady. I'm waiting until I find someone exactly like you.' Unfortunately he rather spoilt this charming compliment by adding, 'Only much younger, of course.'

Bel laughed. She was delighted with Mr. James. She had been afraid that he might have changed, for he was now a business man pulling his weight in the firm of Copping, Brownlee and Copping, but he had not really changed at all. He still said exactly what he thought without fear or favour, he was still her great big enormous child.

Lunch was a most successful meal, the visitor did full justice to it, especially to the steak-and-kidney pie. Ellis was astonished at his guest's appetite but Bel was not. She had lunched with Mr. James several times so she knew that he required large quantities of nourishing food.

After lunch they went into the garden which was beginning to look quite civilised by this time. Bel was delighted to see that the little 'apricock' trees had arrived from the nursery garden and were being planted along the south wall. Mr. Fuller was there, of course, superintending the operation. Unfortunately he was much too busy to talk to them so they strolled on to the little gate.

4

Presently Mr. James said he must go; he had an important appointment in town (he did not specify the nature of the appointment but Bel had a feeling that it might have something to do with a girl) so they all went into the drawing-room through the glass door.

'Hallo!' exclaimed Mr. James, pausing and looking with interest at the bureau. 'Where did you get that?'

'We bought it from the fellow who sold us the house,' Ellis told him.

'It's exactly like Mother's bureau,' said Mr. James. 'Absolutely identical. Has this one got a secret drawer?'

'A secret drawer!' exclaimed Bel in surprise. 'No, I wish it had; a secret drawer would be rather fun.'

'Perhaps it has,' suggested Mr. James. 'I mean

a secret drawer is a secret drawer. It's only when you know how to open it — '

'How do you open it?' asked Ellis smiling. He was quite certain that Miss Lestrange's bureau contained no secrets for he had examined it carefully.

Mr. James went forward and let down the flap, he put his hand through a little cupboard at the back. 'It's here,' he said, 'or it ought to be here — a sort of little handle — yes, I've got it!'

There was a creaking noise and the secret drawer slid out.

'Oh, how thrilling!' cried Bel. 'Let me see how it works.'

As a matter of fact she was rather disappointed when Mr. James stood back and allowed her to look at the secret drawer for it was small and shallow, little more than a slit.

Mr. James was disappointed too. 'I don't know what's the matter with it,' he said, shaking the bureau and tugging at the drawer, 'in Mother's bureau the drawer is quite a decent size; it slides out much farther.'

'Don't pull it, Jim!' cried Ellis, somewhat alarmed at the rough handling his property was receiving. 'It's a mistake to use force. I expect the mechanism is a bit rusty. I'll get an oil-can and have a go at it.'

'Yes, that's the idea,' agreed Mr. James. 'I wish I could wait and see the result but I shall have to fly.' He glanced at his watch and exclaimed, 'Gosh, yes! I shall have to fly. She'll be frightfully cross if I'm late. You can tell me all about it on Monday, can't you, Mr. Brownlee?'

36

When the Brownlees had seen off their guest at the gate Ellis fetched his oil-can and proceeded to oil the mechanism of the secret drawer. It took him some time because the handle was far back in the little cupboard; he could feel it but he could not see it. Presently with the aid of a feather he managed to introduce some oil into the mechanism and when he had worked the handle to and fro several times the drawer slid out much farther.

Bel had been watching with interest. She now saw that the drawer was not empty, as they had thought. Right at the back there was a long yellow manila envelope.

Ellis had seen it too. 'What's this, I wonder,' he said, picking it up as he spoke.

The flap of the envelope was unsealed; he drew out a parchment document and looked at it curiously, 'Look, Bel!' he exclaimed. 'It's someone's will.'

'Someone's will!' cried Bel. Quite suddenly and for no accountable reason she was frightened. She caught hold of Ellis's arm. 'I don't like it,' she said. 'Ellis, I don't like it.'

'You don't like it? What do you mean?'

'There's something horrible about it.'

'Nonsense,' said Ellis smiling. 'Why should it be horrible? Look, it says 'THE LAST WILL AND TESTAMENT OF HELEN FRANCES LESTRANGE'!

Isn't that queer? She must have hidden it in the secret drawer and forgotten all about it.'

'What?'

'Put it in the fire,' she repeated urgently.

'But, Bel, why should we — '

'Because I'm frightened of it!'

'But we can't burn it without — '

'We can! We can!' cried Bel frantically. 'Give it to me, Ellis. I'll put it in the fire.'

'I don't know what's the matter with you,' declared Ellis in amazement.

'I want to put it in the fire, that's all.'

'You can't burn people's wills.'

'She's dead!' cried Bel. 'She's been dead for years and years. That paper belongs to us.'

'Belongs to us?'

'Yes, of course. You bought the bureau and its contents, so the paper belongs to us. We can burn it if we like.'

'No, darling, honestly — '

'Yes, we can. I want it burnt. I don't want to read it — or anything. I just want to burn it.'

'You can't burn people's wills.'

'It's all over — long ago,' said Bel breathlessly. 'It's been there for years and years.'

'I know, but — '

'Listen, Ellis. You said you would do anything for me. You've said it over and over again. I want you to burn that paper.'

'We can't — really.'

'You didn't mean what you said.'

'Darling Bel, of course I meant what I said. You know I would do anything for you.'

'Well, then, please burn that horrible paper.

I'm asking you to do it, Ellis.'

'But I can't,' said poor Ellis. 'It's Miss Lestrange's will. You can't put a will into the fire. It wouldn't be — '

'Nobody would know! Nobody would ever have known anything about it if you hadn't found the secret drawer. Oh, how I wish it had never been found!'

'Bel, do be sensible. What's all the fuss about?'

'I want to burn that paper.'

'It wouldn't be right to burn the old lady's will. Don't you understand, darling? I couldn't do it because it wouldn't be right.'

'You'll regret it,' began Bel. 'You'll be sorry . . . you didn't . . . listen . . . ' Her voice died away. The room was beginning to get dark. Her knees were trembling. She sank on to the sofa.

'Darling, what's the matter?' cried Ellis.

'I feel — rather — queer — '

Ellis looked at her in alarm; her head was drooping side-ways against the cushion, her face was as white as paper.

'Bel!' he cried, seizing one of her hands. He was horrified to find it was as cold as a stone — cold and limp — there seemed to be no life in it.

Ellis raised her feet on to the sofa and tucked a cushion behind her head. He rushed to the cupboard and poured out a glass of brandy. Her lips were quite blue and tightly closed; when he tilted the glass a few drops ran down her chin. He was terrified — she was dying — he was sure of it — Bel was dying. His heart was thumping against his ribs with fright. What could he do?

364

Should he run and telephone for the doctor? But how could he leave her like this? He seized her hands and rubbed them, calling her name. He moistened his handkerchief and dabbed her forehead . . .

After a few minutes Bel's eyelids fluttered and she gave a little sigh.

'Bel!' he cried. 'Speak to me, darling!'

Her head moved a little and her eyes opened.

Again he held the glass to her lips. 'Just a little sip, come on, darling!'

She managed to drink a few drops.

'A little more,' Ellis pleaded.

She drank a little more and turned her head away.

'I know you don't like it, but it's doing you good,' he told her. 'Do try and drink it, there's a dear. I'm going to ring up Dr. Armstrong and ask — '

'No,' said Bel feebly. 'Don't leave me — hold my hand tight.'

He knelt beside her, holding her hand, gazing at her. She was better, he could see that. The colour was coming back into her face. Yes, she was better — his heart stopped thumping madly.

After a minute or so he managed to make her drink a little more brandy.

'Ugh — nasty — ' she said, and smiled wanly.

'My best brandy,' Ellis told her squeezing her hand. He added, 'Gosh, what a fright you gave me!.'

They were silent for a little while.

'I felt — so queer,' said Bel at last.

'Better now?'

'Yes, much better. It was horrid, Ellis. Everything got quite dark — all of a sudden.'

'You were upset, that's all.'

'Yes, it was that will. Couldn't we burn it?'

'No, darling. You can't burn people's wills.'

'You keep on saying that.'

'There's nothing else to say.'

She sighed. 'What are you going to do with it?'

'I ought to take it to Mr. Tennant.'

'No, Ellis. If you won't burn it you must read it. Read it now,' she added.

Ellis picked up the document and unfolded it. He stood and read it carefully. After a few moments he looked up and said, 'This is most extraordinary. I don't understand it at all. She seems to have bequeathed Fletchers End to her sister. It says, 'To my dear sister Mrs. Dora Jane Harding.''

'I thought it might be — something like that,' said Bel in a shaky voice.

'Did you know about this?' asked Ellis in bewilderment.

'No, of course not. I just thought — I mean when I saw it I felt terribly frightened.'

'I don't understand,' said Ellis frowning. 'If she bequeathed the place to her sister how did it come to Roy Lestrange? It belonged to him, didn't it? He sold it to us, so it must have belonged to him.'

Bel was silent.

After a few moments Ellis walked over to the window and stood there looking out. It was beginning to get dark and had started to rain; the heavy drops were pattering on the window. 'Yes,'

366

said Ellis at last. 'Yes, I see. It didn't belong to him. This will cancels the other one.'

'You can still — burn it,' said Bel in a very small voice.

'You know that's impossible, don't you?'

'I suppose it is.'

'Quite impossible. We would never have another happy moment.'

'Ellis, what will happen? It doesn't mean we shall have to leave Fletchers End, does it?'

'I'm afraid it looks like that.'

She had known it, of course. The fear of having to leave Fletchers End had been there, in her mind, but it was far worse now when it was put into words. 'Oh, I can't bear it!' cried Bel. 'I love it so dearly! The poor old house was so miserable when we got it — and now it's happy! I can't bear to think of leaving it and going away. I can't bear it!'

'Perhaps we could make some arrangement with Mrs. Harding. I mean if she doesn't want to live here — '

'She will!' exclaimed Bel. 'She'll want to live here.'

'How do you know?' asked Ellis in surprise.

'Mr. Harding told me.'

'Mr. Harding?'

'Leslie Harding — Roy's cousin — the one he was staying with in Oxford. He told me that his mother was terribly disappointed when she heard the place had been left to Roy.'

'I see,' said Ellis. 'That's definite.'

'I suppose it is quite definite? I mean the will — '

'We had better face it, Bel. This document is the last will and testament of Miss Lestrange and in it she bequeathes the house to her sister. What could be more definite than that? She must have signed it and put it in the secret drawer — a foolish thing to do!'

'She ought to have given it to Mr. Tennant?'

'Yes, of course.'

'Ellis!' cried Bel. 'Perhaps she changed her mind! Perhaps she didn't want anyone to find it! If so, it's all right, isn't it?'

Ellis shook his head. 'I'm afraid it isn't any use thinking things like that.'

'No, I suppose it was silly of me.'

'You see, Bel, the last will that a person makes cancels all the others. I know that much. So it looks as if the house never really belonged to Roy Lestrange.'

Bel nodded, 'So he had no right to sell it to us.'

'None at all.'

'It's awful for him, isn't it?'

'Awful for him? I think Roy Lestrange has done pretty well out of it,' said Ellis grimly. 'He sold the house and paid off all his debts. We needn't waste any sympathy on Roy Lestrange.'

'But he'll have to return the money, won't he?'

'How?' asked Ellis. 'The money has gone, hasn't it. The man hasn't a penny left — you told me that yourself.'

'Ellis! He'll have to pay — '

'My dear girl, you can't get blood out of a stone.'

'But that's dreadful!' cried Bel. 'Perhaps Mrs.

Harding would — '

'Bel, don't you understand? If *this* will is the last she made it cancels the other will, and the house belongs to Mrs. Harding. You couldn't expect her to buy her own house.'

'What are we to do?' asked Bel in consternation. 'Ellis, what are we to do?'

For a moment or two Ellis did not reply; he was still gazing out of the window at the falling rain. Then he said, 'I had better see Mr. Tennant. He will know what to do.'

'Yes, perhaps you had better see him.'

'He has got the other will,' continued Ellis. 'The one in favour of Roy Lestrange. It was in the file with all the other documents when I bought the house, so he's the man to ask. He'll be able to tell me where we stand — legally, I mean. I shall go now,' added Ellis with decision.

'Now!' cried Bel. 'It's too late! He won't be in his office.'

'I shall go to his house. I must see him to-night; I shan't be able to sleep a wink until I've seen him.' Ellis hesitated and then added, 'Of course there's just a chance that the other will, leaving the house to Roy Lestrange, may be a later one — '

'Oh!' cried Bel eagerly. 'Do you really think so?'

Ellis did not really think so — and what was the use of raising her hopes? He said doubtfully, 'Well, it might be. It all depends on the date — you see that, don't you?'

Bel saw. She had no hopes. Ever since her talk with Mr. Harding the fear of losing Fletchers

End had lain at the back of her mind.

There was a short silence and then Ellis turned quickly and took her hand. 'Darling Bel,' he said. 'Don't worry too much. Whatever happens we've got each other. That's the main thing.'

37

When Ellis had gone Bel lay and thought about what had happened. It had all happened so suddenly that she could scarcely believe it. It couldn't be true, she thought. It couldn't possibly be true. Less than an hour ago they were happy — having fun with Mr. James — and now it seemed as if the skies had fallen. Less than an hour ago they were comfortably settled, looking forward to a long life in the dear old house — and now they would have to leave it. There was no hope — none at all, thought Bel — if Fletchers End belonged to Mrs. Harding she would want to live in it herself.

Ellis loved Fletchers End too; they both loved it. The house was so beautiful now; they had done so much to make it beautiful; they had planned every detail together. It was their very own dear house. Must they give it up? Would they have to go away and never see it again? We've been too happy here, she thought. We've been too happy!

Bel was weeping now, lying on the sofa and sobbing. She had managed to keep back the tears until Ellis had gone — Ellis hated tears — but now she could keep them back no longer . . . and there was no need, because Ellis would be away for hours. Ellis would go to Mr. Tennant's house and show him the will and discuss the matter with him. It would take hours.

She wondered vaguely what Mrs. Warmer was doing and why she had not come to say that dinner was ready, and then she remembered it was Mrs. Warmer's night out — it was the night of the meeting of the Women's Institute in Shepherdsford. Bel was glad of that. She could not have faced Mrs. Warmer.

Ellis was not away for hours. He was back long before Bel expected him. She was still sobbing uncontrollably when the door opened and he came in.

'Mr. Tennant wasn't there,' said Ellis. 'He's gone away for a holiday. I could see his partner of course, but that wouldn't be much use — besides I don't like the man. Oh, Bel, don't cry like that, darling! You'll make yourself ill.'

'I can't help it.'

'We had better try to eat some food.'

'I couldn't.'

'It might do us good,' said Ellis. He took her hand and helped her to get up from the sofa.

Mrs. Warmer had left their supper on the dining-room table: cold chicken and salad; a plate of sandwiches, covered with a napkin, and coffee in the percolator ready to be heated up.

'We must eat something,' said Ellis firmly. 'I'll give you a little piece of chicken, shall I?'

Bel had managed to control her tears. She said, 'I'll eat something if you will. I could drink some coffee.'

They went on talking while they were having their meal. Ellis had the will in his pocket, he took it out and showed it to Bel. Miss Lestrange's signature was witnessed by James

Fuller and A. S. Whittaker.

'It couldn't be old Mr. Fuller, could it?' said Ellis.

'Yes, it is. He told me about it one day when I was talking to him in the garden.'

'Told you he had witnessed Miss Lestrange's will?'

'Not exactly,' she replied thoughtfully. 'He talks on and on, you know. I wasn't really listening properly . . . he said she called him in from the garden to write his name on a paper . . . and Dr. Whittaker was there. He said there had to be two people.'

'Yes, of course. There must be two witnesses to a will. What else did he say? Try to remember, Bel.'

'That was all, I think — except that she gave him 'ten bob' — but you could ask him, couldn't you?'

'No, we mustn't speak to anyone about it until we know exactly how we stand,' said Ellis firmly. 'We must wait until Mr. Tennant comes home. The whole thing is such a muddle and I don't know enough about law to see my way clearly. It's very serious, Bel.'

'Of course it's serious!' she exclaimed.

'It's more serious than you think. You see, Bel, I borrowed from a building society to buy the house — it's a sensible thing to do and it's done every day by thousands of people who don't want to touch their capital — and in addition to that we've spent a great deal on doing up the place. I felt perfectly justified in these measures because the house was a valuable asset.'

Ellis paused. He got up and walked to the end of the room and back. He said, 'I don't know where I am. If the house doesn't belong to me what am I to do? I suppose I shall have to pay back the loan from the building society. How am I going to do that? I haven't got the money to do it.'

'Yes, I see,' said Bel, gazing at him in dismay.

'A good deal depends on Mrs. Harding,' continued Ellis more calmly. 'I don't know whether she would be reasonable to deal with. Perhaps she could be made to pay for all the repairs we've done to the house . . . that would help . . . but of course we've done a good many things which weren't absolutely necessary.'

'You mean the bow-window?'

'Yes, and the central heating and the new bathroom. I don't suppose she could be made to pay for things like that.'

'Why not? Why shouldn't she pay for everything that's been done to her house?'

'She might say she didn't want the things done.' Ellis sighed and added, 'I wish I knew more about the legal aspect of the case.'

'Mr. Tennant — '

'Yes, I shall go and see him the moment he comes home, meanwhile we must just go on as usual.'

38

The Brownlees had decided that they must not mention their troubles to anyone until Ellis had consulted Mr. Tennant, so they pulled themselves together and endeavoured to go on as usual. Bel finished making the curtains and hung them up. It seemed rather a silly thing to do, but she did it all the same. The 'chaps' came and worked in the garden under the supervision of Mr. Fuller, who seemed to be under the impression that he was now in full control — perhaps his mind had gone back to the days when this was the case. Mrs. Warmer cooked delicious meals (which unfortunately were not appreciated as they should have been); she scrubbed and swept and polished and sang cheerfully as she went about her duties. There was no cloud in her sky.

Bel wondered what would happen to Mrs. Warmer. Would she too have to leave Fletchers End? Perhaps Mrs. Harding would keep her on and if so Mrs. Warmer would continue to be happy and contented. It was the old house that Mrs. Warmer loved.

Ellis did not agree with Bel in this. 'It's you she loves,' declared Ellis. 'She'll be miserable when we leave the place. It's a pity we couldn't take her with us, but that's impossible of course. I'm afraid it looks as if we shall be very badly off. I can't tell exactly; it depends upon so many different things. I've been thinking what we should do and where we should go. Perhaps we could take a small flat in London, we were very happy there last winter, weren't we?'

'Yes,' said Bel. It was true that they had been happy; but the flat in Mellington Street had been only a temporary lodging, they had been looking forward all the time to their permanent home in the country. That made all the difference in the world.

'You wouldn't mind living in town, would you?' asked Ellis anxiously.

'No, of course not, Ellis,' she replied. 'We'll be together won't we? That's the main thing,' she added, trying to smile.

Several days passed. Ellis was obliged to go to his business and went off as usual every morning. It was good for him to have his work to do and to get away from Fletchers End. Sitting in his office with his mind concentrated upon business affairs he had little time to brood. Bel's case was very different; all day long she was in the house or the garden; all day long she wandered about miserably, thinking of the trouble that had come so suddenly like a thundercloud in a summer sky. The house felt strange to Bel; it was different, not happy any more. To Bel's disordered mind the house seemed to be waiting.

Sometimes Bel looked at the bureau standing near the window; she could not be bothered to look through the letters and diaries in the drawer. If only she had not urged Ellis to buy it the wretched thing would still be in the warehouse, mouldering away amongst all the other furniture, with the will safely hidden in the secret drawer. It would not have been found for years, probably it would never have been found, thought Bel.

One morning she and Ellis were having breakfast together; on Bel's part it was a mere pretence of having breakfast; she was drinking a cup of coffee and crumbling a roll of bread to pieces on her plate.

'Do try to eat something,' said Ellis. He was terribly worried, not only about the house and the prospect of losing a great deal of money but also about his wife. She was pale and languid with blue shadows beneath her eyes. 'Do try to eat something,' he repeated. 'You can't go on like this — '

'Ellis, we can't go on — like this,' declared Bel with a little catch in her breath. 'It's the uncertainty that's so terribly hard to bear. I keep on wondering all the time — I can think of nothing else. It's like a huge dark thundercloud in the sky. Couldn't we do something? Must we wait until Mr. Tennant comes home?'

'I think it would be better to wait. You see Mr. Tennant knows all about it so he's the right man to consult.'

Bel put her elbow on the table and leant her head on her hand.

'I suppose I could take advice from another lawyer,' said Ellis, looking at her in alarm.

Bel did not reply.

'Perhaps I had better do that,' he suggested. 'I could ask Singleton, he's a very good fellow — I know him well. I could put the matter to him and see what he says. Would you like me to do that, Bel?'

She looked up doubtfully, hesitating, trying to make up her mind what to say. Would it be better to know quite definitely that they must leave Fletchers End or to remain in suspense?

'I'll see him,' declared Ellis with sudden decision. 'I'll ring him up this morning and ask him to have lunch with me at the club.'

'Ellis, I don't know! Perhaps you shouldn't — '

'I've decided,' said Ellis firmly. He kissed Bel and added. 'I must go now or I shall miss my train. Do take care of yourself darling and try not to worry too much.'

2

The other days had been bad enough but this was the worst of all. The thundercloud was bigger and blacker than ever. Ellis would talk to Mr. Singleton — and then they would know for certain. It would be worse to know for certain that they must leave Fletchers End. Bel wished — now when it was too late — that she had not urged Ellis to 'do something about it.'

It was when she was dusting her dressing-table that she glanced out of the window and saw Mr. Fuller in the garden accompanied by a very large and hefty young man. Bel had seen the young man before; it was Bert — Mr. Fuller's youngest grandson. The two were busily engaged unpacking some plants. The rose-bushes of course! In normal circumstances Bel would have been pleased and excited at the arrival of Ellis's rose-bushes, but to-day the sight of them added to her gloom. However it was necessary to go out and speak to the men. They would think it strange if she showed no interest in what they were doing.

Mr. Fuller was in his element, measuring the ground carefully and directing the digging of the holes. His manner towards Bert was extremely autocratic, he found fault with everything the young man did.

'That 'ole's too deep,' declared Mr. Fuller in his squeaky voice. 'You ain't planting a tree — not as I knows of. It's too deep and ain't wide enough to spread out the roots. Roses likes their roots spread out noice and comferble. Just like 'uman beings, they are.'

' 'Uman beings?' asked Bert pausing in his labours and looking at his grandfather in bewilderment.

'You don't like your roots cramped up in tight shoes — he, he, he!' exclaimed Mr. Fuller chuckling at his own excruciatingly funny joke. 'And don't you stand there gawping like a zany,' said Mr. Fuller with a sudden change of tune. 'These luvverly roses got to be planted 'ere an' now — not nex' week nor the week after neither. You get on with your digging, Bert.'

'Luvverly roses!' muttered Bert beneath his breath. 'Foolish liddle sticks — that's all they be.'

'What?' asked Mr. Fuller. 'Why can't you speak right? Mumble, mumble, mumble! You don't never open your mouth proper — 'cept when you're 'aving your dinner . . . '

All this would have amused Bel considerably if it had not been for the black thundercloud in the blue summer sky. To-day nothing could amuse her; certainly not the planting of Ellis's roses. The 'foolish liddle sticks' which were being bedded in so carefully would grow into healthy bushes and bear beautiful blooms — but Ellis would not be here to enjoy them.

3

Soon after lunch there was a telephone-call. Bel lifted the receiver hopefully. It was Ellis, she was sure. Ellis was ringing up to say he had seen Mr. Singleton and everything was all right and they would not have to give up Fletchers End. It must be that, thought Bel as she waited for the call to come through.

But it was not Ellis; it was Louise.

'I haven't seen you for days,' declared Louise. 'I've had a perfectly sweet letter from Alec with all sorts of interesting news. He says things are beginning to look a lot better already. That man, Wilkie Bates, is doing tremendously good work and several big orders have come in — a specially valuable one from a firm in London. He says that's Ellis. Did you know about it?'

'Ellis has been talking about 'Drummond's' to people that's all.'

'That's all!' exclaimed Louise. 'It's everything. It means a frightful lot to Alec — and to me too, of course. I can tell from the poor darling's letter that he's feeling ever so much more cheerful. Listen, Bel, I want to come and tell you all about it. I thought I'd come over to tea if that will be all right.'

Bel hesitated. She did not want anybody — not even Louise. 'I've got a very bad headache,' she said. It was perfectly true; her head ached and her heart ached; she felt cold and shivery. 'I don't think it would be much good your coming,' she added. 'I really feel rather awful.'

'Poor darling!' exclaimed Louise in anxious tones. 'Perhaps you've got a chill or something. You had better take two aspirins and go to bed.'

'Perhaps I should.'

'Are you sure you wouldn't like me to come just for a few minutes?'

'I'd rather you didn't — honestly.'

'Well, I'll come over to-morrow and see how you are.'

'Yes,' agreed Bel, 'perhaps I'll feel better to-morrow.'

Perhaps she would feel better to-morrow or perhaps she would feel worse, thought Bel as she put down the receiver.

Louise had told her to go to bed — and like most of Louise's plans for the comfort of her friends it was sound and sensible — but it would worry Ellis if he came home and found his wife in bed and poor Ellis had quite enough to worry him already. No, thought Bel. Bed was out of the question. Instead of going to bed she went into the drawing-room and sat down by the fire with a book.

'You-go-and-have-a-nice-sit-down-with-a-book,' thought Bel as she turned over the pages listlessly. Dear Mrs. Warmer! How sad it would be to say good-bye to her! Nice Mrs. Warmer!

Presently Mrs. Warmer brought in the tea-tray and arranged it conveniently on a table near the fire. 'You're looking very poorly,' she said in sympathetic tones. 'To tell the truth you haven't been looking like yourself at all for several days. It's to be hoped you're not in for 'flu.'

'I've got rather a bad headache,' admitted Bel.

Mrs. Warmer nodded. 'It might be 'flu — or it might be your eyes,' she said. 'I used to have dreadful headaches till I got my spectacles. Why don't you ask Dr. Armstrong and get your eyes tested?'

'Perhaps I should,' said Bel.

Mrs. Warmer continued to talk about headaches. Her mother had been a martyr to headaches — sick headaches they were. She couldn't hardly lift her head off the pillow. Her brother had headaches too — they were in the family — his headaches came on all of a sudden so bad that he could hardly see out of his eyes . . .

Mrs. Warmer's voice went on and on — all about headaches and the different members of her family who suffered from the affliction.

Bel had almost reached screaming-point when at last she made up the fire and went away.

She went away and there was peace. Silence was heavenly, thought Bel. There was no silence so heavenly as the silence of Fletchers End. She took two aspirin tablets and drank her tea and leaned her aching head upon the cushion.

39

The silence in the drawing-room continued. There was no sound at all except the crackle of the wood burning in the fire — a nice comfortable sound. After a little the pain in Bel's head receded; she was almost asleep when the door opened and Dr. Armstrong appeared.

Normally Bel would have been delighted to see him — she was very fond of the big doctor — but to-day she would much rather he had not come.

'Don't get up,' said Dr. Armstrong. 'I just came in for a minute, that's all. Lou seemed a bit worried. I didn't say anything to her, but I thought I'd have a look at you.'

'How kind,' said Bel.

'A bad headache, Lou said.'

'Yes, but it's a lot better.'

He sat down and took her hand. 'You don't seem to have any fever,' he said, looking at her doubtfully. 'All the same I think you'd be better in bed.'

Bel had not wanted anybody — peace was all she had wanted — but there was something very soothing about the doctor and now that he was here she wanted him to stay.

'I think you'd be better in bed,' he repeated.

'I'm not ill — just a bit worried,' said Bel trying to smile.

'What's the trouble, Bel?'

She hesitated and then said, 'I'm afraid I can't tell you; it's a secret.'

'Doctors are quite good at keeping secrets.'

Bel hesitated. The desire to confide in Dr. Armstrong was overpowering; she had talked to nobody about the trouble, nobody except Ellis (their discussion had been unending of course, it had gone round and round and arrived at no conclusion). What a relief it would be to talk to Dr. Armstrong! He was so sensible, so wise, so trustworthy! It could do no harm to confide in Dr. Armstrong; Bel was sure of that.

There had been a short silence, but now Bel said, 'It would be a great relief to tell you about it — but it's a long story and terribly complicated. Oh, dear! It's so terribly complicated — I don't know how to begin!'

'Begin at the beginning,' he suggested. 'How did the trouble start?'

'Well, it all began with that horrible bureau,' declared Bel. 'If only we hadn't bought it — '

'That bureau!' exclaimed the doctor in surprise. 'It's rather a nice piece of furniture. Miss Lestrange had one exactly like it and it stood in exactly the same place. I can see her now, sitting at it and writing.' He got up as he spoke and went over and looked at it closely. 'By Jove, it's the same one! I remember that chip off the corner. Did you buy it from Lestrange?'

'Yes, I wish we hadn't.'

Dr. Armstrong knew a good deal about people who were in trouble — people who had secrets on their minds. Some people found no difficulty in pouring out all their worries into a sympathetic ear — they were only too ready to do so — others found it difficult to begin. Bel was the latter kind of person. When he had soothed her down and made her feel more comfortable she would be able to confide in him. He was thankful that the trouble had nothing to do with Ellis — thank God for that! The trouble could not be anything very serious if the bureau was at the bottom of it.

There was a short silence.

Talk, said Dr. Armstrong to himself. He said aloud, 'So Miss Lestrange's bureau has come home! She was a curious old lady. I think I told you that she was my patient for the last few months of her life, so I used to see her quite often. I had to keep an eye on her because she had an unusual heart condition which necessitated care. I knew that with care she might live for years but there was always the possibility that she might die suddenly. She knew that herself; Whittaker had told her, hoping that it might make her take more care, but it had no effect upon her at all. One day when I came to see her she laughed and said, 'Well, here I am, Doctor. Not dead yet.''

'It was brave, wasn't it?' said Bel.

'Oh, she was very courageous. I admired her courage tremendously, but unfortunately she was a very bad patient, medically speaking, irascible and easily upset. She was always quarrelling with somebody or other, which of course was the worst thing for her.'

'Quarrelling with her relations,' said Bel nodding.

'Yes, quarrelling with her relations and changing her will,' agreed Dr. Armstrong smiling. 'Miss Lestrange enjoyed making wills, it gave her a feeling of power. She was really a 'dictator' in her own limited sphere.'

'A feeling of power,' said Bel thoughtfully.

'Yes, I happen to know that quite definitely. You see I was here when she signed her will.'

'You were here!' exclaimed Bel in astonishment.

'I witnessed it,' he told her.

Bel was gazing at him with startled eyes. 'But you didn't!' she exclaimed. 'Dr. Armstrong, you didn't witness it.'

'I can assure you that I did.'

'But Dr. Armstrong — '

'My dear girl, I see you don't believe me, but I can tell you exactly what happened from beginning to end. It was more than six years ago but for several reasons the affair made such an impression on my mind that I can remember it as if it had happened last week. It was an afternoon in January; we were having a cold spell so I called in to see Miss Lestrange — cold weather didn't suit her at all — but in spite of the weather she was in good trim and exceedingly cheerful. She could be very amusing when she felt like it and that afternoon she was very amusing indeed. I wondered what had happened to make her so lively — and quite soon I discovered the reason. When I had finished my examination she produced her will and asked me to witness her signature. She smiled and said she enjoyed making wills; she said, 'It amuses me to change things about.' As I told you before, it gave her a feeling of power. She could make one person happy and another person miserable with a stroke of her pen.'

Dr. Armstrong paused for a moment thinking rather sadly of the indomitable old lady. She had suffered a great deal of pain and borne it courageously; her bitter tongue had alienated all her friends; she was lonely and often miserable; sometimes she was cross and disagreeable but all the same he had liked her quite a lot. And he had missed her. Life had seemed a bit flat after she had died.

'You were going to tell me about the will,' Bel reminded him.

'Yes,' agreed the doctor. 'Well, of course it was essential to have two witnesses, so she called old Fuller who was working in the garden and told him to clean his boots and wash his hands and come in. Presently in came Fuller; he was quite composed and confident — not a bit surprised or embarrassed — it was obvious to me that he had done this before and knew the procedure. He watched Miss Lestrange sign the document and immediately sat down at the bureau, put on his spectacles and, breathing heavily, wrote his name in the correct place. Then it was my turn, so I sat down and signed my name below his.'

'Dr. Armstrong, it wasn't — '

'Wait,' he said. 'Let me finish my story. Miss Lestrange gave Fuller a ten shilling note. He took it as a matter of course, put the note carefully into the case with his spectacles and went away. It had happened before — more than once — there was no doubt about that. I couldn't help being amused. When Fuller had gone Miss Lestrange handed me the document and told me to read it. I explained to her that it wasn't necessary for me to read it but she smiled rather mischievously and said, 'I know that, Doctor. There isn't much I don't know about wills — but I think it will interest you.''

'You read it!' exclaimed Bel.

He nodded. 'Yes, and I was rather distressed.'

'Distressed?'

'It wasn't what I expected,' he explained. 'You see I happened to know that she had intended to leave her property to her sister. I knew Mrs. Harding and liked her. She came to Fletchers End when Miss Lestrange was laid up with a bad chill and was very kind and sensible, so naturally I was distressed to discover that Miss Letrange had changed her mind.'

'Changed her mind!' echoed Bel in bewilderment.

The doctor nodded, 'I was sorry about it,' he said.

Bel was completely muddled. She did not know what to say so she went over to the bureau and took the will out of the secret drawer and handed it to Dr. Armstrong without a word.

'What's this?' he exclaimed in surprise. He unfolded it and added, 'Oh, this is a different one.'

'A different will?'

'Entirely different. As you see, this will has been witnessed by Whittaker and old Fuller. I told you that Fuller was quite accustomed to signing his name and getting his ten bob, didn't I? The will I witnessed was the last she made?'

'The last — she made,' echoed Bel in a faint voice.

'The very last,' declared Dr. Armstrong. 'I can tell you that for certain because the poor old lady died the following day.'

'What!' exclaimed Bel.

'It wasn't really very surprising. She had that curious heart condition, you see, but I felt unhappy about it because I had upset her. She was angry with me and it wasn't good for her to be angry. I won't bother you with technicalities, but it was a valvular disease — '

Bel was not interested in technicalities. 'Oh, Dr. Armstrong, are you sure?' she cried. 'Are you positive? Are you absolutely certain?'

'Of course I'm certain,' said the doctor, looking at her in surprise. 'What's the matter, Bel? Is it so important?'

'It's frightfully important,' she declared. 'The last will cancels all the others, doesn't it?'

'Yes, of course. This document isn't worth the paper it's written on.'

Bel was silent. She could not have spoken to save her life. The room seemed to be going up and down in an alarming manner. It was making her feel quite sick.

Dr. Armstrong took her arm. 'Come and sit down,' he said. 'I don't know what it's all about, but we had better try to straighten out the tangle.'

She allowed herself to be led to the sofa and they sat down together.

'Now then,' he said, taking her hand and holding it in a firm clasp. 'Now then, tell me why it's so frightfully important.'

Bel moistened her lips, she said: 'That will — we found it in the drawer. We thought — we thought it was the last she made.'

'Well, it wasn't,' declared the doctor. 'If you had asked Tennant he could have told you that. Now tell me why it matters. Why is it frightfully important?'

'Because,' said Bel. 'Oh, Doctor Armstrong, don't you see? Roy Lestrange sold us Fletchers End . . . but if it didn't belong to him . . . if it wasn't his . . . ' her voice altered and stopped.

'Oh, I see!' exclaimed the doctor. 'Good heavens, I never thought of that. If the house didn't really belong to Lestrange he had no right to sell it to you. No wonder you were upset! When did this document come to light?'

'I'll tell you all about it in a minute, but first — ' said Bel breathlessly. 'First, please tell me about the other will. You said you read it and you were distressed because the place hadn't been left to Mrs. Harding, but you didn't say who — '

'In the will I witnessed Fletchers End was bequeathed to Roy Lestrange — and it was the last. There's no doubt about that whatever.'

Bel could not speak.

'So you see it's all right,' he added. 'You needn't worry any more about it, need you?'

Bel tried to answer, tried to thank him, but she could not utter a word.

The doctor put his arm round her shoulders

and gave her a big hug. 'Buck up!' he said. 'It's all right, I tell you I There's no need to worry any more. Why, I believe you're crying, you silly little goose! Here, take my handkerchief — women's hankies are absolutely useless to mop up tears.'

'So silly of me — ' sobbed Bel. 'So frightfully silly — but — but the last few days — have been — dreadful. You can't imagine — how dreadful — '

Dr. Armstrong let her cry. He sat beside her in silence, holding her hand.

It was some little time before Bel was able to pull herself together, but presently she sat up and blew her nose vigorously. 'There, I'm better,' she said.

'Good,' said the doctor smiling. 'Now you can tell me all about it, can't you?'

40

There was now no difficulty in telling Dr. Armstrong all that had happened; Bel began at the beginning with the arrival of the bureau at Fletchers End. She told him how the secret drawer had been discovered and how they had found the document which had caused so much trouble and distress, and how she had besought Ellis to burn it — but of course he wouldn't. She explained how Ellis had taken the will and gone to see Mr. Tennant, but had not been able to see him because he was away from home, so they had just made up their minds that they must wait until he came back, and carry on as usual.

'Waiting is horrible,' said Bel.

'The sword of Damocles.'

'Yes, just like that. I wandered about, I couldn't settle down to anything, I couldn't sleep. Ellis was miserable too; you see we both love Fletchers End so terribly much — we couldn't bear to think of going away and leaving it. This morning was worst of all.'

'Why was it worst of all?'

'Ellis's little rose-bushes arrived and I went out to see them being planted.'

'Quite unbearable,' said the doctor nodding understandingly.

'Yes, quite unbearable,' agreed Bel with a little sigh.

It was now Dr. Armstrong's turn to take up

the story. There were all sorts of things Bel wanted to know.

'You told me Miss Lestrange was angry with you,' she said. 'Why was she angry?'

'Because I spoke my mind. I told you that I was distressed when I read the will and saw she had left the house to her nephew. I said, 'But I thought you intended to leave your property to Mrs. Harding!' I shouldn't have said it of course — it was no business of mine — but I said it without thinking.'

'It was unreasonable of her to be angry,' declared Bel. 'She told you to read the will, so — '

'She was a very unreasonable woman,' Dr. Armstrong replied. 'I knew that, so it was foolish of me to say it and to tell you the truth I still feel uncomfortable about it; I still regret those foolish words. Doctors should never speak without thinking.'

He paused for a moment and then continued, 'She was furious with me — absolutely furious. She said she supposed she could do what she liked with her own property! Dora hadn't been near her for months — she had gone to Guernsey for the winter with her nincompoop of a son. She said that the only member of the family who had taken the trouble to come and see her at Christmas was Roy — and if she wanted Roy to have Fletchers End when she was dead and buried it was her affair and nobody else's. She said, 'Roy is a Lestrange. He may not be an angel, but he has got some spunk in him.'

'I tried to pacify her but it was useless, she

became angrier than ever and exclaimed, 'If I leave the place to Dora it will belong to Leslie when she dies — there isn't a doubt of that! Do you think I want Fletchers End to belong to that miserable little worm?'

'At last I managed to soothe her down. I apologised for what I had said and agreed that it wasn't my business. Her rages were furious while they lasted but fortunately they never lasted long. I was alarmed because it was the worst thing for her to get excited and I was annoyed with myself for having made such a gaffe. I talked to her about other things — I forget what — and after a bit she recovered and seemed quite like her normal self. All the same I was worried, so I advised her to take a sedative and go to bed. I said I would look in and see her in the morning. So then she smiled quite amicably and said, 'Yes, Doctor, come and see me. Perhaps I shall be in a better humour to-morrow morning.' There was something very nice about Miss Lestrange in spite of her fiery temper,' added Dr. Armstrong with a sigh.

Bel made no comment and after a moment's silence he continued his story.

'I was just going away when she called me back and asked me to post her will, so I waited while she put it in an envelope and addressed it to Tennant. 'Don't forget to post it,' she said as she gave it to me. 'It's very important that he should get it safely.''

'As if you would forget' exclaimed Bel indignantly.

'She was like that,' said the doctor smiling.

'She told people what to do and expected them to do it straight off. Some people resented her arrogant manner but it didn't worry me.'

'So you posted it for her.'

'No, I didn't. She had said it was important and in my opinion it was much too important to be posted in a pillar-box — without being registered — so I took it to Tennant's office then and there and gave it into his own hands. As a matter of fact it was after five and he was just going away, but he took me into his room for a chat. I like Tennant, we've always been friends. When he saw the will he said, 'Oh, she's signed it, has she? I thought she might change her mind.' I said it was a pity that the place wasn't being left to Mrs. Harding, and he laughed and said, 'Don't worry, she may get it yet.' Then he told me that exactly the same thing had happened before; she had been annoyed with Mrs. Harding for some reason or other and had made a will in favour of her nephew — cutting out Mrs. Harding altogether — and then, a few days later, she had come to his office and torn it up.

''And made another will in favour of Mrs. Harding?' I suggested. I was rather amused to tell you the truth. 'Oh, yes, of course,' said Tennant gloomily. I told him I saw no reason for him to be gloomy about it, as of course he must be making quite a good thing out of the old lady's wills. I said it as a joke, but he didn't laugh. He said it worried him. 'It's a sort of game to her,' he said, 'but it isn't a game to me. She's got that other will somewhere in the house

— goodness knows where! I did my best to make her give it to me to keep safely for her but she wouldn't.' Then he said, 'It's all very well for you to laugh but perhaps you don't realise that if Miss Lestrange had died suddenly I should have had to ransack the house to find it. I've had to do that before, for another client, and believe me it wasn't a pleasant job.'

'I said, 'But it's all right now, isn't it?'

''Oh, yes,' he agreed. 'This will cancels the other.' He put it in his safe and added, 'The other will isn't worth twopence, but all the same I should like to have it — or else see it torn up. It isn't a sound thing to have stray wills knocking about the place. It's apt to cause trouble.' '

'He was right, wasn't he?' exclaimed Bel who had been listening with rapt attention.

'Yes, he was right,' agreed Dr. Armstrong. 'I see that now. At the time I thought he was being too particular — and I said so. He replied that he liked things done properly and added very emphatically that anyhow he wasn't going to let the new will out of his clutches until he got hold of the old one . . . 'But you can't reason with that woman,' he said.

'I knew that only too well,' added the doctor ruefully.

'What happened next?' asked Bel.

'Oh, nothing much,' he replied. 'I remember I gave Tennant a lift home and we chatted about Miss Lestrange and the difficulties of dealing with her vagaries. Tennant said she was more trouble than all his other clients put together.'

Dr. Armstrong paused in his story — he thought he had told Bel all that was necessary — but Bel wanted more.

'You said Miss Lestrange died the next day, didn't you?' asked Bel.

'Yes,' replied Dr. Armstrong sadly. 'Yes, she died the next morning. The housekeeper rang me up early in the morning and said Miss Lestrange seemed very ill. I went at once of course and found the old lady unconscious with a very weak and erratic pulse. I gave her an injection, but there was no response to the treatment so I sat down beside her bed and waited. Presently she stirred and opened her eyes and said, 'Dora!' She said it urgently as if she were calling to her sister. I bent over her and said, 'You want Dora, don't you? You want Dora to come. I'll send for her at once.'

'She said it again quite clearly — 'Dora!' Then she relapsed into unconsciousness and died a few minutes later.'

'Oh, Dr. Armstrong!!' exclaimed Bel looking at him with wide horrified eyes. 'Do you think she was sorry? Do you think she had changed her mind?'

Dr. Armstrong had thought just that, but he was too wise to say so. 'We can't tell, can we?' he said. 'Perhaps she just wanted to see her sister. I think Mrs. Harding was the only person in the world she was really fond of.'

'You thought Mrs. Harding should have got Fletchers End, didn't you?'

'Yes, I told you that. You can understand my point of view, can't you, Bel? It seemed better that the house should belong to someone who would live in it and enjoy it rather than to a young naval officer who had no use for it at all. Afterwards whenever I happened to pass the place and saw the old house standing empty, getting more and more shabby — all the paint peeling off the woodwork and the gate falling to pieces and the garden a wilderness of weeds — I felt guilty. I felt as if I were to blame. I felt as if I ought to have been able to do something about it — but of course I couldn't have done anything, really. As Tennant said she wasn't the sort of woman who would listen to advice All the same it made me feel sad.'

'You don't feel sad now, do you?' asked Bel anxiously.

'No, of course not,' declared the doctor smiling at her very kindly. 'I feel very happy and the house is happy too. You mustn't worry about Mrs. Harding.'

'I can't help feeling a little worried. I feel Mrs. Harding has a right to the house. I mean it was her home — '

'You needn't feel worried about that,' he told her. 'Mrs. Harding hasn't a shadow of right to the place. It was left to Roy Lestrange, and you and Ellis bought it, so it belongs to you — and nobody else.'

'Yes, but perhaps Miss Lestrange would have — '

'Bel, listen. Miss Lestrange didn't want Leslie Harding to have Fletchers End. It's obvious from what she said to me that she disliked him intensely and I'm pretty certain that was the reason she didn't leave it to his mother.'

For a few moments Bel was silent. She, herself, had liked Mr. Harding, but she realised that he was not the sort of man who would appeal to a woman like Miss Lestrange. No, thought Bel, Miss Lestrange would have no use for weaklings, no sympathy for people who were unable to stand up for themselves and hold their own. She would rather have a man like Roy Lestrange who knew what he wanted and took it — yes, a pirate, thought Bel. All the pieces in the puzzle were falling into place and soon the whole picture would be complete.

'And another thing,' continued Dr. Armstrong. 'You must remember that a will is a legal document; the executors are bound to carry out its instructions to the letter, no matter what they think, no matter how unreasonable the instructions may seem to them. 'Theirs not to reason why,'' he added with a little smile.

'Wills are terrifying, aren't they?' said Bel in thoughtful tones. 'I wonder how many people would regret what they had put in their wills if they knew what happened after they were dead.'

'Quite a lot, I should think.'

'If Miss Lestrange could have seen Fletchers End all falling to pieces — '

'I know,' agreed the doctor. 'But fortunately that doesn't concern us, so we needn't worry about it. The place was bequeathed to Roy Lestrange — and that's that.'

Dr. Armstrong did not stay much longer; he

said Lou would be wondering where he was and what he was doing.

'Take care of yourself,' he said as he rose to go. 'I could give you a sedative but I don't think you'll need it.'

'I shall sleep like a top,' said Bel. She put her arms round his neck and looked up into his face, 'Thank you — for everything. I love you very much — but you know that, don't you?'

'Dear little Bel!'

They were silent for a moment or two.

'You're quite happy about Louise, aren't you?' said Bel at last.

'Goodness knows what I shall do without her! — but, yes, I'm happy about her. She couldn't have chosen a better man, I'm sure of that.'

'He's good all through and absolutely reliable,' declared Bel, paying Alec Drummond the highest compliment she knew.

'Yes, he's the right one,' agreed the doctor. 'I thought at one time — but, no matter. It appears I was wrong. It's been Alec all the time.'

'Ever since Drumburly,' nodded Bel.

'I must go,' he said. 'Lou will be wondering — but first I want to thank you for all your kindness to my child.'

'Kindness?'

'For going to Edinburgh with her and taking such good care of her. I'm pretty certain that quite a lot of things happened in Edinburgh — things that Lou knows nothing about.'

Bel smiled up at him affectionately, but did not answer.

'Yes, I thought so,' he said with a little chuckle. He bent and kissed her and went away.

3

When the doctor had gone Bel sat down in her usual chair by the fire. It was not yet time for Ellis to come home, but it would not be long. She must listen for the car and the moment she heard it stop at the gate she must run out and meet Ellis and tell him the wonderful news. Ellis might have seen Mr. Singleton but that did not matter now. It did not matter what Mr. Singleton had said about the legal aspect of the case; all that mattered was the date upon which Miss Lestrange had signed her last will and testament — and that was definitely fixed.

Bel had said to herself that the pieces of the puzzle were all falling into place. She wanted to collect them and make a picture of them, but there were so many pieces that it was not easy. Miss Lestrange was the centre-piece of course. Everything that had happened had been caused by the curious personality of the frail old lady who had loved power. Bel had heard so much about Miss Lestrange that she felt as if she knew her quite well, felt as if she had seen her and spoken to her. It was almost impossible to believe that she had been dead for six years. (Perhaps people like Miss Lestrange are never really dead, thought Bel vaguely. There is so much of them alive in the minds of those who knew them).

Bel had heard about her first from Roy Lestrange and remembered his description of her — very good-looking with white hair done in curls on the top of her head and a straight back like a Guardee — and she remembered Roy's story about the Egyptian scarf, she had looked magnificent in it! Roy had said, 'You can imagine her, can't you?' and Bel had been able to imagine her vividly.

Since then other people had added to the portrait; Margaret Warren with her account of her visit to Fletchers End on Poppy Day; 'She was rather a wicked old lady,' Margaret had said. She was also very amusing. 'You never knew what she was going to say next.' She had been kind to the twelve-year-old Margaret and, in spite of the horrid tea, Margaret had enjoyed herself.

Then there was old Mr. Fuller with his description of Miss Lestrange walking down the garden path 'in a grey dress with a red thing round her neck' — and her imperious command, 'Do it now, Fuller.' And there was Lady Steyne — she had made a considerable contribution to the portrait — and there was Mr. Harding. Poor little Mr. Harding! His recollection of 'Aunt Helen' was a very unhappy one. She had hated him, she was jealous, she had broken her promise to leave her property to his mother; 'Doesn't it seem unfair?' he had exclaimed. Dr. Armstrong's contribution to the portrait was most important of all; he had seen Miss Lestrange clearly with all her faults and failings but all the same he had been very fond of her.

They had all seen her differently, thought Bel, but really and truly that was not as queer as it seemed, for of course human beings are composite mixtures of good and bad qualities and show entirely different aspects of their personalities to different people.

Yes, all the pieces of the puzzle were there, thought Bel, and when she had talked to Ellis and told him everything they would make a clear picture. Meantime she could let her thoughts wander, and enjoy the relief of knowing that everything was all right and there was no need to worry any more. How wonderful it was — almost too good to be true!

Almost too good to be true? Bel sat up suddenly — supposing it wasn't true? Supposing Dr. Armstrong had made a mistake? It was six years ago — and six years is a long time. You could easily make a mistake about something that had happened all that time ago . . .

But fortunately the intrusive doubt was easily banished; Bel knew and trusted the big kind doctor; he was absolutely reliable. He had told her everything that had happened on that cold January afternoon — every smallest detail — and it had all fitted in with what she had known before. He had said that for various reasons the affair had made such a deep impression upon him that he remembered it as if it had happened last week — and obviously this was true — so it was all right.

It was all right, thought Bel, leaning back with a sigh of relief. Fletchers End was safe.

Bel's thought wandered. All sorts of things

chased each other through her mind, one after another . . . all the things she loved about Fletchers End; all the things which together constituted the enchantment of the old house; the friendly feeling when you came in (as if it were welcoming you home) . . . the old oak beams . . . the curve of the staircase and the smoothness of the banister-rail beneath your hand . . . the morning sunshine pouring in through the windows and shining on the polished floors . . . the singing of the birds at dawn . . . the clock on the tower of St. Julian's striking the hour . . . the crackle of logs burning in the big stone fireplace . . . the gentle creaks and sighings as the old house settled down for the night . . .

Bel thought of Mrs. Warmer — nice kind Mrs. Warmer — and Mr. Carruthers talking about 'chimbleys' and little Mr. Fuller walking about the 'garding' and enjoying the 'luvverly flowers' — invisible to everyone except himself. They were all part of Fletchers End. She thought of the aspen tree outside the staircase-window and the rustle of the wind amongst its leaves; she thought of the roses, Ellis's roses, which would bloom for him next year. She thought of the 'apricocks' on the south wall — not next year, but perhaps the year after, their branches would be bowed down with little golden globes 'Which, like unruly children, make their sire Stoop with oppression of their prodigal weight.'

For days and days — it seemed like weeks — Bel had not been able to think of these things without misery, but now she could think of them with happiness. Happiness filled her heart to overflowing — for Fletchers End was safe. It belonged to her and Ellis, it was their very own. They would live here and enjoy its peace and beauty all their lives . . .

Presently Bel became aware of the scent of violets, it was faint at first — perhaps it was just imagination — but gradually it grew stronger until the delicious fragrance filled the room. Bel glanced up at the picture and it seemed to her that Mrs. Lestrange was smiling.

We do hope that you have enjoyed reading
this large print book.

Did you know that all of our titles
are available for purchase?

We publish a wide range of high quality
large print books including:
Romances, Mysteries, Classics
General Fiction
Non Fiction and Westerns

Special interest titles available in
large print are:
The Little Oxford Dictionary
Music Book
Song Book
Hymn Book
Service Book

Also available from us courtesy of
Oxford University Press:
Young Readers' Dictionary
(large print edition)
Young Readers' Thesaurus
(large print edition)

For further information or a free
brochure, please contact us at:
Ulverscroft Large Print Books Ltd.,
The Green, Bradgate Road, Anstey,
Leicester, LE7 7FU, England.
Tel: (00 44) 0116 236 4325
Fax: (00 44) 0116 234 0205